This is a work of fiction. All characters and events are either a product of the author's imagination or used fictitiously, and any resemblance to real people or events is entirely coincidental.

PARAGON OF SHADOW

Cover art by Michelle Ong

Edited by Amanda Dimer Silva

First Edition: November 2024

ISBN-13: 978-1-952145-34-6

PARAGON OF SHADOW

SPECTRUM LEGACY BOOK FIVE

BETH ALVAREZ

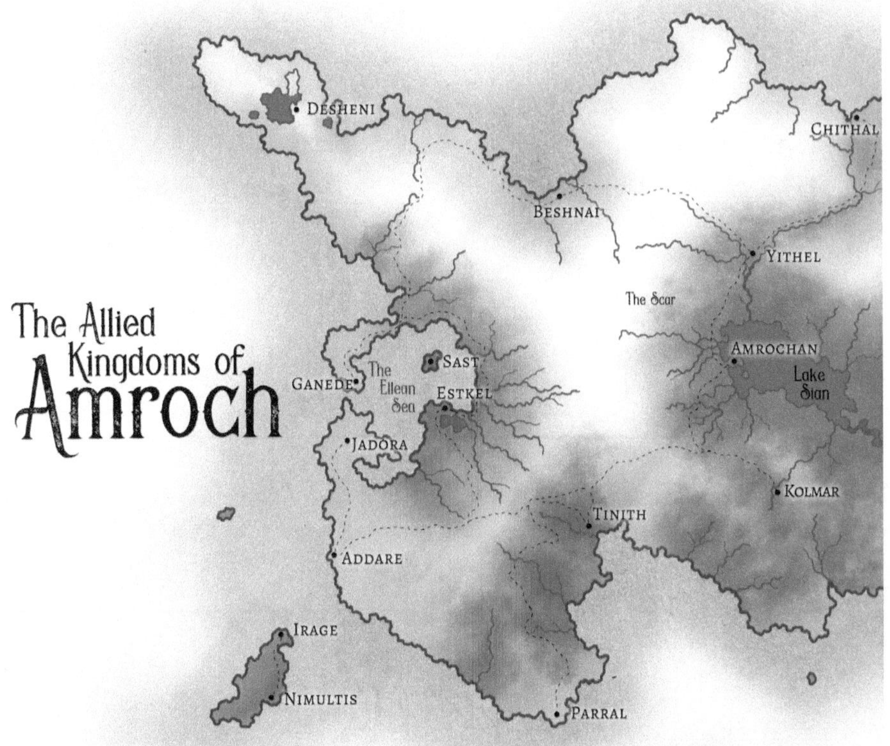

The Allied Kingdoms of Amroch
DESHENI
CHITHAL
BESHNAI
YITHEL
The Scar
AMROCHAN
Lake Sian
GANEDE
The Ellean Sea
SAST
ESTKEL
JADORA
KOLMAR
TINITH
ADDARE
IRAGE
NIMULTIS
PARRAL

CHAPTER ONE

Pain radiated up Zaide's arm. He had not dared to look at it, but it hurt almost as much as the knowledge of what he'd done. Instead of looking at his hand, at the fingers that were simultaneously numb and throbbing with the burns that had to be there, he kept his eyes closed and suffered the visions that replayed in his head.

He deserved it.

He deserved every ounce of pain and worse.

The image of the fear on Lark's face etched itself a little deeper into his brain every time the memory repeated. Worse than the fear her father had shown, though the king had been the one to die.

He hadn't seen Sendassian's face. Instead, his eyes had been on Lark—on all of his friends—the moment he'd driven the Spectrum Blade through the man's back.

The moment the sword had rejected him.

He flexed his hand.

The skin was blistered. He knew that much without looking. The blade had responded with more power than he'd ever imagined its dormant form could bear, and now he understood why the princess had never dared touch it.

But he'd been chosen. The blade had called him, had selected his hand to wield it, and he...

Zaide couldn't squeeze his eyes shut any tighter.

He had failed.

Voices carried from somewhere nearby, harsh words in a language he couldn't understand. Others moaned or cried, those belonging to Amrochan soldiers who pleaded for their lives—or begged for their misery to end. Zaide sympathized with them. He wanted nothing more than for the cold stone beneath his body to open up and swallow him whole, to let its weight mirror the burden of his guilt and failure and crush his bones to match his spirit.

But it wouldn't. The floor was as solid and real as he was, and just as unforgiving as his own thoughts.

He pressed a hand against the stone and spread his fingers wide. The rough skin of his fingertips did not snag, leaving him to wonder how many other hands had been there to rub the surface smooth. He did not know where he was, though he'd been awake when they'd taken him there. Or, he thought he'd been awake; he'd heard things, had been aware of them in the vaguest sense, and he knew his eyes had been open. Yet the moments after the Spectrum Blade had rejected him were obscured, nothing but a sheet of strange, crackling gray laid over his awareness.

The thought of the sword renewed the ache in his chest before it had a chance to fade, but he could not wallow. He was awake. Alive. And from the sharp, sudden screams that echoed off the stone, he could surmise not everyone was so lucky.

Zaide swallowed against the dryness of his mouth and struggled to push himself upright. His eyelids did not want to open, and when he forced them, they scraped back like sandpaper and left his eyes watering.

Bars. They'd taken him to the prison. He should have known that, should have remembered, but no matter how he tried to focus on the gray haze that clouded his memory, he could not penetrate it.

No sooner than he'd realized where he was, a figure stepped into view and his stomach gave an uneasy flop.

The man-sized goborrin unlocked the cell door and Zaide half expected the creature would bark orders at him in Torec or some language of its own. Instead, another goborrin—a towering beast, like those he'd seen on the day Kolmar was razed—ducked to step inside.

Zaide's stomach sank and he lurched backwards, but the cell was small and the goborrin snagged him by the leg before he could find his feet. His hand flew to his belt, but the Spectrum Blade's empty scabbard was missing and his Jadoran long knife was gone. Had the knife even been on his belt? He touched his leg and his other side, desperate for a weapon.

The goborrin dragged him along the floor, ignoring his frantic search as it pulled him toward the hall.

Both of Zaide's hands shot out to seize the bars of his prison cell, but the pain in his blistered left hand weakened his grip and his fingers lost hold of the iron in an instant. He clutched tighter with the right and gritted his teeth as he hauled his free leg back and kicked his captor's wrist with all the strength he could muster.

The massive goborrin grunted as if mildly inconvenienced, then jerked so hard that Zaide's shoulder popped and his fingers spasmed. He gasped and curled in on himself out of reflex, and the brute carried on as if nothing had happened.

Zaide lurched sideways and kicked again, but the goborrin did not react, even when the heel of his boot slammed into the creature's fingers. He gritted his teeth and twisted to claw at the stones in the floor, but they were worn smooth from years of traffic and he found no purchase.

He couldn't escape like this. He had to get a weapon. His eyes darted around the prison as he was dragged past each cell, but it was a fool's hope. He found nothing but the faces of other prisoners, each of them a mixture of anger, hatred, disgust, and fear.

Fear of the goborrins.

Hatred for *him*.

He saw it in the way more than one man glowered back with a curled lip.

They knew. They knew what he'd done, how he'd failed, how this—whatever this was—was his fault.

No, he told himself. He'd tried to kill Gadranus. He should have killed him. His sword had been poised in midair, and then... what? He didn't know. He couldn't remember, the moment hazed with the same sense of gray and twisted time that blotted out his memory of what had come after he'd collapsed. The Spectrum Blade had hovered above the enemy's back, and the next thing he knew, the blow had landed and it was Sendassian, instead.

It wasn't you. Zaide tried to roll up and grab the goborrin's hand around his ankle, but his reach fell short and he collapsed backwards as they spilled out of the prison and into a wide room with high ceilings and a bloodstained floor. The scent of death hung thick on the air and he would have retched if the goborrin hadn't flung him into the center of the room.

Zaide rolled over once and fought the heaving of his stomach as he landed on his hands and knees. His back was bruised and raw from being dragged, but he couldn't spare any thought for simple scrapes now. The door through which they'd entered slammed shut, and a wave of inhuman cheers and laughter rose as he found his feet.

Goborrins crowded near openings at the top of the room, jeering and gesturing in ways Zaide didn't understand but assumed meant nothing kind. Balconies, he decided, the openings a good twelve feet up and higher than he could hope to reach. An arena. He'd never imagined Amroch's palace would hold something like this.

He turned in a slow circle, letting his eyes skim past the solid metal door they'd just closed behind him. The room was empty, save the blood on the stone floor. Another door stood opposite the one he'd come through. It opened as he turned, and the goborrins above roared.

The beast that stepped through was smaller than the goborrin who'd dragged him there, but this one was armored, with a wicked blade in its hand. If not for its exposed hooves and the piglike snout that protruded from its helmet, Zaide might have thought it a man.

He took a step back and the spectators overhead went from roaring to squalling with delight.

Not just an executioner, Zaide realized.

This was entertainment, and he was the next show.

The door slammed shut and the goborrin came at him swinging. Zaide leaped back, his heart already hammering in his chest. He sucked in a deep breath and willed himself to be steady.

It was a goborrin, like any of the others. It moved like the others, fought like the others, in spite of its finer weapon and armor. It would have the same shortcomings and the same weaknesses, and it would bleed the same way. There had to be some gap in its armor, someplace to drive a dagger and end the wretched beast's miserable life.

But he didn't have a dagger. He didn't have anything but his wits, and those did little to preserve him as he leaped backwards again to dodge the monster's blade. The room was large, but not so large that he could back up forever. Another two paces would put his skinned and bleeding back flat against the wall. Zaide cut sideways to circle his opponent and buy himself more room, but he was easy prey without a weapon and the only thing he could do was keep circling.

He had to get the goborrin's blade. That was the only solution. But he had no weapons, no empty scabbards, no armor, nothing to use to try and disarm his opponent. Hitting the creature bare-handed would do nothing with the plate armor it wore.

So he circled. Around and around, keeping as much distance as he could and dodging whatever came close, while the calls from the monsters overhead grew frustrated instead of amused.

The goborrin in the pit with him surged forward in response. It swung more aggressively, tried to back Zaide into a corner, but he was smaller than the brute and he moved too fast to be pinned in one place. He backed up to the middle of the wall, hoping the goborrin might strike the stone and leave an opening, but it didn't take the bait.

The protests overhead grew. What would happen to him if the spectators grew bored? Would they send in another fighter, or just shoot him from above? He scanned the ugly, piggish faces that moaned and squealed their objections, praying none of them had a bow. He'd be as easy to kill as a stag with its antlers snared in brambles.

No arrows appeared.

Instead, a goborrin pushed to the front and flung a knife at the ground. It cracked against the stone and bounced sideways.

Zaide dove past his opponent's blade to reach it and the masses went wild with roars.

An angry bellow escaped the goborrin in the pit, but the introduction of the blade had brought the shift the audience wanted. A fight instead of a slaughter. Above, a goborrin stomped as Zaide's hand closed on the knife's handle. Soon, a hard, steady cadence shook the air, a rhythmic thumping he'd heard before.

Encouragement for the duel. The rhythm of war. The drumbeats of the battlefield and the thudding spears of the goborrins at Kolmar's bridge filled his head and Zaide gave his shoulders a quick shake. His left hand ached, but he wasn't skilled enough yet to fight this thing with just his right hand.

He gripped the knife tight and changed his stance.

He'd fought enough goborrins now to see the openings it left in its angry swings, but it swiped several times before he dared to try one. The monster swung and he dropped low to dart beneath its blade and stab at a gap in its armor. The fit was different from what he'd expected and the knife glanced off, but he flowed into the motion and slid around the goborrin's back.

Excited howls echoed off the stone walls, growing in volume until they hurt his ears. He couldn't afford to let it distract him, couldn't risk flinching or turning away.

The goborrin in the pit spun to slash at his midsection and Zaide barely slipped beyond its blade. The tip of the sword snagged and sliced through the front of his shirt. He bounded forward at the end of its swing and tried to drive the knife into the space beneath the monster's arm, but there was something hard in the gap and it did nothing but bruise.

Spittle flew from the goborrin's mouth as it snarled and swung its arm back hard. It caught Zaide before he could escape and its elbow struck the side of his head. Pain shot through his eye as the plate armor rang against his skull and Zaide staggered.

The roars overhead grew even louder.

It took two steps to right himself, but Zaide stayed on his feet and scrambled backwards. His vision wasn't right in one eye. He shook his head and blinked hard to try and clear it, but the goborrin was on him in an instant and it was all he could do to parry its strikes with his pitiful knife.

His eye.

That was it; that was the weak point.

Zaide ducked sideways instead of trying to deflect a blow, then sprang for the monster head-on. Its wet mouth dropped open in surprise, but he was too small and quick.

He brought up his arm and stabbed hard.

The goborrin crumpled and the screams overhead were enough to shake Zaide to his core.

They were cheering.

Cheering for him, for the death of their comrade at his hands.

Zaide stepped back from the monster's corpse before he realized he should take a weapon. He lunged for the sword his opponent had dropped, rather than the knife embedded in the goborrin's face, and his hand closed around the hilt the moment the door opened again. No; it was both doors. A pair of goborrins strode in from either end of the room.

He braced for combat and his heart lurched as his vision went gray.

The next thing he knew, the goborrins were dragging him again. There were two this time, one holding either ankle, and his back burned so badly as they pulled him over the stone that he gasped and arched.

One of the beasts looked back and said something to its companion. The second goborrin chuckled, the sound so low and close to human that it threatened to make him sick.

Then they swung him in through a cell door and slammed the bars behind him. Zaide groaned and turned onto his side. His weapon was gone, his hands empty again, though now one was smeared with the coppery brown blood of the monster he'd slain.

The goborrins on the other side of the bars exchanged words —harsh, guttural, an uneasy cadence that made it more primal noise than speech. One departed, and the other stayed to tie a colored scrap of cloth to the door's bars. Zaide stared at it as the second beast walked away.

"The flag means victory," someone said. A human voice, a familiar one. "I'd congratulate you, but I don't think you've won."

The cell directly across from Zaide's was empty. He tried to stand but his legs felt strange, as if he wasn't quite in control of them, so he dragged himself to the bars on his hands and knees to peer out. To the right, another colored cloth decorated a cell door, though the man on the other side of the bars looked anything but victorious, his face contused and caked with dried blood.

Zaide's stomach dropped. "Lieutenant?"

"Aye." Raddan offered a weak smile in greeting.

As far as Zaide could remember, the last time he had seen the man had been on the battlefield outside Amrochan. He opened his mouth to say he was glad the lieutenant-medic had survived, then shut it just as fast. Such accolades seemed in poor taste, given where they were. "How long have we been down here?"

The lieutenant raised a brow. "They knock you out?"

"I—I think so." Zaide had no other explanation for the gray haze over patches of his memory. He didn't recall the goborrins getting close enough to hit him, but his head was odd after taking that armored elbow to the temple. Thinking of anything clearly now would be hard.

"A few hours, maybe. Feels so much longer that it's hard to tell. The city went down fast, and there are a lot of them. More than I ever imagined." Raddan's volume dropped as he spoke and a moment later, a goborrin strolled past, dragging an Amrochan soldier by the ankle in the same fashion they'd dragged Zaide.

They remained silent until the monster and its captive were gone, then Zaide pressed close to the bars. "Where's Lark?"

"Don't know." The lieutenant's tone grew gruff and he pulled back from the door of his cell. "Best save your energy, lad. They're planning something for us, and I doubt it'll be good."

Zaide started to protest, but a shadow fell over the hall and he retreated out of reflex.

A pair of goborrins stopped outside his cell and exchanged words in that harsh language again, then nodded in conclusion and reached for the door. Crude batons hung from their belts, but Zaide's eyes latched onto the whip in the larger goborrin's hand.

The lieutenant was right.

He'd won his fight, but there were no prizes at all.

CHAPTER TWO

Smoke clogged the streets of Amrochan, the same choking clouds of yellow-gray that had covered the fields for weeks. It was thick enough that Lark struggled to see, but worse was how difficult it was to breathe. Still, she leaned toward the window until her cheek pressed against the glass. No matter how she tried to get a glimpse of the palace, she saw nothing but smoke and combat.

Hands grasped her by the shoulders and dragged her back. "Your Highness, you must stay out of sight."

She did not know the soldier's name, but he was one of the roughly twenty men who had swarmed to her defense the moment she'd been dragged from the throne room. They were a mix of soldiers and palace guards, all of them varied in age and skill, but she was glad to have them—even if they had no sense of propriety. She shrugged away from his hands and turned to glower. "We have to go back."

The soldiers shifted in discomfort and said nothing.

Lark had given the same instruction a dozen times or more, yet every time, it went ignored. She had screamed it as Andriun carried her from the palace, slung over his shoulder like she was a sack of grain or the game taken in his latest hunt. The Shaman had disregarded her, even when she begged. Even when she'd slammed an elbow into the back of his head and driven her knee into his chest.

He disregarded it now, too. Andriun squeezed water from yet another cloth and helped tie it around a soldier's face. Most of them wore wet cloths now; he'd claimed it would help them breathe without being smothered by smoke.

Tula, on the other hand, stood by another window and stared at the sky with such intensity, it was a wonder every fire in the city did not extinguish on the spot. Andriun had assigned that task, too, encouraging the Magister to figure out how to control the flames and smoke to aid their escape from the city.

Somehow, everyone listened to Andriun. They all ignored her, despite the fact she was their princess.

No; she was their queen. Her father was dead. The king was dead, and the crown was hers. These people should have been on their knees before her, instead of dragging her away from windows like she was some disobedient child.

She drew herself up and glared straight at the Shaman. "I said, we're going back."

Andriun glanced her way and for the first time, she saw hesitance in his eyes before he looked away. Hesitance and something else. Guilt? Shame?

Whatever it was, it sent white-hot anger prickling up the back of her neck.

Her shoulders tensed and her hands curled to fists at her sides, but the moment she drew breath, he spoke.

"We must leave the city, Your Highness. Your safety must be our first priority." At no point did he meet her gaze. Instead, he dipped another cloth into his bowl of water and prepared it for the next soldier.

"So you just mean to leave him there?" She could hardly believe it. This was not the team she had led. Tula put her head down, too, meek and chastised. The Jadoran girl had not spoken a word since their departure from the palace.

These were not the Paragons Lark knew.

"You would be wise to listen to the Desheni Shaman's counsel, princess. At this point, you don't even know if that broken-born is alive." That sour opinion came from one of the men who'd joined their ranks once they'd passed the palace gates. She should have been glad to see Admiral Warinal had survived. He bore fresh injuries that promised he'd fought as hard as anyone, and between his skill with a blade and his experience with her father's armies, he was a valuable ally to have. It was only his disposition toward her that made her displeased by his presence.

Resia sat with him in the corner, bandaging what he would not allow her to use magic to heal.

Lark turned toward the admiral with her jaw clenched. As negative as his words were, she hated that they reflected her own fears. They didn't know if Zaide was still alive. But if he was, there was no guarantee he would stay that way for long. If they did not rescue him... She shook her head to dislodge that thought before it could take root. They knew. They all knew. Yet for all they'd decided she was all that mattered, they offered her no respect. "Queen," she said.

The corners of the admiral's eyes tightened with an unspoken question.

"My father is dead," she added, tone flat. "That means the crown is mine, and I am now Queen of Amroch. I will forgive you for such insolence only once."

A sober hush fell over the room. If there had been any morale left in the troops before her, it evaporated now. Many bowed their heads or let their shoulders slump.

What a way to start her rule.

"Forgive me," Admiral Warinal said, then added with a measure of caution, "Your Majesty."

Andriun squeezed water from a cloth for her and crossed the room to offer it on upturned palms. "All the more reason we must leave, Your Majesty. You must let the soldiers out there know that you still draw breath, and you will lead them to victory."

Victory felt so far off, she couldn't imagine where it might be. Gadranus had seized the palace the moment her father was struck down. There would be no burial, no goodbye. Despair clawed at her heart. "Victory is in the palace behind us. Victory is supposed to be in that blade." She jabbed a finger toward the table, where the dormant Spectrum Blade lay atop a piece of fabric with its empty scabbard beside it. She did not know who had retrieved the scabbard or when, but someone had placed it beside the sword, and none of them had been willing to touch the blade to sheath it.

"Then it will come when you have the strength of heart to raise it," Resia put in quietly from the corner. "Andriun is right. For as long as you draw breath, there is hope. You are not yet defeated, but for now, we need to regroup."

Lark could scarcely believe what she heard. "And you would leave our Bladebearer behind to do that? Abandon him to the hand of Gadranus? Your own brother?"

The Kolmari Elder's brows drew together in sorrow, but she nodded.

Tula, too, nodded.

Had Lark's heart not already broken, it would have shattered then. "Does he mean nothing to you?"

"You misunderstand," Andriun said calmly. So little seemed to bother the Shaman; she wished she had his equanimity. "We run not because we wish to abandon him, but because I made a promise, and I will see it fulfilled." He offered the cloth again.

She faltered. "What are you talking about?"

"We promised," Tula echoed.

Lark turned her way.

"He made us," Resia added.

All around them, soldiers stood silent and solemn, waiting to see how their queen would respond.

She wanted to scream. She wanted to seize the Spectrum

Blade from the table and fight her way back to the castle on her own, to break in through the throne room's doors and put Gadranus to his end. She wanted Zaide by her side, ready to act, like he always was.

None of those things were within reach. Just keeping her breath even was a struggle, but she held her chin high and tried her best to look as if she deserved the deference the soldiers gave her.

"What do you mean?" Lark asked at last.

The Paragons exchanged worried looks. Tula shrugged and again, it was Andriun who spoke.

"After he saw the state of things here in the capital, Zaide took me aside for a word in private. He made me promise to put your safety before that of anyone else, Your Majesty." The honorific was awkward on his tongue, both unfamiliar and uncomfortable. Perhaps she had been too lenient with those in her group, letting them speak to her as they pleased for so long. Then again, of the three Paragons, only he met her eyes. Andriun wet his lips with his tongue and went on. "I swore on my life, before the Maker, that if anything happened to him, I would see that you escaped. That if Amrochan fell, I would get you out of the city. At any cost."

A heavy sensation pulled inside her chest, an anchor of dread dragging her down.

Had he known? Zaide had been the only one to speak with Gadranus in private, to have heard their enemy's plans and guess what was to come. A hint of shame heated her neck. More than once, she'd been too fast to dismiss his concerns. Her gaze slid to Tula.

The Magister nodded. "He made me promise. On all the books in the Great Library, on every scale on Vorkaris's hide, and every grain of sand in the deserts of Jadora. No matter what happened, I would get you out."

The sinking feeling didn't go away. Lark turned to Resia last, but the oaths had already made her feel small and miserable.

What had she done to deserve such an honor? She'd failed Amroch—failed *them*—every step of the way.

The Kolmari Elder nodded, too. "On every tree in the Maker's forests, on our family and the Maker and the Spectrum Blade itself. He made me promise, Your Majesty."

"Why?" The question rasped in Lark's throat, so coarse she thought she might choke.

Resia's gaze slipped past her to rest on the sword that lay on the table. "Because he believes in you. In your ability to restore that sword and bring peace to Amroch."

Then he was the only one who did. Lark made herself look at the Spectrum Blade. If anything, the color on its surface was even fainter than before. It was barely iridescent, and the colors did not move. They had not for a long time.

She struggled not to laugh.

All of this, and her power still had not manifested. That confrontation in the throne room should have been the last. She should have restored the blade's strength and Zaide should have struck Gadranus down. Instead, it lay depleted, so unremarkable that it could have been mistaken for any antique blade.

She'd been unable to protect her city, her father, or Zaide.

And now, as her city fell around her, she ran.

"Do not misunderstand him," Andriun added. "Or us. Zaide will do what he must to protect himself, as we will do to protect you."

Yet that she needed protection brought no comfort at all. She was powerless to stop the war outside the empty house where they hid. The home's occupants had already fled, though to where, she could not fathom.

"Scouts," the admiral said.

Half the people in the house's shabby front room turned toward the dirty windows. Outside, a few men in light armor skittered down the edge of the street, casting wary glances into every nook and cranny. One of the soldiers in Lark's company hurried to the door to peer outside and flag them down. They needed every soldier they could find if they were going to make it out of the city.

Andriun muttered something and went looking for more cloth. Lark still had not taken one, but every time they flagged down another wandering soldier, she was glad for it. Like all the others they'd picked up along the way, the three scouts lit up when they slipped through the front door and saw her there.

Maybe the Paragons were right. As long as she was alive, there was hope. She saw it in the men's faces.

"Admiral," one of the scouts offered in greeting. He coughed to clear the smoke from his lungs as he turned to bow. "Your Highness."

Lark was more willing to forgive the common soldiers for addressing her that way. Most of them still had no idea their king had fallen, and she was not eager to share the news. She didn't know how to greet him, though—she saw no insignia on his armor, nor was he a soldier she recognized. Instead, she merely smiled. "I'm glad to see more of our own alive."

"There are still a few of us, Your Highness, doing our best to hold fast." The man paused to cough again. Most of the soldiers they'd encountered looked ill, but they'd been breathing that infernal smoke for weeks now. Their health had to be suffering.

"And I thank you for it," she said, "but there's been a change of plans. How much of the city have you seen?"

A flicker of uncertainty touched the faces of the newcomers. "A change, Your Highness?"

"Evacuation and retreat," Admiral Warinal said before Lark could answer. "Her *Majesty* must be aided in escaping the city. The Paragons, as well."

The way he tacked them on as an afterthought rubbed her the wrong way. The Paragons were the strongest defense they had. She would have glared at the man, but the scouts had turned to her with looks of caution and dismay.

Almost at the same time, the three men bowed to her. "Your Majesty," they murmured in turn. The one in the front must have been chosen as their group leader, for he lifted his head first and addressed her with a solemn face. "We shall do our best to serve you however we may, my queen. As far as the city goes, we have not seen much, but the situation makes little sense. The goborrins that breached the city seem to have no interest in it. They hold the gates against interference from the army, but they make no effort to impede the common folk."

The admiral frowned. "They don't kill them?"

"They act as if they hardly know the city's people exist, Admiral. Whole families run right through their armies to flee without the beasts so much as looking their way. They'll fight a lone soldier to the last breath, but they don't seem to care if the city they claim is emptied."

Lark was not surprised. Gadranus had taken the castle and, by extension, the throne. He already had what he wanted. The presence or lack of peasantry made no difference and he lost nothing by letting them flee. She was the only one he would want. Her, and maybe the Paragons. "He's not after the people," she said at last.

As expected, the statement earned her a few confused looks.

"They have orders to take the city, not its people," she added. "The presence of people is an inconvenience. If they take the city without us in it, they'll only have themselves to worry about feeding."

"They will be eager to let the common folk go, in order to gain absolute power over the city with no chance of a rebellion from the inside," Andriun mused. "But perhaps that is something we can use to our advantage. If the soldiers remove their armor and leave their weapons, we will not have to fight our way past the walls."

"Leave our weapons?" The admiral's face grew so red, Lark fancied he was an overripe tomato about to burst. "We'd be leaving ourselves completely defenseless, and lose the capital in the process!"

Lark sniffed. "You assume we haven't already lost it."

The soldiers grew grim but remained silent. Of course they did; it wouldn't have been proper for any of them to argue with their superiors.

Andriun resumed wetting cloths. "We should leave at once. Before these face coverings dry out."

"I don't want water smacked over my face," Tula muttered. "I'll suffocate."

"As the Paragon of Fire, you're unlikely to be harmed by a little smoke. The rest of us are better served by keeping our lungs clear, though." Lark crossed to the Shaman's side and made a show of accepting the next cloth he prepared. On second glance, she thought it was the same one he'd offered her in the first place. She should have taken it then.

"Is that it, then? Your plan?" The admiral's tone almost dripped with contempt.

"At the moment, I believe it's the best chance we have. There are other places to find weapons and armor. You'll be harder pressed to find trained soldiers, and we have no hope of retaking the city without men who know how to fight." She smoothed her hair and allowed Andriun to tie the damp cloth over her face. The next breath she drew was cool and humid, and she hoped he was right about the water protecting her lungs. "We will preserve whatever portion of the army we can and regroup. Those of you who intend to stay here may do as you please. I won't make you come with me. But we will flee under the guise of being commoners, leaving our weapons here. Whoever escapes, however you manage it, come and meet me in the marshes just south of the city. Even the goborrins still don't dare to step off the road there."

Resia cleared her throat. "Just one question, Your Majesty."

"Speak it."

The Kolmari Elder offered a sheepish but nervous smile. "If we're leaving weapons behind, how do you mean to get the Spectrum Blade beyond the walls?"

"Leave that to me," Andriun said. "It will be hard for me to go unnoticed no matter what, so I may as well take the blade along. I will move alone, in order to reduce my chances of being seen, and I will meet with the rest of you in the marsh."

"Very well." Lark cast the Spectrum Blade one last look, but it remained unchanged, as still and silent as ever. She had to wake it soon, whatever that took.

They were out of time to stop Gadranus's advance, but it was not too late for the man to die.

CHAPTER THREE

Nᴏɴᴇ of the soldiers were pleased about leaving behind their weapons and armor, but none of them dared look at Lark as they muttered and grumbled and stacked their things against the wall. One or two tried to remain optimistic, explaining how leaving things behind meant they'd have a stash of gear waiting for whenever they returned. Lark admired the confidence with which they spoke; she wasn't sure they'd be returning at all.

In the end, all of them had agreed to flee the city and reconvene in the marsh. Admiral Warinal's face had taken a more sour twist than ever at such a conclusion, but he did not protest, either.

"We won't be able to escape in a group this large," he said as he coiled both hands around the hilt of his sword. "We'll have to divide into clusters. Two, no more than three men in each."

Resia raised an eyebrow. "No plans for the women, I see." She delivered the statement without a single drop of venom, yet more than one man flinched. Piece by piece, she returned her supplies to her bag. Only when everything was stowed and ready for their impending escape did the Elder lift her head and smile. "Well, there are only three of us, so I suppose we'll go together."

Which meant Lark's group would be either the safest or the most dangerous of all, hosting her and two of the Paragons Gadranus was after. Not that she would have desired it any other way. She trusted the skill of the men before her; they'd held Amrochan for this long and had more than proven their competence. Yet they were all strangers, and at least she knew the Paragons and their limits. "The goborrins should be less likely to bother a group of women, if they truly aren't disturbing the common folk. Even so, we'll take two men along with us, just to be certain."

A handful of soldiers shot to their feet even before she asked for volunteers.

Resia cracked a smile, but Tula rolled her eyes. Neither of them thought the soldiers would be needed. Lark wasn't so certain. The Paragons could handle themselves, she was sure, but she was less certain about herself. Without her knives, she was helpless. At least the men would have been trained in some form of bare-handed combat.

She tried to keep that in mind as she made her choices. "You two." She singled out the men with a finger, one after the other. "You'll come with us. The rest of you, divide yourselves into small groups. Whenever you believe you are ready, you may begin working your way out of the city."

"The only means of escape is through the front gate," Admiral Warinal added. "There are no remaining ships in the harbor by which you can flee. You'll have to determine for yourselves how you'll pass the gates. The goborrins will have them closed, but if you make it out, begin spreading the word that the army outside the walls is to fall back and regroup in the south marshes after dark."

Lark pursed her lips. She didn't like the man giving orders when she was right there, but she couldn't think of anything she would do differently. Waiting until nightfall to regroup meant whoever made it out of the city unarmed would have a better chance of escaping before the enemy determined what they were doing.

Rather than objecting on the basis of who gave the directions, she gave a slow nod. "Further, if you encounter any soldiers inside the walls on your way out of the city, relay the plan to them as well. We want as many people out of the city as possible. Any soldier who stays here and stays in armor risks death. I doubt Gadranus will leave any of us alive."

"All the more reason for you to leave at once, Your Majesty," the admiral said.

Tula drew back from the window before Lark could protest. "Agreed. The smoke is getting thicker, and I can't seem to catch any of it. I don't think they're burning the city, but they're definitely trying to smoke us out, and you'll get sick if you stay much longer."

Lark glanced to the others, but Resia was already gathering her things, and Andriun was attempting to maneuver the Spectrum Blade into its sheath without touching the sword. She considered offering help, but he was so intent on the effort that she doubted he would have heard her, anyway.

"Fine," she sighed. "We'll go." She had little to prepare, herself. She eyed the bag she'd been fortunate enough to carry into the throne room for a moment, then took it from the table and thrust it into Resia's hands. It still held the Sunshard and Shadowsliver, and she suspected they would be better entrusted to someone with magic to protect them.

"In less distinct clothing, maybe," Resia suggested as she accepted the task.

For a moment, Lark thought the Elder meant her. Instead, a stricken gasp came from beside the window. Tula grasped her ornate, gold-embroidered coat in both hands and held it close to her body. "I can't leave this behind, it was a gift when I became Magister!"

"And there will be more gifts for Magisters who make it out

of the city alive." Resia's words stayed sweet, despite the severity of their meaning.

Lark, on the other hand, would have gladly changed into something more practical than the dress she'd been unfortunate enough to wear for the end of all things. The pale pink silk rustled as she shifted to look down at herself. She would have given almost anything for the comfortable trousers she'd worn for her expeditions across Amroch. Or any trousers, really. "Unlace the back of my dress, Tula, would you?"

More than one of the soldiers squirmed in discomfort.

Tula did not hesitate. She slid to Lark's side and started in the middle, where the ends of the laces had been tied off and tucked inside the bodice.

"Underlayers fit for a queen will be as fine as any commoner's dress," Lark muttered as the gown came loose, half to reassure the soldiers who politely averted their eyes, half to convince herself it was a better idea than running across the city in finery that might make her stand out. Tula peeled the dress downward and the fabric pooled on the floor, leaving her in plain ivory linen that was, she admitted, far less noteworthy than what she'd been wearing.

"Hang on," the Magister said. "There's something in the pocket, do you need that?" She stuffed her hand in after it and made a strange face when she produced something wooden.

Lark snatched it from Tula's grasp. "I do, thank you." Her heart twisted as she curled her fingers around the small hair fork, but she moved without missing a beat. Her free hand swept her hair up the back of her neck and worked it into a loose bun she could pin to her head. "That should help me convince those goborrins to let me pass."

"You certainly don't look like a princess," Admiral Warinal said dryly. "Or any decent woman, running about in your underwear."

"Then it's fortunate we aren't in need of decent women at the moment. Only decent leaders." Lark glowered back, though she lifted her chin and squared her shoulders with a confidence she didn't feel. "I'm ready. Let's go."

Andriun made a small sound of triumph as the Spectrum Blade's hilt clicked into place and he stood holding the sheath with both webbed hands. "Be safe, Your Majesty."

"You, as well." She mustered a smile for the Desheni Shaman, and the ache in her chest made her fear it might be the last time.

He nodded back.

She turned toward the soldiers. "The rest of you, be cautious, but have confidence in your mission. Do not provoke any goborrins, and they should let you pass. I pray that I will see you —all of you—in the marshes tonight."

Her chosen guards moved to her side as she turned for the door. Tula hurried forward to open it, and Resia paused to get a wet cloth for her face before she joined them.

"Lead the way, Your Majesty," the Elder whispered. "You know the way better than any of us."

Lark hoped that was still true.

She strode into the smoke-hazed street and marveled at the way the cloth covering her face helped. She would thank Andriun for that later, when she saw him.

When she saw him, she repeated firmly in her mind. They would make it. They all would make it, and they would be reunited. The Paragons first, and then Zaide. She cast one final look toward the palace. "Be safe," she whispered.

Then she turned west.

The streets were cluttered with the bodies of fallen soldiers. People scuttled from alley to alley, hiding their faces and peering about as if they feared a darkness that wasn't there. Or maybe it was there; maybe it was the black, crushing tide of goborrins that filled the city's streets.

Lark kept her head down and mimicked the commoners,

though she did not fear the monsters that marched toward the palace. She kept her head down, lest she spit at them, lest her hate burn through and reveal her for who she was.

"Clear," Tula whispered.

Their tiny group shuffled along in the wake of the latest goborrin band to pass by. They paused out of the way of each column that marched and pretended they feared death or trampling. The men Lark had chosen to accompany them always put themselves at the front of their group when they hid, and she found she was grateful for it; it was easier to hide who she was when she could pretend to cower behind them.

As the group they'd picked up at the house had claimed, the goborrins were wholly disinterested in the people who shuffled from one street to the next, looking away from the marching squadrons as if not looking at the monsters meant they ceased to exist.

Halfway across the city, Tula ducked farther back into an alley and finally removed her ornate coat. She mumbled to herself as she folded it onto itself and stuffed it into a bag she'd turned up from who knew where. At least Resia's bag made sense; Zaide had intercepted her as she'd helped the Kolmari pack for their escape. Lark shut her eyes and bit her lip, wishing she could shut out the sound of clanking armor as she prayed for the safety of the Kolmari. They'd had an early start. Maybe they'd made it, and were safe across the water.

"Clear," one of the men whispered.

Lark still didn't know their names. She should have asked sooner; there was no way she could pause for introductions while fleeing for her life. The next alley wasn't far ahead, but the road was clear, and the group collectively and silently decided to keep going.

The gates were just ahead. Lark had expected to see people clustered around them, struggling to find a way past the goborrins and into the scorched fields beyond the city. Instead, all she saw was a horde of goborrins storming in, with two groups of the monsters ready to close the gates at a moment's notice. The only bodies on the ground were those of her father's men.

One of her escorts leaned in to whisper close beside her ear. "The guard house to the left. It has a triple door that opens into the gap between the layers of the gate."

She glanced back, surprised. "It has what?" She'd never heard of any such thing, nor had she seen any doors when passing through the thick walls that sheltered the city. Then again, she had never devoted that much time or energy to studying the city's defenses, and her father had never pushed her in that direction. Unpleasant emotion tied a knot in her throat at the thought. Had he ever believed she could be a competent leader? All her education had been focused on governance and political maneuvering, never on tactics or warfare. Perhaps that was why Admiral Warinal was so comfortable speaking over the top of her. He and the other officers had been trained to lead the armies in her stead.

"Follow me." The man waited for the latest band of goborrins to pass through the gates, then sprinted toward the guard house's door. It stood open, the station's soldiers long gone. Blood on the floors and walls promised the goborrins had emptied the space as soon as they'd breached the city. Now, instead of armored guards, families shuffled through its halls, unhindered by their invaders.

"Looks like it's open," the man whispered. "People getting out that way."

Good. If others flowed out of the city that way, they would be less remarkable. Maybe the goborrins wouldn't even notice them. They hadn't drawn attention yet; perhaps that luck would hold.

They were halfway to the doorway in the alcove her escort had pointed out when a strange yet familiar keening reached her ears. She froze in the middle of the hallway.

"What is that?" the other soldier with them murmured, puzzled.

Lark ducked out of the hallway and ran toward the sound. A vague protest rose behind her, but she ignored it as she ran from door to door within the guard house. Most of them were open, the rooms beyond bearing signs of bloodshed. Some held families who cowered in the corners for a moment of rest, but none of them held the source of that pitiful, moaning wail that rose with persistent despair.

At last, she came to a narrow door barring what had to be a storage closet, and here, the groans were accompanied by a steady scratching.

Lark seized the door's handle and let the poor thing free.

A surge of white sprang from the room and the two men at Lark's back gave a cry and lunged forward, but she was in no danger. The beast she'd freed continued its yowling complaints as it circled her legs, tail wagging so hard its whole body swayed.

"Daisy!" Tula squealed.

"So this is where he left you." Lark bent to bury her hands in the dog's thick mane and regretted it immediately, for Daisy tried to lick her in the face.

One of the guards sighed. "Please, Your—" He caught himself just before the honorific slipped free and cast a wary look back the way they'd come. They had to be careful; all it took was one goborrin hearing them refer to her that way. "Your friends are waiting," he finished lamely.

Lark wished he was right, but the only thing awaiting her outside the city was more trouble. "We're going. Resia, mind your brother's dog." She pushed the canine away and stood, pretending she didn't care.

"The door is this way. Stay close." The nameless guard led her back through the hallways to a doorway so narrow, she wasn't certain the men would fit. He went first, proving her wrong.

As he'd said, the passage bore three layers of defense. An iron grid waited just behind the wooden door, and another door of what appeared to be iron waited at the far end. It stood halfway open, and someone ahead of them in the passage squeezed out without pushing it any wider. That left the man at the forefront of their party to open it further, and he grunted with effort when he pushed.

It was no wonder, Lark saw as she came close; it was iron on one side and stone on the other, so it would blend into the wall when it was closed. She stepped into the space beneath the city's wall as she looked at it, right into the path of a goborrin.

CHAPTER FOUR

"Watch out!" Tula leaped forward to seize Lark's arm as the goborrin snarled and raised its weapon toward her, but it was the dog who came to her rescue.

Daisy launched herself at the monster, snapping and growling with all the hair on her back raised. She'd never looked so angry or vicious, and even the goborrin was taken aback. It stepped sideways and lifted a crude club, but another goborrin shoved its shoulder and snapped something before it swung.

The offended goborrin looked back at the dog and then Lark with its lip curled, exposing ugly peg teeth in a mimicry of Daisy's snarl.

Lark took the hint and hurled herself after the dog, looped both arms around the animal's neck, and dragged her backwards.

Daisy resisted, but not for long. She licked her teeth and kept them bared, but moved backwards at Lark's behest.

The goborrins moved on.

"Maker's mercy," one of the men whispered. "They really don't care about us, do they?"

"Be glad they don't. That was too close." The other shook his head and urged their group onward.

They pressed close to the side of the gateway leading through the city's wall and shuffled single file toward the exit. The outer portcullis was open, a ring of goborrins beyond it to keep Amrochan's soldiers at bay.

How fast the tide had turned, that it was Amrochan's army—Lark's army—that now struggled to gain access to the city.

The dog growled at another goborrin that came too close.

"Daisy, come," Lark said absently. She sort of recalled Zaide giving the dog orders, but she didn't remember what the animal knew and could only hope she would respond. To her fortune, the white dog moved closer to her legs and walked right beside her. Or perhaps that was her misfortune; Daisy hung so close that she threatened to trip her every step of the way.

"Keep left. Push south as soon as we break beyond the line," the man leading them said.

They squeezed around the corner and the devastation of the battlefield came into view. Broken bodies of men far outnumbered the corpses of goborrins on the battlefield, and combat rang loud and heavy in the air. Lark's stomach turned and she put her head down, but it gave her heart no respite, for the earth underfoot was dark with death.

This was her fault.

Her failure.

If she'd only managed to awaken her power, if she'd had the skill to replenish the sword...

Tula screamed.

Lark tore from her self-pity as Daisy hurled herself toward the goborrin that had seized Tula by the hair and dragged her backwards. The dog's jaws snapped shut on the monster's arm and the goborrin reeled back with a howl.

"Go, go!" the unarmored guards shouted as they leaped to Tula's side, but fireballs ignited in the Magister's hands. She launched them toward the beast that had dared to touch her, and a panicked cry rose in the throats of the ring of goborrins nearby.

"Tula!" Lark cried, half in fear and half in frustration, but it was too late to change anything now.

They were found out.

A bellow of warning tore from the goborrins nearby and a portion of the ring defending the gate broke toward them, crude swords raised.

Daisy released her opponent and retreated to Lark's side, the pale fur of her jaws stained an ugly copper brown. Lark started to reach for the dog, but one of her guards seized her arm and spun her toward the south.

"Run!" the man screamed as a second wave of fire poured across the monsters nearby.

Lark turned, but there were already beasts there, closing in on them. She shrank back a step as fear swelled in her chest until she couldn't breathe.

Then, a burst of wind poured forth from behind her, two high, shrill notes piercing the sounds of war.

The Hymnflute. The knot of fear released in an instant and a bright, startled laugh escaped her throat.

Wind forced the goborrins back and then whirled between the beasts and their party, wrapping itself into a barrier around their group.

No matter how many times they used the artifacts, Lark always forgot what they could do.

Tula gave a frustrated cry as the barrier sealed them off from the enemy army, but she dropped her hands to her sides and let her prepared fireballs dissipate.

Between them, the two guards gaped.

"We have to move fast," Lark said, raising her voice to be sure they heard her over the Hymnflute's song. "She won't be able to keep it up forever. Make for the marshes!"

Neither of the men protested, and their party pushed swiftly to the south.

Daisy tossed her head and keened along with the barrier

song, and Lark pitied her sensitive ears, but there was nothing else she could do.

Resia remained steady and unruffled as she played, but goborrins threw themselves at the barrier with new vigor when they saw how their weapons bounced back.

"I saw this before," one of the guards said, somewhat shakily. "When you arrived with the Bladebearer, you used this, didn't you?"

Some part of Lark was surprised to hear it, but so many had seen it. It had changed the city's morale for the better, too. What would it do to the remaining guards to see the same power used to escape, leaving them behind?

The moment that guilt set in, the patch of goborrins to their right suddenly split and a cluster of guards in Amrochan armor spilled into the gap.

Tula gave a whoop and jumped on her tip-toes, but her enthusiasm was short-lived. "We can't let them in. Even if they could pass through the barrier, we can't make it any bigger. They won't fit."

"They don't need to. They just need to move along with us." Lark waved at the men and pointed south, praying someone would recognize her and accept the order.

If they did, she didn't know, but they fell in around the barrier's bubble and pushed back when the goborrins surged.

More men streamed across the battlefield, pressing toward their shelter to join its retreat. Or perhaps they came to aid its defense—Lark didn't know if it made a difference, but she could explain when they reached their destination.

The growing number of soldiers slowed their progress and the barrier faltered. Lark fell back to offer a hand and Resia gladly relinquished the Hymnflute for her to play.

"Good work," Tula said, though her hands flexed with a desire to do something.

"Cover the dog's ears," Lark ordered before she began playing.

The Magister made a face when Daisy's keening resumed with the first notes, but she shoved a hand deep into her bag and produced a scarf. The animal looked ridiculous a moment later, with bright Jadoran cloth wrapped around her head and holding her ears flat against her skull, but Daisy lowered her head and tucked in her tail and slunk along without more than a miserable whine.

Lark and Resia traded the Hymnflute back and forth several times before one of the unarmored men within the bubble spoke. "The marshes are just ahead," he called over the music. His arm swung up to point, but Lark couldn't see it anyway, the path ahead obscured by the number of soldiers who had joined them. So it came as a surprise when a few minutes later, the men in front of the barrier plunged off the edge of the road and into knee-deep water.

The men beyond the barrier were beaten and wearied, but they trotted along with a steady pace and managed to keep the goborrins off their backs as they marched. And the monsters tried to ride their backs; they hung close, pursuing them to the very edge of the water and then beyond it, but their heavy bodies and narrow, hooved feet were ill-suited to the marsh and they toppled, one after another.

All around them, goborrins squalled as they spilled into the marsh and sank like stones, falling over one another and tangling themselves in the mud.

Cheers rose among the Amrochan soldiers and they marched onward with renewed vigor until the last of their collected number reached the water and passed beyond the flailing goborrins.

For now, at least, they had escaped Gadranus's hand.

Lark let the barrier fall and sucked in a long, gasping breath to steady herself. Mud sucked at her ankles and threatened to pull her under, but she sought firmer ground with her toes in every step and eventually set herself on a path where she did not sink.

"How long do you think we have before they find a way to cross the marsh?" Tula asked softly, the question meant for Lark's ears alone.

If the goborrins still floundered in the mud behind them, Lark could not see, but the soldiers behind her seemed in good spirits.

"I don't know, but we don't need long. A few hours to let Andriun join us, then we can move." They could take as many soldiers as would follow them then, and a few could be left behind to share instructions and help the remaining men on the battlefield escape. Part of Lark wished she could stay to oversee that aspect of the plan, too, but if she was going to lead them, she needed to push forward.

"People!" Resia exclaimed.

Lark had been walking with her head down, watching where she stepped, but she lifted it now. The ranks of men ahead of her had thinned, and past their shoulders, she saw what the Kolmari Elder meant.

A mixture of soldiers and refugees from the city stood on an elevated section of land in the middle of the marsh, and a man in officer's colors waded out to meet them. He asked a question that didn't quite reach her ears and the procession ground to a halt around her.

"An escort party, not just a retreat," one of the men in her own group called as answer. "Getting Her Majesty to safety."

Lark was grateful the title told them everything they needed to know. It spared her from repeating the story over and over— or from having to hear it from those who might be less impartial. She didn't know how to explain what happened. She didn't know how to stave off the rumors that would inevitably rise, casting doubt over Zaide's integrity.

The officer's eyes swept to her and his face grew grim, then resigned. The swarm of wet and muddy soldiers parted to let him through and he strode closer before he crossed an arm over his chest and bowed. "Your Majesty."

She nodded back. "Officer...?"

"Karj," he supplied, then cleared his throat. "Sergeant. One of the commanders ordered me to gather some men and escort escaping refugees into the marsh. Looks like you had the same idea, Majesty." He didn't seem as if he knew how to speak to her, alternating between something weary but casual and a stiffer, formal tone.

"Thank you, Sergeant. Yes, the goborrins seem averse to the marsh and even the forests that border it. They're the best place for us to use to regroup." Not that Lark wanted to enter the forests. She'd already seen some of what hid within them, back in Kolmar's temple. Even the goborrins had feared that.

Karj nodded. "The city?" He looked between Lark and the soldiers for confirmation.

"Lost," Lark answered, though admission of their defeat was bitter on her tongue. "The army and the city's guards are being cut down, but unarmed commoners are being allowed to pass. There will be many refugees for you to gather, and if you mean to help them flee instead of fight, you'd be better served by taking off your uniform."

His grimace was mirrored by at least a dozen others. He did not protest, though, and there would be time to explain everything while they waited for Andriun to join them. "And where are we retreating to, when all our refugees are gathered?" The sergeant asked that part more slowly, as if uncertain how the question would be received.

Lark hesitated. She'd tried to think of their options as they pressed through the battlefield and made the long trek to the marsh, but options were few and she had not been in Amrochan long enough to be sure of the state of all the cities that were now hers to rule.

More than a few expectant gazes turned her way, some mixed with such uncertainty and hopelessness that it made her heart ache.

"Jadora," she said at last.

Tula's head whipped around.

Lark ignored her and went on. "The Watcher is a secure city, and it has a dragon overseeing its safety, besides."

"Jadora?" Karj frowned, then rubbed his forehead as if he could smooth the creases that formed between his brows. "The city was infiltrated by Gadranus not even that long ago. If we go all the way across the desert and find—"

She raised a hand to cut him off. "The Oracle of Nimultis told Magister Vorkaris that the city would remain standing with him as its leader until beyond what she can see. Do you mean to doubt a vision given to the Oracle by the Maker Himself?"

The doubtful lines in his forehead only increased, but she suspected the target of his skepticism had changed.

"We will go to Jadora," Lark repeated, louder. "And my group will depart as soon as the Paragon of Water escapes the city and rejoins us. In the meantime, we will organize ourselves, determine where our refugees will be sent, and establish orders for the soldiers who will remain behind. If anyone has questions, bring them to me. I am in charge now."

"Of course, Your Majesty." The sergeant bowed again with his arm over his chest.

Lark drew herself up at the display of deference and tried to look regal, though it was the farthest thing from what she felt. There she was, clothed in undergarments and muddy from the knee down, queen of a burning city and all the hopeless people gathered before her to huddle in a swamp.

She forced herself to smile at them, though she felt her mouth draw tight and the expression was more grim than reassuring. But she was their queen now, for better or worse, and she allowed herself one harsh, silent laugh in the depths of her thoughts.

Long live the queen.

CHAPTER FIVE

THE SHARP SNAP of the lock jarred Zaide from sleep. He rolled onto his stomach and tried to drag himself onto his hands and knees, but the goborrin that came through the door seized him by the leg. It hauled him backwards, rucking his shirt up his chest and scraping his bare stomach across the floor.

He couldn't shout; his breath left him in a long, pained hiss instead.

They'd given him no time to recover, though he didn't know how long he'd slept after they'd cornered him in his cell. The goborrins had spared him the whip that time, but from the way one had continually brandished it at him in warning, he doubted he would be so lucky again.

Not that the scrapes and welts that covered his body were *lucky*. Lucky would have been falling in that arena, being sent back to the Maker for his soul to be venerated or condemned based on the things he had done.

Odd that he'd think of that now. Before his first encounter with the goborrins, back on the day of the Spring Choosing, he hadn't been sure he believed there was a Maker at all.

Or a Gadranus, for that matter. Now, he was afforded no such luxuries as skepticism, and he fought to turn onto some part of him that was less scraped and bruised. Somehow, he got his hands under himself and managed to lift his upper body. The goborrin dragging him set a hard pace to follow, but he walked his hands against the floor to keep from losing the rest of his skin. His free leg hovered awkwardly and he struggled to hold it aloft.

He made it halfway through the prison before his arms gave out and he fell back to the stone, and the slow scrape of movement bloodied the rest of his back.

The goborrin hauled him into the arena and dropped his leg. It continued on through the far door without ever looking back, leaving him spread on the floor like a starfish on the beach.

Overhead, there was less jeering. The goborrins gathered on the balconies were less interested in him today, their ranks filled with what struck him as casual conversation, peppered with unsettling laughter.

Zaide shut his eyes.

Had it even been a day? He had no way of knowing how fast or slow time crawled by in the dungeon, but a day seemed right.

A day since the confrontation he should have won.

A day since he'd helped destroy the kingdom he'd fought so hard to save.

He swallowed against the thick, dry feeling in his throat and made himself sit upright.

A few murmurs of notice followed. Spectators turned toward the railing to see what would come of this fight. Then, to Zaide's dismay, a door creaked open and his next opponent stepped inside.

Getting his feet under him was a struggle, but he stood. His breath came hard and his whole body simultaneously ached and burned, but he could not surrender now. Not yet, not when he hadn't determined if there was any way out.

Not until he knew Lark was safe.

He readied himself for the monster's first attack, but instead of striking, it strode forward with one hand out, palm toward him.

This one wore less armor. If Zaide could get a weapon, killing it would be easier. Already, he scanned its body for weak points. He backed up as it approached, but paused when it did not strike. It halted a few steps away and reached for the weapons at its belt. An axe rode on either hip—not the great, two-sided battle axes with a speared tip that he'd seen occasionally on the field, but a small, hatchet-like weapon of finer make than what goborrins typically carried.

It gripped one by the axehead and drew it from its ring, then offered it at arm's length.

Zaide stared at it, confused.

The goborrin grunted and gave the axe a shake. Its handle bobbed in invitation.

It wasn't a battle like before.

It wanted to spar.

Slowly, Zaide lifted a hand and curled his fingers around the smooth wooden grip. The goborrin nodded its approval and retreated a few steps before it drew the other weapon from its side.

Above, their audience grew quiet, save a few murmured speculations that were in an unfamiliar tongue but easily identified by the musing in their tone.

Did they want to test his skill? Was showing them what he could do with an unfamiliar weapon a bad idea, or did it matter at all? He hadn't seen if any of the other survivors had been taken from their cells a second time; he had no way of knowing what to expect. At this point, maybe it didn't matter. Zaide paced backwards and shifted his hand on the axe until it had a good balance in his grasp.

He'd never fought with an axe before, but if they thought he'd be easily conquered with a new tool in his hands, they were in for a sour surprise. The axe he'd been given wasn't so different from the one he'd used in chopping wood back home, and he'd fancied that a tool for chopping through goborrins more than once in the days he'd spent pining for battle.

He'd been a fool, craving this. Now, he never tasted anything else.

He made the first swing.

A few surprised grunts came from overhead, but the opponent in the arena adapted quickly to the apparent comfort Zaide felt with the new weapon. The monster came at him with a few aggressive swipes, forcing him back, testing his agility. It was no harder to be nimble with a small axe than a small sword, and Zaide darted and ducked the same as he ever had.

But the monster was only testing. Zaide was fighting, and the first opportunity he had to dive in, he lunged forward and buried the axe in the goborrin's side.

The goborrin howled and staggered and shouts of alarm burst overhead. The doors to the arena sprang open and more monsters in heavier armor rushed in to seize his arms.

Zaide kicked and thrashed against their grasp, but they were stronger than he was, and more plentiful, besides. One snagged his legs when he tried again to lash out, and three of the monsters together carried him out of the arena by the limbs.

They'd expected something different from that encounter. He didn't know what. He didn't understand anything the monsters said, and he was a prisoner—why would he react any differently to being given a weapon? Yet they spoke amongst themselves in quiet concern as they toted him back through the prison, past his cell and past that of Lieutenant Raddan, who rose to his knees in worry when he saw them go by.

Then the lieutenant's face slipped out of view and Zaide made himself stare at the ceiling instead.

The three goborrins carried him through a new doorway and deposited him on his feet. There was another goborrin there, hunched over a table populated with bottles and jars and who knew what else. It barked a quiet order and the goborrin that had held Zaide's legs gave a crude bow, then hurried out the door. The moment it was shut, the two that held his arms let go and shuffled backwards until they stood guard.

Slowly, the goborrin at the table turned to look at him.

Zaide stared back, startled.

The monster wore spectacles.

It grunted something, not quite a word, and motioned toward something at the side of the room.

Zaide didn't want to look away, but he wasn't safe to stare; there were the goborrins behind him, too. He angled himself to be able to see both those by the door and the one at the table in his peripheral vision, then glanced to whatever sat beside the wall.

A wash basin.

His brow furrowed and he gave the spectacled goborrin another glance.

It motioned more vigorously, and when he didn't move, it rolled its head in an exaggerated gesture of annoyance and pushed itself up from its stool.

The goborrin was old, Zaide realized. Its face was wrinkled and weathered, with more coarse white hair than normal along its fat lower jaw, and it moved with all the grace of an arthritic man.

He'd so rarely thought of the goborrins as anything but monsters, but the one before him now was different. It behaved almost human, with the way it pressed a hand to its stiff lower back and shuffled forward as it found its balance. Then it moved a little more easily, though it hobbled, and it reached for Zaide's arm when it came close.

He pulled back, unwilling to be touched, but the beast was not deterred. It snagged him by the wrist, then pointed at his torn and bloodied shirt and said something else.

"I'm not bathing here," Zaide snapped back.

The goborrin peered at him, its beady black eyes magnified by the round lenses. Then it huffed and reached for the hem of his shirt by itself.

He recoiled, but it already had him, its fat hands peeling his shirt upward. The cloth stuck in places he'd bled and each time it pulled loose, Zaide sucked in a hissing breath. It scraped over his raw skin and pulled tight across his bruises, managing to hurt in every place possible before it came off over his head.

The moment his upper half was bare, the goborrin made a stern sound of disapproval. It said something in what Zaide thought was Torec, its voice so phlegmy and thick that it gave him a shudder.

When he did not reply, the beast waved a hand at him in dismissal and stooped to take a cloth from the water. The cleanliness of that tub looked questionable and Zaide tried again to back away when the goborrin turned toward him, but the two acting guards by the door moved to intercept him. To his dismay, they caught him by both arms and held him fast as the elderly goborrin washed the blood from his skin. The frigid water gave him goosebumps and it stung on his scrapes, but it brought relief, too.

There were worse things than a bath, he decided. At the same time, he concluded this was an infirmary. It didn't look like it had been equipped by Sendassian's men, hastily set up and missing most of the tools Zaide would expect to find in Resia's bag of healing supplies, but maybe some of those jars and things on the table contained a healing salve. There was a mortar in the midst of them, he noticed now that he looked again. He had no idea if human remedies worked for goborrins. Perhaps the old one had been preparing something for one of their own.

Zaide nodded toward it. "Medicine?"

The old goborrin paused to squint at him.

Why had he bothered? He had to be losing his mind, trying to speak with a goborrin. Or maybe it had already been lost, and that was what landed him in this situation to begin with. He spoke again, though his throat had grown raw with thirst. "Do you understand my language?"

A sound like a question bubbled in its nose, drawing forth

another shudder from Zaide. Even if he could understand them, he doubted speaking with a goborrin would be pleasant.

"Only Torec?" he asked.

For a moment, the monster's black eyes brightened. "Torec?" The word came out with all the finesse of a brick striking stone.

Zaide shook his head.

Whatever light had sparked in the thing, it faded. "Torec?" it asked again, though this time, it shook its head too, as if to confirm the answer was a negative.

Zaide didn't know how else to say no, but the shake he answered with now was smaller, hesitant.

It patted a clean spot on his shoulder, as if to reassure him, then said something to dismiss the two armored beasts that held him. They returned to their positions by the door, while the old goborrin rinsed the cloth and continued cleaning. It said something each time it moved to a new spot on Zaide's skin, and it wasn't until one of the words repeated while it cleaned his other arm that he realized it was giving him words for the different parts of his body. His brow crinkled and he touched his arm and repeated the last thing it had said.

The goborrin grunted in approval.

Maker's mercy, what was he doing? A bloodied prisoner under the castle he'd inadvertently helped their enemy seize, tested twice in arena combat, barely clinging on to survival, and now he was taking lessons in what should have been his mother tongue from a *goborrin*? The absurdity made Zaide dizzy and he pressed a hand to his forehead.

The goborrin tapped the top of his skull and gave him the Torec word for *head*.

Zaide repeated it, then made a twirling motion with one finger.

Another disapproving grunt. It seized his arm and steered him toward the stool beside the mortar, and did not resume cleaning him until he sat down.

When he got out, this was going to be a strange story to tell.

It scrubbed his whole upper body clean, then pointed at his pants.

Zaide shook his head with enough vigor to make his dizziness worse, but it would not be dissuaded, and it was not long before the goborrin had removed his boots and trousers, too. His lower half had not been so scraped or bloodied, so cleaning took less time, and the old goborrin finished its ministrations by slathering every wound with a thick, foul-smelling paste. Then, at last, his clothes were returned to him and the goborrin motioned for him to get dressed.

It was strange to pull his torn and dirty outfit back on over freshly washed skin and sticky medication, but he had to admit his injuries felt better already. All that was left was the question of *why* they were better. What good did it do for the goborrins to clean and treat him? He hadn't seen Lieutenant Raddan come back washed.

Then again, the lieutenant hadn't been taken for a second round in the arena. Not yet. Maybe that was still to come.

Zaide was ready and unsurprised when the goborrins by the door took him by the arms again, though their hands were gentler on his biceps this time around.

They started to move him when the old goborrin grunted and called for his attention. It made an odd pinching motion at the side of its head.

Out of reflex, curiosity, or some blend of both, Zaide lifted his hand and found his ear—not the blunted one, but the one that was whole. His fingertips grazed the bluish-silver ring through the lobe and the goborrin grunted again.

"*Takk,*" it said, nodding with staunch approval.

Zaide touched the metal for a moment longer, then lowered his arm and let the armored goborrins take him back to his cell.

Was that why they'd pulled him out and cleaned his wounds? Because they recognized something that had become theirs more than it was his? Or did it have more to do with his second victory in the arena?

The goborrins locked him back in his cell and left without another word.

Across the hall, Lieutenant Raddan watched until they were gone, then pressed close to the bars of his own cell. "Are you all right? What happened, boy?"

Zaide stared after the guards and wished he knew.

CHAPTER SIX

"YOUR MAJESTY, we cannot afford to wait any longer."

The sun had already set and the last rosy glow of twilight gave way to the lights of the marsh-wisps floating above the water. They had a haunting sort of beauty, something that Lark watched emerge in the growing dark with a sense of both wonder and trepidation. The people feared the wisps; they huddled close on their tiny island in the middle of the marsh, clinging to each other and making themselves small. It worked, from what she could tell. The wisps ignored them, so long as they did not move.

"Your Majesty?" General Jobe prompted.

Lark had been glad to see the man, though she had been less glad for the way he hovered beside her, as if she was a lamb in need of a shepherd. But Jobe was level-headed and polite to her, at least, something Admiral Warinal was not.

The admiral had made it out of the city with every last one of the men they'd gathered along the way.

On the other hand, few of the palace guards had survived to escape with Jobe. His had been a harder fight, from what little he had shared. The admiral had endured his share of combat, but he'd been in the courtyard, halfway out of the palace when things turned sour. Jobe had been just outside the throne room, one of those who held back the tide of goborrins so Lark could escape with the Paragons in the first place.

The knowledge that one of the officers had fled while the other struggled to ensure her safety made it clear which one she was more apt to listen to, but they'd already chosen to use that against her. She'd overheard the general and the admiral whispering, and they both agreed they could not wait for Andriun. Then they agreed that Jobe should be the one to tell her, for she was more likely to cooperate with him.

Lark would not be played. "We will stay here as long as necessary, but we will begin preparation for departure. Where is Sergeant Karj? He was the first to help refugees escape into the marsh. He should be given the choice of whether he stays to stabilize the situation here, or if he helps escort Amrochan's people to Jadora."

Jobe's face stayed placid, though he was clearly dissatisfied with her answer. "I will find him. Please consider our next actions carefully, Your Majesty." He crossed an arm over his chest and bowed before he excused himself.

Tula tossed a pebble into the water behind him, her only contribution to the interaction. She'd posted herself close by Lark's side, but had little to say. Instead, she'd plucked dozens of pieces of marsh grass and torn them to bits, the tiny shreds of green floating atop the water at the edge of their muddy island. "His name is funny," she muttered.

A complaint about the situation or a bit of worry over Andriun's absence would have been more in line with what Lark expected. Her brow crinkled. "Jobe?"

"Karj. It's like if you turned your name around backwards, so the L turns into a J."

"That would be Kraj," Resia put in from behind them.

"Oh. Well, I never was that good at spelling. Or a lot of other librarian stuff." Tula plucked another blade of grass and looked wistfully to the north.

Lark put a hand on the Magister's shoulder. "He'll be along. Don't worry." She didn't have it in her to doubt. She no longer had the strength or energy to despair over what might have happened to delay Andriun with the sword, and assuming the best was all she had left to do.

"Uh-huh," Tula responded half-heartedly.

Well, let her sit and pine. Lark had other things to worry about now. "Resia, how do things look?"

"Few injuries, blessedly," the Kolmari Elder began, ticking off her fingers as if she spoke of some mundane inventory instead of a group of people that had swelled to hundreds, if not thousands at this point. "Mostly among the soldiers, but none who made it were wounded so severely that they need healing. The others are primarily women and children. Not many elderly, and those who did make it are spry."

It felt wrong to be glad for the news, but it sounded as if the group would be easy to move. Lark worked her fingers through the hair at the nape of her neck, below the bun still pinned with Zaide's wooden fork. "What do we have as far as provisions?"

"Virtually nothing." Resia flinched as she said it, too. "I'm competent with foraging, as all Kolmari are, but for this many people..." She didn't need to finish. There was no hope of feeding so many.

"Then we'll have to subsist our way to a city where we can gather supplies." Tinith was the only nearby option, but did it still stand? The last Lark had heard, the city had been as overrun as the southeastern forest.

Resia twisted a curl of her hair around her finger. "Perhaps I could send a messenger to Kolmar? If any of them have made it safely back to the forest, the Vale is protected enough that they should be able to comb the forest for supplies."

The barrier sheltering the forest had not crossed Lark's mind. She tilted her head to one side, briefly considering, but she had already seen Kolmar. Even at its most developed, as it had been the day she'd first seen it, the forest village would not have been able to house so many people. Even if they'd utilized the temple as shelter, there would not be enough room. But anything they could offer would be helpful, and if Tinith had been reclaimed by her father's men, perhaps the Kolmari could meet them there with supplies. "Of course. Speak with one of the officers and have someone sent immediately. I'm sure you'll be happy to know your people made it home safely, too."

A hint of red rose in Resia's face, turning her browned skin dark. "Yes, Your Majesty. I would appreciate that."

"You don't have to call me that," Lark muttered. "I'd prefer if you didn't."

"And I'm more than happy to speak with you on a familiar basis, but I suspect some people will benefit from reassurance that we have a leader." The Kolmari Elder mustered a smile, but it faded the moment General Jobe returned with the sergeant in tow.

"Your Majesty." Karj bowed deep. "The general has told me your offer. If it would please you, I'd prefer to stay here and assist in recovering as many of our people as possible. There are a lot of wounded men on the battlefield, and I'd rather not let the goborrins burn their bones."

That wasn't the only thing goborrins did with bones. Lark fought back a shiver at the recollection of the old Magister's demise and made herself nod. "Very well, then. Assemble a team from those willing to stay here and aid you. Your efforts here are just as valuable as the work of getting these people to safety." She was less certain that was true. Perhaps it would have been wiser to send soldiers back to summon as many fighters as possible, and reassemble them in the desert.

"Where are we going to safety?" Andriun asked.

"We're—" Lark began, but Tula's shriek of delight cut her short.

The Magister flung herself at the Desheni Shaman, wrapping her arms around his neck in a gleeful hug that ignored the fact he was dripping wet.

He cautiously extricated himself from Tula's grasp. "Hello."

General Jobe looked the Shaman from head to foot, his lip curled. "Maker's mercy, did you swim all the way here?"

"It did seem the most practical solution. Lake Sian is right beside the city, and then there are the rivers that feed the marshes." Andriun's long black hair had come loose from its braid and laid plastered against the side of his face, across his shoulders, and twisted around the backs of his arms. He pulled each strand free, one at a time, until he had untangled himself. For all that he was rumpled, he was in one piece, and the Spectrum Blade's sheath hung at his side.

He caught the way Lark looked at it and offered a sheepish smile as he grasped the scabbard and tilted it upward, letting a stream of water pour from its top. "I would recommend finding somewhere to let it dry. I do not know if legendary blades can rust, but I suspect it would be displeased with us if we try and find out."

Jobe's brows knit. "*It* would be displeased?"

"The sword bears some level of sentience," Lark said. "How else did you think it chose a wielder? It grants permission and retaliates against those who dare to touch it without its approval."

The general stared at the sword, troubled.

In truth, it troubled Lark, too. In their current situation, she was more bothered by herself, though. Her own reluctance to try and handle the blade had become an inconvenience, and she could not expect Andriun to carry it at his hip forever.

But that was a problem for later. Right now, she needed to answer the question the Shaman had posed, which had gone without answer. Lark tore her eyes from the sword and raised them to his face. "Now that you're here, we can prepare for departure. We're taking the refugees to Jadora."

Until that moment, she had not realized the Desheni could blanch. A strange, murky gray tinted his face. "The desert?"

Guilt slumped through her like sludge. She hadn't

considered his comfort at all when she'd made that decision. Out of everywhere she could have chosen, the desert would be worst for him.

"You don't have to stay with our group, if you don't wish to go." She tried to sound amicable, but she already knew he would refuse, and the offer did nothing to assuage her own embarrassment at making such a choice without consulting him, too.

But he hadn't been there. She hadn't known when he would return, and decisions still had to be made.

Andriun frowned and looked no less ashen, but his voice was steady. "I will go wherever I must to see this to the end."

"We'll figure out a way to make things comfortable," Tula chimed in as she sidled close and took his arm in both hands. "We can get a big barrel of water for you to sit in during the ride."

One side of his nose wrinkled. "I am not that fragile."

"But you'll dry out like a starfish on the beach!" The Magister dragged her hands down her face, distraught.

Lark did not usually mind Tula's antics. Today, they wore thin. "If he says he will be all right, then he will be all right. Besides, we don't even know if we'll have to cross the desert. The road takes us near Tinith. We'll send scouts to see if the city is held by my father's—by my men, then plan accordingly. If there are ships in Tinith, we will make for Jadora by sea."

None of the Paragons flinched at her mistake in the middle. It would be difficult getting used to seeing them as her soldiers, but she was the queen, and she would not make those kinds of errors for long.

To her relief, Jobe nodded his approval. She didn't need it, but things would be easier if she received no friction from her officers.

"There are some experienced scouts in the party I brought out here originally," Karj said. "They were invaluable in finding a safe spot in the marsh. I can send a pair of them to Tinith at once and have them return to meet you on the road."

Lark gave the general no chance to interject. "Please do, then assemble a team of volunteers from any of those present who wish to stay here and aid the evacuation of Amrochan."

The sergeant blinked in surprise. "Am I to lead the group? With so many high-ranking officers, I thought..." He trailed off and turned to Jobe as if he expected a scolding.

"I will need General Jobe and Admiral Warinal with me in Jadora," Lark said. "You've already proven your competence in managing refugees. Not only do I have need of those sorts of skills, but I will see they are rewarded once Gadranus is defeated."

Karj straightened at the way she finished that sentence, and his reaction bolstered her confidence, too. That was what the Paragons meant. The more certain she was they would reach victory, the better the soldiers would perform.

"Go on, then." Jobe waved the man on with a gruff edge to his voice and the sergeant saluted before he jogged back to the cluster of soldiers resting beside the huddled families.

Lark cast the general an expectant look, prepared for more complaints.

Instead, the man gave a weary smile. "I'll speak with Warinal. If anyone can secure ships, it will be him. Depending on what those scouts have to say, it may be best if he's got a party ready to send to Tinith ahead of the rest of us so transportation can be arranged."

"You mean to stay with the rest of us, then?" Lark suspected he meant to shepherd her some more and was unsurprised when he nodded.

Having him in the role, rather than the admiral, would be tolerable. It would not look bad to have a trusted officer hanging close by her side as she accompanied her people to safety, and it would give her an upper hand with the men, too; few would dare disrespect their queen to her face, but they were used to following General Jobe's orders, and his presence would smooth the transition.

"Very well." She almost sighed, but it would have been unbecoming. "Organize the people into groups and assign soldiers to escort and aid them. We have no provisions, so we'd be best served by moving at once. The marsh has no food to offer, and I would not drink the stagnant water."

"I want to be a scout," Tula put in.

Lark was surprised she wanted to be parted from Andriun so swiftly, considering how worried she'd been. "I would rather have you here. There's something I'd like to do before we depart, and I would appreciate having the three of you present."

Resia started to question, but Lark's eyes fell to the sword at Andriun's side, and that conveyed enough.

The Desheni reached for the belt that held the scabbard in place. "It would be good to tend the blade, anyway, as I have said."

He would get no disagreement from Lark, but she admitted her reasoning was not so altruistic toward whatever consciousness the sword possessed. There was one last chance for her to turn the tide of war before they tucked tail and ran, and she would not let it slip by without trying.

Andriun pressed the scabbard into her hands. "How many of the artifacts do we have? I had not thought to ask."

The sword felt heavier than she recalled and she tried to reassure herself it was only the extra weight of the water in the sheath. "The Molten Dagger and the Vale Hymnflute are accounted for," Lark said slowly. "The Captured Spring..."

All of them grew sober. No one had mentioned what Gadranus had done to the slender magical vial, and now that she addressed it, Andriun's expression grew pained. Of course it did; it was his loss, more than anyone's. The artifact that had been entrusted to the Desheni Shaman, which had guaranteed the safety of his people for generations. That he had allowed her to borrow it had been enough for his people to exile him. What would they do when they learned it had been destroyed?

"That is my problem to solve," Andriun said without elaboration. "What of the others? The shard and the sliver?"

"I have them. Or, rather, Resia has them in her bag." Lark seldom let them out of her presence, and they had been in her pockets at the end, for all that it had helped. Without the pockets of her dress at her disposal, entrusting them to the Kolmari Elder and the medicine pouch that never left her side had made the most sense.

Though Lark had not asked for them, Resia drew her bag forward and withdrew the two stones. Neither was necessary for what Lark intended and she shook her head.

Frowning, Resia put them away again.

"Keep your healing poultices ready in case this goes poorly." It was an attempt at humor, but Lark did not feel like laughing. Nor did any of the others, she assumed from their silence. She let her hand hover over the hilt of the Spectrum Blade as she gathered her courage. It had let her touch it once before, but it had rejected her before, too.

She held her breath and wrapped her fingers around the grip.

Tula blew out a long, hissing sigh of relief, but the others remained silent.

Slowly, Lark drew the blade from its beautiful scabbard. She tilted the sheath so the rest of the water could drain out as she turned the sword's tip toward the sky.

The colors on the surface shifted, but it was only the play of the night's feeble light.

If I have any hope of ending this at all, please *speak to me,* she begged, pushing the thought toward the sword with all her mind and soul.

She closed her eyes and waited.

The blade remained silent.

CHAPTER SEVEN

"Scouts," Andriun called.

Lark lifted her head, but he stood on a rise some distance ahead, and she saw nothing but the hill. He'd joined the soldiers in their rotation of pushing toward the front of the group as they marched the long, winding road that led toward Tinith. He kept the pace longer than any of them, too, trotting well ahead of the rest of the refugees for hours on end, ensuring the way ahead was clear.

They'd encountered few goborrins along the way, but that they encountered any at all left Lark unsettled. The first wave that attacked the capital had swept up from Kolmar, but after the city had been reclaimed and the protective magic over the forest restored, the onslaught had come only from the north. For more goborrins to strike from the south end of Lake Sian, they'd have to be coming from Tinith—or from Kolmar again. Her stomach roiled at the thought of losing the forest again. Especially after the Kolmari had fled Amrochan by ship. She chanced a look at Resia, but the girl's face told her nothing. She remained serene and steady no matter what they faced.

How was it everyone did a better job of filling leadership roles than she did?

Lark resisted a frown and hurried ahead, one hand on the hilt of the Spectrum Blade to keep it from sliding around. It had not responded to her, but it hadn't rejected her either, so she'd elected to carry it herself. It felt silly and was a hindrance more often than not, the belt too big for her and strapped over the undergarment she still wore as a dress, besides. It tried to slide down her hips when she walked and the blade knocked loose against her legs, but seeing her with the weapon that represented their salvation had brought her people some peace.

She scaled the hill and shaded her eyes against the morning sun to see when Andriun pointed into the distance.

Sure enough, the scouts they'd sent ahead to Tinith some days before were on their way back. Making good time, too, though she wondered if the way they ran was a bad sign.

Before she'd decided what to do, General Jobe appeared beside her. He, too, raised a hand above his eyes to blot out the sun. He wore a frown, but it was pensive rather than concerned, and she chose to take it as an indication she should not be worried. He was comforting that way, steady when the other officers were stormy, calm and decisive when all the soldiers inevitably looked to him for guidance. He had not tried to steer them her direction for leadership, but he had explained the men were used to answering to officers. Sendassian had been king, but rarely had he interacted with his armies directly. For many of those who walked with them, this was their first time sharing the field with a member of the royal family. Few of them knew what to do.

"Let's go greet them," Lark said at last. The others started down the slope without question or comment, leaving their party to trudge downhill in silence.

It was one of the easier parts of the trek. The road was smooth and her trip along it before had met no challenges, but there had only been a handful of them then. It was different with half her city's population at her back. They could not have moved swiftly if the Maker Himself had appeared to drive them along with thunderbolts. Or lightning bolts, she supposed. Thunder was only the noise.

And what does that matter? she chided herself in silence. If that was the sort of thing that concerned her, she'd grown far too tired.

"Hail, Majesty," one of the scouts called as soon as he came close enough to make himself heard. He waved an arm overhead in greeting, too, but his voice brought her comfort. If he was willing to shout, there were no goborrins ahead and no need to worry about who might overhear.

Lark drew to a halt and let them close the rest of the distance between them. Both scouts bowed and she flicked a hand to bid them rise. Only then did they lift their heads so she could see their grim frowns. Whatever sliver of optimism she'd scrounged up crumbled to dust.

"It's not good, Majesty. General." The scouts both gave Jobe a greeting that wasn't quite a bow, but it wasn't a salute, either.

"You made it all the way to Tinith and back?" Lark could only hope it was not so severe that they'd never reached their destination.

"To the city's edge. The market remains, there are people in the city, but it's occupied by goborrins. Lots of them."

Somehow, she'd expected him to sound apologetic. Instead his report was flat and factual. He barely looked her way, but that bothered her less. He was there to report to his commanding officer, who would be the one to sort things out with their queen.

"The shipyard?" Jobe asked.

The scout shook his head. "Empty, save the frigate they came in on."

Lark didn't know whether to be disappointed or relieved. If the goborrins had arrived by ship, it meant Kolmar's Vale was still intact and the Kolmari would be safe. "How big of a frigate?"

"One of the biggest ships I've ever seen. It actually looks

more like a war galley, but I've never seen one so large. A thousand men could row that ship at once."

She pursed her lips. "Shall I take that to mean there are a thousand goborrins in Tinith, then?"

"More than that, I'm afraid. I'm sorry, Your Majesty. The city appears to be firmly within Gadranus's grasp." The scout touched his fingertips to his heart and gave an awkward and apologetic half-bow.

Lark resisted the urge to sigh. She had hoped for better news. They could not continue into the desert without supplies, and she did not know where else to find them if not the markets where she'd hired a caravan and stocked their wagon once before. Then there was the matter of weapons and armor for the soldiers who had abandoned theirs to flee the city. They could not be left without equipment forever. She lifted a hand to rub her brow.

Jobe was less concerned. "Any signs of wreckage in the harbor? Indications of battle that may have taken place?"

"None, sir. The people of Tinith are still there, but there was no sign of our soldiers or any indication that merchants had tried to flee or had stock destroyed. Goborrins were present, patrolling the city, but folk went about their business as usual. The market was stocked, but no trade was happening without visitors. It was like everything had been put on hold." The scout paused, then shook his head. "If any battles took place, they weren't in the city."

"Combat against more than a thousand goborrins would leave scars on the landscape," Lark protested. "You saw no signs anywhere around the city?"

"None, Your Majesty." The man's face twisted with apology before he returned his eyes to the general. "We believe the reinforcements King Sendassian deployed to Tinith never arrived. The guard presence there normally wouldn't have been enough to stand up to that sort of invasion. They could have been taken prisoner and let Gadranus and his forces seize the city with minimal effort."

"Reinforcements in the numbers the king sent don't just disappear," Jobe said.

"No, sir," the scout agreed, but it was clear he had no idea where the missing soldiers could have gone.

The general nodded slowly, then pointed back over the hill. "Admiral Warinal is currently positioned at the rear of the procession with the Magister. Report to him. Tell him what you've told me, answer his questions, then take your rest. Her Majesty and I will take this time to determine the best way forward."

"Thank you, General." The scouts bowed in unison and departed, one after the other.

Lark turned her head to watch them go, but found herself gazing thoughtfully at Resia and Andriun instead.

"What is that look?" the Shaman asked warily.

She hadn't realized she had a look, but she hoped it was determination. "We're still going to Tinith."

"With the city overrun by goborrins?" Resia twisted a curl of her hair over and over again. "Are you thinking they'll leave us be, the way the ones in Amrochan did?"

"Perhaps they would, but that's not the plan. We're taking back the city." Her fingertips drummed against the Spectrum Blade's hilt as she trudged back up the hill.

Jobe followed right on her heels. "With what army?"

She stopped at the peak and cast a speculative eye across all the people shuffling along the road. "That one, General."

"Thousands of commoners don't make—"

"Thousands of commoners is only the beginning of what's down there. Don't forget how many soldiers we picked up on our way out of the city, and how many have come to join us in the days following." Lark gestured with a spread hand, rather than pointing. She did not want to do anything to make anyone watching concerned. "More come from behind us every day as the battlefield empties, and the enemy's armies do not follow."

"They come injured and ill-prepared," he replied flatly.

Lark raised her chin. "Even accounting for injuries, exhaustion, and those who were forced to leave behind their weapons and armor, we'll have thousands of ready soldiers by the time we reach Tinith. We will not give them the opportunity to crush us between two occupational forces. We will reclaim the city and its market before we continue to Jadora."

"You speak with great certainty, Your Majesty." Andriun halted at her side and studied her instead of the masses of people. "You have a plan?"

"Yes, although I cannot be certain it will work until I see the state of the city for myself. General Jobe, please retrieve Admiral Warinal and Magister Tula, and select five of your best officers to organize soldiers. Each should choose fifty soldiers to accompany us."

Jobe grimaced. "So few?"

"Two hundred and fifty is more than a few men. Besides, I want them for our initial visit, not to reclaim the city. Enough to defend us, should I need to retreat before my plan is fully formed." She smiled sweetly, knowing it would unsettle him.

His eyes narrowed, but he placed a hand over his heart and bowed. "Of course, Your Majesty. I'll see to it at once." He managed to sound subservient, but his back was straight as a blade when he turned to march downhill and find the admiral.

Lark allowed herself a tiny snort.

"What about the people?" Resia came up on her other side, her hands clasped before her. Had her brown knuckles not grown pale, she would have appeared calm.

"We will allow them to continue forward for now. They will not reach Tinith any time soon." It was miraculous if they covered a few miles in a day. Lark had spent the last handful of days wishing they moved faster, but now she decided their sluggishness was a boon. Soldiers could be mobilized independently of the refugees. All their practice marching meant they'd outpace the rest of Amrochan's people easily, and if all Lark had in mind went smoothly, Tinith would be long reclaimed by the time her people arrived.

"Onward, then." Andriun shrugged and resumed walking. "Will you enlighten us as to what your plan entails?"

"Soon," Lark promised. She gripped the sword to keep its belt from sliding and jogged down the hill to put herself at the head of the procession.

In truth, she would not.

Not until she laid eyes on the city and knew just how mad she'd become.

CHAPTER EIGHT

SEVERAL DAYS LATER, Lark huddled flat on her stomach and stared across the fields. Swaying grasses obstructed her view, but she dared not stand yet. Regular patrols circled the market, though their numbers were few. The way the goborrins ambled around the city reminded her of how they'd circled Kolmar's temple, and how she and Zaide had climbed to evade them.

There was no evading these.

For one fleeting, heart-wrenching moment, she wished for one of Zaide's absurd and spontaneous plans. Then she drew a breath, steeled herself, and looked again. Tinith was low and perched at the edge of a forest, but they'd come in from the eastern plains so they'd have a view of the harbor. The goborrin warship was immense, looming over the city like a shadow.

She inclined her head toward the vessel. "Can you sail that?" She kept her voice low, though they were too far off for any of the goborrin sentries to hear.

To her right, on the other side of Resia, Admiral Warinal gave an agitated snort. "I can sail anything, given enough hands to man it."

That wouldn't be a problem. "We'll have plenty of hands as

soon as the rest of our people arrive. Andriun, can you sense the water from here?"

Andriun, belly-down to her left, nodded.

"Can you tell if there are any other ships in the water?" She didn't know what all his power could do, but it didn't strike her as an unreasonable question.

His mouth twisted to one side. "There are many ships in the water. The problem is that they all seem to be beneath it, rather than floating on top."

So the goborrins had arrived and sank anything that could have been used to escape. That struck her as odd after what transpired in Amrochan. Why hold the people of one city hostage and let the others flee? "Do you suppose they aimed to trap the people of Tinith so no one could come to our aid?" It was the only thing that came to mind, though it seemed unlikely. Her father had spread soldiers far and wide, but their greatest help would have come from Jadora, where Elsanna kept her own army. Or, where she kept Tula's army. Before long, the Jadorans would discover Elsanna was not their true Magister.

"That seems far-fetched," the admiral said. "Not a soul in all Amroch would expect the capital city to need help defending itself."

Lark disagreed, but now was not the time for arguments over political posturing. "I think we should approach from the north. Through the thickest part of the trees."

Warinal shook his head. "This field makes a better location for battle."

"But the trees give cover and will help disguise our numbers. They won't know how many of us there are and they won't be able to organize their attacks in the woods." Plus there were the Paragons. Lark did not add them to the equation, unwilling to plan for their involvement until she had a chance to speak to them without the admiral there. She had no doubt they would accept any order she gave, but she didn't want to order them about; she was the queen, but they were the only ones who had supported her when she wasn't.

"The forest would be better for me," Andriun put in. "There is more water to be found under the trees, and that path will take us closer to the river. I will be most useful if I can follow the western edge of the woods, where the river flows down from the mountains."

Resia nodded and pointed with one delicate finger. "The forest is ideal for me, too. My magic will be strongest there, and I'd be able to manipulate the plants to aid us."

Beside her, Tula huffed. "Well it's not great for me. Green timber doesn't burn well."

"We need you to burn goborrins, Tula, not the forest around us." The reckless nature of the Magister's power was the primary reason Lark had elected to leave Daisy behind with the civilians. The last thing she needed was for Zaide's dog she was supposed to be looking after to be roasted. She studied the path of the goborrins that circled the edges of the market, then bit her lower lip. It would be better for Tula to go in with full freedom over her fire magic, but could they afford to split what soldiers they had? Losing any after they'd escaped from Amrochan struck her as too high a price. Her gaze traveled past the market to the enormous ship in the harbor, and a new thought sprang to mind. "But don't worry. I have the perfect way to ensure you can."

The admiral's face turned so sour, Lark expected him to spit.

She smiled warmly at him, just to get under his skin, then turned her attention to the Kolmari Elder at her side. "Resia, you help the men through the forest. Anything you can do to aid the soldiers as Admiral Warinal leads them through. Clear paths, topple trees on goborrins, anything."

Alarm wrenched Warinal's eyes open wide. "We don't have enough soldiers with us to—"

Lark continued as if he hadn't spoken. "Be coy with the monsters when they come after you. Do as much as possible to hide our numbers and give the impression it's just a small band of men on a supply raid. Tula and Andriun, you'll be with me."

"Not beside the river?" Andriun asked.

"This is ridiculous," Admiral Warinal said at the same time. "There's no way we have the numbers needed to take a city of this size on our own."

"You'd be ashamed of those words if you had any clue what we've gone up against before." Lark shifted to point through the grasses. "The moment the goborrins move in response to the soldiers in the woods, the Desheni Shaman, the Jadoran Magister, and I will head south across this field until we reach the shore. Andriun, you'll get the three of us onto that warship."

The Shaman's dark eyes traced a path across the grasses, then hung on the ship. "I can do this, but there may yet be many goborrins on the vessel. Are you sure we should...?"

Tula made a soft *psh* and waved a hand. "We'll take the Hymnflute with us and you two can hide in the barrier while I take care of them. I'll burn the whole ship down."

"Please don't, we will need it to sail to Jadora. I'll explain the rest along the way. Admiral, Elder, please begin. I trust you are experienced enough to know when it's time to draw the men forth to attack." Lark pushed herself to her hands and knees and inched backwards down the hill to let the city slide out of view.

"Your Highness, I cannot allow this," Warinal snarled. "This foolishness will get all of you killed, and we cannot afford—"

"Your *Majesty*," she snapped back. "And you will do as I say, unless you want to be stripped of your rank immediately."

The man blanched and she knew she'd won.

As soon as she no longer saw Tinith, she stood and gave him an imperious frown. "Now, go. We'll watch for the enemy to respond to your bait, then we'll enact our half of the plan."

Whatever surprise she'd stirred up in him, it soon melted into a dark scowl, but he said nothing as he found his feet and made for the cluster of soldiers who waited out of sight at the foot of the hill.

Resia flashed her a nervous grin before she trotted along after him, sure of foot and with her head held high.

Lark hated to push the girl into battle. In truth, she and Resia were close in age, but the Kolmari girl was short of stature and slight of frame, and it was hard to imagine her going up against goborrins at all. She touched a hand to her heart and sent a silent prayer for Resia's safety.

Only once Warinal had departed with the soldiers and the Elder in tow did Andriun speak. "What exactly is this plan meant to do?"

"Pull the goborrins out of the city, so we can eradicate them without putting the people of Tinith at risk. They won't know we're headed for the ship until we're there and they can't stop us from boarding. Don't forget, goborrins can't swim. We'll destroy their rowboats as they cross to the ship, and I'm willing to sacrifice the docks in the harbor to Tula's flames." Lark spared the Magister a smile and Tula's eyes grew bright.

"So I can torch all of them in the little boats, but not the big one." Tula appeared satisfied with that. "But what do we do about the goborrins on the big boat?"

Lark started to speak, but an odd prickle coursed up her side and stole a gasp instead. Both Paragons grew concerned, but she raised a hand and tilted her gaze toward the sword at her side. "Should I take that to mean you'll help?"

The Magister clapped both hands to her mouth. "Is it —did it—"

A gentle wave of energy followed, so soft it almost tickled. Lark rested a hand on the Spectrum Blade's hilt. "I see why Zaide struggled to explain what it was like handling the sword. It's certainly not what it has been, but a blade is a blade, and it will let me wield it." For now. Her fingers tightened around the grip.

Andriun's shoulders bunched up and he crossed his arms over his chest to hide the way they rose. "I do not like this plan. It sounds like... almost like..."

"A Zaide plan," Tula finished for him. Her fingers still hovered before her lips, her eyes round.

If only it was. Lark's throat tightened, but she made herself move. She wouldn't pretend to know how, but his plans always worked. Perhaps that was the sort of impulsive madness they needed right now. She paced north, around the hill, to search for a new place to lay in wait. "This way. We have to watch for the goborrins to cross into the woods."

The soldiers moved in small groups, keeping their movements quiet. There was still a good distance between them and the city down the slope, but the noise of an army carried, and the less they made, the better. Had she waited for all the men Warinal had wanted to bring, they never would have been able to get so close.

As if the tension in the soldiers leached into her, too, Tula kept her voice near a whisper. "Right, so, how are we getting onto the ship, exactly?"

"Do you remember the battle in Ganede?" Lark asked, though she gave her no time to reply. "Andriun will have to lift us with the water."

Tula's nose crinkled with displeasure.

"I will carry you on my back, if that will be more comfortable," Andriun said.

"Can't you carry me in your arms? Like a damsel in distress?" The Magister pressed the back of her hand to her forehead and pretended to swoon.

He was unconvinced. "Neither one of those words could be used to describe you."

Tula let her arm drop and this time, her whole face scrunched. "Yeah, well, the story books never said anything about the handsome prince being a fish, so I guess you're not cut out for the role anyway."

"Here," Lark said. "This is a good spot for us to keep watch. If you would, please save your bickering for later."

"I am not bickering. She is being disagreeable on purpose."

"Am not. I don't *need* a prince to come rescue me, but it would be nice sometimes, you know?" Tula rubbed her arms and grew still as she settled in to wait.

Lark did not agree, but there was no point in continuing the argument. As far as she knew, she was the only one who had been to Tinith, which meant planning their route around the city—and across the docks to the ship—was her responsibility. "Worry less about handsome princes and more about all the people we're responsible for right now. They're the ones who need to be rescued, not us."

A hint of guilt drew across Tula's face, but it didn't stay long. A moment later, she grinned. "Maybe the pretty princess can be the rescuer this time, then."

"Pretty queen," Andriun murmured and nudged the Magister with his elbow.

Neither description felt accurate, though his was closer. Lark hardly felt like a hero in her dirty and worn underdress, her tangled hair pinned up on the back of her head and a borrowed sword hanging from her waist by a belt that didn't fit. Heroes were supposed to have an air of... well, heroism. She had no doubt she looked as uncertain and ill-equipped as she felt.

But uncertainty didn't spare her from what she had to do, and once her people were safe and they had a chance to structure a proper plan from the safety of Jadora's walls, there was one more rescue she'd need to mount. Her eyes flicked north, though even the smoke from the fires that took Amrochan were no longer visible from where she stood. *Just stay alive that long,* she thought—begged—as if the words might reach him. *I'll find you. I'll help you. I promise.*

"Look." Andriun's webbed hand swept toward the trees. The goborrins had seen the first of the soldiers filter into the woods. Now they marched across the field, calling warnings, drawing others from the city. They'd already taken the bait.

Lark turned toward the open field and took hold of the Spectrum Blade so it wouldn't bounce as she ran. "This way."

They went single-file, though the high grasses slowed them down. At that rate, the city would be devoid of goborrins by the time they reached the shore.

The alert rose across the city as drumbeats—familiar and yet unwelcome—carried across the rolling earth.

By the time they were halfway there, sweat stuck Lark's dress to the middle of her back and made loose hair cling to her face. "As soon as we hit the sand, get us to that ship," she panted. Even Tula wouldn't complain about how refreshing the water's touch would be.

They gave the city a wide berth, though the farther they went, the more visible they were. Tula's hair glowed like a torch under the sun, and Andriun—well, there was no hiding how blue he'd become, no matter where they were. Had they gone under the cover of night, perhaps it would have worked better, but she had not dared waste a moment for fear goborrin scouts would spill out of the city. Or, worse—for reinforcements to arrive and trek north to crush anyone who escaped from Amrochan.

Rather than a smooth slope, the shore dropped hard. Lark misjudged the height of the ledge and tumbled into the sand with a yelp, but water swept up a moment later to curl around her body. It tightened like a hand and lifted her off her feet. Tula's startled cry behind her promised the Paragons were at her back. The wave rose, carrying the three of them toward the ship that loomed larger with every passing moment, and for the first time, she second-guessed her plan.

The warship was large enough to house a city. Maybe it still did, for as the warning cries rose all across Tinith, goborrins poured from the ship's hold.

Dozens.

Hundreds.

"Hang on," Andriun said.

"To what?" Tula shrieked.

The wave crashed over the warship, sweeping goborrins

against the rails and leaving the three of them in the center of the deck.

Lark did not so much as stumble when the wave receded, and the Spectrum Blade glinted in the sun as she tore it from its sheath. "Hope."

CHAPTER NINE

After all the times Lark had seen Zaide wield the Spectrum Blade, she should have expected what it would be like to have it in her hand. She was not skilled with swords, more used to having her twin knives in her hands, but it was short and light and close enough that she adapted fast. But the charge that tingled up her arm as she spun to strike her first foe was like nothing she'd ever experienced, like lightning in her veins.

It crackled through her body as she drove the sword into a goborrin's gut. It tore through the leather armor like a cat's claws through sheer silk, and while the wound did not burn with light when she withdrew the blade, the monster fell, all the same.

So this was what she'd failed to grasp. What had escaped her, every time she'd tried to claim it.

Why now? She could not help the surge of bitterness that welled inside her as she twirled around to strike again.

It had refused her when she needed it. Had sparked against her hand and refused to accept her as Bladebearer in her father's stead. Only now, when he was gone, had it deemed her worthy.

Her jaw tightened. No; that wasn't true. It had let her handle it before, when she'd needed it to unlock the Sunshard's hiding place. Her father had still lived then.

Was it her, then? Had she done something to sour the blade's opinion of her before she'd even so much as found it?

A strange sensation brushed her mind, almost a sound. A descending note, like disagreement—or disappointment.

She almost scoffed. What was that supposed to mean?

Water swirled ahead of her to snag a goborrin and fling it overboard. It twisted back like a liquid snake.

Lark shuddered and tried to stay focused. The others would fight how they pleased. She was the one in the thick of things, surrounded by goborrins that raced in from every side. Fire shot past her ear and stole a yelp from her throat.

"Sorry!" Tula shouted.

Just stay focused. Lark tried to ignore everything but the monster ahead of her. The Paragons had her back and the blade was in her hand. The Hymnflute hung against her side in the holster Zaide had crafted for it, ready to shield her the moment she grew too tired to fight.

Every goborrin she faced went down in one hit, sliced or skewered like soft fruit. It was no wonder Zaide had been able to fight so hard and so long. He'd been good with a blade from the moment they'd met; with the Spectrum Blade in his hand, he'd been all but unstoppable.

Please give me the same strength. My people need this. She didn't know who she begged—the sword, herself, the Maker, the monsters—but it didn't matter. Fear was what answered, clawing at her insides the way it always had.

Fear of failure.

Fear she wouldn't be enough.

Fear the sword would change its mind, and all would be lost.

"Boats coming!" Tula already had fireballs in both hands as she sprang for the railing.

Good. Lark swallowed hard against the rising tide of doubt that rose within her. Distress bells rang out across the warship's deck, the noise all but lost in the roars of pain from the monsters she felled. She tried to see who rang them, but her eyes caught on something else instead.

A banner bearing a tusked ram's skull flowed in the wind overhead.

The enemy's flag.

Inspiration sparked in her chest, bright as Tula's flames. Lark shifted her path to carve her way toward the mast where it billowed.

Tentacles of water lashed out beside her, knocking goborrins off their feet. "How many are there?" Andriun asked, though she suspected the question was not for her.

She didn't know, nor did she want to. She just wanted her arm to hold out long enough for the Spectrum Blade to do its work.

What had it been like when it was at its full strength? When it had been powerful enough to rake beams of pure power across ships like these and sink them into Ganede's harbor?

A sting in her palm reminded her to focus on where she was and the size of the task before her.

Fine, she thought at the sword, though the word came with determination instead of petulant spite. *You've lost so much of your magic. It just means I have to be your light now.*

The power that scorched through the evil of the monsters before her. A force she'd never touched on her own, but maybe this was different. Channeling it through the blade, pouring all her hope and frustration into every stab and sweep.

Heat itched between her shoulder blades and swelled within her chest. Inch by inch, she fought her way toward the ladder that led to the platform above the folded sails.

She'd draw the goborrins back to the ship and she would destroy them. All of them.

Two more of the monsters fell to the blade and she all but leaped onto the ladder. *Goborrins can't climb,* she reminded herself as she scaled the thing. That was important; she'd seen that as a fact in Kolmar's temple. They couldn't swim and they couldn't climb, which meant there had to be human members of the crew somewhere.

"Watch for broken-born," she shouted over the rush of Andriun's water magic and the whooshing booms of Tula's fire, but she dared not look back to see if they confirmed the order. Instead, she paused to return the sword to its scabbard and free her right hand, then scaled past the rigging and the sails so large, the canvas could have draped the entirety of the castle courtyard back home. Her heart hammered against her ribs and tried to climb into her throat. She couldn't let it choke her. Nor could she look down.

"Just keep moving," she breathed.

As if that was easy. Now that the sword was out of her hands, she noticed the way her arms and shoulders burned with fatigue, but she'd gone too far to stop. The fight went on without her and she almost glanced toward the harbor, thinking to see how many rowboats Tula had set alight with goborrins in them, but to look would mean seeing how high she'd climbed and she did not think she could bear to know.

Give them a sign. Draw them all near. Then they can drown. And her people could reclaim what the hand of darkness had stolen.

At last, she reached the platform. It was not until she was so high above the deck that she realized how the ship rocked on the waves that came into the harbor. The platform swayed viciously beneath her, upsetting her stomach and threatening to cast her into the sea.

Yet the flag bearing the mark of Gadranus furled in the wind just above her head. She stayed on her hands and knees until she'd caught her breath by the tail and dragged it back into her lungs with all the force she could muster. Then she stood and seized the banner.

It fought her.

She fought harder, twisting the cloth, tying it down.

The last knot tightened and she fell back to her knees for a moment of respite.

The enemy's flag still flew above the warship, but now, it flew upside-down.

"The first taste of distress you'll get," she told the flag, as if Gadranus himself might hear. "But it won't be the last."

A fireball streaked past the edge of the platform and Lark stifled a shriek. That had come too close to be anything but deliberate.

She glared down at the ship's deck and regretted it at once.

"Hey! Get down here, we need you!" Tula called from below. Or, one of the Tulas shouted, or maybe both—she split before Lark's eyes as dizziness and nausea swept over her.

Down. Of course. Lark opened her mouth to reply and shut it just as fast when her stomach heaved.

So much for that moment of victory. She grimaced and turned onto her belly so she could slide one leg out long and search for the top of that ladder. It had to be there; she'd just come up it, hadn't she?

"Just get down. Just the way you came. It's perfectly safe, goborrins can't climb." But people could, and she already knew they had to be there, or else no one could hoist the sails.

Her toes found the first rung and she worked her way backwards to find the next. Going down would be easier with handholds, or a railing, or—

Something grabbed her waist and Lark flung herself back against the platform with a shriek. It wrapped tight and dragged her back and the moment her body left the solid wood, her voice failed and she waited to fall. Darkness surged in from the edges of her vision and colors flashed before her eyes. It was not until the coil of water left her that she realized she'd been carried, not dropped, and she collapsed onto the deck with a shuddering gasp for air.

"Sorry," Andriun said with no remorse at all. "Go with Tula. I'll hold them off."

"What—" Lark managed, though she couldn't summon

enough words to finish the question. What urgency had driven him to speak that way? Andriun never—

Tula seized her by the arm and dragged her to her feet, then pulled so hard she thought she might fall over again.

"Hurry," Tula urged.

As if she meant to dally. Lark staggered along in the direction the Magister pulled her until her vision cleared and she gathered her wits enough to draw the Spectrum Blade again. They dodged dead goborrins and felled half a dozen more before they reached a door into the hold.

"Andriun took out one of their leaders," Tula explained as she slammed a foot into the door twice and busted the latch. It swung open with a groan and she turned her palm upright to cradle a flame to light the way. "They've got prisoners."

"Prisoners?" Lark repeated. That put more power in her step, though she dared not hope what they might find.

The locked hold was all but empty, most of the goborrins already pitched into the choppy waters beyond the ship's hull. They ducked low beams and squeezed between crates of supplies as Tula led the way with far more certainty than she should have held.

Finally, Lark huffed and made herself ask. "Where are we going?"

"I have no idea, but if I was going to keep prisoners in a great big boat, they'd be just about..." The Magister rounded a corner and pointed with her free hand. "There!"

Lark's mouth fell open as the firelight glinted on metal bars and polished armor.

Amrochan armor.

"Your highness?" one of the prisoners nearby exclaimed as he leaped to his feet. His face was tired and worn, but he was alive, and at his voice, dozens more men surged to the fronts of their cells.

"I know you." Lark stumbled over a barrel of something in

her haste to reach the bars. "You're one of the officers my father sent, one of—Maker's mercy, you're the missing army!"

"And you're a miracle for weary eyes to spy," the man laughed. "We're rescued! We're saved!"

Enough soldiers to reclaim a city and hold it against enemy forces.

Lark laughed, too. "And so is Tinith."

The men were haggard after however long they'd been imprisoned, but there was no force in the world that could stand against the vigor and excitement that blazed in the rescued soldiers' eyes.

The tiny flame of hope within her heart grew a shade brighter.

CHAPTER TEN

DAYS CLAWED their way past with little change. Sometimes Zaide was dragged out of his cell and made to fight. Sometimes he did not see the goborrins for what felt like ages, and his bruises had time to start healing before they pulled him out again.

Other prisoners came and went, but he recognized none of them. The lieutenant remained in his cell across the hall, but the goborrins never came for him. After his first battle, he'd been left to rot. Everyone had grown to look scraggy, but the steady influx of new prisoners gave Zaide a little hope. There had to be people fighting outside, people still struggling to regain control of the palace.

Yet no news came from beyond the palace walls. The men who ended up in cells close enough to speak with him had nothing to share beyond what he already knew: Amrochan had been lost to Gadranus's forces, and the man had claimed the throne.

"Hard to understand why we're still fighting," the newest arrival mumbled as he lay facing the ceiling, downtrodden and exhausted.

"Because we're not the only ones doing it," Zaide said. He always kept his voice low, afraid of what the punishment might be if their captors overheard them talking. The goborrin patrols through the prison were few, but they came at random intervals, so there was no telling when or if they were safe to speak.

The soldier harrumphed. "How do you figure?"

"Gadranus is still alive? Still in control of the palace?"

Slowly, the man turned his head to squint across the hall. "He is."

"Then that means Dasienna is alive." And she was the last. The last heir to the throne of Amroch, the last ruler that stood in their enemy's way. Zaide hated to think of what pressure she faced now, trying to evade the crushing forces that had overwhelmed the city, so he didn't think of it at all. He put it out of his mind and told himself there was nothing else he could do. "For as long as she lives, we have a chance to make it out of here."

A moment of silence came, followed by a scoff. "She won't save us. We'll die in here. You, me... all of us will die here. He's in charge now. We've already lost."

Zaide leaned against the stone wall at the back of his cell. "He took Amrochan. That doesn't mean he won."

The only response he got was a skeptical *tch*.

He couldn't fault the man for doubting. Few others knew their enemy's true goal, and the princess was one of them. Or, the queen, he supposed. He flinched at that thought and rubbed his face. Amrochan had been lost, but parts of Amroch still stood to resist Gadranus and his forces. She was the only remaining heir, so she would be their queen now, leading them from... where? He stared at the floor and considered where she might have gone.

There were a few options. They'd just come from Nimultis, and he did not think the Oracle would refuse her if she sought shelter in the west. Kolmar was another choice, now that the protective barrier had been restored to hold enemies at bay. Jadora was less practical, though having Vorkaris nearby would be a boon. But Kolmar was the closest and it was guaranteed to be safe. If he made it out—*when* he made it out—he would start his search for her there.

"Keep that spirit up, lad," Lieutenant Raddan said softly from across the hall. "I think you're going to need it." His head turned.

A moment later, Zaide caught the clack of cloven goborrin feet against the stone.

He groaned.

They arrived at his cell before he made it to his feet, and one of the beasts seized him by the arm and pulled him off balance so he could not stand.

Zaide snarled his frustration as he tumbled, but the second goborrin snagged his other arm before he landed and together, the two brutes pulled him into the hall.

"Let me up," he snapped, though they did not react. He struggled to find his feet, and they set such a brisk pace, he could barely keep up while pedaling backwards. He hated this, hated being wrestled and manhandled. At this point, he would have preferred to walk. There was nothing he could do to escape them and no point in trying, for the harder he resisted, the harsher they were in their handling.

He knew the route to the arena by heart now and even being dragged along backwards, he was not surprised when they pulled him through the door and let him drop. He toppled onto his back with a displeasured grunt and cast a baleful glare at the goborrins in the balconies overhead.

How many times would they bring him here? Until he failed? Until he died? With the sparse rations they gave him, it was only a matter of time before he didn't have the strength to fight. Even now, he found it harder to rise than it should have been.

Yet he still dragged himself upright. He stayed on his knees for a time, letting his eyes rove the goborrins gathered along the balconies. There had to be something he could do, something that didn't involve just rolling over and quitting, but he hadn't found it yet. Even if he'd been able to escape the goborrins in the halls, there was no clear escape from the prison, and the place was crawling with so many goborrins that he would have been caught in an instant.

The balconies, too, offered no way out. Even if they hadn't been full of monsters, he saw no way to reach them. He'd spent trip after trip studying doors and halls and corridors, hoping for some weakness in the way they managed things, but he'd found nothing.

Nothing on this side of the arena, anyway. He turned his head, just far enough to watch for the opponent he knew would come out the other side. They'd never taken him that direction. If there was an escape route to be had, maybe it was on the other side of that door.

Zaide forced himself to climb to his feet and waited for his opponent to slide in.

The fight was like all the others. A goborrin stepped in, someone provided him with a weapon at some point, they battled until his enemy was felled. All the times he'd faced them in combat had begun to blur together until he couldn't distinguish one match from another. Sometimes they used axes. Sometimes it was swords, sometimes knives. They all ended the same way, with a goborrin either dead at his feet or grievously wounded. Then they'd spirit him off to the old goborrin on the other side of the dungeon, where he'd be scrubbed clean, rubbed with foul-smelling healing salves, and sent back to wait another turn.

The old goborrin's infirmary had become the only thing he looked forward to.

Every time he was washed and treated, the beast taught him a few more words. Zaide had thrown himself into listening, clinging to every scrap of linguistic knowledge he could gain.

Now and then, the goborrins that passed through the prison's hall spoke. Rarer still, one of the broken-born commanders would make an appearance and whole conversations would reach Zaide's waiting ears. After the first week of listening and learning—he was convinced they dragged him to the arena and their healer more than once a day—he'd started to pick out a few words, and others hung at the edges of his understanding.

He had to have known it at some point. He'd been small when his mother fled with him to Kolmar, but the harder he thought and tried to remember, the more he was certain pieces of the language were familiar. He'd only forgotten, that was all. How old had he been when his mother died? The memories had grown hazy, but he was certain he'd been no more than five. Old enough to speak. Old enough to understand. His head dropped into his hands and he strained to listen to every distant voice, praying it would unlock some of what he needed now.

The cycle went on and on. More fights. More monsters. More words in Torec with more repulsive medicine. More prisoners from outside, more haggard and hopeless faces.

Then one day, not all the words were Torec.

Zaide wasn't the only one in the prison who sat straighter at the sound of the princess's name. Dread lodged itself in the pit of his stomach, a cold and bitter mass that threatened to make him ill. He inched closer to the bars and listened hard, relieved to see his own uneasy expression mirrored on the face of the lieutenant across the hall.

A pair of broken-born officers meandered down the corridor, one twirling a ring of keys around his finger while the other stopped at each cell and took notes. They spoke as if bored, but Dasienna's name came up again, followed by several words the old goborrin had taught him.

Dasienna. Sword. Goborrins dead. Tinith lost.

The dread that poisoned his middle cooled to icy uncertainty, but he strained to keep listening and struggled to pick out anything else he could understand. There was something about battle. Someone was unhappy. Dasienna's name again, and something else about a sword.

Not a sword. *The* sword.

Dasienna had the sword, and the sword had cost them Tinith.

Zaide choked a laugh and covered his mouth to stifle it further as the officers worked their way down the hall. They lingered outside his cell and he pretended to clear his throat. He dared not look at their faces, lest they realize he was learning. So he kept his head down and let them make their notes, listening all the while in hopes he'd hear something to answer the thousand questions that burned in the forefront of his mind.

Rather than giving him time to stew, one of the broken-born called for a guard. A goborrin appeared a moment later and the man asked something—Zaide picked out the Torec words for hand, goborrin, and what he'd come to assume meant fight. Maker's mercy, how long would it take for him to recover the rest of the language he'd lost?

The goborrin guard grunted and held out a hand. The second of the broken-born handed over the ring of keys, and the monster turned to unlock Zaide's cell.

That interaction meant something. He was so close to grasping the conversation, even without knowing all the words, yet it still managed to evade him.

He stood before the goborrin had the door open and for once, he paced toward the door as it opened instead of trying to figure out a way to escape.

Dasienna. The sword. Tinith. He had a rough idea of what it all meant, but he knew someone he could ask, and the only way to get there was to play along.

When the goborrin reached to seize him, Zaide offered his arm. Both white-haired men in the hall between cells made noises of surprise, but he did not look their way again. The goborrin wrapped its painfully strong hand around his elbow and gave it a twist, forcing him to stumble.

Zaide sucked a breath in through his teeth, but he recovered his balance two steps later and managed to stay on his feet. They'd always dragged him, but he'd never gone willingly.

This time, the monster merely escorted him through the

prison, to the door into the arena that had grown so familiar. Another pair of goborrins waited outside and his escort relayed some sort of question or order before it shoved Zaide through the door and slammed it shut behind him. It took more than two steps to right himself this time, and he stopped in the center of the bloodstained room.

He'd just squared his shoulders when the opposite door opened and his opponent slid in.

Zaide stared, uncertain.

The goborrin that stepped toward him bore no weapons and no armor. It was scarcely even clothed, nothing but coarse linen trunks to keep it from being naked. It grunted as it approached and squatted to put them at eye level. The hard cords of muscle that drew tight in its arms and thighs seemed at odds with the blobby proportions of its torso and its fleshy jowls.

Uneasy, Zaide stepped back. He'd planned to take a hit from a weapon, earn a cut and be taken to see the goborrin medic. How was he supposed to do that when his opponent was unarmed?

Another grunt escaped the goborrin's throat and it said something in Torec. Zaide thought he caught the word *hand* before the monster resumed that strange stance and bent its arms upward, its hands loosely curled.

Martial combat, then. Another way of fighting they'd thrown at him. By now, he was certain they were testing his proficiency, though he couldn't fathom why. Knowing what he could do made little difference; he'd already been captured, and clearly none of the combat skills he possessed had helped him escape.

Still, Zaide had no choice but to go along with it. He could always get himself a new scar next time. There would be a next time, he was sure. There always was.

He inched backwards a little farther and shifted to a combat-ready stance. He knew little about fighting bare-handed, but he understood the concept.

The goborrin across from him grunted in what sounded like

approval. It shifted sideways, examining his position and footing before it went in with a jab.

Zaide ducked sideways, but that simple attack highlighted the trouble he was in. The monster's arm was as thick as one of his legs. How was he supposed to best something so much larger than him?

Another strike came, almost before he was ready, and he knocked the goborrin's arm aside. He'd have to deflect, not block; any attempt to stop a strike instead of merely skirting it could end with him just as injured as if he'd taken a hit.

Two more punches came his way before he dared to retaliate. He swept in past them and drove his curled fist for the center of the goborrin's chest. His knuckles made contact with a dull smack and pain shivered up his arm. The monster might have looked flabby, but beneath the fatty skin that rippled with the blow, his fist found a solid wall of muscle and bone.

Squalling laughter rose from the goborrin in front of him and those overhead. Heat crept up Zaide's neck, but he backpedaled and shook his hand as if to shake off the pain.

He didn't get time to retreat before the goborrin came after him. It drove a flurry of strikes for his head, but it lacked speed and most were easy to dodge. Zaide waited for an opening, but nothing came—the goborrin was relentless, tireless, and gave nowhere for him to answer with another jab. A knuckle grazed his jaw in a way that would bruise; a rough fingernail on the monster's meaty hand scraped across his cheekbone and drew blood. Overhead, grunts or harsh barks sounded with each punch that missed or made contact, but it was not the sort of rowdy jeering that had accompanied his sparring matches before.

Zaide stuffed that thought into the back of his mind. He didn't have time to think about it now, not when one punch from the beast in front of him could be enough to shatter his skull. That sort of strike was not what he wanted to send him to the infirmary; a hit like that would knock all the questions right out of his head. It wasn't even one of the big goborrins, no taller than his foster father or any of the guards locked up in the castle prison.

He ducked a swing and spotted his opening. It repeated moves in a pattern, and it had recycled the same sequence three times in a row. After the third swing, it changed its stance before its other arm moved. The gap wasn't long enough to retaliate with a strike, not without leaving himself wide open, but he could change how he defended.

The goborrin swung, and Zaide grappled its arm instead of deflecting, then twisted his body to sling the monster over his shoulder.

Or, that was what should have happened. He hadn't planned on how much the goborrin would weigh, and instead, he jerked on its arm and only succeeded in pulling it off balance.

Howls of amusement surged overhead. Even the goborrin he fought bellowed a laugh. It stood and raised its arm until it pulled Zaide off his feet. He dangled for only an instant before it whipped its arm sideways and slammed him into the wall.

Pain burst from every point of contact and odd lights flashed in front of his eyes. Zaide blinked twice, staggered, and fell to his knees.

Wild snorting and keening laughter roared overhead, but it didn't matter. The fight was over and two of the goborrin guards were already on their way in to claim him.

Rather than lifting him, they dragged him to his feet and waited for him to steady. He wobbled, then gave up. There wasn't a speck of blood on him and there were no cuts or scrapes for the medic to treat, save a scratch on his cheek. If they thought him severely injured, they'd be more likely to take him where he wanted to go.

Neither of the beasts caught his ruse, and when they chose to drag him along, he pretended to be too dizzy to fight them. His head didn't feel good after that blow, but if anything made him dizzy, it was the rush of thoughts that ran through it.

Who else was in Tinith? How long had they been there? Had he assumed correctly, and what he'd heard meant the city slipped Gadranus's grasp? Had Lark taken an army in hopes of finding supplies? He tried to sort out what he needed to ask while the guards carried him to the old pig-medic.

The spectacled goborrin sat on his stool by the table when they arrived, as he always did. He glanced back and grunted, then motioned for them to leave Zaide in the middle of the floor. They did that, sometimes; dropped him wherever there was space and took up their post by the door.

As soon as they released him, he tried to get to his knees.

A few words of scolding came from the old goborrin as he pushed himself up and hobbled over to take Zaide's head between his hands and check his eyes.

Zaide grabbed the medic by the wrists and struggled to think of all the words he'd need to ask his broken question. "Dasienna," he started.

The medic's dark eyes blinked behind the dirty round lenses of his spectacles.

He did not appear to be put off, so Zaide pantomimed a crown over his head with both hands. "Dasienna?"

The goborrin repeated her name, prefaced with a title he assumed meant *princess*.

"Princess Dasienna," Zaide repeated. Her name came easy, but the Torec words still felt odd on his tongue. He pushed them out anyway, wishing with all his might that he'd taken the time to have Andriun teach him more words. "Sword fight Tinith? Tinith no fall princess?"

With every word, the medic's eyes grew wider. For one instant, his mouth split with a wide grin, exposing ugly teeth. Then he sobered and moved his hands from the sides of Zaide's head to his shoulders. "Yes." The single word came out smooth, a sharp contrast to Zaide's efforts. When the goborrin went on, it was in crude language compared to how the others spoke, simplified for ease of understanding. "Tinith fell, yes. Hold city no more. Battle lost."

Zaide tried to hold his excitement at bay. Maybe if he masked it, made it sound like concern... "Dasienna hold sword? Sword light, colors?" He gestured to indicate the weapon's size, then wriggled his fingers to mimic the way the iridescent colors flowed across the surface. How else was he supposed to describe the Spectrum Blade?

The medic grunted. "Yes. Dasienna blade holder."

And she'd used it to take Tinith. The first shred of news that had come from outside, and it was good. Tinith was the closest city to Kolmar. If she'd reclaimed the market, maybe Zaide's guess of where she'd sought shelter was right. Not that it mattered. What mattered was she was alive, she was safe, and she had...

His excitement drained as he thought that over a second time.

Lark had the sword.

He turned his hand to examine the ugly marks left on his palm. The blisters left by the Spectrum Blade's rejection were gone now, the last of them mended by the old goborrin's nasty salves, but scarring still remained. A permanent mark of what he'd done.

Of what he'd lost.

Zaide curled his fingers into his palm and shut his eyes.

He'd known it could happen. That should the wielder be deemed incapable of brandishing it, the sword would choose a new hand to be its bearer. Somehow, he'd assumed he would escape and things would be the way they'd always been. That he was merely rendered temporarily incapable by circumstances, not that he'd become unfit.

But Dasienna had the Spectrum Blade. It had rejected him.

Replaced him.

He didn't know whether he was hurt or relieved.

The old goborrin patted his shoulder and Zaide was startled

to recognize sympathy. "Boy good fighter. Boy hold swords again. Many swords." He spread his hands wide apart to indicate the number, in case the word hadn't been clear.

That, too, brought no comfort. Zaide sank back to sit on his heels and opened his hand to stare at it again.

"Boy good fighter," the medic repeated, as if to reassure him. "Only boy Torec bad."

If that was supposed to be ribbing, it fell short of the mark. Zaide hesitated, then glanced up. "Speak more Torec. Many speak, Torec no bad."

The old goborrin's fatty brows rose and it gave a snuffle that was wholly pig, instead.

Zaide touched a hand to his chest. "Zaide." Then he pointed to the medic's chest and made a questioning sound.

Round black eyes stared back at him.

He tried again, tapping his chest with more insistence. "Zaide. Mmm?" He reached toward the old goborrin and let his fingertips hover just above its ratty shirt.

The medic raised a hand to touch his own chest, then made a sound so far from being a human word that Zaide couldn't help but laugh.

"All right," he said, dropping back into the language he spoke best. "I guess Whok is the closest I'm going to get."

The piglike ears atop the goborrin's head quirked at the approximation of its name.

Zaide cleared his throat and pointed at the table. "No medicine." Those words came out a little better in Torec; he'd used them often enough. "Zaide no hurt."

"No hurt?" Whok asked before he prodded at Zaide's ribs with one thick finger. "Zaide no hurt in heart?"

It was a perceptive question, but not one he intended to answer. After all, how was he to explain to a goborrin that he'd been replaced?

CHAPTER ELEVEN

"Are you certain we need to stop?" Lark watched the soldiers milling about the warship's deck as she traced the edges of the Spectrum Blade's hilt. It was far more comfortable wearing the sword on a belt that fit. Never mind how much better it felt to wear proper clothing. She'd traded her travel-worn underdress for the best Tinith's market had to offer. The loose-sleeved shirt, brocade vest, and sturdy trousers were much more in line with the sort of things she'd worn for the early part of her adventure. She still missed having her knives sheathed at her thighs, but that was one thing the market they'd reclaimed lacked. There had been armor aplenty, but the weaponry was gone, all of it commandeered by the goborrins that had taken the town.

All the more reason she'd been glad to find the soldiers on the warship. Their blades had been stashed nearby, rather than turned over to goborrin hands.

Admiral Warinal scarcely turned his head. "You'll have to trust me, Your Majesty. It would be foolish to continue on to Jadora without at least pausing to schedule shipments of food. We're carrying a lot of people with us, and you can't possibly expect the desert to support them all."

She still didn't like it.

They'd departed from Tinith a scant few days before, leaving the army they'd freed to defend the city in their absence. A great many of the refugees from Amrochan had been left behind, too; there simply hadn't been room on the ship for all of them. Jobe and Warinal had selected a combination of soldiers and families to bring along for the first voyage. Those who remained in Tinith had been promised shelter and boats that would carry them farther.

That was half the reason Warinal had decided to stop in Parral. It was the first major city along the coast, and the last anyone had heard, Parral had not suffered the same fate as Tinith. Why the goborrins would have sailed past that coastal city to land in another, she didn't know. She could only assume it was because Tinith was so much closer to Amrochan. If they had intended to push north, using the great warship to move faster made sense.

Lark bit her lip and drummed her fingers against the top of the sword's scabbard. "Do you think Parral will have enough ships to carry everyone? All the refugees behind us?"

"No. But not everyone will wish to go. Some will settle in Tinith. Others will push east toward Kolmar, and many will move from Tinith to Parral and stop there. I wouldn't expect more than half of Amrochan's people to go all the way to Jadora, and a number of your soldiers will be seeking permission to stay with them. They'll want to remain near their families after everything that's happened. You would be wise to consider granting some of them that wish." The admiral always sounded like he was bored, as if he was explaining common knowledge to children instead of discussing war and resource management with his queen.

Whether that was insolence or just his personality, she had yet to determine. "Well, I suppose that's something to attend to after we make landfall." It would not be long before that happened. Already, Parral sat on the horizon. They'd hugged the continent's southern coast and made good time, no doubt thanks to Warinal's experience manning such ships—and Resia's gifted use of the Vale Hymnflute.

Lark had always known the artifact could manipulate air, but she had not realized that with the right melody, it could alter the wind patterns and weather themselves. It would have been useful to know that sooner.

To Resia's credit, she had tried to help and had been surprised by their lack of knowledge. The songbook she had entrusted to Zaide along with the artifact had held information on all of the Hymnflute's uses—and he had ruined that book shortly out of Kolmar.

"I shall let you know as soon as we reach the harbor," Warinal said. "We'll want to send scouts to be sure the city remains free of the enemy's influence, but I don't anticipate problems."

Naive for such an experienced man. Lark held that thought to herself. "Very well. I'll leave you to it." Not that she wanted to leave his side at all, but the trip made her restless.

She hadn't wanted to leave Tinith, either. Leaving the city so soon after they'd reclaimed it had felt wrong, but every inch they sailed also widened the space between her and Zaide. Lark gazed northeast as she descended from the helm and made her way toward the cabin.

How long would it take before word of Tinith made it back to Amrochan? Would he hear? Would he be encouraged by the victory, or would he think she was running away? He wouldn't be wrong if he did—she was fleeing like a frightened dog with her tail tucked between her hind legs. It didn't matter that it was the best and wisest thing to do right now. It made her feel like a coward, and she feared she wasn't wrong.

Lark opened the door to her quarters and grimaced when a white blur leaped out to greet her. "Off." She planted a hand atop Daisy's head and pushed the dog down, though that only resulted in her hand becoming the target of wet kisses, rather than her face. She made a sound of disgust as she stepped inside and shut the door.

"She missed you," Tula said sing-songily.

"I had hoped I wouldn't need to deal with her again after we left her with the civilians outside Tinith." Lark wiped her hand on her hip and crinkled her nose, but Daisy was undeterred and stared up at her with her tongue lolling and her pale eyes alight.

"Deal with her?" Andriun asked in a murmur. "Aside from letting her sleep in here, you have had nothing to do with her. Who do you think has gotten stuck cleaning up after the dog on the ship?"

Lark turned toward him with a protest on her lips, but she paused when she saw him hunched over the cabin table with a book and papers spread before him. "What are you doing?"

"If I tell you the answer, you will become very unhappy with me." He never so much as lifted his head.

"I'll become unhappy with you if you're hiding something from me, too." She started to cross her arms, but it made her look pouty, and she was trying to preserve some air of authority. She settled for resting one hand on her hip instead, letting the other dangle beside the Spectrum Blade's hilt.

Andriun hesitated, then turned the page.

"He's looking for clues." Tula turned on her bunk until her head hung upside-down off its edge, her red hair pooling on the floor.

Lark had not regretted asking for the three Paragons to share her cabin. It was the largest space on the ship, intended for the captain, and provided more than enough room for the lot of them. The only downside was a lack of privacy. It would have been nice to sit on her own bed and sulk for a while, but their presence meant she had to sit at its edge like a proper lady. Daisy trotted over to sit by her feet and she reached out unconsciously to stroke the dog's ears. "Clues for what?"

"Stuff about Gadranus we might use to our advantage whenever we head back to Amrochan. We're going back to

Amrochan, right?" The Magister twisted her head to look in Lark's direction and made herself look like a contortionist in the process.

A shudder rolled down Lark's spine and she masked it with a small shake of her head. "Not any time soon, at this rate. I should have stayed behind in Tinith and gone back on my own."

"I do not think you would be able to breach the city's defenses on your own." Andriun tapped one finger against the page, then finally raised his head. "There are things we do not yet know about our enemy's power. We should engage with great caution."

As if she didn't already know that. It wasn't just his power that was a mystery; the way Gadranus intended to manage and defend the city was still as unknown as his next move. Lark shifted her hand sideways to scratch the spot beneath Daisy's ear that made the dog kick. "What are you reading and why do you think it will help?"

Andriun's face grew guarded. "I suspect you will be unhappy with me if I tell you the answer to that, as well."

"It's Zaide's father's journal from the time he was an officer in Gadranus's army," Tula provided.

Lark's brows shot upward.

The Shaman gave Tula a dark glare, but the red-headed girl was already turning herself upright and did not seem to notice.

"I mean, we haven't gotten to discuss it a whole lot because Andriun has to translate it as he goes and his Torec isn't perfect yet, but it sounds like they were really good friends up until the part where Gadranus killed him." Tula touched a fingertip to her chin and her eyes drifted upward. "Actually, maybe they weren't that good of friends."

"I beg your pardon?" Lark almost choked on the words and she didn't know whether to glower at them or storm over and snatch the book from his hands. "Where did you get that?"

"Zaide gave it to me," Andriun said defensively.

"When?" Perhaps that would have been a better question to lead with.

"When we were in Amrochan. Before the part where I helped him pierce his ears." The Desheni laid a hand over the book. "He asked me to translate it because he could not read it. We did not know what was inside. I had been carrying it, so it was in my pocket still when we left the city. I had hoped it might offer some insight into what to expect for when we..." He trailed off and his dark brows drew together in doubt.

Lark drew her shoulders back and tried to summon some of the authoritative spirit she used with her frustrating officers. "We are going back. That's for certain. No matter what happens between here and Jadora, we are going back."

Tula pursed her lips, but nodded. "I guess it makes sense to go there first. Maybe we can convince Vorkaris to help."

Nothing would have pleased Lark more, but she dared not hope the dragon would volunteer to mount a rescue. Vorkaris had never been fond of Zaide. "Right now, the plan is to establish a transport route for refugees as they continue to find their way to Tinith. Some will work their way to Parral, too, which is part of why Warinal wishes to stop here. We'll ensure transport is available, let your sister and Vorkaris know what has happened, and then we will take a ship from Jadora and travel down the northern river to Lake Sian."

"We did that before, going to Jadora. It took weeks. Can we really wait that long?" Tula glanced to Andriun, as if the Shaman might have the answers instead of her.

Lark tried not to bristle. "What choice do we have?"

"Little now. But perhaps that will change." Andriun shrugged and returned to his studies.

The steady scratch of his pen against paper was the only sound in the cabin for a long time, but eventually, voices rose on deck, calling out their arrival for their first stop.

～

Lark did not leave the ship when they docked in Parral. Nor did she disembark when they reached Addare a number of days later. The arrival of the goborrin warship with the enemy's flag flying upside-down over its sails caused a stir in both cities and both Jobe and Warinal told her she should be proud of what it had done to morale. But their ship carried the news of her father's death, too, and she could not bring herself to face her people knowing how she had failed.

It was strange how no one spoke of that. How she had failed to restore the Spectrum Blade, failed to best Gadranus in the throne room of her own palace, failed to prevent her father's death despite all the prophecies and warnings that should have given her time. What the Oracle had told her in Nimultis did nothing to ease her guilt; she had known, and she had still failed. She could avoid facing it as long as she stayed on the ship, but the wooden hull would not protect her forever.

"Are we certain sailing a goborrin warship into the Ellean Sea is wise?" Andriun asked as they reached the narrow mouth of the bay.

Lark thought a better time for such protests would have been days ago, before they reached the gap between the two sister cities and their harbors. It was too late to turn around, even with the Hymnflute's power over wind.

"They'll have spotted us days ago," Admiral Warinal said with a dismissive wave of his hand. "The standard we're flying shows something is amiss, and if this Elsanna you've left in charge of Jadora is any sort of leader at all, she'll have figured out whose side we're on."

As if he didn't know who Elsanna was. She had headed the Magister's guardswomen for years; Lark had heard the woman's name long before they met, and her father rarely told her anything.

She resisted the urge to sniff, lest she come across as haughty. "Knowing Elsanna, they'll be preparing a banquet for us already. We should worry about how we're going to move so many people across the desert, first. It's a long walk from the cliffs to the city."

Getting the people up the cliffs was another problem. Some people had chosen to stay behind in Addare and Parral, but nowhere near the number Warinal had claimed would desert the ship, and every inch they had vacated had been packed full with supplies. Transporting that many goods in addition to so many people would present a challenge. When Lark and Tula last came this way, just getting a cart full of books to the city's gates had been hard.

"I would recommend leaving most of the people aboard the ship for another day. If we request assistance from Jadora's army, it should be easier to move people along in one simple line." Warinal paused. The faint lines that deepened at the corners of his eyes were the only sign of uncertainty he gave. "How do they typically transport goods from the docks? Sleds pulled across the sands?"

That would have been a better question for Tula, but the Magister was in the cabin, tending the dog. Lark shrugged. "Sometimes they use wagons and hand carts with wide wheels so they roll better on the sand." That was what she'd been given before, and what the caravans in the desert had used.

Andriun turned a slow circle beside them, examining the rising cliffs and the ocean waves. "I will stay with the ship and oversee moving things across the desert. It should be easy to manage, but it will take time."

"An expert in freight management, are you?" Warinal asked dryly.

"Perhaps not, but I am experienced in the management of people, I possess the skills needed to move things across sand with ease, and I am a leader in the eyes of those aboard this ship." Andriun met the man's stare with such a calm determination, Lark could not help but admire it.

"I will entrust you with the task, then." She nodded toward the Jadoran coast. Already, its cliffs towered, but they were far enough out to sea that the city's plateau was still visible. "As soon as we dock, I will take Tula, General Jobe, and a contingent of soldiers to the city to request guards and guardswomen to supervise the placement of Amrochan refugees."

The admiral snorted. "This ship will not *dock*, Your Majesty."

"Why? Do you lack the ability to manage it?" She couldn't resist the jab, but he did not rise to it.

"Jadora's harbor is too small to accommodate a ship of this size, unless they have undergone radical expansion in the last few years. Given the state of things in the world, that strikes me as unlikely." Warinal nodded toward the bay where dozens of merchant ships sat on the water, dwarfed by their stolen vessel. "The spacing between docks is designed for ships like those, and I suspect the Magister would not appreciate if I chose to make room for myself."

From anyone else, that would have been a joke, but Lark did not believe the admiral even had a sense of humor. She shrugged it off. "Very well, then. I shall see that the general is prepared to row me to shore. Best of luck managing the ship and its passengers, Admiral Warinal. Shaman Andriun." She bowed her head in acknowledgement of the Paragon, but not Warinal, and a petty part of her hoped he noticed the slight. He would get used to her being in charge eventually, but she would not fawn and beg in hopes it would happen sooner.

When she reached the cabin again, she held out her hands in anticipation of Daisy's greeting, but the dog was not on the other side of the door. Instead, she was sprawled on Tula's bed with the Magister's legs draped over the top of her ribs as she read. Daisy's head snapped up to look at her, but she did not move.

"Gather your things, Tula. We're heading to the city as soon as the admiral drops the anchor." Lark made quick work of gathering her own supplies. Everything fit tidily into a bag she'd procured in Tinith's market. All that was missing was the Hymnflute, but that was in Resia's hands.

Tula slid from her bed with a groan. "What about the puppy?"

"Andriun is staying here. He can look after her." If he was transporting cargo, it was best for him to transport the dog, too. Lark didn't know how to get her across the hot sand without burning her paws, but if she remained with Andriun, at least she could ride in a wagon.

"How many of us are going?" Tula turned in a circle before she seemed to decide what she needed to pack. She, too, had little to bring.

"Not many. Some soldiers and the general. Most people will be staying here until we know where to put all of them. We can't just meander in through Jadora's gates and pick somewhere to live." Lark did not doubt there would be space for them in the palace, but her people were another story. They couldn't all live in the palace, nor should they.

The Magister frowned, but slung her bag over her shoulder and trudged toward the door. "I sure hope there are gates again."

Lark reached it at the same time. "I trust Elsanna will have taken care of that by now." She still felt bad for the state in which they'd left the city. Between the fires and the goborrin bombs, repairs would have kept Jadora's people busy for weeks.

By the time they returned to the deck, General Jobe had already gathered a number of soldiers and prepared half a dozen vessels to see them to shore. He stood beside one as men boarded and prepared for departure, his hands clasped behind his back.

"It seems we should have purchased another flag for the ship while we were in port elsewhere," he remarked, never blinking.

Lark craned her neck to follow his gaze. Armor glinted on the docks. Regular soldiers, rather than Elsanna's guardswomen. "After the attack on Ganede, I'm not surprised to see they've increased security. Put me and Tula on the lead boat. It'll be hard to mistake her for an invader."

"And if they do, I'll just torch them." Tula took a running start and leaped over the railing into one of the waiting boats. It lurched, drawing shouts from the men already seated inside it.

"We will refrain from torching." Lark followed more sedately, and a soldier stepped forward to help her climb into the boat.

The next thing she knew, they'd been lowered to the water. The other boats inched down the side of the warship on their pulleys. General Jobe put himself in a different boat, but he relayed instructions the moment they landed.

"Shouldn't he be with us?" Tula whispered.

"He fears our boats may be fired upon. Putting himself in a separate vessel increases the odds one of the leaders of this delegation makes it to shore alive." It might have been offensive under other circumstances, but who knew what to expect now? Lark shifted toward the front of the little boat as the soldiers rowed. Her hand settled on the Spectrum Blade and she braced herself for disappointment. She didn't need much. Just a hint of cooperation. A little color glinting on its surface so they knew what she held.

Slowly, she unsheathed the blade. Sleepy, faint iridescence still marked the steel, but it was no greater or less than it had been since it accepted her hand.

Come on, then, she thought at it. *Let some colors flash.*

She raised the sword overhead and tilted it in the light.

Flashes of gold and green, purple and pink reflected the sun and across the bay, the soldiers on the harbor burst into a frenzy. Excitement, not distress. Carrying the good news. Relief flowed through her, warm and soothing as the waters of the bay. She remained on her feet, but lowered the blade to her side until they finally reached the docks.

"Thank the Maker," was the first greeting out of a soldier's mouth.

Lark tried to smile, but an odd sense of uneasiness tingled down her spine. "Sorry to give you a fright. I turned the flag over in hopes it would signal we'd taken the ship, but we came with such speed that we didn't have time to replace it."

"No apologies necessary, Your Highness." The man flashed her a smile and his shoulders relaxed as if a great burden had been lifted. "I never thought word would reach you so swiftly. How did you make it here with such speed?"

"Word? What word?" Tula asked as she scrambled to her feet. Their little boat bumped against the pilings and threatened to spill her into the sea, but she leaped from its edge and landed on the dock with a clumsy thump.

The soldier's good cheer faltered and he glanced between the Magister and Lark with a shadow in his eyes. "That is why you're here, isn't it?"

Lark's ascent to the dock was more graceful, assisted by four men at her back. "Forgive her. We've dealt with a lot the past few days, receiving so much information from so many places that it becomes difficult to keep straight. What she means is, are there any updates?"

Her feigned knowledge worked well, for the man relaxed and nodded. "Of course, Your Highness. Forgive me. No changes yet, though it doesn't seem to matter how many times Magister Vorkaris wipes them out. There are always more. Though if you've taken one of their ships, maybe that will slow things down." His attention drifted to the warship in the harbor, a thoughtful tightness to his lips.

"One of their ships?" Tula repeated, puzzled.

"The goborrins," the soldier said.

Lark smiled despite the sinking of her heart.

More goborrins.

Of course.

CHAPTER TWELVE

"I GUESS we shouldn't be surprised," Tula murmured when the goborrin encampment came into view. "Ganede had just been attacked when we left."

Lark counted the tents and wagons while General Jobe halted the soldiers he'd brought along as their escort. It was always strange, seeing a goborrin camp. They were so tidy and structured that she always expected to see broken-born among them, yet she had seen enough such camps by now to know that they were not always accompanied by human officers. It was hard to imagine the beasts might be so civilized.

Then again, maybe they were just well-trained.

"It's not as many as I expected," she said after she completed her tally. "Only five hundred or so, from what I see. So few shouldn't be a problem for Jadora."

The soldier who had accompanied them from the docks hummed a note of disagreement. "Sometimes it's as few as a hundred, sometimes two thousand. It doesn't matter. Vorkaris comes out, Vorkaris destroys them, and as soon as the next day, they're back again. We don't know where they're coming from."

"And how does Ganede fare?" Lark asked. She hadn't had a

chance to visit Jadora's sister city, but from the bay, things had looked placid enough.

"They face the same issue. There's an encampment on the north side of the city over there. But theirs come by land. Ours don't seem to be coming from the docks, and they don't have the resources to be coming across the desert. From what we've heard, Addare doesn't seem to have any goborrins about." The man scratched the nape of his neck as he spoke. No doubt he was sweating in that armor, even though the desert had begun to cool as evening set in. The sand was still scorching underfoot and Lark shifted back and forth in hopes of relieving some of the heat.

A bead of sweat trickled down her own brow and she swiped it away with the back of one hand. "Well, we'll solve it, but we have to make it into the city, first. I don't suppose we can just walk by."

"That's part of what makes them an issue. Every blasted day, we have to step outside and flatten yet another drove of stinking pigs before we can go about our business. They delay everything. It's gotten hard to transport goods up from the docks." The soldier gave a helpless shrug. "Magister Vorkaris helps, but every time we call for his aid, we hinder his ability to do... well, everything else."

"We have more than enough soldiers on the ship to take care of them, but I'd prefer not to leave the ship without its full defenses." Jobe scanned the switchbacked road that climbed from the desert to the city walls, then returned his attention to the goborrins and frowned.

Tula shrugged. "We won't need them. Vorkaris is on his way."

Lark turned to her with her brows raised. There would be no hiding Tula's role as the human Magister before long, but she hadn't thought it would be revealed so soon.

Rather than explaining, Tula grinned and pointed skyward.

The dragon's scales glowed in the sunset, or maybe it was

just his own light. He'd always dulled the smoldering fires of his wings when Lark was near, reluctant to risk any burns. Now, there was no such risk. Ash rained from his great wings as he dove toward the goborrin encampment. His maw split and fire raked across the tents—and the monsters around them.

A number of goborrins rushed to take up arms and answer the dragon fire with hurled spears, but Vorkaris was nimble in the air and not a single spearhead touched his luminous hide.

Tula bounced on her feet and cheered with both arms overhead.

The soldiers at their backs merely gaped.

"Well, they should be distracted enough for us to head up." The dock guard adjusted his belt and started forward.

Lark didn't know whether to follow. Vorkaris raked back and forth across the encampment, incinerating every inch, and the last thing she wanted to do was put herself in a position where she might be doused in flame. But General Jobe signaled his men forward and when the guards began their march, she let herself be swallowed by their number.

Tula hung close to her side. "Vorkaris will want to speak with us in the palace. Elsanna will meet us at the gate."

"Can you warn her about what we have waiting in the bay?" Lark asked in a murmur. The dock guard was far enough ahead that she didn't think he would hear, but she did not know how much was hers to tell. Everything would change for Tula once her identity was known and she was expected to stay and lead.

The Magister squinted. "Um, I can't think stuff at her like Vorkaris does."

Of course she couldn't. Lark snorted at the very idea. "What I mean is, can you ask him to relay a message?"

"Oh. Well, I probably could, but he seems a little busy right now. I guess we'll just march up to the gates and tell Elsanna by ourselves, and he'll meet up with us after he..." Tula paused mid-stride and her face twisted with disgust.

Lark managed to keep her pace steady, but she stared straight ahead, lest her companion's expression make her blanch. "Do I want to know?"

"Nope. You sure don't." Tula stuck out her tongue and shuddered, eliminating any chance that anyone might ask.

The stench of smoke and burning goborrin flesh hung low on the desert sand and Lark was grateful when they'd gone far enough up the road to the city to leave the smell behind. Everyone stole glances at the goborrin camp as they climbed— even the general, though his age-worn face remained placid.

The trek itself was as hard as Lark remembered, and all of them were sweating and a little short of breath by the time they arrived at the city's gates.

There was no line of merchants waiting for access this time, no guard taking notes on a board of wax, and no portcullis with complex guard stations and interviewing rooms behind it. Instead, massive bronze doors guarded the way into the city, without so much as a sentry outside.

Lark's procession stopped before it and all of them stared. The doors reached higher than the biggest goborrin's head. Large enough for Vorkaris to pass through, though the dragon's wings meant he'd never have any need to enter the city that way.

Tula shuffled her feet. "So do we knock, or...?"

"Over here." The dock guard motioned for them to follow as he strode off to the side, toward a divot in the stone wall.

Lark followed. It was more than a divot; it was a deep hole. "What are you looking for?"

"The chain. Would you like to do it, Highness?" He stepped back and gestured to the slot with one hand. "No scorpions in there. I already checked."

The risk of scorpions had never crossed her mind, but she made a mental note to never be the first to reach into that thing. She leaned forward to peer inside, but saw nothing. Slowly, she slid her arm into the gap and let her fingers explore. After a moment, she found the chain. "Here it is. What do I do?"

"Pull it toward you, real hard. That'll let them know we're here." The guard grinned.

Puzzled, Lark wrapped her hand around the hard links and pulled. Somewhere overhead, a bell clanged so hard, it vibrated in her bones.

Stone rasped and a piece slid back and disappeared into itself. The new hole was no larger and every bit as dark, and when a voice came from somewhere on the other side of the opening, it echoed hollowly against the rock. "Who's there? Step back so I can see you."

She blinked twice and shuffled back a few steps, unsure how far she needed to go. "I am Dasienna, the—"

"Princess!" the voice exclaimed. The stone clacked back into place and a strange banging rose behind the doors.

Lark had not yet drawn a full breath before the doors groaned on hidden hinges and the hair-thin line between them grew to a modest gap.

"Who else would it have been?" a familiar voice chided.

Tula squealed and leaped for the space between the doors. She squeezed through before they were open enough to admit anyone bigger and threw herself at Elsanna for a hug.

The guardswoman laughed and accepted it, more good-natured than Lark recalled. She looked less like a guardswoman, too, clothed in the fine silks befitting a Magister, her red hair coiled atop her head and filled with golden forks embellished with ornamental chains and jewels. "Vorkaris told me you were coming. Welcome back, my little librarian. And you, too, Your Highness." Elsanna did not bow, but she did bend her knees just enough for it to be considered a curtsy. It was probably hard to do anything else with Tula wrapped around her.

"Thank you, Elsanna." Lark was not sure she considered the two of them friendly enough to use each other's first names, but referring to her as Magister when the real Magister was right there struck her as wrong.

If Elsanna was bothered by the familiarity, she didn't show it.

"I see a good number of new faces," she said as she gingerly grasped Tula by the wrists and peeled her off. "And one that seems to be missing."

An unwelcome train of thought. Lark's cheerful mien faltered, so she drew herself up and tried to look regal instead. "I'll explain everything, of course. It sounds as if there's a lot of updates for you to share with us, too."

"Yes, but I assure you that a fair number of them are good, despite what you see out there." Elsanna waved a hand at the smoldering campsite below. The smoke rose dense and black in the dusky sky.

"I look forward to hearing it. Shall we make for the palace? I'll be happy to leave my soldiers in your barracks or deploy them around the city as you see fit." Lark was pleased when the woman turned without hesitation to lead the way. She fell in step alongside Elsanna and ignored the dour look General Jobe turned her way. He could fuss all he wanted about her moving soldiers about, but they were her men, and even he answered to her authority.

"The barracks will be fine. We'll have plenty of cool drinks for them, and they can have some time to rest before we decide what we're doing." Elsanna's own retinue consisted of all guardswomen, and they glided along almost silently in comparison to the heavily-armored men.

Lark had always admired the guardswomen's grace, as well as their bravery. Leaving so much skin exposed made sense in the desert heat, but that they could fight without any need for armor was a testament to their level of skill. She dared not plan for it, but allowed herself to ponder whether they would help train her in use of the sword.

They ambled along at a casual pace and the great bronze doors were closed behind them. It was not until after they had passed through the thick wall that Lark thought to look back. Several more layers of defense closed behind them, locking any surviving goborrins out in the desert. Locking Amrochan's people out, too. Lark tempered her frown. They'd be safe on the ship; with the Paragon of Water guarding it on the sea, there was nowhere safer they could have been.

"As you can see, the city has already been fully restored," Elsanna said with great pride. Her shoulders squared and her chest rose as she gestured to the streets and the many buildings that lined them. "The librarians are hard at work preserving the books in the library that were damaged and making new copies to keep in use. They'll be done within a month."

"That's a great deal of speed." Lark had the heart of a scholar and had been wounded by the damage done to the library. To know that, too, had been restored brought her no small measure of relief.

"We have a great number of librarians. Since your last visit, we have also refined our army, ensured our ranks are filled with loyal Jadorans, and corrected several history books on the role the great Magister Vorkaris plays in relation to the city and Jadora's leadership." The woman delivered that with a wink toward Tula, who beamed.

"The city looks beautiful. You've done such a good job. Is the palace all fixed, too?" Tula tucked her hands behind her head and walked with her elbows out to either side, her Jadoran silk coat billowing behind her as she walked. Its color matched what Elsanna wore, only serving to make their connection as sisters more evident.

"Of course," Elsanna said. "Vorkaris called for a number of improvements, too. I believe you'll be more than pleased with everything we've gotten done."

Lark suspected Tula wouldn't be hard to please. After everything they'd been through, even an ordinary bed at an inn would have been a luxury. In the palace, they were likely to grow spoiled.

The palace gates had been replaced, she noted when they arrived. The new ones were a finer bronze than what guarded the city's entrance, and rather than being a solid piece or merely bars, they were an elaborate scrollwork in the shape of two fire-breathing dragons.

"Modeled after Vorkaris, of course." Elsanna elbowed her sister and the two shared a giggle as the guardswomen ushered them through.

"I'll settle the men," Jobe said as they filed into the courtyard. His voice held a gruff edge, but he said nothing to offend.

"Good. See that all their needs are catered to, and should Elsanna send word that they are needed anywhere in the city, make sure we oblige. We are here to help, after all." Lark smiled sweetly and did not bat her eyes, but she did peer at him from beneath her lashes in a way she knew he would hate. If he wanted to be short with her, she'd make him suffer. From what she'd seen on the ship, kindness got under his skin worse than anything else. The same went for Admiral Warinal, but she found it harder to muster the same enthusiasm to play the game with him. At least she *liked* General Jobe.

His mouth tightened, but he bowed before he split away with all their soldiers in tow. Elsanna's guardswomen were more than enough to keep them safe within the palace walls.

They scarcely set foot inside the palace before another handful of guardswomen appeared to greet them, escorting a particularly tall and dark-skinned man.

Elsanna greeted him with a kiss on the cheek, which he bent obligingly to receive. "You remember my husband, Moros."

"*Husband*?" Tula shrieked. She clapped her hands to her cheeks and looked as if she might melt into the floor. "You got married without me?"

"A story I'll gladly tell after we take care of business," Elsanna said.

Moros folded an arm over his chest and offered a deep bow. Lark thought he sported more scars on his face than he'd had when they'd parted, but she could not be certain. Rather than armor or a uniform, he now wore silks to match his wife, and though his head was shaven clean and left him with nowhere to keep any ornamental forks, he wore a fine gold torque around his neck that was modeled after a dragon, too. It seemed Vorkaris had left his mark on as much as he could.

"It's good to see you again, Moros." Lark gave her head a gentle incline, acknowledging his manners. "Would that I came with as much good news as Elsanna has already delivered. Shall we speak in private?"

"I can't believe you got married without me," Tula whined.

"It was not our intention to rush, but there were things that made it expedient." Moros did not smile—Lark wasn't certain she'd ever seen him smile at all—but there was a new softness to his dark eyes that warmed her heart.

Elsanna smirked. "What he means is he was an influential part of the previous Magister's guard force, which came to be seen as oppositional to the guardswomen after my unfortunate disappearance and the formation of factions within the city. What better way to break down the walls between factions than to have them merge at the very top?"

This time, instead of whining, Tula stifled a gag. "Politics? Ew. What a terrible reason to get married. What happened to true love?"

"When you're older, maybe you'll understand there is room for both, but they must be navigated carefully. Come, we'll meet in Magister Vorkaris's private parlor." Elsanna led the way, though Lark and Tula both already knew where the Magister's quarters were.

Once they reached the doors, Elsanna gestured for the guardswomen who had accompanied them to take posts outside. "Dasienna's general may join us when he is finished seeing to his men. Otherwise, we will receive no one but Magister Vorkaris himself."

"Yes, my lady," one of the women confirmed. They all bowed, and one held the door while Lark's group slipped inside, but the Magister's quarters were blessedly empty.

For the first time in what felt like ages, Lark allowed herself to relax. They were safe here, if temporarily; she'd have to set out again soon enough. "Well, let's get to it."

"Shall I brew tea?" Moros offered.

Tula shook her head. "Nah, I think we have a lot of business things to do. You know, the kind of political stuff that *doesn't* involve getting married without your sister there."

Elsanna rolled her eyes and made for the low table and sank to one of the cushions with a casual grace. "Fine, we'll start. I was surprised when Vorkaris said you were here. I admit I felt ashamed to send word to Amrochan, seeking advice on the goborrin issue. I never would have imagined it would be you who might answer."

The cushions were soft enough that Lark struggled to hold back a groan as she sank into one. She settled cross-legged and leaned against the table. "And I wish I could say that was why I am here. I fear I carry no good news, Elsanna. None at all."

"As I feared." The former guardswoman's eyes slid to the sword at her side. "Your party is missing someone."

Lark's throat tightened.

"Tell us," Moros said as he knelt beside the table and took a seat of his own. "Where is Zaide?"

It took all her strength to summon her voice and even then, it trembled. "He has fallen." Tears brimmed on her eyelashes until their faces became a blur. "And so has my father."

CHAPTER THIRTEEN

EXPLAINING everything that had transpired took nearly an hour. Lark did her best to remain composed. Tears still flowed down her cheeks now and then as she recounted it all, but she grew to feel disconnected from herself and the salty droplets that dripped from her jaw as she spoke. So much had happened that it hardly felt real. She no longer knew how long it had been since Amrochan's fall; the days all ran together in her head, smudging their time in the palace backwards into their visit to Toren. Her voice cracked a dozen times over as she explained her father's death and the way Zaide had collapsed. The words pulled the memory into sharp focus and she could not keep the image of him on the floor out of her head.

He had to be alive.

She could accept nothing else.

As the explanation went on, Elsanna's face shifted with growing concern. Moros frowned, too, but that expression came more naturally to him. General Jobe had arrived at some point, and she had just reached the conclusion of her story, detailing their arrival at the docks, when the doors opened and the dragon himself appeared.

Lark faltered, unsure if she should continue or start over. In her moment of confusion, she forgot to greet Vorkaris when everyone else bowed. Heated embarrassment rushed up her neck and she scrambled for words.

Peace, Majesty, the dragon's voice rumbled in her thoughts. *I have heard everything through Tula's ears. One convenient effect of our bond when we are this close together. There is no need to speak. It would seem your words have already caused you grief.*

Deep appreciation swelled in her chest. She pressed a hand to her sternum, shut her eyes and gave a single nod.

The dragon strode past them to settle on the cool tiles of his chamber. The way he crossed his forepaws reminded Lark of a great cat, but she silenced that thought as soon as it appeared, lest he hear it in her mind.

"I hate to say it, but you were telling the truth when you said you brought no good news," Elsanna said slowly. "It certainly puts our little goborrin problem in perspective."

"But at least that problem, we can solve fast." Tula shifted to stretch her legs out long. Moros gave her a hard look and she grinned back. "Sorry."

She must have kicked him.

Elsanna ignored the interaction. "I hope that's true. I feel terrible to bring this up after all you've been through, though."

"Don't," Lark managed. She wiped her eyes with the heel of her palm and drew a deep breath to calm herself. "Tell us what you've tried, and we'll figure out what else can be done. We can send a messenger to the harbor to let Andriun know it's safe to come, and he'll bring Resia, too. We may be short a Bladebearer, but at least we've got three Paragons."

But are you truly short a Bladebearer? Vorkaris asked.

Elsanna's gaze slid to the Spectrum Blade, its hilt peeking just above the edge of the table.

Flustered, Lark put a hand atop it and pushed it down out of sight. It didn't protest, either way; it had been silent since the skirmish on the warship. "Tell me what you've found regarding your goborrin camp."

Elsanna tilted her head back as she sorted out her thoughts. "We started by searching the area around the bay, then expanded along the Ellean Sea's coast. We sent scouts all the way to Estkel, but the swamp held no sign of goborrin passage. There have been no more goborrin ships in the harbors since those that attacked Ganede, and after we sent reinforcements to help hold Ganede against attack, no goborrins have made it past their defenses."

"So they have to be coming from the desert side," Tula concluded.

"As far as we can tell," her sister agreed. "Vorkaris reopened the way into the tunnels below the city to search them, but he found nothing. The crater remains undisturbed, and every passage we sealed to prevent them from entering the city has remained sealed. They circle the plateau sometimes, and I fear the tracks they leave behind may be obscuring signs of where they're coming from."

I have flown across much of the desert and have seen no sign of them crossing from elsewhere, Vorkaris added. *But I have seen ships off the western coast. The sea is vast and I cannot monitor all of it. They may be coming up the cliffs.*

"They couldn't," Lark said with an absent shake of her head.

Elsanna and Moros both stared. Eventually, a faint crease etched itself between the former prison warden's brows.

"Goborrins can't climb." Tula grinned. "Or swim. Their big bulky bodies and little tiny pig feet don't work well for ladders or swimming. So that can't be it. Got any other tactical ideas to suggest, General?"

Jobe did not reply.

Lark hadn't noticed his silence until that moment. She expected to find him stewing in deep thought, but instead, she found him gaping at the dragon.

"What's the matter, General?" Tula leaned forward across the table and tried to catch his eye. "Never seen a dragon?"

He did not look at her, or anything other than Vorkaris. "I... I thought they were extinct."

"So you just thought all your men were liars when they told you a dragon helped raze the enemy's armies outside Amrochan?" Lark arched one delicate brow, but he didn't glance her way, either.

"No, I simply..." He trailed off, distant and dumbfounded.

"Forget that. It doesn't matter." Elsanna gave her hand a sharp, cutting swing. "We'll come back to the goborrins when everyone is here to make a proper plan. For now, we need to send a messenger to this Paragon of Water, and we need to determine how we're going to manage the influx of refugees. Jadora's supplies are already strained, considering the difficulties we've had with this wart of an army out there."

Tula raised a hand.

Lark caught her by the wrist and made her lower it. "You're the Paragon of Fire, Tula. You don't need permission to speak."

"Oh." The Magister blushed. "Well, Vorkaris is more Paragon-ish than I am in that regard, actually, so I thought maybe I should ask for permission before I volunteer him to help."

The dragon's tail lashed. *I beg your pardon?*

"Well, you've got wings, it's not like goborrins on the ground are going to do anything to you." Tula flapped her hands beside her shoulders. "Why don't you just carry goods up from the harbor yourself? You're strong enough to carry a whole wagon at a time."

"Not incorrect," Moros said slowly, "but presumptuous, given you're speaking to an ancient fire-breathing dragon."

"An ancient fire-breathing dragon who picked me as the human he likes best." She tilted her head to one side and batted her eyes.

Vorkaris stared back, unimpressed.

"I am sure Magister Vorkaris has enough on his plate already, given all he does for Jadora." Lark chose her words with caution.

The dragon had always deferred to her, for some reason she could not fathom, but she had come to his territory with a large request this time.

His great head swiveled toward her and thin curls of smoke drifted up from his nostrils. *Fortunate for the lot of you that a dragon requires a very large plate.* He adjusted his wings and let the tip of his tail curl and swish like that of a cat. *But if you're truly concerned about the availability of my time, let's strike a bargain. You take over a task for me, and I'll see that imported supplies are carried directly into the city and managed by my staff, to ensure they're distributed fairly.*

"The goborrin encampment?" Lark guessed.

Precisely. The dragon's tongue flicked and again she thought of a cat, preening his whiskers as he conned someone out of a bite of fish.

"More than fair. Once the other Paragons reach the city, we'll organize a plan of how to flush them out and eliminate them. As soon as it's settled, I'll need to set sail, but whether or not the Paragons accompany me will be up to them." She had no doubt Tula would need to stay behind to help manage things in Jadora. Resia would likely want to stay put and wait for word from the Kolmari, since their messenger would know to seek them in the desert. The only one she was counting on going with her was Andriun, and then only because she could not picture a Desheni staying in such a climate with any sort of comfort.

"Set sail for what?" Moros asked. His words were always so flat and unamused that for a moment, Lark felt as if the question was a scolding.

She raised her chin to meet his gaze levelly. "As of right now, we have no reason to believe Zaide is not alive. A few soldiers that escaped Amrochan and caught up with us in Tinith said that some of the palace guard had been taken prisoner. It's quite possible he is among them."

Elsanna scoffed. "He is one of the greatest threats Gadranus could face. Why would he keep him alive?"

Lark had not been sure of the answer herself until she'd caught Andriun translating that journal and learned what was inside. Perhaps it was foolish to think a man like Gadranus would feel kinship with a fallen comrade's son, but it gave her hope in a situation where there was little to be found. She folded her hands together and rested them against the edge of the table. "I suspect he'll be seen as valuable."

"As if you aren't?" Jobe tore his eyes away from the dragon at last and pinned her with a disapproving stare. "It's far more likely that he'd be held as bait, and you're ready to sail straight into whatever trap he's set."

"Of course he's trying to lure her back." Tula hunched over the table and peered at the gray-haired general through narrowed eyes. "You think we didn't know that would happen as soon as we left? The moment we set foot outside the throne room?"

"Maybe you should have considered that before you abandoned him," Jobe replied dryly.

Tula's eyes widened and her nostrils flared. Heat swelled around her alongside her temper.

Lark put a hand on her shoulder, though she half feared she might be burned. "They were complying with the Bladebearer's combat plans by fleeing without him. He made the decision that getting me to safety was more important than ensuring he escaped. Do you disagree?"

His lips pressed tight and the lines around them multiplied.

"We are the leaders of our people now, General. You don't have to like it, but the time for your generation to act has passed. This was never meant to be our fight, but it is now." The Oracle had given all of them that message, as far as Lark knew. It had been comforting, in its own strange way; it was easier to accept that she had no idea how to manage the task before her when she understood it had never been intended as hers to accomplish.

"Yeah," Tula added. "And that means I'm the one who's

going to be in charge of Jadora's resources, whether you like it or not, and I get to decide what we support. Her Majesty will have whatever ships she needs to mount a rescue, and whatever other support she needs from us."

Elsanna motioned for her to settle. "Of course she will. Jadora has always been proud to serve Amroch's crown, and that is not going to change, even if the wearer of the crown has."

"Which is another thing that must be discussed." Jobe's expression softened. "Morale among both our refugees and our soldiers is incredibly low. We've been running from problems, only to land in a place that was supposed to be sheltered and discover problems waiting for us here, too."

Hardly Lark's fault, but she gestured for him to continue.

He nodded back. "After everyone is here and settled, before you try to take off and get yourself killed, it would greatly benefit our people if we were to hold a coronation ceremony to officially declare you queen."

The others looked at Lark with varying levels of expectation. Tula seemed hopeful; Elsanna struck her as reserved. Vorkaris... well, the dragon's expression rarely changed at all.

"We'll need to have a new crown forged." It was the first thing that crossed Lark's mind, though it struck her as frivolous.

"There are illustrations of the various crowns of Amroch in the library's books," Tula said. "I'll see that they're brought to the palace for the acting Magister's inspection." Her eyes cut toward her elder sister.

Elsanna nodded. "I'll commission the finest jewelsmith in the city. And we'll discuss how to handle the Magister situation when we have time to sit alone with Vorkaris."

Jobe pushed himself up from the cushions on the floor with a grunt. "I will send word to the harbor and let the admiral and Paragons know it's time to unload the ship."

The dragon, too, rose. *I suppose I shall survey the city and select a convenient staging point for the refugees.*

"And I—" Moros rose to his knees, then paused and released a sigh that made his shoulders droop. "I will make us that tea."

Lark could not do more than muster a smile.

Her people to settle. A goborrin problem to solve. A coronation to hold, and then at last she could do the one thing that clawed at her heart with an ever-growing need.

Just stay alive a little bit longer, Zaide, would you?

CHAPTER FOURTEEN

BLOOD SPATTERED the gritty stone floor. Zaide stared at it, at the filth beneath his fingernails and the veins in the backs of his hands. Another drop of red fell from his brow and hit the floor.

He had to get up. He had to keep moving. They were going to kill him.

Slowly, he dragged a foot forward. If he could get one under him, use it to push up...

He lurched sideways instead and grimaced when his shoulder hit the ground. His breath still escaped him. The split in his eyebrow leaked into his eye and tinted half the room a strange shade of yellow-orange before the burn forced him to squeeze it shut.

A knife. He'd had a knife when he fell. Where was it? Where had it gone? He tried to get back onto his hands and knees, but his arms shook and couldn't support his weight.

This was it. They'd done it.

He'd finally lost.

"Over," a goborrin in the balconies called in Torec.

A moment later, fat, fleshy fingers seized him by the hair and for one painful instant, Zaide didn't know if the sensation in his chest was fear or relief.

Over. It was over. He shut his other eye and released what little breath his lungs held as he waited for the monster to crush his skull or slit his throat.

It dragged him upward and the goborrin's other hand slid beneath his arm. To stab him in the ribs? Make his suffering short? That didn't seem like the monsters he knew.

Yet no knife followed. Instead, the beast hoisted his arm over its shoulders and heaved him upward.

Zaide tried to stand but his legs gave out. He was too tired, too worn down after weeks of struggling against the beasts in the arena both day and night.

Another goborrin took his other arm. He couldn't make himself wrench open his eyes, yet he would have known the smell of the creatures anywhere.

"Good fight," the newcomer said.

The goborrin that bested him grunted its agreement. "Long fight."

Not all of them spoke Torec as well as Whok, and though Zaide could make out the words, they slurred in animal mouths that weren't made for human speech.

"Don't drop him."

"Watch his legs."

Zaide couldn't even feel his legs. They dangled as uselessly as the rest of him as the goborrins dragged him out. The monsters continued their conversation, simple and terse, as most of their speech was.

"Strong, for a human."

"For a small human."

"Big or small, he knows a strong warrior."

"Mmm. Always has."

If there was more said, Zaide didn't know. Gray shadows crept in around the edges of his mind, blurring the space between awareness and nothing. The sharp smell of Whok's infirmary hit his nose and made him flinch, but he still couldn't get his eyes open. One still burned, and the other saw only that cloudy gray that tried to swallow his thoughts.

His head listed when they put him on the floor. He tried to brace himself with his arms, but couldn't muster the strength—or the will.

They should have killed him.

He wished they had.

Instead, he grimaced as one of the goborrins turned him onto his back. A second later, his nose was assaulted by something so odorous and vile, it made his empty stomach heave.

Maybe they just weren't done with him yet.

"Open," the medic's familiar voice rasped.

Zaide clamped his mouth shut instead. A strong hand gripped his jaw and fat fingers dug against his cheeks to find his teeth. They squeezed there and wrenched downward until his lips were forced to part. Whok crammed a glob of thick, gritty herbs past his teeth and under his tongue.

The taste was so bad that his whole body convulsed, but there was nothing in his stomach for him to purge. Yet a moment later, his tongue grew numb, and the ability to taste subsided as the creeping lack of sensation spread throughout his body.

"Good." Whok patted his cheek—it was more like a slap, really—and left him on the floor.

Pain ebbed, but its retreat brought back no strength. Zaide struggled to turn onto his side so he could spit out the greenish-brown mass of herbs. None of Resia's medicine could do that, and he did not believe a goborrin could be a more sophisticated healer. He still couldn't get his blood-stung eye to open, but at least the shadows were gone from the one he could use. He watched as the old goborrin collected bottles from the work table.

When the creature turned and found him staring, it froze, then raised one of the bottles in its too-human hand. "Good medicine. Help for Zaide's hurt."

He didn't understand. Helping him made no sense. Healing

made no sense. They'd driven him beyond what he could defend, had their opportunity to kill him, and just... didn't. Hadn't his death been the goal? That eventually, he wouldn't best his enemy and would become just another blood stain in the arena? Maybe he'd misunderstood. Maybe this was the only form of torture the goborrins knew.

Zaide stared at the bottles and struggled to find his voice. Though he'd made great strides in understanding Torec, his use of the language was clumsy on a good day. With his mouth numb, getting the words out was harder than ever. "No medicine."

The old goborrin stared back, his beady eyes made huge by the lenses of his spectacles.

What was the word for poison? Zaide didn't think he'd ever heard. He'd have to find some other approximation. "Bad medicine."

Whok blinked at him, then looked at the bottle in his hand, puzzled. "No, all good. Helps with hurt. Medicine heals."

Zaide shook his head. "Goborrins give death."

The goborrin's brows rose, making its magnified eyes look all the more ridiculous. Then it seemed to realize what he was trying to say, and it let out a squealing wheeze of a laugh. "No, no, no. No death." Whok clopped over to crouch beside him and pour thick, greenish sludge from one of the bottles. It stung when applied to the cut in Zaide's eyebrow, but the sensation was short-lived. "Zaide is strong. Survives all fights, makes Gadranus happy."

That was the last person Zaide wanted to please. He winced and turned the other way, but it did nothing to free him from the goborrin's ministrations—or from the weariness that had settled in his bones.

Exhaustion was what had done him in. The fights had gotten longer as opponents he went up against were more skilled, and eventually, he simply could not muster the strength to keep going. That fight should have been easy. He had a knife to use against his opponent's short sword, both of them weapons he understood well. But familiarity couldn't save him from fatigue. It had made his movements too sluggish, his strikes too weak.

Any other time, he would have considered it a blessing that the goborrin had chosen to finish him by cracking the pommel of its sword's hilt against his face, rather than simply running him through. Laying on the floor of Whok's infirmary, he suspected the latter would have been the true blessing.

"Why?" Zaide asked.

Whok paused. "Why happy?"

"Why fight? Why medicine? Why Whok's help? Why learn Torec? Why Amrochan? Why war? Why?" Frustration poured out with the questions until Zaide wasn't sure why he bothered to ask. Half of those, he already knew. The war was unavoidable. For the same reason, so was the invasion of Amrochan.

"Many questions," the goborrin muttered. The creature's fatty jowls made the words almost sticky. "But Zaide survives. Questions later."

"Questions now," Zaide snapped.

Again, Whok paused. His chin rocked from side to side a few times without his mouth opening, then he gave a helpless sort of shrug and lifted his head. "Clothes."

Zaide started to ask what that was supposed to mean, but it had been an order, and not for him. One of the guard goborrins by the door nodded and slipped out.

"Many questions, but no answers here." Whok offered an ugly grin and a raspy snort of a laugh, then licked his nose with a tongue that should have been too broad for his mouth. "Whok is only a goborrin, eh?"

A goborrin and the closest thing to a friend Zaide had outside that Maker-forsaken prison cell. He shut his eyes and wished for a moment that the creature had brought poison, rather than treatment for his wounds.

Whok continued cleaning and dressing each injury with his nasty poultices and sludgy salves. The goborrin made thoughtful sounds as he mulled over an ugly cut on Zaide's jaw and returned to the swollen split in his eyebrow. "New scars."

"Only if I live that long," Zaide muttered in his own tongue.

"Eh?" The goborrin leaned closer, cocking an ear as if he hadn't heard.

Instead of repeating himself in Torec—or trying, anyway—Zaide simply shook his head.

Every injury had been cleaned, his eye wiped clear, and Whok was in the middle of smearing the last of the medicine across his skin beneath a broad thumb when the door opened. The guard returned with folded garments, and the old goborrin pointed and grunted something that was not words. Only after the clothing was deposited on his table did he turn back to Zaide. "Sit?"

Zaide thought he could, but he didn't want to. First he'd sit up, then he'd be given some bitter tea, then he'd be dragged back to his cell until the next fight, and the next, and the next. He stayed on his back, contemplating the ceiling with as much interest as if it had been patterned Jadoran tiles.

Eventually, Whok snuffled in displeasure. "Up." He grasped Zaide by the arm and pulled. For all that he was old and stiff, he was as strong as any of the other goborrins. Resisting would have been useless.

"Up," Zaide repeated with a groan as he was pulled upright, then dragged onto his feet.

Whok examined him, gave another displeased sniff, then pointed to the clothing. "Dress."

After all the battles he'd been in, his own clothing had been reduced to filthy rags. The thought of something new was appealing, but he paused when he saw what the guard had brought.

Dark colors in a cut he'd seen before, worn by the broken-born officer who had led them to Toren.

He retreated from the table, shaking his head. "No."

The old goborrin looked to the guard and asked something

Zaide didn't quite catch. The other goborrin's response wasn't much clearer, but Whok gave a grunt and looked to Zaide again, his beady eyes beseeching. "Clothes for now," he explained with a placating pat of his hands. "Dress for now. Go up. Zaide's room. Clothes there."

"My room?" It had been weeks. Had the guest rooms gone untouched for all that time? From what he'd heard from others, the entire palace had been ransacked. Yet if that was the case, Whok would not have known the place existed. Surely they wouldn't have kept his things there under the assumption he'd be back for them. Zaide looked at the clothing and considered.

"Dress for now," Whok coaxed.

It seemed like a trap, but the only alternative was going back to his cell wearing tatters. If he wore what they wanted and they took him upstairs, at least he could get a look at the state of things and update the others.

The fleeting thought that he might never return to that cell crossed his mind, but he dared not hope they'd turn him free. Instead, he assumed they wanted something and would kill him once they got it.

Die in the dungeon, or die in the palace.

"What a choice." He rubbed the back of his neck, then sighed and took the uniform from the table.

The goborrins watched in silence as he clothed himself, and only after the last button was fastened did Whok finally seem pleased. Then, in the single most disgusting action Zaide had seen since his arrival, the old goborrin licked his thumb with his wide, too-wet tongue and used it to slick back an errant strand of Zaide's hair.

It was all he could do not to shudder.

"Good, good. Go now. Take questions with you." The goborrin medic wheezed with laughter as the guards moved to intercept Zaide in the same practiced pattern they'd exercised for weeks.

They took him by the arms, though they no longer dragged

him. He walked between the armored goborrins and remained stone-faced as they led him past the rows of cells. Dozens of frightened and dismayed soldiers looked his way, but he dared not let himself see them. All of them who remained sported strips of colored cloth on the bars of their cells. All of them had succeeded in the arena, but to his knowledge, only once. The single word *why* nagged at his thoughts so incessantly, he thought he might go mad.

The goborrins led him to the familiar arena, but its balconies were empty. Was one of his guards still the goborrin he'd fought? The one who had helped carry him to the infirmary? He stole glances at them from the corners of his eyes, but he could no longer tell. With the exception of Whok, they all looked the same. Bigger or smaller, but always the same, with the same pink flesh and fatty faces and flat pig snouts that glistened with saliva or snot.

Then, at last, they led him through the far door, confirming everything he'd suspected about the dungeon. There was only one way out. The stairs beyond the arena led to freedom, but it was on the other side of death.

Both goborrins tightened their grip on his arms as they escorted him up the stairs, and he allowed himself a stroke of wry amusement at how off-balance they grew as they scaled the narrow steps. Only he remained sure-footed, lending him the notion they held on to him for assistance rather than to keep him from escaping.

Yet their grips did not ease when they emerged into the halls of the palace and wound their way up more and more stairs. Zaide had learned a few routes through the palace, but this was not one of them, and when they stopped before a carved wooden door, he was uncertain where they had taken him.

"In," one of the goborrins croaked as it pushed him forward.

This was not his room. "Where—" he started, but the monster just grunted and pointed at the door.

He grasped the handle and let himself into a fine parlor,

where sunshine poured in through tall windows and spiced tea scented the air.

Across the room, a man looked up from the book in his hands and straightened in his chair. "Zaide," he said with a note of delight in his voice. "What a pleasant surprise."

All reason fled and Zaide threw himself at Gadranus with a scream.

CHAPTER FIFTEEN

THE CHAIR FLIPPED BACKWARDS as Zaide crashed into its occupant. He landed two punches before Gadranus flung him off, but he was ready for the flip and rolled to land in a crouch. A porcelain tea set lay in pieces on the floor. He snagged a shard from the plush carpet before he launched himself at his enemy again.

Gadranus was strong, but he was older, bigger, slower. Everything that put the goborrins at a disadvantage worked against him, too, and Zaide dove in with the shard clenched tight in his fist. He gritted his teeth and drove it at the man's throat, but hands seized him from behind and dragged him backwards.

He hadn't even heard the goborrins come in.

Slowly, Gadranus got back to his feet, a low chuckle welling in his throat. "I see what they meant when they said your determination was a problem."

Zaide strained against the guards, but he couldn't reach.

He spat instead.

Gadranus did not so much as flinch. A hard smile coiled at the corners of his mouth and he flicked the slime from his shirt with a fingertip. "I take this to mean your testing is complete?"

"Testing?" Indignation surged as white-hot as Zaide's anger, but even his outrage couldn't give him the strength to break free.

"They're testing all the captives, of course. Learning which fighters have merit, which should be kept alive, which will be of no use. But I requested that their examination of your skills be expedited. You have been their main focus since I took power here, and from what my officers have told me, you did not disappoint." A cold glint sparked in Gadranus's blue eyes. Then he drew back and righted his chair.

Zaide could scarcely believe what he heard. "I've fought dozens of times. Killed dozens of your soldiers. Don't their lives mean anything to you?"

"On the contrary, boy. You are not familiar with goborrin culture yet, but you will be, and then you will understand the great honor I gave them by allowing them to die. Not only did they bring themselves valiant deaths, but they did so in service to their leader, and there is no better reward for a goborrin than to die a hero's death." Gadranus returned to his seat, though he left his book abandoned on the floor alongside the broken tea set.

"Maybe you should join them," Zaide snarled through clenched teeth.

Another low chuckle. "That is the goal, isn't it? But not yet. I've taken Amrochan, slain its king, and yet the crown eludes me."

An odd pang ricocheted inside Zaide's chest. Lark. She was still alive, then, even after whatever happened in Tinith. He hadn't found her, hadn't captured her. Not yet.

Gadranus stared at him, his unblinking gaze all too knowing. "I don't suppose you wish to tell me where she may be?"

"Kiss a goborrin," Zaide said.

"You're only making things difficult for yourself."

"I'll kill you."

"Something we both desire," Gadranus said. "Now is simply not the time. Not when I—we—are this close to freedom. We both seek the same thing, Zaide. I've explained it to you before. Why do you resist?"

"Why did you lock me up in a prison cell and have your monsters beat me?" He jerked forward as he spoke, but the goborrins kept him from moving so much as an inch.

"To ensure you are worthy," Gadranus replied simply.

Zaide's breath hitched. "Worthy of what?"

Gadranus smiled in response. "Power."

There were a thousand explanations he'd been ready for. That hadn't been one of them. Zaide fought to keep his brow from furrowing. "What do you mean?"

"Isn't it obvious?" The man glanced down and gestured to Zaide's outfit with a sweep of his hand. "I've chosen you, Zaide. You are my heir."

Confusion tangled with disgust and knotted them both around his thoughts. Zaide gave his head a slight shake. "A slaughtered king leaves nothing behind to inherit. Dasienna still bears her crown. When I kill you, she will rise to power."

A brighter, mirthful laugh escaped as Gadranus leaned back in his chair and drew up one boot to cross his ankle over his knee. "I never said anything about a crown. Power, Zaide. When I die, my magic will move on from me. Just like every Paragon. And you... you will inherit my strength."

This time it was Zaide's turn to laugh. "Think again. I'm not a mage. I can't learn magic."

"So you believe."

"So I know," he replied hotly. "I was held back from my Choosing and made the Elder's apprentice. You think I haven't tried? You think I didn't spend every waking hour for months on end trying to make something happen? I have no magic. Not a drop. You chose wrong."

Gadranus never stopped staring at him, a comfortable smile on his lips all the while. "I cannot fault you for believing this. It's all you know, so it's what you cling to, regardless of its inaccuracy. But all you know of magic is what has been passed to you, and such is the same for all those who came before you. You will know power, Zaide. There is no other choice."

"I don't believe you." Zaide pulled against the goborrins that still held him. They had not taken the shard from him, and he turned it over in his hand, adjusting his grip, grounded by the way the rough edges dug into his fingers and palm.

"Your belief is not a necessary part of the equation, but you will find it makes sense as you think on it. Your Elder, his peers —they struck you as so wise, so capable, yet even they could not prevent knowledge from slipping through the cracks of time. Consider, if you would, who must know more. Someone with wisdom and skill earned through the ages, or those who no longer possess so much as a history book that recounts a time where I did not exist?" The smile Gadranus wore widened, yet it fell short of smugness.

Zaide hated to admit it made sense. He shook his head, refusing to let the thought even take root. "And what if your goborrins killed me? What then?"

"They were instructed not to. To test you, see where you lacked skill and formulate plans to further your training, but even without power, you are too valuable to kill."

Valuable how? He was just an orphan from Kolmar, barely a man by anyone's measure. He'd seen a fleeting life of value with the Spectrum Blade in his hand, but that was over now. The sword had rejected him, and Lark...

Lark. Zaide's breath caught and he shut his eyes.

"Precisely," Gadranus said. "She will come for you."

"The Paragons won't let her. They swore they'd take her away from Amrochan. Away from you."

The man shrugged. "Then I will pursue her. I will chase her to the end of the world, seize power however I must, and see that things end. Is that what you desire? For your princess to be struck down?"

Fear lanced Zaide's heart at the very idea. His arms slackened in the goborrins' grips.

"Then you see how I am doing you a favor." Gadranus scarcely moved a hand and the guards let go, though they remained close enough to act should Zaide try and strike again.

Zaide saw no such thing. "What favor?"

"A chance to hone your skills beyond anything you've ever dreamed, to experience your first taste of magic, to work with me so we may continue toward this goal we share. You can try again to convince her to cooperate. To protect her. That's what you want, isn't it?"

More than anything. Zaide scarcely caught the words before they traveled to his tongue.

The retrieval of the artifacts. All the monsters he'd faced, the battles he'd fought, the injuries and terrors he'd endured. Everything he'd done had been for Lark's sake.

That wouldn't change now.

"Isn't it?" Gadranus prompted gently.

Instead of answering, Zaide spun sideways and plunged his porcelain shard into a guard's thigh. The goborrin howled and doubled over. He dove into the opening and came up with the guard's sword in hand.

The other goborrin flung its injured companion out of the way and drew his weapon, but Zaide leaped forward before its tip left its sheath and stabbed the goborrin in the throat. It toppled with a gurgle and he rounded on the first one to end it before it could stand.

Gadranus flew to his feet and drew his own sword, not a hint of surprise in his cold blue eyes.

Zaide gave him no chance to act. He jumped the dead goborrins and landed in one of the sword forms he'd learned from the Oracle's guards, and the fluid and twirling movement of the blade drove his enemy back.

There was little space for Gadranus to retreat, nothing behind the chairs but the tall windows overlooking the garden where Zaide and Lark had once met in secret. How fitting it would be to strike him there, to fling him out through the glass and let him die where the princess once begged for help in stopping him.

It wasn't so easy. His stolen blade rang against the one Gadranus held, the dark-haired man's a better weapon by far. Zaide set his jaw and flowed through a series of practiced movements he hoped would be unfamiliar. He'd scarcely had time to tap into his knowledge in the fight they'd had before, and he dared not make himself predictable.

"Fool," Gadranus spat. "I've already told you I will not die yet."

"And I already promised to kill you." Zaide swept in for a stab and adapted when his opponent parried. "One of us has to be wrong."

The heat of anger robbed Gadranus's eyes of their icy chill. "I will not let you throw away everything I have done. Not now, not when I am so close." He deflected another strike, then launched his own.

Instead of blocking, Zaide dove forward and let the sword cut into his side as he lunged. The edge of his blade sliced the skin on Gadranus's cheek, then claimed half his left ear.

The man's bellow was enough to shake stone. "Enough!" Black coils of shadow burst forth from his feet, snared Zaide's arms and twisted the blade from his hand. The sword hit the floor with a clatter as more guards poured in through the door.

Hands replaced the tendrils of shadow that held Zaide captive as Gadranus turned to glare at him.

All Zaide did was smirk.

"Return him to the prison," Gadranus said as a broken-born officer slid into the room. "Begin his training immediately. He will cooperate, whether he wants to or not." He pressed a hand to his cut and bleeding ear, then looked at his fingers. A shadow of disbelief haunted his face.

"You'll get used to it," Zaide said as the goborrins dragged him toward the door. He relaxed into their grip and turned his head to display his own ear, shortened so long ago. "Guess we're even now."

The enemy leader's face crumpled into a scowl.

Good. Zaide stared back without blinking.

He could play their game, weather their training and come out stronger.

Then, next time, it wouldn't be his ear.

There was no return to his room, no change of clothes waiting. Just an escort back to the prison, where the uniform he still wore drew startled looks and frowns of confusion from many of the prisoners they marched past. Zaide couldn't fault them. He had to look rough, his face sporting new bruises and ugly gashes that were now crusted with Whok's strange medicine. Combined with his outfit and the fresh cut across his ribs, they'd either mistake him for a broken-born officer who had done something to earn a beating, or they'd recognize his face—ugly as it had to be—and wonder what hare-brained scheme he'd tried to pull that had ended with him disguised as an enemy soldier. Those who remained alive weren't foolish enough to think he'd turned on them, or so he hoped.

The goborrins and white-haired man who escorted him back to his cell remained silent, even as they locked him back in the cramped and dirty little space he'd begun to think of as his quarters. He stayed standing until they left, stubbornly determined to watch them retreat. Only after they disappeared did he allow himself to sink to the floor and lean back against the stone wall.

Weakness took his limbs now that his heart no longer pounded. All his anger drained and left him more exhausted than he'd ever been, and he found he could not even raise his arm to brush his disheveled hair from his face.

Perhaps that was for the better. The brownish blood of the goborrins he'd slain still marred his hands.

"Maker's mercy, boy," Lieutenant Raddan murmured across the hall. "What have you done?"

Zaide's eyes, too, were heavy. As soon as he found the will to move, he would lay down and sleep, maybe for the rest of his life. He kept his eyes closed and stayed where he was. "They took me to see Gadranus."

He expected questions, an exclamation or an oath—something, anyway. Instead, all he got was a taut silence.

Maybe he'd been too generous with himself. Maybe they did think him a traitor. Thoughts of everything Gadranus had said and offered surfaced, and he tamped them down with the memory of the sword in his hand. His fingers twitched and he forced his eyes open, locked gazes with his friend across the hall. "I cut off his ear."

Raddan's brows climbed, but the first response didn't come from him. Instead, it came from the stranger across the hall, the man who'd been hopeless, who had sworn they would all die in those cells.

His laugh echoed off the stone walls, long and carrying and filled with a kind of delight Zaide had never dared hope to hear in a place like this.

"What? What's happened?" someone farther down the corridor called.

Zaide sat in silence as the message was repeated and more voices rose, carrying it off into the depths of the prison and beyond what he could hear.

They needed it. They'd all craved something that could be taken as good news. Yet if he were to be honest with himself, he'd failed.

Had he managed to strike a few inches lower, it would have been the man's throat and not just his ear. He could have stopped this, saved Amrochan, freed them from the clutches of the Rise.

Or maybe that was just wishful thinking. He thought again of all Gadranus had said, how he'd claimed Zaide would be his replacement. It was nonsense. It had to be. Yet it brought questions to light, things he'd never considered, things Lark would have answers for that he did not.

"Lieutenant?" he asked softly over the shouts and laughter that still rippled through the air.

"Hmm?" Raddan answered.

Zaide struggled to keep his eyes open, but he dared not let them shut, lest fatigue take him while questions still burned in his mind. "What happens to the goborrins after Gadranus dies?"

The lieutenant stared for a time, then tilted his head. "We kill them, what else?"

"No, I mean—I know that." Zaide fought back a wince, sure the man thought him a fool. "But where do they go when we drive them to retreat? What do they do? Why don't they continue to strike Amroch after he's slain? Who leads them until the next Rise?"

"I don't know, lad. Can't say I've ever thought about it before."

Nor had Zaide. He tilted his gaze to the ceiling as the words hung in his mind, shrouded in the smoke of the promise of power Gadranus had given him.

You are my heir, the man's voice whispered, so crisp and clear that Zaide could have sworn he'd heard it out loud.

Heir to his power. Heir to that legacy. Heir to all the Shattered Lands and every unknown thing that lay beyond.

Zaide shut his eyes and prayed whatever darkness swallowed him as he succumbed to his exhaustion, it would never let him wake.

CHAPTER SIXTEEN

No matter how many times Lark refused, someone refilled her teacup. She didn't want more, yet she found herself drinking it without thought, and now she had a stomach ache to nurse along with her headache and the growing cramps in her neck and shoulders. A wave of her hand dismissed another member of Elsanna's staff before the woman could refill the cup yet again, though there was no doubt someone would sneak in before long and fill it while she wasn't looking.

"Water, please, if anything," Lark said absently. She caught herself reaching for the cup out of habit and pushed it farther across the table so it sat outside her reach. By now, she'd done that a dozen times.

The maps of the remaining tunnels beneath the city were convoluted, but after a thorough explanation from Moros and the guardswomen who had combed through the space in search of goborrins, they had plotted out each passage and connection with different colors of chalk.

They had also concluded there was no way the goborrins could have exited from the tunnels beneath the plateau. Vorkaris had sealed every passage that opened to the outside, forcing magma into the tunnels and letting it cool. Lark preferred not to think of what sort of power was necessary to do such a thing, but she was grateful it was a force on her side.

If only the advantage Vorkaris offered had let them unravel the problem on their own.

"Well," Tula sighed as she slumped over the table, "I still don't see anything useful, and we've been at this all day."

"It is better than searching the desert," Andriun muttered. He'd lain sprawled out on the stone floor since his arrival, swearing it was the only place he could find that wouldn't cook him alive. Lark had never known him to be dramatic, which made everything worse. If even the reasonable member of their party had reached his limit, what did that mean for the rest of them?

"Unfortunately for me and Tula, I believe searching the desert is our next course of action. Vorkaris has flown over a portion of it, but there must be something he's missing." Lark was grateful the dragon was out fetching things from the harbor, lest he take her words as criticism. She didn't mean it that way, but everyone was tired and irritable, and she had little time to develop a plan before her officers returned from... wherever they had gone. Off to settle refugees or organize soldiers, but she couldn't recall which of the men had gone where, nor did it matter. It was easier to think without them questioning her.

"There must be, or else there wouldn't be another batch of goborrins out there right now." Tula pointed at the dark rectangle on the map. It hung outside Jadora's gates like an ugly stain on the fine paper.

Lark tucked in her chin and examined that spot again. According to reports, it had not been a large group, but plentiful enough to indicate there was a steady supply of reinforcements hiding somewhere. They had moved in during the night, yet somehow, no one had seen them approach. She sighed and scrubbed her face with both palms. "It feels as if it should be obvious, but every single one of the volcanic tunnels has been closed. If not the tunnels and not the desert and not the bay, how else are they supposed to get here?"

"And they cannot swim, so I would not think it is the river," Andriun said.

Both Lark and Tula turned toward him, faces blank.

He didn't notice, his eyes trained on the ceiling far overhead. His blue skin had taken an odd sheen beneath the knotted-rope shirt he'd been given in Nimultis, and Lark wondered absently if Desheni could sweat.

"Andriun," Tula started, her tone almost a reprimand, "you know what the word *desert* means, right?"

"It is a place where very little rain falls."

The Magister's nose crinkled. "Which means no water, which means no rivers."

"But you do have water," Andriun said. "Your people do not carry saltwater from the bay and distill it. You have dozens of wells."

"Yeah, because if you dig down deep enough, you'll find water underground. Even in a desert." Tula made a show of rolling her eyes.

Lark frowned. "The reservoir beneath the city—are you saying it's connected to a river somewhere?"

The Shaman turned his head to look at her. The angle of his mouth was cross. "Yes? I just explained this."

Her fingers tightened against the edge of the table. "Underground?"

"As Tula just explained. If you do not wish to listen, I would prefer not to speak right now. I believe I now understand the misery that is suffered by a beached whale." His attention returned to the ceiling, but it didn't stay there long. He jerked in surprise when Lark leaped up from the table.

This was it; the obvious thing they'd all been missing. It had to be. Lark gripped the Spectrum Blade and tried to still her excitement. "Tula, fetch either Elsanna or Moros. Whoever you encounter first. We need equipment. Weaponry. Lanterns, ropes. A handful of guardswomen or soldiers would not be amiss."

The Magister snapped a salute and bounded off to do as she was told.

Lark turned to the Shaman next. "Andriun, come here. Are you able to sense the river from where we are?"

"Yes," he said slowly as he turned onto his stomach and reluctantly got to his feet.

"Show me where it is. We'll mark it on this map and determine the best point of entry from there." She extended a piece of blue chalk in one hand.

"And when you say we, what you mean is you will make me do it, as I am the one who can breathe underwater?" Andriun asked glumly.

Lark hesitated, but he wasn't wrong. "I would have thought you'd be glad for that, given how miserable you looked on the floor."

"Water will not drown me, but it can kill me many other ways. It is foolish to dive into an unknown current, even for one of my kind." In spite of that risk, he took the chalk and leaned over the table. His head tilted to one side, as if he was listening, and he carefully considered what he heard before he made the first mark.

Inch by inch, the river's path overlapped the ink outlines of the city, then trailed into the desert beyond. She studied it as he drew. The shape made little sense to her, and while she was no expert when it came to terrain and natural structures, it didn't follow what she knew of the land. Even subterranean rivers had to form in logical ways, didn't they?

"The end of the river is beyond what I can feel easily from here, but I believe it would terminate here." Andriun finished by circling a point at the western edge of the continent, where the high, rocky cliffs met the sea.

The blue path did not pass underneath the goborrin camp,

but it was close enough. Lark stared at the dark rectangle until her eyes blurred.

Andriun waved a webbed hand before her face and brought her back. "You are making the plan face again."

"Sorry," she said out of reflex. She wasn't sorry at all. "I was just wondering how plausible this is. They must be coming up through the river, don't you agree?"

He did not say anything at first, though his dark eyes fell from her face to the map. He examined it for a long time before he tapped a nail against the edge of the table. "It is the only viable path I can see. They do not cross the desert, they do not come from the harbor, and they cannot come from the tunnels the dragon has closed. There are no other options. This must be it, although..."

The way he trailed off left Lark unsettled. "Although what?"

"I cannot see how." He tapped the table a few more times before he tilted his head again. Second-guessing his senses? Double-checking to make sure he'd drawn everything right? Whatever it was, he eventually sighed and pointed at a well etched in the center of what appeared to be a plaza. "Here. This is where we will enter. I will go first, but only after I am certain you will be able to retrieve me if something goes wrong."

"We would never abandon you." She thought it would reassure him.

Instead, the look he gave her was flat. "I am aware you still have need of me."

Lark slammed her hands down on the table. "That's not the reason! We'd aid you no matter what happened, no matter what else waits ahead of us. No one else gets left behind." Her voice cracked. She hated herself for it.

No one else, she said. As if the first had been acceptable, as if she could take it in stride.

She squeezed her eyes shut and cursed herself for ever leaving Amrochan.

"I am sorry." Andriun's voice came softer this time. Sincere.

"I did not mean... that is, forgive me, Your Majesty. The weather here, it makes me cross, but I am too old to behave in such a fashion."

And she was too much a leader to allow such emotions to rule her. Sometimes sacrifice was necessary. Her father's willingness to forsake her should have taught that. She steadied herself with a breath and chose diplomacy. "You are allowed to find conditions unfavorable. Don't feel as if you must hide your lack of comfort because of me."

"I'm back!" Tula announced in a bright, melodic tone. "Look who was in the hallway on her way over here." She gestured to her sister with a broad sweep of her arms.

Elsanna's smile was polite, but strained. "I've already called for what you requested. You've found something?"

"I believe so," Lark said. "I suppose we'll find out shortly. Come. Let's go."

The well was less impressive in person than it had been on paper.

The plaza had been bustling when they arrived, ringed with vendors peddling wares and people perusing their carts, but the guardswomen had chased all of them away and filled the space with soldiers instead. Their numbers were split equally between being Jadoran forces and part of Lark's own army, an arrangement she had no concerns with, though the admiral did not agree.

He had complained the whole way through the city and did not stop now. "Water is my domain," he groused as they stood beside the stone-walled well. "This should be my call."

Lark did not dignify him with eye contact. Instead, she watched as a pair of guardswomen helped Andriun secure his strange rope harness. "It is his domain, Admiral Warinal, unless you can prove you are better suited to investigating a previously unknown river than a Desheni and the actual Paragon of Water."

The man floundered and turned red when he found no words. He would likely be less considerate when they spoke in private later, but for now, she enjoyed his silence.

"Are you ready?" Lark asked as Andriun made a few final adjustments for his comfort.

"Almost. I will need Tula's assistance before I can descend." He beckoned for her to come closer, then pointed to one of the lanterns that sat beside the well.

Puzzled, Tula crept forward to take it. "What am I supposed to do?"

"Light it. Then, we tie a rope to the ring on the top. The lantern will be lowered into the well, and you will use your magic to track its flame. The moment the flame is extinguished, you will tell us, and we will draw the lantern back up." He readied a rope to help.

Lark watched the two of them prepare the lantern and felt useless. She struggled to remind herself she was overseeing the project, as was befitting a queen. "But what will that do?"

"If the lantern is wet when it is raised, we will know it was the water that extinguished it, and we will know how far down I must go before I reach it. If the lantern is dry but the flame still dies, we will know there is poison in the air, for a flame cannot breathe where man cannot."

"And if it explodes, we'll get a really interesting show," Tula added.

Andriun was not impressed, but he held his tongue. He waited for the lantern to be lit and then swung it over the edge of the pale stone wall. "Are you ready to follow it?"

Tula nodded. "I'm watching. Feeling. Magic-ing."

Inch by inch, he fed the rope into the mouth of the well. The opening was scarcely three feet wide. When he went down, it would be an uncomfortably close fit.

The plaza fell silent and the rasp of the coarse rope as it slid across the stone grew as grating as if it raked across Lark's nerves instead.

All the while, Andriun watched Tula's face. She remained focused on the well with stoic determination.

"Still?" he asked in a murmur when the rope had gone far enough that it could have stretched from one end of the large plaza to the other.

"It's still burning." Her brows drew together.

Everyone remained quiet.

How far did the city's people lower pails to retrieve water? Lark hadn't thought to ask and the guardswomen nearby offered no information on their own. They watched, too, silent and uneasy, unwilling to distract Tula from her task. Even the admiral stayed silent, though he shifted back and forth on his feet.

Would they have relaxed if they'd known Tula was Paragon of Fire and not her sister? Elsanna had not made the trip to the well with them. As far as Lark knew, her identity had not yet been disclosed—nor had the women discussed how they would go about passing power and authority from one to the other.

"Oh—" Tula jerked forward. "It just went out. I felt it."

Andriun paused long enough to mark the rope, then started reeling it back in. "I suppose we should be thankful there were no explosions involved."

"Really? I'm actually a little disappointed." The Magister peered down the well. She stayed there a long time before the lantern resurfaced, water pooled in the plate beneath the wick. Her nose wrinkled with displeasure.

Lark leaned forward to dip a finger in the water and was startled by its chill. "I take that response to mean you won't be going down with us?"

"Well, someone has to stay up here and be in charge, right?" Tula shuffled backwards as the guardswomen advanced and watched with a wistful eye as they made sure there was enough rope connected to Andriun's harness to pull him to safety.

The look struck Lark as painfully familiar and she hated that she knew what it meant.

"I will call for you if it is safe and beneficial for you to descend," Andriun said as he removed his boots and swung a leg over the side of the well. He gave the opening a dubious frown before he climbed the rest of the way in. Lark thought the guardswomen would lower him, but instead, he bent his legs and pressed his back to the wall to shimmy down on his own.

Unsure how to respond, she simply nodded and watched as the guardswomen gave him rope a little at a time.

The sound of movement echoed and Tula shuffled forward to look down again.

Lark looked, too, but he had already vanished into the dark so she returned her attention to the Magister on the other side of the well. "You're very fond of him, aren't you?"

Tula glanced up, startled. "I'm fond of looking at him, if that's what you mean."

Hardly the response Lark expected. "What?"

The Magister pursed her lips and averted her eyes. "There was one time—a long time ago, long before we left for my first real adventure—that my sister told me Desheni men were the most handsome in the whole world. She was right."

Lark's brows shot upward.

Then Tula caught her gaze and held it, her expression uncharacteristically deadpan. "But he is a fish. Do you know how bad it would taste to kiss a fish?"

"Is it going to be extremely embarrassing if I make you aware I am still within hearing distance, or should I pretend that I am not?" Andriun's voice rang hollow from the depths of the pit before them.

Lark and Tula both startled, and if the Jadoran girl had been serious before, the hard glint in her eyes now said things were beyond grave.

"Drop him," Tula told the guardswomen. "I can't allow him to live after that."

A few of the guardswomen grinned back, but they continued to feed rope into the well at a steady pace. Eventually, what they offered went slack. They slowed and gripped the rope tight, waiting.

"Does that mean he's at the bottom, or did we lose him?" Lark stared into the dark and wished the sun was higher overhead so she might see more than blackness.

"I am here," Andriun called back. His voice was fainter than before, though it carried easily in the still. "And I think you will wish to know about this."

That was the point, but she bit her tongue and leaned forward to shout back. "I'm coming down."

"What?" He sounded alarmed. "Your Majesty, there is no need for that. I can investigate and come back to describe—"

She didn't hear the rest; the guardswomen were already retrieving more rope and looping it around her body to create a harness like what they'd made for him. It pulled uncomfortably tight, but she was more concerned with how she was going to make it down after him. Belatedly, she realized he'd gone down without any light. "Prepare a lantern." She pointed at one and Tula was quick to retrieve it.

Something echoed in the well.

"What was that?" Lark asked.

"He said he's going to drop into the water to make room for you." Tula pointed a finger at the lantern's wick and it sparked to life. The gesture was wholly unnecessary, given what she'd shown of her power before, but she seemed to delight in the little flourish of her hand that followed.

"Your Majesty, this is idiocy." Admiral Warinal stepped in between her and the well. "Send some of my men, let them come back and report."

That would have been wiser, Lark agreed, but she did not intend to change her mind now. Later, when she had time to sit and reflect on the sudden desire to be reckless, she would determine how to deal with the new and hungry need to be in control of every situation. For now, she took the lantern and pushed past the admiral to climb into the stone-rimmed opening the way she'd seen Andriun do. "What am I to do to signal I need to be pulled back up?"

"I dunno, scream?" Tula suggested.

Lark gave her a blank look, but the Magister only smiled back at her. If they had established a way for Andriun to communicate that need, she hadn't heard it. "I suppose I won't be able to pull the rope if I'm hanging from it, so perhaps calling for assistance is the best option." In a dignified manner. Not screaming.

"Your Majesty, please," the admiral said, though there was no pleading in his tone, only force.

She would not be bullied. "We will call for soldiers and guardswomen when we have evaluated the best way to bring them down." Then she began her slow descent, resting the glass-paned lantern against her front and shuffling downward and only then realizing her mistake.

Yawning blackness waited beneath her, a depth she could only imagine and dread, and there was no easy way to go back now. Fear fluttered in her belly and churned it up, but she swallowed hard against the rising nausea and forced herself to keep going.

The distance swallowed the sunlight, yet she'd expected it would be dark below her. Instead, a soft, warm light grew below. It struggled to compete with the lantern she carried, but the farther she went, the more pronounced it became. Had Andriun taken a lantern of his own after all? She certainly hadn't noticed him carrying one.

"Come slowly," the Shaman called as the light grew brighter, illuminating him and the ripples on the black surface of the icy water that surrounded him. "I will help you when you drop, but you will go under the water for a moment no matter what. Do not panic."

That would be easy; Lark was afraid of heights, not water.

Then she glanced down again and changed her mind. The water had to be fifteen feet below her, and she had run out of well.

"Do not panic," Andriun repeated. "Just drop."

"Easy for the man who breathes underwater to say," she muttered. "Catch my lantern. Put it wherever your light is, if you can."

He moved directly underneath her and held up a hand. The rope still fastened to him bumped against her face and she squeezed her eyes shut to protect them as she dropped the lantern. No splash followed, though she heard movement in the water and the slack rope smacked against her cheek twice more before it grew still.

When he spoke again, he was underneath her once more. "It is on the dock."

"Dock?" Lark asked in surprise. That was enough to spur her to action. She held her breath and let herself drop. The frigid water stung her skin when she hit.

A moment later, strong hands drew her above the water and she gasped and shook droplets from her face.

Now that she was in the water, she could see clearly, and she understood what he'd wanted her to see.

Docks.

Ships.

CHAPTER SEVENTEEN

"Well no w-wonder they're getting here in such n-numbers," Lark managed through chattering teeth. The water was cold enough to make every hair on her head prickle.

Andriun put an arm around her and helped steer her to one of the low docks, mindful not to let the ropes go taut. Bit by bit, the guardswomen aboveground gave them slack, allowing them to move. When they had enough, he pushed her up onto the wooden platform and then followed, a hard shiver coursing through his frame. "I did not expect the water to be so cold. I am not adequately blubbered for this temperature."

"I wonder what Tula would think if you were." Lark wiped her nose, then sniffed hard. She scarcely had a chance to gather her hair in her hands before magic prickled against her senses and the water removed itself, leaving her dry. One benefit of working with the Paragon of Water.

He dried himself next. "Do not encourage her."

"I was not planning to." She stood and turned a slow circle, taking in the cavern and the docks that ringed its edge. Lit lamps that were not their own illuminated the dock and the shadowy shape of ships that floated on the night-black water. She studied those the longest.

Perhaps to call them ships was generous. They were long, low, and narrow, of a make she had not seen before but too polished to be goborrin workmanship. For that matter, she did not think any boats were goborrin-crafted. They did not seem eager to explore water without Gadranus snapping a whip at their heels. But their origin was of little importance. What mattered was that they were empty, tied to the pier with long ropes. Narrow tunnels branched off to either side of the cavern, connected to what she could only assume were similar spaces, all filled with water. The icy scent of it stung her nose.

"This appears to be recently constructed," Andriun murmured as he pushed his bare toes against the wood.

Lark found herself looking at his feet instead of the docks. She should not have been surprised to see his toes were webbed like his fingers, but it still struck her as strange.

The most handsome of men in the world, Tula had said. Lark wondered at her taste, then made herself look away. "When the false Magister was in charge, perhaps. Why do you suppose Vorkaris didn't find these tunnels when he was sealing those linked to the city?"

"Either they are not related, or they sealed themselves off so long ago that the dragon did not know they remained present. Magma flowing outward from the plateau's volcanic column would solidify more readily against the water and eventually close up those passages." Andriun examined the walls as if looking for signs that may have happened.

"All your time spent with Tula has you sounding like a librarian, too." Lark pointed down the wide main passage before them, where the tied boats sat. "Can you feel if there's an opening to the sea in this direction? Something they could simply sail through?"

He turned that way, but shook his head. "I can sense water, not openings in the stone. I can try to trace it, but I would be better served by swimming the passage after we determine where the goborrins go after they leave their boats here."

A hint of color warmed her cheeks. Of course; letting him explore the water by swimming would be far more effective. It was the whole reason they'd chosen to send him down. "Very well. Can you tell anything about the direction they may have gone? I don't know if the water gives you access to any traces you might follow."

"It does not. I suspect our legs will serve us better in this regard."

Lark scanned the docks. "Doubtful. If they went anywhere, it had to be through water."

"Swimming?" Andriun asked, skeptical. "I am sure their bodies float, but they are not known to stay calm in water."

"Then we either have a new problem to worry about, or we're missing some boats. There have to be smaller ones, right? How else would they get from those to here?" She pointed at the ships and swung her finger to the dock under her feet.

"Rafts, then." He turned toward one of the side passages, then the other. "It was not this direction."

"Wouldn't it be easier to tell me which direction it was?" Lark shook her head in exasperation and strode to the end of the dock. There were no lamps in the other tunnels, nor did the light from those behind her carry far enough to show her what waited down that waterway. "Do we swim?"

The Shaman snorted. "*We* do not do anything. I will swim the length of these passages, now that I know the current down here is safe. You will return to the city, send soldiers down to investigate these boats, and convene with your military leaders to determine the best course of action. Once I know where these tunnels lead, we can take care of the rest."

"But I want to help," she protested. The moment it left her mouth, she realized how petulant it made her sound and her ears burned. All she had ever been was a demanding princess. She didn't want to sound like a spoiled child, but how else was she to share her thoughts?

"And you are," Andriun said gently. "It was your idea to

look here, was it not? I am ashamed, for I am the one who immediately discounted the river as a possibility. Now all we must do is determine where it opens to the desert above, and you will have fulfilled your promise to Vorkaris and found the source of the infinite goborrins."

True as it was, it brought no reassurance. "I'll be leaving the work to others, hiding behind a stone wall while they face danger."

He waved a hand in dismissal. "You will have more than your share of danger when we return to Amrochan for Zaide's rescue."

Lark straightened. She hadn't yet asked him to accompany her and hadn't expected he might volunteer. "You're coming with me?"

"It is as you said." He shrugged. "No one will be left behind."

Whether he meant Zaide or that no one would stay behind in Jadora when she departed for the rescue, she wasn't sure. She opened her mouth to ask when Tula's voice echoed down the well.

"Hello-o-o-o? Are you two doing something down there?"

"I'm not kissing the fish, if that's what you mean," Lark shouted back.

A high-pitched shriek of embarrassment answered.

Andriun stared at the column that was the well, his mouth pressed flat as he chose his words. When he spoke, they were calm, measured, and wholly unbothered. "While I appreciate the compliment she has given me, I do feel the need to defend myself. I am positive I would not taste of fish."

"And I have no interest in kissing you or anyone else, but she sets herself up for antagonism far too easily, making it impossible to resist." Lark adjusted the rope that she could only assume the guardswomen still held. "Fine. I'll go up. I'll send others down so they can aid you in returning to the surface, just in case you can't find another way out."

The Shaman nodded and splashed back into the water with practiced ease.

Lark followed with more care. The water was still unpleasantly cold and she would relish the Jadoran heat when she was pulled back out through the top. She paddled back to the space directly beneath the well with Andriun's assistance.

"Dasienna is ready," he shouted as he helped her stay afloat. "Pull her up."

Her rope went tight in an instant and she lurched upward, out of the water. She twisted to grip the rope with both hands and hold herself steady. "Be careful down here."

"I am a fish in water. I will be fine. Even if it is cold, that feels more like home than the desert above." He flashed her a grin, then returned to the dock to begin untying his harness.

A moment later, she was drawn into the stone-walled portion of the well and he vanished from sight. She trailed her fingers over the stone, wondering at the craftsmanship and puzzling at how it had been bricked from top to bottom. The well had to be as deep as the Jadoran plateau, though it certainly didn't feel it. There was no way the rope had been that long.

"Puzzles for another time," she sighed. Then she burst into daylight and the desert heat.

Jadora's palace offered no view of the city. Lark had spent so much of her life sheltered in the towers of Amrochan, peering beyond the castle's walls and into the city that would be hers to lead, yet she'd never thought she would miss it. It had always been burdensome, a weight on her shoulders, seeing all the people who were meant to answer her call. Here, she felt like a rabbit hiding in a hole, shut safely beyond the reach of all the problems they faced.

She could not see the soldiers who bore her standard as they marched off to solve the problem of the goborrins. She could not watch the distribution of the supplies Vorkaris carried in from the port that clung to the cliffs. She could not answer questions, offer reassurances, or even smile at her people in hopes it brought them comfort. All she could do was stand in one place as a tailor made the last few adjustments to a lavish gown of bold blue Jadoran silk. Maids tittered and fussed as they practiced styling her hair and buffed her fingernails until they shone, and through it all, she bore only one thought.

This was not how she was meant to rule.

"The skirt isn't made for a belt to go over it," one of the ladies lamented as she looked between Lark's dress and the Spectrum Blade that lay on the table nearby. "Wouldn't it be better to leave the sword here while—"

"The sword's presence is non-negotiable," Lark said before she could finish the question. "I will carry it during the coronation. If fashioning a belt for it that can lay over a skirt is beyond the capability of the leatherworkers here, then I will carry it in my hand."

The tailor paused mid-stitch, then hurriedly continued without a word. Two of the maids ran for the hall, though. There was no doubt they intended to fetch a leatherworker and have something made for her that instant. Lark had no qualms with asking for what she desired, nor did she care if others got their feathers ruffled over a brusque presentation of her opinion. Even better if it got results.

"Just one more hem along the bottom edge, Your Majesty, then the dress is complete. Shall I have you take it off and finish hemming elsewhere?" The tailor lifted her head, though she remained on her knees with the skirt and a threaded needle in her hands.

Lark shook her head. "Finish it now. I have no desire to sit." Sitting would force her to stew over everything happening outside the palace walls. As long as she remained clothed and standing, she could think about the dress and the coronation to come.

She was queen with or without it, but she agreed the formality would help. Her soldiers would eliminate the goborrins outside the city, her people would settle and become productive citizens, and perhaps having a crown atop her head would make her stand with a little more confidence.

The tailor did not respond, just set to fixing the silk in place with stitches tiny enough to be invisible. Lark stayed still with her head high and her gaze set on nothing as the woman worked.

She was so close. Everything she needed lay just beyond her fingertips. She could almost see the ships in the harbor now; she'd choose one that was light and fast, one to sweep them around the continent's northern rim and down the river to Amrochan. She'd take the Hymnflute, influence the winds and let Andriun shift the water. There would never be another ship that traveled so fast, and no one would be able to spread word of their approach before she arrived in Lake Sian with the Spectrum Blade in hand.

"Your Majesty," General Jobe began as he stepped through the door.

She hadn't heard anyone knock.

He crossed an arm over his chest and dipped into a bow. "I've brought news from the Paragon of Water. There are goborrin warships off the coast where the river terminates, allowing them to bring an endless stream of soldiers to Jadora's gates. The Paragon and Admiral Warinal have found the route the goborrins take through the underground river to emerge into the desert. The Admiral advises sealing the passages, but the Paragon advises against it. What are your orders?"

Lark practiced looking down at him with a queenly air. It was easier to summon in a fine dress, that was for certain. "I trust the Paragon's advice when it comes to this. The river runs beneath the city and cannot be interrupted. Sealing the passages would mean destroying Jadora's access to water, which is too valuable to sacrifice."

The general nodded as if he'd assumed that would be her answer. "How shall we proceed?"

That he offered no suggestions struck her as noteworthy. A test, perhaps. Judging how well she made decisions based on limited information. There was no way Andriun and the admiral had reached their conclusions with so few and simple of words.

She pivoted on her heels when the tailor motioned for her to turn. "The coastal opening and the one the goborrins are using should remain open. Determine the best course of action to eliminate the goborrins in the underground river, then establish guards at both ends. Ask the Paragon if he has suggestions for how the coastal point may be defended. The desert point will be easier to manage with guards, but it will be up to Magister Vorkaris to decide if that point of access would benefit the city by allowing greater access to water. He may choose to have it sealed and that will be his prerogative."

"As you wish, Majesty. Any further orders?" What he thought of his instructions, he did not say.

"Yes. Find all possible additional access points and seal them off, as long as they don't interfere with the flow of the water. Refer to Shaman Andriun's expertise in that respect." She didn't like shrugging off so much of the effort, but the Paragon's unique sense of water made handing the task to him the best decision.

"Very well. I will see it done and inform you as soon as there are updates." He nodded, but lingered in place.

It took Lark a moment to realize he was waiting for permission. Odd; the two officers did not treat her as if she held any true authority. Perhaps the dress and the regal air worked better than she'd hoped. "Good. You are dismissed, General."

Jobe bowed again and excused himself from the room without any further comment. She stared after him with an odd sense of discontent brewing in her chest.

So, this was it; this was being a queen, the future of

everything she would do. Swathed in silk, surrounded by servants, hiding in lavish parlors while others shed sweat and blood on her behalf. Her eyes drifted to the Spectrum Blade and constriction knotted around her heart.

Leadership should have been different.

CHAPTER EIGHTEEN

"No good," Whok said as he sprinkled a yellow powder into his newest salve before he spread it over Zaide's ribs. It was bitter-smelling and foul, but so was everything else in the bottles and bowls spread across the table. "Come sooner next time. Come fast, not so bad. Come slow, then this. All red. All ugly. No good."

Zaide dutifully held his shirt while the goborrin administered treatment for the cut on his side. It was shallow, but Whok was right; it would have been wiser to have it looked at sooner instead of waiting a full day.

Not that the decision had been his to make. The shift in how things were managed through the dungeon had been evident immediately after he'd been returned to his cell. The guards had returned, but not for him, and someone else had finally been given a second round of testing. Zaide had done his best to explain what it was, but it was hard to ensure long strings of information reached people soundly. The only person he could be sure understood was Raddan in the cell across the hall.

Raddan had gone first.

Zaide himself had gone back to the arena, too, though things had been far different. Not only had they allowed him to walk, they had gone from testing his limits to expanding them. Rather than goborrins intent on wounding him, he'd been taken to see a broken-born officer whose aim was to teach him something new. The man spoke Torec clearly, compared to the goborrins, and it was incredible how much easier it was to understand the language when it came from a human mouth. It was that officer who had elected to cut training short and have the cut on Zaide's side tended before they resumed.

"Come fast next time," Zaide agreed. "No red... ah..."

"Redness," Whok provided. "But much blood still, yes. Zaide is man, man blood is red."

An observation? Or an explanation of what to expect from an injury? It was far from the first Zaide had received after Amrochan's fall. "Goborrin blood is brown," he replied, unsure whether he meant it as a question. Maybe it was just an observation, too.

The old goborrin blinked at him, then adjusted his spectacles and offered a broad grin that displayed all his ugly teeth. "Yes, yes. Goborrin blood brown. Goborrin blood..." He raised one fat finger and scanned the table. A soft, pleased grunt rumbled in his throat when he found what he was looking for. He plucked a bottle from the table and held it out for Zaide to see. "This."

Rather than crushed herbs or odd liquids, the bottle was filled with something else. "Dirt?" Zaide asked, surprised. He took the bottle and turned it in hand, letting its contents move. That was certainly what it appeared to be. "Earth?"

"Earth, yes! Yes, goborrin blood earth." Whok nodded vigorously and then took back the bottle. He held it protectively, cradled to his chest. "Earth bottle Whok's. Goborrins all have. Big bottle, little bottle."

"Bottles of earth?" Zaide studied it, puzzled. "Home?"

"Yes." Again, the goborrin grinned. "Goborrins have home in bottle. Goborrins keep. Goborrin blood earth, goborrins from earth. Goborrins die, blood go back."

"Man die, blood go back to earth too." The medicine on his

side had begun to dry, so Zaide let his shirt fall. "Zaide die, body go in earth." He worked charades with his hands as he explained.

Rather than agreeing, Whok looked troubled. "All body go to earth?"

Zaide nodded.

The goborrin shook his head and returned his bottle of dirt to the table. "Goborrins die, blood go back. Body go to goborrins."

So they bled their dead and returned the bodies to other goborrins. For what, Zaide took the feeling he did not want to know. He eyed the old goborrin with a hint of wariness and steered the conversation in a new direction. "Not soon? Whok not die."

Whok gave a wheezy laugh. "Whok die soon. Whok have many summers."

The season should have been an unfamiliar word, yet it sprang readily from elsewhere in Zaide's memory. It wasn't hard to tell the goborrin was old; Whok resembled the Kolmari Elder who had taken Zaide as apprentice what now seemed so long ago—in the way he hobbled and cradled his aching back, if nothing else. "How many summers?"

The goborrin offered a thoughtful hum and lifted his hands to count on pudgy, human-like fingers.

Zaide's brows climbed when he stopped. "*Nineteen?*" He slipped back into Amrochan's common tongue. "You're nineteen? That's—" A year older than he was. Far less than he'd expected. The creature in front of him was hunched and wizened, grizzled and arthritic. He stared in disbelief.

"Old. Old, old, old." Whok laughed again, the breathy, rasping squeal grating on the ears. "Whok die soon, blood go back to earth. All good. Strength to goborrins. More come, new goborrins. Many more. Stronger."

And none of them would live longer than the average wild boar.

"Medicine done," Whok declared, providing an end to the conversation. "Zaide go back. No see Whok soon."

That part wasn't instruction. If he was training instead of fighting for his life, the likelihood of being injured was reduced. Without injury, there was little need for tending.

Somehow, Zaide thought he'd be happier when this stage of his life came to an end.

"Have question." There had to be a smoother way to say it, but he hadn't worked it out yet. How much harder would it be to learn proper Torec now that he'd gotten most of his lessons from a goborrin?

Whok peered at him from the corner of his beady black eye. His ears twitched, silent indication he was listening.

Zaide struggled to think of the right way to pose his request and fell short. In the end, he pointed at the ceiling. "Zaide go up, see Gadranus?"

The old goborrin's ears quirked again, this time in surprise. "Guards. Guards take. Ask guards."

Good enough. If he was lucky, it would be more of the broken-born, those who were more likely to understand the language he was actually fluent in. "Thank you."

"No thank. Whok heal." The creature waved a hand in dismissal. Just his job, then. Nothing more to it.

"Thank you," Zaide repeated with a half-smile as he pushed himself off the stool.

Whok waved him off again and busied himself with work, but Zaide caught the old goborrin looking after him as he rejoined the guards by the door.

For the first time, they didn't drag him back to his cell. He walked between them with his head up and his shoulders square, and the uniform they'd given him offered the illusion he was in the lead. More than one of the imprisoned soldiers saw him and backed away. For all that they'd seen him countless times as they hauled him to and from the arena, they didn't seem to recognize him now. It stuck in his chest like a branch from a briar, but he tamped down the pain. It was better that way.

He'd spent the night stewing, but it had only been after Raddan was taken to the arena for continued evaluation that he determined the best course of action.

He was going to get them all out of there.

No one was going to like what it would take.

But the lieutenant was back in his cell when Zaide returned to his own, and Zaide did not ask to be taken to Gadranus yet. He would speak first, give the lieutenant time to grapple with the unpleasant decisions that had to be made, and then after his next training session, he would finally make his move.

He had time to settle down before the guard goborrins disappeared. His side pulled uncomfortably, but he admitted it did feel better, and there was a soothing warmth in the herbs Whok had applied. Altogether, it was not unpleasant, and it would just leave another interesting scar to match the ones he'd have on his jaw and cut through his brow. Zaide thumbed the scab on his jaw absently while he waited for the clacking footfalls of the goborrins to fade away.

Normally, Raddan greeted Zaide with encouragement whenever he came back from his fights. This time, it was the other way around. Zaide sidled up to the bars of his cell and peered across. The color of the cloth flag on the lieutenant's cell had been changed and the man leaned against the wall on the far side of his cell.

Zaide skipped the greeting and went for the first positive he saw. "You made it back."

The lieutenant opened his eyes a crack, though it only served to etch the lines of exhaustion a little deeper on his face. "Almost wish I hadn't. Maker's mercy, boy, I can't believe what they've put you through."

The same wish had been heavy on Zaide's heart since the early fights. "They take you to see Whok?"

Raddan squinted. "Who?"

"The old goborrin with the spectacles. His name is Whok."

"Oh. Aye, I saw him. Nasty brute." The lieutenant grimaced. "Didn't know they had names."

"I don't know if all of them do. He'll keep you patched up, though." Zaide doubted that would be a comfort, but it was all he had to offer.

A wary light touched Raddan's eyes. "You sound like you won't be there to see it."

"I won't. But with luck, you won't be, either." There were few ways for the conversation to go, but it didn't matter. Zaide had already made up his mind. Whether others were on his side or not didn't matter.

The lieutenant grunted and forced himself across the floor. He hung against the bars of his cell, exhausted and concerned. "What do you mean, lad?"

Zaide lowered his voice. "I think I know how to get us out, but nobody's going to like it."

"No?" Raddan asked cautiously.

"I'm going to join Gadranus."

For a long time, there was only silence. Then the lieutenant leaned his forehead against the bars and gave Zaide a long, hard frown. "That's not funny."

"It's not a joke. He offered me..." Zaide trailed off, unsure how to describe it. Power? Magic? They'd laugh at him or call him mad. Maybe he was; maybe he'd been struck in the head one too many times by the goborrins that dragged him off several times a day. "He offered to give me a position leading part of his army. I'm going to take it." That it would eventually be all of that army hardly mattered.

"And become a traitor?" Raddan's nostrils flared. "Turn your back on all of us?"

"No," Zaide snapped back.

"Then what? You're a fool if you think he'll keep his word. He'll kill you, just as soon as he'll kill all the rest of us."

"Then I'd rather die out there than in here." Zaide drove a

finger against the stone floor. "If my choices are death or death, then I'll accept whatever outcome I get, but I'll also take my chance to help get people out of here."

The lieutenant scoffed. "And how do you think you're going to do that? One man against an entire army? You're good with a blade, boy, but you're not that good."

"I don't have to fight anyone to make it happen, I just need to play along. The same goes for you. They want to draft you. All of you. They want everyone who makes it through their testing alive to join the army, and it's a lot easier to escape if it's a matter of being a deserter instead of trying to make a jailbreak."

Raddan's expression grew stony, but it grew thoughtful, too. He was considering it.

"I'll go first, because he's already invited me," Zaide said. "I don't want to. It's the last thing I want, but I can be useful by going first. I was the Bladebearer, remember? A beacon of hope for all these men." He spread a hand toward the prison. Several other prisoners had moved closer and listened to him speak, but he dared not address them now.

"And you're in prison now, same as the rest of us, with no blade at all," Raddan replied.

It stung, but it was true. "That shouldn't matter. All of you know how hard I've fought. I need you to think of that now, when I ask you to trust me. I'm going to meet with Gadranus and tell him I've decided to accept. I'll see if I can get him to let me oversee the testing matches in the arena. And then all of you can declare that you want to follow me."

The lieutenant shook his head, both resigned and disappointed. "It won't work, lad. He's too smart for that."

"How do you know it won't work if you won't give me a chance? If I can persuade them to give me power over how all of you are handled, I'll be in a position to vouch for every soldier here and give you a chance to get out from behind bars. You have to trust me, lieutenant."

Again, Raddan shook his head. "Don't be naive, boy. You're doing exactly what he wants."

"He'll think I'm doing what he wants. There's a definite difference there. What I'm doing is getting out and getting us back to Dasienna." The name felt wrong on his tongue and Zaide scraped it against his teeth as if to shed some bitter taste. She would always be Lark to him, spirited and determined. His jaw tightened and he made himself go on. "You're free not to believe me. But I'm positive this is the way I can get us out, and I'm giving it a try whether or not you agree. When you see me in the stands, trust me."

The lieutenant had nothing more to say, but Zaide caught the whispers of the other prisoners.

Maybe that was all it would take for him to make a difference. Maybe they would play along, seek him out and find a way to get themselves out of Amrochan after he set them on the path. He understood Raddan's reservations, but there was already no doubt in Zaide's mind that his scheme would end with him dead. Better to die in service to his queen, he thought with a grim smile.

In that, he was no different from the goborrins.

Zaide sat back and waited for the guards to come while new rumors swirled through Amrochan's depths.

He'd be a hero or a villain before this was over, and he was not sure which.

CHAPTER NINETEEN

The palace had changed.

Zaide had never grown intimately familiar with the place, his visits few and often short, but he'd learned his way through some of the halls in the days that led up to the siege. Those hallways were unrecognizable now, stripped of everything that had made the palace seem fine or lavish.

It was strange; nothing in Toren had been so bare. The lack of tapestries and rugs made the hallways echo, each footstep sharper than it should have been. The clacking hooves of the goborrins that formed Zaide's escort grated on the ears, but he did his best to ignore it.

He'd been to the room they guided him to before. Sendassian had used it as a war room, and when the goborrins paused outside and gestured for him to knock, he wondered if it had been stripped of every trace of the old king, too.

His knuckles cracked against the wooden door. No answer came, but the goborrins pushed forward anyway, wrenching it open and forcing him through.

Inside, little had changed. The long table remained, as did the dark, heavy drapes that lined the room and deadened sound. The same map Lark had helped expand lay waiting for plans, though most of the pewter figurines that had served as markers lay toppled. Rather than goborrins, half a dozen broken-born officers—men who looked so much like Zaide—hunched over those markers and shuffled them about. All of them stopped to stare.

Gadranus stood beside the map, one such figurine in his hand. He weighed it in his palm as he lifted his head. Slowly, he placed the marker atop the square depicting Amrochan. "Had a change of heart, have you?"

Zaide dared not step any closer. He lingered by the door and his escorts lingered beside him. From the way the officers glowered at him, it was clear he'd interrupted something. "I just have some questions."

Inch by inch, Gadranus straightened. It was odd; he'd seemed so large as the shadow in the depths of Kolmar's temple. In reality, he was a scarce few inches taller than Zaide. "Very well. Come. Sit." He motioned toward a sitting area to the side, something Zaide was relatively certain had not been there when Sendassian had stood beside the same table. "Ask whatever it is you desire, but do not make me wait. As you can imagine, there is much for me to do."

The officers drew back at some silent command or a gesture Zaide had missed. They filed toward the door with dour expressions.

Zaide stepped aside to let them pass. "I don't know where to start."

"At the beginning, perhaps. Whatever made you reconsider what I had to say." Gadranus stalked over to one of the chairs and took a seat without waiting to see if his instructions were heeded.

"Goborrins," Zaide said, casting a frown at the taller of the beasts that had escorted him. It seemed they would not leave him alone this time. There was nothing to be done about that; he had brought that trouble on himself.

Gadranus said nothing, merely laced his fingers together before himself and raised a brow.

Zaide had no desire to sit with the man again, not like they had in Toren. It had been too easy. Too comfortable. He did not want either from this meeting. Yet he did not feel safe with his back to the door. If he crossed the room and sat, at least he wouldn't feel a constant need to look over his shoulder. He crept to the chair directly across from his enemy and sat. "You want me to take your place. You lead them. Why would they follow me?"

"Ah." The man moved his head, not quite a nod, but some sort of affirmation that he understood. "Theirs is a simple way of life. Strength means everything. They follow whoever is strongest, largely without question. I proved my strength long ago."

"But how am I supposed to prove they should follow me?" With the way the two goborrin guards loomed over his chair, Zaide could not fathom giving such monsters orders and expecting them to obey.

"Again, simple," Gadranus said. He reclined into the high, cushioned back of the chair he must have moved from elsewhere. Perhaps that was why the rest of the palace was so bare. Vanity and redecoration. "They recognize me as the strongest warrior they have ever encountered. You are going to be the one to kill me." A ghost of a smile brushed across his lips. "So what does that make you?"

Oh. A hint of color rose to the tips of Zaide's ears. He had come to understand how much the goborrins valued strength; he should have known. At the same time, he'd never stopped to consider how that might be used against them. Useful knowledge. Something worth passing on. "How many of them are there?"

Gadranus raised his shoulders an inch. In the fine black coat he wore, the movement hardly showed at all. "More than we could likely imagine. I gave up counting long ago. They are animals, and they breed and grow as fast as animals. Eight to a dozen or so in every litter, mature enough to fight or bear their own young after a year."

The thought was enough to make Zaide's head reel. "Where do you keep all of them? The amount of resources that would take—"

"They are relatively self-sufficient," Gadranus provided before he could finish. "I leave them to their territory and they merely answer my call. Do not forget, Zaide. Amroch is the only part of the world that has yet to bow to me, and it is but a fraction of what exists. They have vast expanses of land at their disposal."

More than once, Zaide had felt as if the monsters were innumerable. He could not fathom the size of the world beyond the Shattered Lands; the space between Kolmar and Toren was vast enough. Knowing how much more territory belonged to the goborrins was enough to leave him cold. "They could crush us if they wanted."

Gadranus nodded in agreement. "Which is why it is important for someone to lead them and keep our kind safe. I assume this is the concern that crossed your mind."

It had been, though Zaide found he couldn't make himself confirm it. Where would the goborrins go when everything was over? Without someone to hold the beasts at bay, they would topple straight from one war into another. His tongue pressed tight to the roof of his mouth and it was all he could do to nod back.

A low chuckle welled in Gadranus's throat. "You're a better man than me, selfless to the very end."

"Someone's going to have to manage them," Zaide replied, though his voice had grown hoarse.

"Indeed. I would not have expected that would be what might sway you, but if it ends the senseless strife between us, I will accept your humanitarian sacrifice in the honorable way you intend." Gadranus raised a hand as if to offer a toast, though he held nothing.

Zaide fought back his disgust at the arrogance. "I'm not agreeing just yet."

"Then tell me. What else is needed to convince you?"

"Two things." Zaide wouldn't push his luck, not yet. Authority over the soldiers in the dungeon below would have to come later. "First… I want you to teach me. I've only fought you briefly, but I've been told your swordsmanship is unparalleled. So, teach me. Show me how to fight."

Again the dark-haired man shrugged, as if such a request was of no consequence. "Of course. It would be an honor to shape you into the greatest swordsman to ever live. And the other?"

"Proof."

That seemed to still the man's ego a moment, for Gadranus gazed at him in expectant silence.

"You said you mean to give me magic," Zaide continued. "I've always heard that wasn't possible. If you're really as powerful as you claim, it won't be hard to prove you can just choose to give me magic."

To call the expression Gadranus had worn before haughty would not have been accurate, but whatever it was, it cooled into an unreadable mask at that request. "A demonstration, then," he concluded dryly. "Are you certain that's what you want? A taste of what is yet to come?"

Zaide made himself meet the man's stare. It was what he wanted, wasn't it? A chance to make a difference? To set free the innocent soldiers who'd been made prisoners of what had once been their home city? To save those he cared about, the only way he knew how?

His throat tightened, but he made himself speak. "Yes."

Gadranus held his gaze without blinking. "There is no going back from this, Zaide. Once you know the taste of magic, this can never be undone. That which is awakened may never sleep again. You are absolutely certain this is your request?"

"Yes," Zaide repeated, irritated.

For a time, Gadranus stared. Then, ever so slowly, the corners of his mouth coiled into a cold facsimile of a smile. "As you wish." He extended his hand, an invitation to shake on the agreement.

Zaide stared at it. There was no way this would end well, but there were no other paths forward. He bore the power to aid those trapped with him, to save a friend and remove one more problem from the ever-growing list of them Lark had to solve. She had everything else she needed—three Paragons by her side, the Spectrum Blade in her hand, and clues toward what was required to restore it and set them all free. He had helped her gain all of it, and now he stood to give her more. Every time Gadranus drew a blade to train him, it would be another chance to strike him down, to overtake him and buy them time before another Rise.

There were worse ways to meet one's end.

"Proof or no deal," he said.

"Agreed."

Zaide leaned forward to take the enemy's hand.

His grip was firm and warm. They shook once and Gadranus did not let go.

Warmth became heat, and the burn crawled up Zaide's arm. It spread through his shoulder and chest, bringing pain and something else that streaked through his senses like lightning. His hair stood on end and his heart raced as if it might escape the confines of his ribs, and still the sensation spread.

"It will be heady at first," Gadranus said, still holding fast. "Those of us born with such power become accustomed to it. For you, though, it will be all-consuming."

The words faded in Zaide's ears as his head spun and shadows crawled down Gadranus's wrist to twine around his arm and sink into his flesh. It was ice against the heat, and if he'd thought the sensation powerful before, now it grew to unbearable heights. Colors flashed and twisted in his eyes as his body flushed with scorching strength and frigid shadow. It flowed to his fingertips and toes and spurred his pulse to climb until his whole chest ached and clenched.

Magic surged in his senses in ways he'd never imagined. Sounds grew sharper, his vision brighter, and shapes crackled all around him in masses of prickly gray. People. Mages. Elements around him. He collapsed, gasping for air, and Gadranus released his hand.

"There," the man said, as mildly as if he'd signed a contract with ink instead of transforming the whole world. "A fragment of power to call your own. It will grow weaker over time, as the energy you now hold works its way back to me. I suggest you enjoy this, for the sensation will not always be so strong."

Zaide stared, but he no longer saw his enemy's face. Instead, a roiling shadow that sparked with power hung where Gadranus should have been, looming like a storm on the horizon. The same shadows crawled over him, tingling painfully as they burrowed into his skin.

He tried to reply. He couldn't speak. He could scarcely breathe, every inch of him twisting on the floor in an exquisite blend of agony and pleasure that words would never describe.

Gadranus chuckled softly to himself and the shadow of his form drifted across the room to return to work.

Zaide did not know how long he stayed on the floor. Sounds and colors swelled and faded, pushing him to the brink of consciousness and then retreating until he was almost aware. Shadows and power nestled into his bones, leaving him with flesh broken by goosebumps and sweat beading on his brow. Voices rose and fell at the edge of his awareness, filling his ears with words he almost understood. Then, slowly, everything faded until the magic all around him became nothing but a hum that vibrated in the depths of his being, a latent *something* that begged to be touched.

He opened his eyes and found his breath steady and his body cool, for all that he felt as if he'd just woken from a fever.

A shadow stirred above him and resolved into the now-familiar figure of Gadranus. "How does it feel?" the man asked softly, conversationally.

Zaide pushed himself to his hands and knees. Cooled sweat dripped from his brow and he stared at the darkened spot it made on the plush carpet that tickled his palms. A haze of disorientation still clouded his head, but his muscles answered readily when he moved, strong and sinuous and touched by a grace he'd never felt before. "Good," he answered in a rasp, and it was the truth.

Magic—*his* magic—crackled up the nape of his neck and down his arms, and Zaide knew he had made a mistake.

CHAPTER TWENTY

No one wanted to be responsible for the crowning of the queen.
Lark struggled not to take it personally; she understood their
concerns, but the situation was just another hitch in the long
string of catastrophes that had come to mark each point in her
life.

Resia felt she did not know her well enough for the honor.

Tula thought it would be best if Elsanna handled it, as her
position as Paragon had not yet been revealed.

Elsanna thought it would be an inappropriate gesture for her
to be viewed as an authority to crown the queen she was
supposed to serve.

Andriun did not believe he held enough honor for such a
task, following the disgrace that had cast him out from his
people.

Warinal said it was not the place of military officers to handle
affairs of succession, and Jobe had said nothing at all.

In the end, they'd concluded Vorkaris was the proper choice,
for no one would question whether a dragon had the proper
authority or credentials to place the crown upon a queen's head.

If only Vorkaris had fingers instead of claws, or forepaws that
were smaller than Lark's entire body.

If only Zaide was here to do it, she thought with no small hint of bitterness. He would have been a perfect choice, bound to her by his role as Bladebearer. He'd always been so fast to offer help wherever he could. She had no doubt he would have offered to aid with the ceremony, too.

But he wasn't there.

She buried her face in Daisy's scruff and shut her eyes tight.

"Uh oh," Tula whispered so loudly, it was no secret at all. "You know it's bad when she's nice to the dog."

Agitation ruffled up Lark's backbone and she raised her head enough to glower at the Magister over the top of Daisy's head. She wasn't mean to the dog; she went out of her way to be polite with the creature. That she had sought Daisy for a single moment of comfort was far from unreasonable, and she resented the suggestion that such behavior was unusual.

She did not like the dog, but the dog and the sword were the only traces of Zaide she had left.

The sword was decidedly less soft and comforting.

Andriun cleared his throat. "Your Majesty, I mean this in the kindest way, but perhaps it would be wise to leave the dog alone so that you are not covered in white hair during the coronation." He adjusted the collar of his new Jadoran coat and examined himself in the Magister's tall mirror again.

They had all been given new finery for the day, all of them dressed in colors appropriate for their station. Tula's bright red and gold coat invoked flames and matched what her sister would wear for the occasion; they would stand together to make their familial bond clear. Resia's silk gown was shades of green and gold that accented the earthy tones of her skin in the most beautiful way. Blue would have been the obvious choice for Andriun, but the rich hues his skin had taken in the desert sun meant it would offer little contrast. He had refused Elsanna's first suggestion of white, saying it was the color of mourning, and instead wore shades of black and gray that had been embroidered with blue patterns that resembled ocean waves.

Lark smoothed her hands down the front of her blue gown and made herself stand. She did not see any of Daisy's fur clinging to her dress, but she supposed maids would brush her down one more time before they let her set foot outside the parlor used for preparation.

As soon as Lark pulled away from the dog, Tula pranced over to kneel beside her and tie a cloth around the canine's neck. It was blue, too, though closer to the color Zaide had always worn. A deliberate choice, Lark suspected, though she lacked the energy to make any such accusation.

"There. Vorkaris says he's ready, so we should head out there and get things started." Tula rose and dusted her hands together, and Daisy stood as if to follow. It was hard to tell when the animal understood things, but she had a way of knowing where the Paragon of Fire was headed and was always quick to tag along.

Lark didn't know whether to be pleased or jealous that Zaide's dog had imprinted on someone else. "Lead the way, then. You know the palace better than I do." Not that it would be hard to tell where they were supposed to go. A massive platform had been erected in front of the Magister's palace, tall enough to raise them above the watching crowd and broad enough to fit a whole dragon.

"I know the way, too." Resia stood, as graceful and placid as ever. It was odd how well all of them fit their roles. Resia reminded Lark of the cool shade beneath a forest's trees or a calm meadow where flowers bloomed. Tula was as spirited and unpredictable as fire, and Andriun was tranquil but bore formidable strength.

Then there was her. Perhaps it was no wonder her magic had never awakened. There was nothing in Lark at all that represented the unwavering presence and stability of light.

Resia put herself in the lead and the group filed out to wind through the halls. Elsanna was already beside the palace's great front doors, her hair pinned up and her neck draped with jewels.

The acting Magister swept forward to greet each of them with an embrace. "Vorkaris awaits us outside. The people have gathered, and all is ready. Just waiting on you, Your Majesty."

Lark said nothing and adjusted the way the Spectrum Blade rested against her skirt as a pair of guardswomen opened the door and the lot of them moved outside.

They had waited until evening to hold the ceremony, the time bringing cooler temperatures and less likelihood that any of them would swoon in their finery. The city was aglow with lights, all of them tingling in Lark's awareness. They were something other than fire, bright and heatless, and she could not help but feel that she should have been able to touch or influence them. She did not try.

Something fell onto her shoulder and she swiped it away with a hand before she realized it was ash from the dragon's wings. Vorkaris sat above them, his flames stifled but his hide glowing as brightly as ever. The stray ash left a smudge on the silk of her dress, so she left it alone. Better to have a small fleck here and there rather than streaks all over, even if she did fancy it looked like a comet in the sky.

Daisy trotted along beside Tula with her tongue lolling, as if the event were to recognize her instead of the queen, and they fell into single file to climb the stairs to the temporary platform. Resia went first, then Tula, her sister, and the white dog. Andriun lingered at the bottom of the stairs, gazing off into the distance as if something had stolen his attention.

"Is everything all right?" Lark asked softly.

He twitched as if startled, then offered an apologetic smile. "Yes, sorry. I thought I felt..." The distant look returned as he trailed off, and she cleared her throat. It jarred him from thought a second time and he hurried up the steps to take his place.

Elsanna had begun a speech. The people were noisy and Lark could not hear it all, but she caught bits and pieces and the sound of her name.

Lark crept up the stairs to wait for her cue. They had already rehearsed inside the palace, where no one could see them falter. She would be called to the stage and kneel before the dragon. Elsanna would speak on his behalf, and he would place the crown. It would be swift and simple, nothing like the coronation she should have had, and she would be grateful when it was done.

The Paragons stood to one side and Elsanna stood to the other, and she could just see them through the space between Vorkaris's half-furled wings. Andriun stood with his head turned, staring out past the gathered crowd. It made Lark's stomach turn and she willed herself not to be ill. There was enough on her plate without more problems, and for something to have his attention that way...

"Dasienna," Elsanna called.

Lark winced. Had she missed the cue, or was that the first time the acting Magister had called for her? She swallowed hard against the fear in her belly and strode up the stairs. The Spectrum Blade's ornate sheath rocked against her skirt and she put a hand to the hilt to still it.

She expected awe or reverence. Instead, the moment she appeared, a roar of excitement tore through the countless people gathered just beyond the row of soldiers encircling the stage. Hands raised and fists pumped in the air and Lark took it all in, bewildered. She had never imagined she might be received that way.

Elsanna motioned to the space Lark was meant to occupy, then stepped back and stood with her hands clasped at her waist.

Lark held fast to the Spectrum Blade as she took her place before the great glowing dragon of Jadora. Her other hand shook so severely that she hid it in the folds of her skirt.

The acting Magister continued her speech, but Lark did not hear it, for Vorkaris whispered into her thoughts.

Do not fear, my queen. This is the first of many good things that shall come your way.

She could not turn to see if Andriun was distracted, but she tried not to let her doubt take charge.

Do not concern yourself with the Shaman. All is well. We have made sure of that. The dragon's mental voice held a touch of smugness. It was more irritating than reassuring.

What is he distracted with? Lark thought back.

You shall see. Kneel, my queen. It is time to receive your crown.

She sank to the platform and kept her head bowed, though her eyes cut upward. The crown looked comically tiny, held between the claws on either of the dragon's index fingers. Index toes? Pointer claws? It was all Lark could do not to snort at the wandering of her own thoughts at a time like this.

The last of Elsanna's speech hummed in her ears and the crown lowered onto the top of her head. Lark closed her eyes as it settled into her hair.

Rise, Queen Dasienna, Vorkaris said at the same time as Elsanna.

Lark stood, and the end of her name was swallowed by cheers.

She turned in place, drew the Spectrum Blade and raised it to the sky. A roar of people unlike anything she had ever heard rose to answer. Jadorans and Amrochanites alike voiced their approval with such ferocity, she felt as if the sound might never stop ringing in her ears.

They see the light in you, Dasienna, Vorkaris whispered.

To know the dragon had heard her sensitive thoughts was embarrassing and she breathed deep, lest it make her blush. *I don't.*

You will, once you learn to open your eyes.

As if she hadn't tried. She'd given everything she could to unlock her power, and the failure to do so had cost her everything. Her jaw tightened as she fixed her eyes on the point of the gleaming sword in her hand, letting it chase away all her bitter thoughts.

All else had failed, but at least she still had a chance to strike down her enemy. It would not seal his power and he would be reborn at once, but it still bought them time. A decade or two would either be enough time to determine where she'd gone wrong, or else enough time for her to find who was meant to replace her.

Such grim thoughts should not be in your head at a time like this, Vorkaris said. *Relish the moment. Then lower your sword, for your arm grows tired, and even queens must rest.*

She'd been doing nothing but resting. It was everyone else who pressed forward, while she hid among luxuries in the palace. Stubborn determination kept her arm aloft for almost a minute more. Then, reluctantly, she let the blade sink. Its surface still bore hints of color, though the iridescence was muted in the magic-made lights. She studied those lights as she returned the blade to its sheath. Before they departed, she would ask who had made them. No matter what Vorkaris said, finding another who bore the power of light could only be a wise choice. If not her replacement, then maybe a teacher.

"Good," Elsanna told her when she turned to go.

Lark forced herself to smile. Tula and Resia departed ahead of her, but Andriun remained fixed in place, a faint crease between his brows.

She cleared her throat and he snapped to attention.

The Shaman mouthed a silent *sorry* and offered his arm. It was not necessary for anyone to escort her down the stairs, but she accepted anyway. It made his pause look more deliberate, detracted from whatever held him occupied.

Behind them, Vorkaris lowered his wings to block them from view. At last, the vibrant cheers began to subside, and Elsanna's strong voice rose above them to conclude the brief ceremony.

Lark wished she could exhale hard enough to deflate, but the bodice of her dress was too snug. She could not even slouch. That stiffness left her grateful for Andriun's support on the way down the stairs.

Still, he looked back, and he did not pull away when they reached the ground.

"What is it?" she asked in a murmur.

"Water," he said. "Water where it should not be."

"The river?" Lark guessed.

Andriun shook his head. "The gates."

A brief pang of fear licked at her heart, though he did not appear troubled. Just... confused. "Then we go to the gates," she concluded. With her free hand, she summoned one of the soldiers nearby.

"What?" Andriun blinked twice and pulled himself from distraction. "No, there is no need. It is your coronation. You should stay here."

"Maybe the new queen wishes to roam the city streets and greet her people." She sniffed and turned to the guard when he answered her call. "We will walk the city. From here to the gates and back, so that all those who could not come to or fit in this plaza might see their new queen."

The man bowed. "Of course, Your Majesty. We will organize an escort for you."

Lark almost dared smile. The speed at which they sorted themselves out and created a ring to surround her was satisfying in a way little had been. If only everyone answered to her so readily. Perhaps more would, now that she had a perpetual reminder of her station she could wear.

"This is not necessary," Andriun said, though he posted himself beside her anyway.

Tula joined a moment later. "Where are we going?"

"The city gates, she said," Resia provided as she pushed into the circle, too. Even Daisy joined them.

Lark half expected Elsanna or Vorkaris to interject, but they said nothing. Were they not concerned about what Andriun sensed? That the dragon already knew about it indicated he had spoken with the Shaman, but he seemed so confident it was nothing to worry about while Andriun was bothered, at the very least.

"Right. Let's move along." Lark lifted her skirt just enough to walk unhindered, and the whole entourage moved like a bubble around her.

The cheers she thought were over returned with a new force as they traveled the streets. Faces appeared in windows and people clustered in doorways to watch as they passed. It was something like a parade, yet altogether more awkward.

She waved, nonetheless.

"It is a great deal of water," Andriun muttered as they walked. "The sand is full, and yet it flows. The heat of the air does not steal it. How...?"

"We'll find out soon enough." Lark was just as confused as he was, but he did not seem disturbed, so she tried to take comfort in knowing that whatever it was, it was only strange and not dangerous.

They wound their way toward the gates at a steady pace, and the Shaman told her the water continued onward, too. It came ever closer, until they finally reached their destination.

The soldiers at the gate—not guardswomen, but soldiers who had been a part of the false Magister's Mage-Guard—barred their way. "Forgive us, Your Majesty," the captain of the small guard team said. "We cannot allow you to set foot beyond the gates. Something approaches the city and we aren't certain what it is. A messenger has been sent to notify Magister Vorkaris so he may investigate."

"That's why we're here." Lark gestured to Andriun with a flat palm. "The Paragon of Water wishes to investigate. I will remain here, but you must allow him to step outside the city and determine what's out there."

The man's mouth worked a moment. "The Paragon of *Water*, Majesty?" It wasn't precisely a question, so much as an expression of concern. There was no mistaking who Andriun was. In a place like this, he stuck out in ways that bordered on comical.

Still, Tula pointed at him and whispered loudly, "He's the blue one."

The guard was not the only one unimpressed, though Resia covered her mouth to hide a smile of amusement.

Now was not a time for mirth. Lark gave the Paragons of Fire and Forest a stern glance and they quieted, leaving her to interpret the man's worry. It wasn't hard, and Lark did her best to remain placid. "Paragon Andriun has informed me that whatever is out there, it is accompanied by a large amount of water. If it poses any threat to Jadora, his talents will allow him to contain it before it gets close."

"Of course, Your Majesty," the man mumbled. His eyes snagged on the crown atop her head before he called for the gates to be opened.

Andriun toyed with the cuff of his sleeve as he watched the two slabs of bronze part. "I will be brief. The moment I have determined what is going on, I will come back to report."

"Take your time," Lark said, though part of her wished she could be by his side in that moment of discovery. How quickly she'd come to miss involvement, even when it put her in danger.

He stepped forward as soon as the doors were open enough for him to slip through the crack and into the desert beyond, and the great doors that served as the gates to Jadora all but slammed shut again behind him.

"Rude," Tula muttered.

Lark struggled to keep from making faces. She should appear composed, not bewildered by her party members. "What do you mean?"

"They didn't even ask if I wanted to go out there." The Magister stuck out her tongue, but the guard's back was turned and he did not notice.

"We don't have to be everywhere, you know," Resia said. Her

smile was soft and sweet. "You should enjoy resting. I get the feeling things won't stay calm for long."

"Do they ever?" Lark asked absently. Her fingers nestled into the soft fur atop Daisy's head. She had not even noticed the dog's approach, nor her own impulse to touch the animal when she sat within reach. She hardly paid attention to the animal, and the dog had been free to roam the palace since their arrival, meaning Daisy was not often by her side. Yet her presence was inoffensive and petting her bordered on reassuring, so Lark stroked the dog's head and velvety-soft ears without comment.

"No," Resia replied with a sigh. "I don't think they do."

One of the gate guards exclaimed something and sprang for the doors. More followed and Lark went stiff. Her hand twitched to the Spectrum Blade's hilt out of reflex, but the sword's cool grip told her nothing.

"Let him in!" one of the guards shouted, and the cluster of armored men parted.

Andriun burst through. "Desheni!" he cried, wide-eyed and wearing a brilliant smile. "Desheni are crossing the desert!"

CHAPTER TWENTY-ONE

Lark shoved guards out of the way without regard for who they served. Men in Amrochan and Jadoran armor staggered back, full of protests, but she ignored them all. Daisy leaped and pranced alongside her as she thrusted her shoulders through the narrow gap between the doors and tumbled into the desert night.

Near the foot of the plateau, she saw them—dozens of figures in pale clothing, their blue skin gleaming in the moonlight. A column of mages walked to either side of the group, pulling water from the sand behind them and sending it over their heads in an arc. Every step they took carried them across firm, wet sand, and their progress was both easy and steady.

"What in all the world?" She ran to the edge of the switchbacked trail to watch as they organized themselves for the climb. The trail was rocky and the water would not be needed to pave the way. Instead of funneling it into the ground, the water mages raised their hands and turned the rippling liquid into some sort of parasol.

"I thought there weren't other mages among your people?" Tula asked, almost accusatory.

"There were no other mages among *my* people," Andriun

said, as if that clarified anything at all. "Of the Desheni in my village, I was the only one."

Tula's head cocked to the side. "Well, you and your father."

"Oh. Yes. But he was a liar and pretended he did not have it." Andriun tipped his head sideways, too, as if that were a new revelation to be considered. "Perhaps he was not the only one who was lying."

"The more obvious answer is that these aren't people from your village," Lark put in. She pointed. "Look."

Resia crept to the edge of the road beside her and took in the scene with the wide-eyed wonder of someone who had seen little of the world. Then again, the Kolmari Elder was newest to all this; prior to this expedition, she had spent the entirety of her life in the forest and had gone nowhere but Amrochan. "They have tails," she breathed in awe.

"Tails?" Andriun's head whipped to Lark and he hurried to join her, too. Rather than wonder, he blanched with dismay.

"All those mages do. Some of the others, too, but not all of them." Tula singled out a few people in the group who appeared to lack them, including one at the front of the procession.

Andriun backed away. "Oh. Oh, this is not good."

For him, it likely was not. Lark knew the Oracle had promised he would reconcile with his people, but the last she had known, Andriun was still dishonored and cast out.

That had been before Gadranus crushed the precious artifact entrusted to the Desheni, which Andriun had been allowed to take.

"Weren't you excited about it all of two seconds ago?" Tula crossed her arms and squinted one eye.

Andriun retreated another step. "That was before I contemplated the ramifications of them coming this way."

"Why are they coming this way?" Lark stayed where she was and her guard entourage positioned themselves around her, though they left space for her to watch the visitors approach.

"That's a good question. I don't think any Desheni have ever come to Jadora before. It's not like we never interact, but it always happened in Ganede when they came south for trade." Tula drummed her fingers against her sleeve. "But even then, it's never been Desheni with tails, or we would have had *that* little piece of information logged in the library's books already."

The group made steady progress up the trail and Jadoran guards filtered out through the gates to greet them.

"Elsanna and Vorkaris have both been called," one of the guards said.

Lark accepted the information with a bland nod. It would be respectful to have the city's leaders present, but hers was the more impressive welcome party. A queen and three out of five Paragons represented most of the world.

That she still only considered her party as holding *three* Paragons stuck out a moment later.

The group of Desheni had just rounded the last turn in the trail when Vorkaris made his appearance. The dragon circled in the air before he elected to land on the high stone wall, just to the left of the doors. His head hung low and the ashes shed from his wings smoldered on the wind and Lark expected Vorkaris would be the first to greet the new arrivals. It was Andriun, instead.

"Uncle Ikan!" He raised his webbed hands to his head in disbelief and hardly seemed to know what to do with his feet. He turned in a circle before he jogged forward to greet the cluster of Desheni, and the tall leader Lark remembered responded with a quick embrace, a slap on the back, and a friendly sort of laugh.

"Thank goodness for family," Resia said with a grin, though she'd never appeared concerned.

Lark smiled, too. Ikan's help had been invaluable in reclaiming the north from the influence of Gadranus. Andriun had come into his power then, had been recognized as Paragon by his people, if not given the title of Shaman. Though the Oracle had referred to him by that title and the rest of them had accepted it, as far as Lark knew, Ikan was the one who carried that role.

She stepped forward, too. "It's good to see you again, Ikan, though I certainly never expected we might cross paths here."

"As it is good to see you, Queen Dasienna. Forgive us, Your Majesty. We appear to be late for your coronation." Ikan's attention drifted to the crown atop her head before his gaze fell to the Spectrum Blade at her side. He did not frown—his expression didn't change at all—but she caught the squaring of his shoulders that promised the unpleasant question would come.

"No one could have expected you would come," she laughed. "Desheni in the desert? It's positively unheard of."

"Well, we are not the first." Ikan thumped Andriun's shoulder again.

Andriun drew back, reclaiming his place in line with the other Paragons. "I do not understand. You have come all this way to see Dasienna crowned?"

"We have come to pledge the service of our people to our new queen, as our leaders once pledged service to her father." A hint of pride drew Ikan up straight, but he grew solemn when he turned to Lark. "We have heard what happened in Amrochan. We would offer our spears, but few of us are land adapted, and I fear we would only hinder you."

Help from the Desheni was one thing she had never anticipated, though the display warmed her heart. "There are ways you can help, don't worry." She recognized him, but the others were strangers. From their age, she assumed they were leaders among their people. Ikan was the youngest in the main group, though their escort was composed of mages of all ages.

"Name your need, Your Majesty, and the Desheni will answer." He laid a webbed hand over his heart, fingers spread wide, and dipped in a low bow.

The others mirrored the gesture and a hint of warmth rose in Lark's cheeks. She was used to deference; she'd gotten plenty as the princess of Amroch. But it was different coming from a group of people who had come to swear themselves to serve her. Would every region present her with such formality? She turned to Vorkaris for guidance, but the dragon merely adjusted on his perch.

If they have offered assistance, accept it. Do not waste their goodwill or their time. The low tone of his voice came across like a whisper, like an advisor speaking for her ear alone.

Very well, she thought back before she spoke. "Our most pressing need is food for Amrochan refugees. We will exhaust Jadora's supplies in no time."

"Keeping a large city fed is a challenge in any time of hardship," one of the other Desheni elders said.

"Indeed." Lark tried to commit the man's features to memory, though she had no name to go with them. She had met so many dignitaries and nobles through the years, it grew difficult to keep them all straight. "It just so happens the Paragon of Water has located a reservoir beneath the city that appears to be connected to the ocean. Is it possible for your people to transport goods through that channel to be lifted into the city?"

"We can do more than just transport, Majesty," Ikan said. "We are skilled as both hunters and gatherers. It would be our honor to help provide food for your people."

The offer was better than she'd hoped for. Just assistance in moving things to the city would be beneficial, but an influx of additional resources brought to their door would make everything easier. "Only as long as it puts you under no strain." She would accept nothing that took food from the mouths of the Desheni. Not after all they had lost.

A few of the elders appeared pleased by her manners, and the same old man answered from Ikan's side. "The sea is bountiful, Your Majesty. Do not fear."

Adjustments can be made to one of the convenient wells within the city, Vorkaris said, and though all the Desheni looked at him, they did not appear surprised by his voice inside their heads. *It will allow us to lift provisions directly into Jadora without your people needing to experience the full heat of the desert.*

"A gracious offer, Lord Dragon," Ikan said with a respectful bow.

Another problem solved. Lark bottled up her excitement, lest she appear flighty, but she could not resist the smile of relief that came with the simple agreement. With the Desheni transporting fresh-caught fish up the underground river and right to the wells of the city, the last of their immediate problems were solved.

The others had remained quiet during the exchange, but now Tula widened her stance and planted her fists against her hips. "I'm glad you're helping and all, but I have a question. If you all live in the ocean, how did you hear there was going to be a coronation in Jadora?"

Vorkaris rumbled in his chest, a sound more like tumbling stones than an animal's growl. *I may have suggested they would be interested in meeting our new queen.*

In a single motion, Lark and the Paragons all turned to gape at the dragon.

"You invited them?" Lark asked.

"Without telling me?" Andriun sounded dismayed.

I do not need anyone's permission to invite guests into my home.

Tula huffed and kicked a rock. "But I didn't have time to get anything ready! Now I'll seem rude. I should have had Elsanna build a pool, or some kind of man made oasis, or—"

"We have brought our own accommodations concerning water. We will be fine," Ikan reassured her. "Crossing the desert was an interesting experience, and it seems our presence will be valued, so it was worth our time."

Behind them, the bronze doors groaned as more guards pushed them wide. Elsanna made her appearance with Moros close at her heels. Neither looked surprised.

You told them you invited the Desheni leaders, didn't you? Lark side-eyed the dragon as she thought at him.

Vorkaris tilted his head back and feigned innocence. *I may have mentioned it to Elsanna in passing.*

And not Tula? Isn't she supposed to be your real partner?

She is, and I am quite fond of her. But she has difficulty holding her tongue, and with all that has happened, I felt it was wiser not to allow your other companion to stew in fear of what he would say to his elders. He spread his wings and held them ready for a strong downstroke, silently warning her of the ashes he would stir. *I will see all of you at the palace.*

Lark shielded her eyes as the dragon took off.

Elsanna did not even blink. "Welcome to the great city of Jadora, my friends. Never has the city been so blessed as we are now, host to so many distinguished guests. I am Elsanna, Magister of Jadora, and it is my honor to provide hospitality while you are here. I would love to offer you a place to stay in the palace. You will find the climate indoors is far preferable to even the night air."

The Desheni did not reply right away. Instead, Ikan and the elder right beside him exchanged glances, then looked to Tula.

Without missing a beat, the former librarian grinned. "I mentioned her when we met before, right? Elsanna is my elder sister, though she doesn't like to talk about it. Maybe it's the elder part." She paused to scrunch her nose at Elsanna, as if that dig was supposed to be revenge. "I'll be taking the role of Magister when she is ready to start her own family. For now, I'm happy to be able to help outside the city." Her chin tucked into her chest, sealing off any further discussion.

Ikan gathered her meaning, for he nodded. "Yes, and your assistance was valuable in the north. We are grateful for Jadora's aid in that time, and it only seems fair that we repay the favor now. We would be honored to join you in the palace and begin plans for how the Desheni may offer assistance at once."

"Excellent. Please, follow me." Elsanna turned to glide up the street, her stride just as graceful and dangerous as it had been when she led the guardswomen.

Lark fell in step behind her, and when the rest of the new visitors followed, the whole city gathered to watch again.

Many Jadorans, if not most, had never seen a Desheni before Andriun's arrival. Now there was a whole group for them to observe and they chattered excitedly as they filtered past with gathered water held overhead.

Lark, too, stole a few glances back at the Desheni behind her. She had met a number of people from Andriun's home village before, and a few of the tailless Desheni bore familiar faces. Most of those present were those from the sea, though, and she could not help her fascination. Their garb appeared to be made of sharkskin and textiles crafted from seaweed, accented with knotted rope, seashells, and colorful beads. The tails were less noteworthy than she might have guessed, but all of them who bore tails were stocky in build and fuller of figure. That must have been the blubber he was always fussing about lacking. All of them had long, dark hair that was tamed by braids like Andriun wore, but they looked altogether softer. Warmer, gentler, as if their lives lacked the struggles Andriun's people had known.

To her amusement, she was not the only one who looked, though they looked for different reasons. Andriun locked eyes with one of the water mages—a girl—and when she smiled, he spun to face straight ahead and shielded his face with one webbed hand, lest the rich purple shade he flushed be too obvious.

Lark refrained from telling him it was too late and everyone noticed.

Tula, always lacking such tact, covered her mouth to stifle a snorting laugh and struck him with her elbow.

Between all of them, Daisy bounded and pranced.

Despite the fascination of the city's inhabitants, the roads remained clear, and they reached the palace before conversation began again. Ikan broke away from the rest of the group to walk beside his nephew. "We are all glad to see you here. And in one piece." He studied Andriun from head to toe and appeared satisfied with what he saw. For all that he had proven a fearsome warrior, skilled with both a sword and a spear, Ikan carried no weapons now. It made him look milder than Lark recalled.

"And I am glad to see you have reunited with so many of our people. Seven..." Andriun paused to count those who followed them again. "No, eight community leaders? And so many mages. All from waters close by?"

"None farther than Addare. Our people are thriving. Both those familiar with the sea and those who are new to its ways." Ikan grinned.

Were his teeth sharper than before? Lark shook it off and stepped aside. It didn't matter, and she felt odd standing beside them to overhear their conversation, but Elsanna had just opened the door to beckon everyone inside.

"I am pleased to hear it," Andriun said.

They remained in the courtyard as the other Desheni leaders moved past them to join Elsanna. Tula and Resia hesitated, too.

A moment passed before Ikan spoke again. "It has not been that long since we parted ways. A few months, but it feels longer. The other elders have asked many questions about you, and I suspect they would appreciate the opportunity to meet you for themselves. If your intention is to stay in Jadora, then having someone to take charge of our group..." He trailed off, his unfinished sentence laden with words too difficult to say.

Lark touched her chest, as if to catch her heart. It was not forgiveness, but it was an offer of acceptance, something Andriun had hungered for since before they'd met. She drew a breath to urge him to take it, but he raised a hand before she could.

"You do not know how I wish I could. The chance to meet so many of our kind and familiarize myself with their ways is something I have longed for, but..." Andriun's webbed fingers curled into his palm and he lowered his hand to his side. "I will return to help when I can, but I am bound by honor to help a friend who is in most dire need."

Ikan's disappointment was obvious in the way his stature shrank. His shoulders sagged and his chin drooped, but he nodded and drew himself up again a moment later. "I should expect nothing less. You have always acted with honor, Andriun. When do you depart?"

Andriun looked to Lark for confirmation, but she had none to offer.

"Tomorrow," Moros announced from the open doors.

Startled, Lark turned with the question of whether he was serious on her lips, but it was foolish. She'd never seen the former jailer be anything *but* serious.

Admiral Warinal stepped forward to join him, an unpleasant hitch to one side of his mouth. "Your ship will be in the harbor come morning, ready and waiting for your departure. I suppose you won't be talked out of boarding it."

"Not at all," Lark said sweetly.

The admiral nodded as if he had assumed as much.

She picked up her skirts and joined them in the palace, working hard to hide her elation as the Paragons trailed in behind her.

At long last, the rescue was about to begin.

CHAPTER TWENTY-TWO

Steel on steel rasped, sending a shiver down Zaide's spine. He rolled his shoulders to alleviate the sensation and adjusted his grip on his sword and shield.

Gadranus circled him, his stride both slow and relaxed. "You are more advanced than I'd realized. I can see you've been training hard."

"Since I was young. More intently, the past few years." Zaide's boots crunched on the gritty earth underfoot. The sound was more pronounced now, accentuated by the tide of borrowed power that lapped against his being.

Rather than sparring in the arena, their training session was hosted by the dusty yard just outside the castle's barracks. Zaide had walked through that part of Amrochan a hundred times in the final days before the city's fall, visiting his foster father in the armory or practicing with the palace guards.

Gadranus darted in, but the swing of his sword was light and experimental and Zaide parried easily. That was all they'd done so far, an easy give and take where they both worked to feel out their opponent's skills.

That Zaide could not read Gadranus well had swiftly become a source of frustration. Everything the man did was smooth and casual. There was no tension in his body to read, no warning signs of how he meant to strike. It kept Zaide on his toes, yet he still found himself surprised by each swing or stab.

"Good," Gadranus said when he lunged and was blocked again. "Now, let's reverse roles. I will defend, and then we'll work on repairing the flaws in your methods."

It was hard not to bristle at the suggestion his techniques were wrong, but that was the point of training. Zaide waited as his opponent drew his sword up to defend. Others would have shifted, drawn themselves back or given off an air of caution. Instead, Gadranus remained as calm and casual as if they were still in a parlor for tea.

There were no openings. No visible gaps in his defense. No hint he even was defending. Zaide tested with a series of cuts instead. He fully expected one of them to be countered, but no reaction came. Just the constant close scrutiny of a well-trained eye. Gadranus deflected every attempt, and through it, Zaide tried to bridle his frustration and hold it close.

They stood facing each other with swords in hand. No distractions. No combat raging around them. No one nearby for Zaide to try and protect.

Now was the time to kill the man, to end their suffering and shake off his yoke. The perfect opportunity to strike him down and free Amroch for a few more years.

Yet Zaide could not touch him. He could not even come close. Every blow was deflected or defended without flaw, and Gadranus did not even wear armor.

Frustration swelled and bubbled over, putting a tightness in Zaide's chest and a pressure in his head. The sensation was new, different, and unpleasant. He retreated a few steps and tried to catch his breath as he raised a palm to his forehead. Another chill rolled along his backbone and drew a shudder from his flesh.

Not a chill, he realized belatedly. It was power—greedy, hungry magic that flicked along his bones and shivered in his muscles, craving a chance to be let free. It hummed along his skin and a cold gray encroached on his vision.

A strong hand landed on his shoulder. The contact tingled like the fizz of fine bubbles, leaving an itch in its wake.

"Deep breaths," Gadranus said. "Press your feet firmly to the ground. Don't lock your knees. Let the magic flow as it pleases or it will make you sick."

Zaide was sick already. His stomach lurched and the underside of his tongue felt odd, as if it was too wet. Too present. Everything inside heaved and he leaned forward to brace his hands against his knees. He didn't know whether he should drop his sword and shield or if he'd be better off dropping to all fours and letting his stomach purge.

Now was the time to destroy his enemy, to save everyone he cared about, and he could not even keep his breakfast down.

"Breathe," Gadranus told him.

Breathing didn't help.

Zaide sank to his knees and marveled at the pathetic irony of his worst enemy being the one to pat his back and soothe him as he revisited the morning meal.

When the sensation subsided, he spat and found that breathing helped a little more. He dared not move too soon, lest it set him off again. "This doesn't happen to anyone else," he grumbled.

"Your power is different," Gadranus said. "When others greet life with magic already within their grasp, you cannot expect your first taste of it will be like theirs. They're exposed to it from the moment they are formed, grow knowing it while still unborn in the womb. For you, this is your very first meal. It is far too rich, and you have consumed more than you were prepared for."

Zaide spat again, then wiped his mouth. "You act like you know what it's like. You were born with magic, too."

"This time, yes. But not the first time. My power was a gift, much like what I've given you now. Something given to me ages ago. I retched then, too." Gadranus gave his shoulder a slap, then stood and retreated. "Do you wish to continue, or shall we halt?"

Zaide wanted to kill him. He wanted to carve the heart from his chest, to watch his last breath, to see his life drain into the soil beneath him. The intensity of the feeling surprised him and put a queasy feeling back in the pit of his stomach.

He gritted his teeth and stood. "Keep going."

Gadranus nodded in approval. "A strong spirit is a sign of a strong warrior. Very well, then. We will continue."

He didn't have to sound so jovial.

Zaide rocked his head from side to side to stretch his neck, then readied his weapon again.

His enemy resumed his place directly across from him. There was no ring marked on the dusty ground, but for the sort of training they were doing, boundaries did not matter. Gadranus twirled his sword in one hand. Whether the point was to limber his wrists or simply show off, it was hard to say. "Your form is excellent and your instincts are good. Your shortcomings are minor and should be simple to resolve."

"All right, then tell me how to resolve them." Zaide righted his shield on his arm. He didn't like it or the training sword he'd been given. Both felt wrong after what he'd grown used to, and they were lower quality equipment, besides.

"You rely on your speed and agility in a battle. There is nothing wrong with either, but it's a good indication that you lack strength, and I have not been proven incorrect in that assessment. Capable, still formidable, but lacking power." Gadranus swung his blade downward in a slow, controlled motion that indicated force. "Without physical strength to support your other attributes, you'll be forced to fight longer and harder, and both of those will cause deterioration of your primary skills."

So be stronger. That was simple enough, though Zaide didn't know how it would help against the enemies he was always stuck fighting. No matter what he did, he would never match the brawn of a goborrin. "More power. All right."

Gadranus twirled his sword again. "There are a number of officers in my army who can assist you in establishing the sort of exercise schedule needed to both improve and maintain more robust upper body strength and physical resilience."

Not ways Zaide wanted to spend his time, but if it put him closer to ending all this, fine. "What else?"

"The most important aspects of any battle. Nothing matters more than timing and reach." The sword in his enemy's hand stretched toward his face.

Zaide took a step back.

The blade lowered. "The latter is possibly an issue that comes from wielding an unfamiliar sword, but it's something that must be rectified. You cannot guarantee the weapon you use will be your own."

At the moment, Zaide wasn't sure he had a weapon he could claim. He did not know what had become of his Jadoran long knife, and Lark had the Spectrum Blade. For all that he'd been disappointed with the sword's size when he found it, it had felt natural after a few days of adjustment. He'd never realized how much the iridescent sword had come to feel like an extension of his own arm.

Gadranus went on. "It's not only your own reach that you misjudge, but that of your opponent. Your depth perception is not something that can be altered, but there are things that can be done to assist your ability to accurately assess the range of both your weapon and your foe's."

"Like what?"

"To begin, fighting with your right hand. Using your non-dominant hand will force you to evaluate everything more closely. It may help improve your instincts." Gadranus paused, then smirked. "Failing that, we shall have you fight with a yardstick instead of a blade."

Zaide did not laugh. He offered no reaction at all, and the man's smile faded. When he spoke again, he was sober.

"Your new magic may be used to augment your senses, but it is not something you should rely on. Power can be fickle. It's better to trust your own innate capabilities. As we practice, that power will manifest on its own and you should allow it to do so. But do not seek it or acknowledge it. Until you are more versed in its handling, doing so will result in more illness." Slowly, Gadranus shifted until he held his sword at the ready.

"So when does learning magic handling fit in with everything else?" Zaide tried to mimic the man's casual stance, but it felt too unnatural. He slid one foot backwards and sank into his heel instead.

"All in time. Use your other hand."

Zaide glanced at his equipment. The shield was fitted for use with his right arm. He shucked it off and turned it upside down to fit on his left.

"That's the sort of open-minded thinking that will aid you in combat. Being able to make quick decisions under pressure is a useful skill." Gadranus tapped his temple. "But it is important to acknowledge that making choices depletes our energy, too. Always enter combat with a number of plans ready."

"Right," Zaide grumbled as he moved his sword to his right hand. He'd used swords that way before, but not often, and he disliked how it felt.

The dance resumed. He defended attacks that came first in a steady cadence, then increased in speed and dropped in regularity, but it became clear early on that the point was not defense as much as learning how to gauge the length of both swords.

Slowly, Zaide adapted. His arm tired faster than he liked, revealing the problem that had been pointed out first. He needed to be stronger. To last longer. He never saw any change in the way Gadranus moved, promising his enemy's battle stamina would far outlast his own. Shy of a lucky break, he would never penetrate the man's defense.

"Will the others train like this?" Zaide asked in one of the lulls he was given to catch his breath.

"Others?" Gadranus asked.

"The Amrochan soldiers in the dungeon. You want them alive, or else they wouldn't be." Sweat stung Zaide's eyes and he rubbed one with the back of his wrist before he swiped his brow.

"Those who prove themselves competent will be given the opportunity to join and train with the rest of my armies. I don't train common soldiers." The inflection on the last two words landed oddly.

From anyone else, praise for his skills would have been cherished.

From Gadranus, it stirred a sudden rage inside Zaide's chest.

"Breathe," the man cautioned.

Zaide had not realized the magic in him surged until it made him queasy again. He sucked in air until his lungs ached, then readied himself to continue battle. Don't acknowledge it, he'd said. It was hard to ignore the sickness and the strange, cold waves of power that radiated down his limbs, but he tried to do as he'd been told and focus on his breath. With time, the illness began to subside.

The practice of defense resumed, back to a slow starting pace, and Zaide trained his mind on the men locked below the palace. As long as he could stay focused on something else, maybe the magic wouldn't enter his thoughts. "What sort of testing do they have to clear? Something like mine?"

"Nothing like that," Gadranus said. "A few simple assessments, then they will be offered the choice between joining us or continuing to fight until they change their minds."

The speed increased gradually, never faster than Zaide could handle, but continually pushing the limit. "So the goal is to break them?"

A single laugh escaped Gadranus's throat. "Such a harsh

term. I prefer to think of it as convincing. Although those who refuse will eventually die in combat, so I suppose in reality they have little choice."

Zaide considered that as he continued to defend. It was harsh, but he expected nothing else from someone who did not so much as bat an eye at the thought of killing countless people to reach his goal. But the subject had already been brought up, and now was an opportunity to propose the second step in his plan. The possibility it was too soon to be asking favors flitted through his thoughts.

"Switch," Gadranus said while he tried to make up his mind. "Try and strike me."

Using a sword right-handed felt wrong, but Zaide swung anyway. It was that way with everything, now; he had to do it, whether he was ready or not. His jab fell short by an inch and he adjusted his footing to slide closer before he spoke again. "I want to take part in the testing."

"For what?"

Zaide's sword made contact with his opponent's blade. Still shorter than what he was aiming for, but if it was close enough to demand deflection, it was an improvement. "Testing what's left of Sendassian's soldiers. It'll help me learn. I'm a better swordsman than most of them, but not with my right hand. I know how they fight and if we're in that arena, they won't hold back."

Gadranus appeared intrigued by the request. "You don't fear they'll name you a traitor?"

"Half of them never liked or trusted me anyway, what do I care what they think?" Zaide still stewed in that resentment, he realized; he'd thought himself past it, but the way some of the captive soldiers had looked at him after a mere change of clothes stirred up all sorts of bitter feelings he had yet to conquer. "They decided I was an enemy as soon as they saw I had white hair."

"Ironic, when you look at me." Gadranus gestured to himself

with a flourish. His long, dark hair was unbound and still in order, in spite of their training.

Zaide darted in, hoping the momentary distraction would give him a chance to make contact. It didn't, and he twirled back. "You're not what anyone expected."

"Good. Never be what is expected."

Two more strikes had to be deflected, but they would not have been severe injuries even if they had landed. Zaide's right arm ached from the effort of fighting when he was unused to using it, but he persisted. "I'm glad we're nothing alike. Even if it means everyone who thinks you're an ordinary broken-born like me is wrong."

"I suspect you have a reason." That Gadranus sounded amused was enough to get under his skin. He was a monster, a cold and violent man who had done nothing but rip the world apart. Who would have wanted to be like him?

Zaide had no intention of replying, but his anger stirred the magic in him again and his breath hitched. He retreated two steps and worked to steady it again. The magic still burned, cold and blistering hot at the same time. Against his better judgment, he decided to speak. Maybe keeping all that frustrated him bottled up inside was a hazard—at least, right now. "My friends thought you might be my father."

"That would have been an honor," Gadranus said simply. Again, he blocked, and Zaide began to wonder how he'd managed to slice his cheek and ear in that skirmish in the parlor.

"For you, maybe." Zaide's next swing was slow and went wide.

"Yes, that is what I meant. There, break." Gadranus raised a hand, signaling for him to stop. "You don't want to push too far past your limits in each session, or you'll do yourself harm. Sore muscles are good. Strained ones are useless."

Reluctantly, Zaide halted. He paced backwards, putting more space between them.

Gadranus studied him for a time before he spoke again.

"Perhaps you will be comforted by knowing I have no children. I've had them in the past, but not this time. It may be unsurprising to know most women are less than enthused to know a potential suitor is a man endlessly reborn in pursuit of power."

"Your kind of power, anyway." Zaide suspected most women would be perfectly fine with a husband who pursued the sort that brought high standing or respect.

"Yes, mine." Gadranus chuckled and smoothed back his hair, though it did not need it. "But I will grant your request. You may train against Amrochan's soldiers. I will make sure my officers know."

Zaide nodded. He would not thank the man, nor would he allow himself to feel a shred of relief or excitement. This was the least Gadranus could do, and if it helped with Zaide's goals along the way, so be it. He held that close, the first scrap of hope he'd managed to recover since that moment in the throne room where everything had gone wrong.

This was the secret. This was what they needed to turn the tide. All he had to do was survive long enough to see it happen. He would learn his enemy's tactics and skills with a blade so he could use that knowledge against him. Then, he would find a way to handle the ugly magic that now thrummed against his bones. For if he succeeded in controlling some shred of the forces of shadow Gadranus held, perhaps he could learn what Lark was missing, and a renewed blade would spell the man's eternal end.

CHAPTER TWENTY-THREE

THE SHIP that greeted Lark in the harbor sent her heart and hopes crashing to her knees. She laced her fingers together in front of her stomach and stared as she tried to determine what to say. Screaming was the first thing that came to mind, but people responded better to honeyed words.

Right now, she couldn't even think of razor-edged ones.

The whole time she'd envisioned the rescue, she had imagined something small and fast, just large enough for her and the Paragons and a tiny crew to sail it. She had resigned herself to the reality that Admiral Warinal would serve as the ship's captain, but his own ship—now abandoned somewhere on Lake Sian—had been one of the most agile on the water.

The hulking thing that waited for her now was anything but agile.

"Admiral," she began in as cordial a voice as she could manage, "is there a reason we are taking the goborrin warship, rather than something that will actually fit down the river?"

Hundreds of soldiers were in the process of organizing themselves on the decks. Far from the small strike force Lark had desired for the expedition, yet not enough to make a difference against Gadranus and his armies, either.

"Do you mean to doubt my ability to steer such a vessel, Your Majesty?" Warinal answered with an antagonizing smirk on his craggy face.

"It's not your steering I am concerned with. More the fact that I requested speed, and you have provided a tortoise." Lark was not sure how long she could be diplomatic. Maybe diplomacy was no longer needed with her father's officers; they were supposed to be hers, now. She had no desire to be a tyrant, but if they meant to find a way to disrespect orders she gave, gentleness would have to go.

"I am afraid the matter is complicated, but rest assured, there are good reasons for the choice. Allow me to escort you to the helm, and I will elaborate there." The admiral offered his arm.

Lark ignored it and started down the dock on her own. Dozens of tiny rowboats skimmed back and forth between the warship and the harbor, carrying soldiers and supplies to support them. More unnecessary weight to slow them down.

By the time she reached the ship, the Paragons had already boarded.

The admiral did not begin his explanation until they stood at the helm and his hands rested on the wheel. "It seems our arrival caused an unnecessary amount of strain for those in Ganede, who were not privy to the fact the goborrin ship in the harbor belonged to the queen of Amroch, rather than still containing enemy soldiers. It has been sorted out now, of course, but Ganede's governor has asked us to remove the ship."

"And that requires us to use it for our journey? I should not have to remind you again that our need is dire and the mission would be greatly aided by speed." Lark managed to hold the irritation from her voice, though she did not know how.

"It is not required, no, but the Desheni leaders brought valuable information with them. I realize your primary concern was diplomacy and accepting their oaths, but we likely would have benefited from your involvement in assessing the state of things at sea." How he managed to sound antagonistic while his words remained polite would forever be a mystery. Lark considered asking, but he went on. "The ocean is teeming with ships flying the standard of Gadranus. You will notice I have had the flag turned right side up."

She had not noticed that at all, but she made a point of not looking. "So you mean to use the ship's appearance to disguise our passage?"

"For now." The corners of his mouth twitched, but he remained stoic. "Once we reach the harbor in Chithal, we will be forced to switch to a smaller vessel. Which is why I bring hundreds of soldiers with us now, rather than thousands. While I whole-heartedly believe myself and my men competent enough to steer a ship of this size against the current and get us to Amrochan safely, our enemy does not appear to have such adept sailors. We would be noticed, and the river's breadth is not great enough to allow us to engage in naval warfare."

Cannons, he meant. Lark knew little about that sort of weaponry; her limited knowledge of the military she had inherited was focused on the foot soldiers who still bore swords. Members of her father's cabinet had mentioned the potential for small cannons that soldiers could wheel about on wagons, but as far as she knew, none had yet been built. The explosive powder was too new. Not, she reminded herself, that the newness had prevented goborrins from using it against them in the siege of Jadora. If this ship was equipped with such cannons, she would not be surprised, but she saw no benefit to having them if the point of sailing it was stealth. "That's all very well, Admiral, but my problem with this arrangement is that sailing around the northwestern edge of the continent in a vessel like this could take weeks. I still believe we would be better served by taking something much smaller. We need to reach Amrochan within days, not some time next month."

"I understand your concern, Your Majesty, but I urge you to trust me to help you reach your destination. Few people know where you're going. You will have the element of surprise, whether you have it now or twenty days from now." The antagonism returned in the way he smirked at her. "Besides, if you believe there's any chance that boy has survived this long, you may as well believe he'll still be there when we reach our destination."

Lark fought the urge to strangle the man and felt herself slipping. She stepped away before she said or did something she might regret. It was easy to see the decision to use the goborrin ship would not be unmade. "I will be in my quarters. Notify me the moment we are to set sail."

"Of course, Your Majesty."

Rather than seeking the cabin she had used during their voyage from Tinith, Lark removed herself from the helm and set to finding the Paragons. They were scattered across the ship, but easy to pick out. None of them fit in with the soldiers and sailors that adjusted rigging and moved supplies. Tula was the easiest to spy, sitting cross-legged atop a large crate and scribbling furiously in her notebook.

The Magister looked up as Lark approached, a grim set to her mouth. "I have some bad news."

"Doesn't everyone?" Lark grumbled.

Tula paused, gripping her notebook with both hands.

Lark had not realized her complaints might silence any of her companions. Average soldiers, yes, but not her most trusted friends. "Go ahead. I'm sure I need to hear it."

"All right. Well..." The notebook tumbled from Tula's grasp as she tried to turn the page. It wasn't like her to be flustered, but her fingers scrabbled at the edges of the paper to hold everything shut when she picked it up again. "I'm sort of estimating the distances based on what I remember, so forgive me if this is wrong, but I asked the sailors how fast a ship like this can go with a crew this size and have been doing math. Assuming less than perfect sailing conditions, since that's what's most realistic, it sounds like it may take us eighteen days to reach Chithal." She winced as she delivered the information, her elbows drawn in and her shoulders raised.

"Unfortunately, I already assumed as much." Lark remembered all too well how long their trip from Amrochan to Jadora had been, and that had been on a more nimble ship.

Tula did not appear comforted by her resignation. She turned between two pages of her book and tapped a fingertip against the mess of numbers. "Even if we get on something smaller and faster once we reach the port in Chithal, it will probably take another week to get up the river. We'll probably be able to shave off some travel time if Andriun can help, but even under perfect sailing conditions, we won't reach Amrochan for around twenty days."

Which was still faster than trying to get back there on foot, Lark reminded herself. She bit her lower lip and turned back toward the city. "I should have asked Vorkaris to carry us. He got us there so swiftly, last time."

"I already did that." Now Tula's knees drew up, too, as if she wanted to crumple in on herself. "We'd have the same number of passengers, and he could drop us right on top of the castle. He said trying that would get all of us killed. Including him."

He was probably right. The goborrins hadn't been expecting an aerial attack when they'd flown in before. Nor had they carried any weapons then that might harm a dragon. Now that Gadranus had taken the city, he had the city's defenses and equipment at his disposal. Catapults and ballistas were more than enough to strike a dragon dead, and she dared not risk Vorkaris. They could land farther away and attempt to steal into the city on foot, but it had been a miracle they'd escaped. Getting back in would be even harder.

Defeated, Lark sighed. "It sounds as if going by ship is still the best solution, regardless of the time it takes."

"I can ask Vorkaris again, if you'd like," the Magister suggested. "If I nag long enough, he might give up. He could drop us down in the marshes, or on the other side of Lake Sian."

"I was just thinking of that, but I don't feel it's wise. It's been some time since we left and Gadranus is guaranteed to have bolstered his defenses. For all we know, he has retaken Tinith and we just haven't heard yet. It would take time for word to arrive." Lark hated how realistic that possibility was. With a solid base in Amrochan, there were few places Gadranus could no longer reach. "If we go by ship, we can still retreat easily if things go wrong. Not to mention it gives us the opportunity to enter from the harbor, bypassing a great number of the city's defenses."

Tula produced a piece of graphite from somewhere inside her voluminous sleeves. "Doesn't that have problems, too, though? I mean, if we go across the water to escape after we get Zaide, what are the odds we can make it back up the river without being caught?"

That was something Lark had not considered. She'd been so focused on the idea of getting *into* Amrochan to retrieve him that she had not put any thought into where they would go afterward. She pursed her lips and scanned the ship's deck. "Let's find Resia."

"She had already gone into the cabin, last I saw her." Tula unfolded herself and hopped off the crate. "The sailors said Daisy was getting in the way, so she took her in there to keep her busy."

Lark's nose crinkled. "Why did you bring the dog at all? Wouldn't it have been better to leave her behind?" Jadora was far safer, and it wasn't as if there weren't people in the city who could look after a pet.

"Resia thinks she might be able to help us find Zaide when we get to Amrochan. You know, sense of smell, or something like that. Andriun thinks she might be too dumb, but he was willing to give it a try."

From what Lark had seen, the creature was useless for any practical tasks, but she bit her tongue. If nothing else, Zaide would probably be happy to see the dog was still with them.

The cabin Lark had shared with the Paragons was unpleasantly familiar, though it brought a shade of comfort too. She already knew she could sleep in that bed, though twenty nights was far longer than she wanted to be in it. Traveling by ship was the reasonable answer, but she was tired of trying to be reasonable. She wanted to be impulsive and furious, to storm her home and fight to victory and find the closest friend she'd ever had.

Then her own thoughts hit her so hard, she thought she might break.

Her friend.

Lark had never had friends. All her life, she had held people at arm's length, ensuring no one got too close. She had always feared the price might be too high, and in that moment, as she realized how easily he and the others had slipped past her guard and embedded themselves in her life, she knew that she'd been right.

Resia was not alone in the cabin; aside from the dog, Andriun had settled there, too. He sat at the table, stringing colored beads and bits of coral onto a necklace, though he paused his work when she arrived.

Rather than addressing either one of them, Lark strode straight across the cabin and flopped face down onto her bed. Even those downy pillows would not have been enough to stifle the scream of frustration that swelled at the top of her lungs, so she swallowed hard against it and wished they'd smother her, instead.

That would be easier, wouldn't it? To just give up, fade away, and let someone else do what she could not? It had been so easy to be angry with those who had come before her, the parents and elders who had been meant to resolve everything and failed. Now she understood their shortcomings in a way that left her wounded.

She was no better. No more competent, despite everything she had sacrificed to try and make a difference. In the end, she'd only robbed herself of the few joys a life like hers had to offer.

The bed shifted, betraying the presence of someone else, but a few beats passed before Tula spoke. "Are you all right?"

Lark was not, nor was she certain she ever had been. She wanted to despair, but she couldn't; her chest ached without any tears forming in her eyes, sorrow chased away by an anger she'd kept to herself far too long.

"No," she all but shouted against the pillow, even as she wadded it up and mashed her face into it hard enough that she could not breathe. Her arms tensed and she held it there a moment longer, then went up for air. "No, I'm not all right. Everything has gone wrong. Even this is going wrong. I can't even properly mount a rescue to help the one person who would give anything to aid me!"

Something rattled at the table, then footsteps. When Andriun spoke, he was right beside the bed. "That is not true. It is not as fast as you might have hoped, but you are going. This has been your intention from the very beginning."

"It's not your fault it took longer than you wanted," Resia added from nearby. "You've done everything you can to set things up so you'd be free to take this voyage. Zaide knows you're the queen. He knows you couldn't just leave."

"And he probably doesn't know I'm even coming." The words felt so heavy in her mouth that Lark wondered how she didn't choke on them. "He probably thinks I failed. That I couldn't do it, just like I couldn't do anything else. We've been together all this time, and never once has he seen me capable of doing anything. I couldn't stop Kolmar from being razed, I couldn't save Jadora from its siege, I couldn't win over the Shaman or save my father or even pour my magic into that blasted sword."

Tula's hand landed on her shoulder and rubbed aggressively, as if soothing someone worked better while their clothing gave them a friction burn. "That's not your fault either. That wasn't your job, and it wasn't fair for anyone to expect you to do it, not when we didn't even have everything we needed. That's the whole reason we went all the way to Toren, remember? To see if Gadranus would give us the other half of the power we needed? The Paragon of Light was supposed to restore the Spectrum Blade, not you."

The words twisted in Lark's chest like a knife. After everything, they still didn't understand—and that was her fault, too. "No," she said, and when she sat up to face them, her eyes brimmed with tears of hurt, frustration, and a disappointment in herself she could never forgive. "It is my fault. It's all my fault, it's all me. Don't you understand? It's me. I am the Paragon of Light!"

CHAPTER TWENTY-FOUR

IN THE SILENCE THAT FOLLOWED, the click-clack of Daisy's claws on the floor was loud. The dog squeezed past the Paragons and clambered onto Lark's bed to whine and nuzzle at her arms.

In spite of the weight of her declaration and the tears it brought, she wrapped her arms around Daisy's neck and buried her face in the thick and wiry white fur of her ruff.

Maybe it was better that she didn't look. That way, she wouldn't have to see the disappointment on their faces when they finally understood.

At last, Andriun spoke, though his voice cracked. "What?"

Lark could say nothing. Her throat had grown too tight. Instead, she nodded and squeezed her eyes shut as Daisy's chin came to a rest on her shoulder.

Beside them, Tula sat frozen, her hand poised as if to offer comfort again—or as if she was uncertain it was deserved. "I don't understand. I thought you said your magic never developed?"

"It didn't," Lark said, and immediately regretted having spoken with the dog right there. She grimaced and twisted her neck to try and scrape her lips against the shoulder to rid them of hair. Several coarse white strands clung to the fabric. "It's like it's there, but I can't do anything with it. It's always just beyond what I can touch. I can sense things, read intentions, feel magic in other people and get a sense of what they can do, but mine is just—it's not there."

"But it must be, or else you wouldn't be able to do those things." Resia inched closer, wringing her hands together in front of her chest. "If magic truly never came to fruition in you, then you'd be like—" Her voice caught and she faltered. "Like Zaide."

Andriun's brow furrowed. "How long have you known?"

Lark freed a hand to pick more dog hair from her mouth before she spoke again. Maybe she should have left it. Perhaps if she did, no one would expect her to speak. But the last of the hair came away between her fingers, leaving her with no excuse. She could not bring herself to look at any of them, so she stared at the curve of Daisy's bushy tail instead. "Always. Since I was a child."

"And you never said anything?" Tula's dismay grew and she rose onto her knees. "Even when we were in Nimultis? You let us believe the Oracle was the Paragon!"

"The Oracle implied that she was," Andriun added, though a thoughtful note tinted the words. "But I cannot recall if she ever said it outright."

Resia looked between the Shaman and the Magister with a doubtful frown. "I can't imagine the Oracle would have lied to you. If she let you think the power was hers, there had to be a reason."

"Protecting me." Lark sniffed hard. "Because she knew I couldn't do it. She saw I would fail. She saw it before I was even born. It was why my mother left the Sunshard there in the first place. They all knew I would fail."

Andriun shook his head hard. "That cannot be. There has never been a Paragon who could not stand to meet the Rise."

Yet here she was. Lark took no comfort in his disbelief, just bowed her head and resisted the want to sniffle like some pitiful child. Hadn't she cried enough already? The last thing she wanted was to be weak.

"Dasienna," Resia said slowly, as if testing the name before she went on. "Your mother passed when you were a child?"

Lark did not understand the point of that question. Everyone in Amroch knew her mother had died, but she nodded anyway.

"Before you became aware of your power? Or after?" the Kolmari girl asked.

"Wasn't she always aware of it?" Tula glanced from Resia to Andriun.

"All mages are born with a seed of power, but sometimes those powers don't begin to grow until a few years into childhood," Resia said. "I was aware of mine for as long as I could remember, but the Elder told me my parents did not know it would manifest as a full gift instead of latent ability until I was three or four years old. All the Kolmari I have ever known were born with that seed, the core possibility of magic, but most never progress beyond an inclination that exceeds natural skill."

Andriun sank to sit on the edge of the bed. "I was nine when my power over water began to manifest."

"Nine?" Tula almost squeaked. "That's so old!"

"I am Desheni," he replied defensively.

The Magister sobered. "My mother said I was born with fire magic already in my veins. I had influence over it when I was a librarian, becoming Magister just amplified it. But fire mages aren't uncommon in Jadora. None as strong as I am now, but you know what I mean. I had a teacher when I was small, someone who showed me how to make sure it never got away from me."

"And we had believed my mother was the last mage in my home village." Andriun smoothed his dark hair with one webbed hand. "She trained me when that power began to swell."

"And the Elder trained me." Resia turned toward Lark and lowered her chin, her face halfway between beseeching and concerned. "So how old were you when your magic woke, and how old were you when your mother passed?"

The point struck like an arrow. Lark's arms relaxed until they slid from the dog, and she wiped her eyes with the back of her wrist. "I could always sense it around me. It was so strong in my mother. She was Paragon before me." It felt wrong to claim the title, given her lack of skill. "But it began to grow stronger after she became ill. I was always afraid her decline in health was her magic leaving her and coming to me. But when she died, the rest of it never came. It was as if it got lost along the way."

"So you have never had instruction," Andriun concluded.

Lark didn't believe that was true, but she did not know how to state her protest. She'd had them, after all; she'd observed them all so closely, asked them questions and received explanations that should have guided her in shaping her abilities into something more. There had been the Oracle, too. Oroduna had been so patient, guiding her through all sorts of meditation and magic-related exercises. None of it had borne fruit.

"We can't expect you to be able to wield magic with any sort of proficiency without having an instructor." Resia, too, crept forward to sit on the bed. The space had grown crowded, yet Lark welcomed their presence.

Tula nodded so aggressively, her red ponytail whipped behind her. "She's right. Maybe we can teach you now. We're not light mages, but Andriun has babbled before about elemental spectrums and stuff. Fire should be closest to light. If there's anything I can do to help, you know I'll do it. You didn't have to be afraid to tell us."

"It was easier if I didn't," Lark admitted. As long as it had been a secret, she'd never had to answer to anyone else for her failures.

Then again, maybe that had been a false comfort. She was answering for them now, and most painfully, she answered to herself. Had she been able to replenish the Spectrum Blade, Zaide would have been able to strike down Gadranus long ago.

She had no doubt of his strength or capability. Had the sword not been depleted of its light, it would have been able to stand against their enemy's shadow, illuminate the dark and let them scour him from the earth.

Instead, he had been vulnerable to that dark force, and she had been powerless to aid him.

"Well, you've told us now, so we can move forward." Resia smiled and clasped her hands in her lap. "We'll do everything we can."

"Thank you. All of you." The burden had not been lifted, but the weight on Lark's shoulders had lightened. One less secret. One less worry in the back of her mind.

"We cannot promise results, as none of us can speak directly to the same magic you possess, but she is right. And maybe we will solve it. Or solve everything." Andriun sat straighter, his posture simultaneously eager and guarded. "Between your magic and the Shadowsliver, we are supposed to have all that we need. If we are able to determine a solution between here and Amrochan, maybe this will be it."

"The end of Gadranus," Tula whispered.

Lark dared not hope for anything so great, but she admitted it sounded good. Daisy wriggled beside her, and she scratched between the dog's ears to settle her.

The Shaman offered a single, solemn nod. "And if that does not work, perhaps we will find answers there."

"In Amrochan?" Resia asked.

"Zaide went to him once before to try and replenish the Spectrum Blade. That was how we got the shadow crystal thing to begin with." Tula craned her neck to look for the artifact, but it was still tucked away and safe inside Lark's bag. "Or, well, I guess we had it, we just didn't know what it was for."

Doubt curled the Kolmari Elder's lips downward. "Is that what it's for?"

"Isn't it?" Lark had warred with herself on that before, but the information Zaide had brought back from that meeting had indicated Gadranus wanted the Spectrum Blade replenished just as desperately as they did. But it was not so simple as walking in and asking him to help. He wanted her crown, too, and she had no doubt he would be willing to strike her down and simply wait for the next Paragon of Light to rise to power in order to restore the blade.

"I don't know. I know we've all looked at it, I just wonder, that's all." Resia shrugged and reached to scratch Daisy's hindquarters. The dog's foot kicked absently in response.

Tula wriggled forward, both hands raised with palms out. "Wait. You think it doesn't do what he said it does? Or that it can't?"

"Or that something is missing." Andriun rubbed his chin. "We have assumed it is instructions, but what if we are supposed to use the artifacts a certain way and have failed to do so?"

"That's why I've felt it's my fault," Lark said. The admission no longer brought the sting of tears, though she felt a stirring of guilt in her chest. "The only thing I'm certain of is that light and shadow have to be replenished in unison, because light cannot exist without casting a shadow. The Oracle explained it, but if I cannot reach my power, how can I cast a shadow at all?"

Resia fidgeted, picking at her nails and twisting her fingers in her lap. "Doesn't that just raise more questions, though?"

Lark waited for her to elaborate. They'd spoken briefly in Amrochan of things the Oracle had revealed, but Resia had not been there. All her knowledge was secondhand, and if some of it had not translated well, no one could be surprised.

Tula was less patient. "What questions? It seems to make sense to me."

"The part about the two powers having to go in together makes sense, but look where we're going and what we're doing." The Kolmari Elder waved a hand, indicating the cabin where they hid. "If shadow can't be managed independently of light, why does Gadranus have power at all if Lark doesn't?"

"But the Oracle said he was the other Paragon." Tula rubbed her neck, rather than scratching her head, but the gesture was just as helpless.

"Did she, though?" Andriun drummed his fingers against his knees. "Because we also believed she had told us she was the Paragon of Light, when that was clearly not as truthful as we believed."

The Magister gasped. "Are you calling the Oracle a liar?"

Lark clenched her hands together and squeezed hard to ward off a shudder. "He's not, but he's right, too." Oroduna had countless years of practice talking in circles, answering questions without really answering, guiding people to their own conclusions. Somehow, they'd missed one that should have been obvious. "The other Paragon... we don't know that it's Gadranus. If that crystal really holds a shard of his power, it may not be what we need at all."

Tula slumped in her seat. "Then why would he lie to us? If he wants us to fix the sword too?"

"I don't know." Lark hated to admit it. Just like that, they were back to the beginning, lost and lacking guidance.

Resia twisted a curl of her brown hair around her finger. "But someone does."

"And we happen to be headed that way," Andriun added.

Uneasy butterflies whirled in Lark's stomach and she tried to steel her resolve.

They had not even departed from Jadora yet, and the impending confrontation had already grown worse.

CHAPTER TWENTY-FIVE

NONE of the training Zaide had ever suffered through had prepared him for life among the broken-born who answered to Gadranus.

A scream of words he only halfway understood jerked him awake and he almost fell from his bunk in the barracks. When Gadranus said he would be trained, he had assumed it meant he'd be taken for sessions in the arena or someplace similar. Not that he would be subjected to... whatever this was.

He jammed his feet into his boots—new ones, a standard issue that didn't quite fit—and donned the uniform he'd been given the day he'd first received the offer that changed the course of things. He'd been allowed to retrieve his clothing from the quarters that had once been his, but he was expected to dress like the broken-born officers at all times. Looking like them was uncomfortable, and he marveled at how his perspective had changed.

All his life, he'd been painfully aware of the things that made him different. None of the Kolmari had mistreated him, but children were sensitive, and he had noticed the differences between them even without the gentle teasing that had come from his peers. He'd both wished to fit in and longed for recognition that he didn't, that he could be Kolmari in name and tradition and everything he knew and yet still be something else. Something other.

Now, he found himself longing for something—anything—that might set him apart from the broken-born officer who snared him by the collar as he tried to slide out to the yard for training.

The man slammed him against the wall of the barracks, shouting something Zaide wasn't entirely sure was Torec, for he did not catch a single word. When he didn't react, the man shook him and snarled something else, then released Zaide's collar and pointed out the door.

Zaide ducked his head and followed the others outside.

He was not the only trainee, though he was the only one who was broken-born. The others were men he assumed were from Amrochan. Some had the bearing of soldiers, while others were younger and wore fear on their faces.

The lack of women came as a surprise; Sendassian had never shied away from granting them access to the military, though Zaide supposed it was possible they'd merely been separated and were kept in separate barracks somewhere. But he'd never seen a woman among the officers that had come west with the goborrins, nor had there been any in the palace in Toren. After traveling with Lark and Tula and seeing the guardswomen in Jadora, it was hard to fathom they would be absent. Or perhaps it was just another aspect of cultural differences he'd have to get used to.

The training itself was the same from day to day, and he was given no time to rest. They ran laps and performed drills before breakfast was served, the meal always the same—cold meat, some sort of vegetable that had been reduced to paste, and an unpleasant pudding that might have once been fruit.

After the bland meal, most of them were put in formation and given instructions while they digested. Zaide alone was pulled out and sent elsewhere in the palace. What appeared preferential treatment had been quick to result in scorn from the other trainees, followed by exclusion. Had they known what those sessions were like, they might have felt differently.

Then again, maybe some of them would have figured themselves honored by daily training sessions against Gadranus.

They always fought in the morning; Gadranus said the hours after breakfast were when Zaide could be judged at his finest. He was awake after the drills, but not yet exhausted, and freshly fed, as if the unpalatable rations they gave him could fill anyone with zest.

Each session began with an assessment of how Zaide fared compared to the day before. He saw no progression in his own skills, but Gadranus appeared pleased, nonetheless.

More than anything, they tempered his patience. The impulsiveness so many of Zaide's companions had identified as his biggest shortcoming was what Gadranus called out, too, and day by day, he learned patience and pacing and came closer to landing a blow that might render his enemy dead.

Yet that killing blow never came, and long days after their sessions began, Zaide began to wonder why he was being played with.

"You want me to kill you," he noted one morning as he and Gadranus moved slow, graceful circles around what had once been the garden where he met with Lark. "Why teach me all this if you have no plan to fight me when the end comes?"

Gadranus laughed, so full of mirth that it put a sparkle in his cold blue eyes. "Consider it my legacy. I already told you, I have no children, and have not for many lives. What lineage I might have left behind has already been extinguished, tainted by what I am and blotted out from the pages of history. No sons or grandsons or ten-times-great-grandsons to inherit all I have learned."

"Then why me?" That question had burned as icy hot as the borrowed magic that simmered in Zaide's veins. There were a thousand others better equipped for such a legacy, even those who might have wanted it. Zaide did not, yet he saw no other answer. Every moment he spent training against the man brought them closer to the end they all craved. He could do little as he was, but a better version of him could offer safety for his family.

Safety for Lark and the others.

For his home.

"I have told you that your father was a dear friend," Gadranus said. "We grew up side by side, and I cherished that. Had things been different, had you not been born to the destiny you were, your father would be alive, and I would have been a presence in your life. I would have taught you swordsmanship either way."

Zaide flinched when their blades met and skidded together, but pushed back and earned himself space. "I thought you said you were from the southern part of the Shattered Lands. The part where people don't look like snowmen."

"That I am."

"And my family was from the north? Somewhere around Toren?" The lack of openings brought Zaide's frustration to a head, but he worked to still his impatience. That was the whole point of his training.

"Ah." Gadranus parried a strike, never breaking a sweat. "I see what you are asking. Allow me to clarify by explaining I was born in the southeastern portion of what is now known as the Shattered Lands. A strange name to me, as they are whole beneath my banner." He smirked. "I was born to a family of wealthy merchants this time. They were in Toren for trade and chose to stay due to my mother's health. A story that sounds familiar to you, I am sure."

If only they'd kicked them out of Toren as soon as they'd realized who Gadranus was. Zaide pulled back another step and reevaluated what he'd been doing. "Who leads the Shattered Lands when you're dead?"

For the slightest instant, displeasure twitched at the corners of Gadranus's mouth. "The period before my new Rise. I am never dead."

Of course. That was why they were here. Why he held Amrochan, why he would continue to push west to bring the rest of the kingdom—and Lark—under his control.

Zaide refused to apologize for the offense. "Who leads? What keeps them from breaking away from your control?"

"The goborrins, largely. By now I have controlled them for so long that my existence is somewhat mythologized." The angle at which Gadranus held his sword shifted almost imperceptibly.

Zaide almost darted in, then thought twice. He was always being tested; any hint of movement outside the norm was meant to distract him or trick him into believing it was his chance to strike. He kept circling, one slow step at a time. "Then what makes you think they'll follow me when you're gone? Why haven't they followed the other people who killed you?"

"They are tied to my magic as inextricably as I am tied to this eternal life. My spirit is bound to this world, and they are sensitive to it. When I am set free and the magic that holds me here is finally severed, they will feel that I am gone and will not return. It is difficult to explain to someone without a foundation in the same sort of power, but when the time comes, you will understand. Your power shall be the closest to mine, but untainted by the curse I bear. Trust me. They will follow you." Gadranus moved an inch to the left and his sword tilted back the other direction.

Zaide didn't fall for that, either, and he asked no more questions.

They circled twice more before Gadranus raised a fist to signal for the session to halt.

Yet another session ended without landing a single blow. By now, the cut Zaide had managed to carve into the man's cheek had healed, and he began to doubt he would succeed in landing another.

He was dismissed without any further conversation and returned to the barracks in silence.

The latter portion of a day's training was always the same. He completed combat with Gadranus, ate a midday meal that was as tasteless as the rest, and spent the rest of the day doing exercise drills with officers barking orders he sometimes understood. He learned more Torec words as he hauled supply sacks to the kitchens or carried stones above his head, along with any other menial tasks they'd decided would make him stronger. All the while, his new magic stung, and still he was not shown how to manage it.

There were other mages among Gadranus's men. He felt them now, detected the tingle of their power whenever it was at use, and he could not help but wonder how anyone ignored it. All around him, people carried innate power, some more gifted than others, but none lacking the way he was. Now that he sensed magic everywhere, a new resentment burned in his chest.

All this time, he had been less, and no one had spared him the kindness of explaining what he lacked. Now he knew, and he hated it and the way everyone had treated him as if he'd been *enough*.

But he wasn't. He couldn't be. How could he, compared to what he was now? With the taste of power bitter and acrid on the back of his tongue?

He struggled to hold it, to call it without flinching, to reassure himself he would be in control and could use what he held to help restore the blade. Yet he was not, and every night, the dark power infested his dreams and he woke vomiting.

"Good news," Gadranus announced one morning when they met to spar. "The first of Sendassian's soldiers is ready for his match."

Zaide had almost given up on that request being honored. He was mindful not to appear eager. "Just now? It's been weeks." Or, he thought it had been; between the hard days and illness-marked nights, he'd lost all track of time.

"You forget that only your testing was expedited. The others have gone in rotation. They will become ready one after another, as they come far enough to be measured against a swordsman of your caliber. You are, after all, not far beneath me."

Not far, yet not close enough to end things now. Every day they crossed blades was another chance to strike him down. Every day, Zaide failed again. He didn't care that killing Gadranus now would render his life forfeit; it was a price he would gladly pay to be free, whatever free now meant. As long as he failed to grasp and control the magic that coursed through him, the possibility of replenishing the Spectrum Blade and redeeming himself was out of reach.

Zaide had nothing to say.

Gadranus went on. "I have a gift for you to mark the occasion. Come." He beckoned with one hand, and Zaide had no choice but to follow.

They departed from the garden—Zaide didn't know what else to call it, though the name no longer fit with all the plantings torn out—and strode through the palace unhindered.

Gadranus was never stopped by any of his officers, or any of what Zaide assumed had become the palace staff. Where the original staff had gone was a mystery, but most had probably fled. The thought of goborrins managing the kitchen might have given him a laugh, but he no longer felt any inclination toward mirth. A sliver of optimism, maybe, as he thought of his impending work to free Amrochan's soldiers from the palace dungeon, but humor seemed so distant as to be unreachable.

They had scaled to the second floor of the palace before Gadranus spoke again. "Thus far, you've been fortunate in battling my officers. No one here means you any harm, as I have forbidden it."

Strange, considering how many times Zaide had been wounded or knocked in the head during his so-called testing.

"The prisoners are guaranteed to see you as an enemy, so they will be unlikely to hold back. With that in mind, it's best if you not enter combat so unprepared." Gadranus stopped at a pair of doors more grand than the rest and opened them with little fanfare.

Where the rest of the palace was almost barren, the chambers beyond those doors were lavishly decorated and stuffed with what might have been treasures. Fine carpets covered every inch of the floor, exquisite vases sat packed into corners around gilded furniture, and polished gold and silver trinkets cluttered every flat surface.

Gadranus led the way through the maze of stolen goods to a chest of fine wood that bore bands of polished brass. He knelt, not seeming to care that his back was turned. Maybe he didn't; Zaide wasn't armed. Or maybe he no longer saw Zaide as a threat after all that had transpired. If they weren't enemies, what were they?

"I had the armor made for you after we met in Toren," the man said as he opened the chest, "but I've had the blade for a long time. I suspect you'll find it better suited to your comfort than what you've been training with."

"Shorter?" Zaide guessed.

"Similar in length to what you're used to, yes." Gadranus withdrew the sword and its scabbard first. He offered it with one hand, scarcely looking back.

Slowly, Zaide took it. He had no desire to receive gifts from the man he hated most of all, but if he was being trusted with a blade of his own instead of being handed practice weapons when it was convenient, it was a step toward what he needed to happen. If he had a sword in his hand, it put Gadranus at risk. Any moment could be the one where Zaide was afforded a chance to surprise his enemy and strike him down.

An ambush was dishonorable.

He no longer cared.

Zaide wrapped a hand around the snake-headed hilt and drew the blade from its sheath of polished dark wood. What slid free was a curious weapon, its blade sinuous and strange in color. He tilted it to examine its sheen.

"It's called the Viper's Tongue," Gadranus said.

"It's gold." Yet it wasn't. It was too heavy, too sharp.

When Gadranus turned, his arms were full. "A unique type of bronze. As hard as steel."

Zaide shook his head. "Can't be."

"I promise you it is, though how it was made is knowledge lost a long time ago. As long as you don't handle it foolishly, you'll be able to fend off men with modern swords." A grim smile painted Gadranus's face and he extended what he held. "Your armor."

The armor, too, was finely crafted, dark leather marked with deep red detailing, but Zaide's eyes snagged on the emblem of the tusked ram's skull that adorned the breast.

He must have grown too still, for Gadranus chuckled. "That, too, will be yours when all this is over."

"No," Zaide said as he jammed the sword back into its sheath and took the heap of armor into his arms. "It'll be a trophy on my wall."

Surprise drove Gadranus's eyebrows upward. Then he gave a loud, hearty laugh. "Still haven't stamped out that fire, I see."

Zaide said nothing and turned toward the door.

"So eager to leave?" Amusement welled in the man's voice and sent agitation crawling down Zaide's spine.

"If they're ready for me to dive into testing Amrochan's soldiers, I don't want to keep anyone waiting." Nor did he want to don the armor in front of someone who stirred his temper, knowing what that did to the magic he still struggled to hold.

"Very well. We resume training tomorrow."

With a new sword in Zaide's hand, something close to the size of the Spectrum Blade. The weight would take some getting used to, but he was supposed to be stronger now. He nodded and took his leave, then worked his way down through the palace.

It was strange to return to the prison and stranger still to stop on the other side of the arena to dress in his new armor and strap the new sword at his side. A handful of goborrins and the officers overseeing them paused to watch as he adjusted straps and tested his range of movement with each piece of armor he added. The mark on his chest bothered him as much as if it had been branded on his skin, but when they saw it, the goborrins thumped their weapons against whatever was closest—the floor, the walls, or their own bodies.

"Ready?" one of the officers asked, his hand already on the door. The first of the prisoners must have already been put there to wait.

Zaide nodded and took his position.

How long had it been since he'd been on the other end of the arena, brought up from the cells and made to fight? It was strange to go back, stranger still to be as pleased as he was, but he rolled his shoulders and braced himself.

The door opened and he stepped inside, his hand on the hilt of his sword.

Then he saw his first opponent.

Raddan.

He'd expected nothing else.

CHAPTER TWENTY-SIX

AT FIRST, the lieutenant did not recognize him. Zaide knew the moment he did from the way the man's whole demeanor fell.

"Look for you in the stands, you said." Raddan didn't spit, but he looked as if he wanted to. "Not where I've been expecting to see you, lad."

"Never be what is expected," Zaide replied dryly as he slid his new sword from its scabbard. The bronze glinted and drew hoots from the goborrins perched above. The monsters leaned against the railing, licking their mouths and slimy noses as if they prepared for a feast.

The lieutenant nodded at the emblem that decorated the new cuirass. "Looks like you've taken that advice to heart."

Zaide ignored him. "Take your blade."

Distrust made Raddan's lip twitch, but he seized the sword the goborrins had provided from the floor.

Now was the real challenge—reassuring the man they were still on the same side without letting the enemy know. Dozens of goborrins hung over the arena, waiting for the battle to begin. A few broken-born stood among them, none of them impressed, but all of them watching.

He'd put himself at a disadvantage. They bore only swords;

neither had a shield. Zaide had little reason to trust Gadranus, so he doubted the integrity of the blade he held. He doubted his certainty with it, too, he decided as he gave it a gentle swish. The length was good, similar to what he'd grown used to, but it felt wrong to hold any weapon that did not bear the same tingling presence of the Spectrum Blade.

Raddan moved first and caught him unprepared. The lieutenant went in with a sweep and forced Zaide back, but then the surprise was over.

Funny; Zaide had only just been lamenting that he had seen no improvement in his own skills. Now that he was faced with real combat, he saw it easily—the way his opponent misjudged his reach and offered too much room for retreat. He flowed into the gap with a jab, not aiming to strike, but testing how fast his opponent moved. He had seen Raddan on the battlefield, but the man was a medic. The sword at his belt had rarely been used when Zaide was there to see it.

The lieutenant put more space between them, either out of caution or that he saw that simple test for what it was—it was hard to tell which. He adjusted his grip on the rough weapon in his hand and it became clear that made the fight unfair from the beginning. Raddan was fighting with a weapon of an unfamiliar make and size. Still, he held it with determination and sized Zaide up, armor and all. "Is it worth what he's given you?"

Zaide snorted softly. Gadranus had given him everything he'd hoped for. A chance to free the soldiers. A chance to gain needed skill. The power needed to destroy him when it was done. "You have no idea." But thinking of the magic was a mistake, for it swelled in response to the attention he'd spared it. It rose like floodwaters, murky and vile, threatening to sweep him away and drown him in the middle of the fight.

He put his head down and swallowed hard against the nausea that rose in his stomach. He had to be patient. Wait for the lessons in how to control it. Only then would what he'd done be useful.

Raddan responded with an annoyed *tch*. "A few meals and a bath? A new sword makes it worth betraying all your friends?"

An unexpected problem rose to the surface and Zaide mulled it over as he circled, waiting for another opening. He'd asked the lieutenant to trust him. Expected him to play along when time came. Now that it was time, Zaide did not know if Raddan was serious or not. Nor could he ask, with dozens of goborrins overhead. Their commentary reached his ears whether he wanted to hear it or not. The long effort he'd put into practicing Torec meant he understood every word, and random pieces burrowed into his mind like wild thorns.

Fights like Gadranus now.

Honored with the emblem.

The emperor's old sword.

He forced himself to ignore it and sneer. "What friends? A few soldiers I met in a dungeon?" Or the ones who had never returned for him?

That heated, bitter thought took him off guard. He didn't think that. He knew why they'd stayed away. He'd begged the Paragons to protect Lark and keep her far from Gadranus. Maybe it took all of them just to keep her safe.

Or maybe they'd forgotten. Or given up, or...

"What happened to the boy I treated beside Kolmar's river?" Raddan asked.

Zaide was grateful for the distraction. "He grew up."

"Into this?"

"Our ugliest fears are of what we might someday be," Zaide said. "But I'm not afraid anymore, Lieutenant. Are you?"

Raddan lunged forward without a response and his unexpected flurry of swipes could have cut if Zaide hadn't ducked aside.

The goborrins overhead burst into cheers, or as close to it as the monsters came. The sounds reminded Zaide of a wild boar impaled on a spear and angrily awaiting its death.

More unsettling was the silence of the broken-born, who

remained in their places. Most had crossed their arms and watched with speculative gazes.

Zaide chose not to disappoint them.

After all he'd been through, it was not hard to see he would outstrip the lieutenant in skill. Rather than destroying him in combat, he shifted his parries and stabs to magnify what Raddan *could* do, ferreting out his strengths and displaying them for the onlookers, one slash at a time.

More than once, their blades met in a clash hard enough to make Zaide wince and worry for the edge of his strange new sword, but the edges of the gleaming bronze seemed little worse for wear after dozens of strikes. Maybe Gadranus had been telling the truth about the sword, too. Maybe it was well-crafted.

No amount of craftsmanship could make a sword rival the Spectrum Blade, though, and again he found himself longing for what he'd lost.

It was a useless longing. He'd been rejected. Used and discarded when the blade was no longer satisfied. And now the man whose fault that was bore the privilege of having his emblem on Zaide's chest and his magic twisting his stomach to turmoil, because those were the only tools Zaide had left with which to help.

The unfairness put a hot anger in his chest, fueled every stab and strike. He pressed harder, working Raddan to the end of his skills, and the combat brought no relief. Every step of the way, he'd been met with failure through no fault of his own. He'd been carried to a strange land as an infant, somewhere he could never fit in. He'd lost his family to illness and war. Lost his chance at the life he'd wanted when the Elder pulled him from his Spring Choosing. Lost his home to goborrins. He'd lost the Spectrum Blade, lost his chance to save the king, lost his friends and his freedom and everything he'd ever dreamed could be.

The sheer exhaustion from it all brought him to the verge of collapse.

All that remained was the snakelike sword in his hand, the

armor he'd chosen, and the borrowed magic he somehow had to wield. It was reckless, desperate, but it was a chance to chip away at some of the destruction from the inside.

The only real problem was he saw no way to wage that destruction without it costing his life.

And what does that matter? As far as anyone knows, you're already lost. He set his jaw and swung hard. Gleaming bronze struck the crude sword in Raddan's hand and the inferior weapon shattered. Shards of iron rang as they hit the floor and the tip of Zaide's sword stopped a hair's breadth from the lieutenant's chin.

Raddan froze, though the cartilage in his throat bobbed as he swallowed.

Above them, goborrins shrilled with glee.

"You have the chance to save yourself." Zaide kept his voice low, though he doubted he could ever sound threatening. "I took it. Will you?"

Slowly, the lieutenant raised his hands in surrender. "Aye, lad. I will."

The words slid the weight of concern from Zaide's shoulders and he allowed himself to relax. It had worked. Raddan had chosen to play along, to give his plan a try. He returned his sword to its sheath at his hip and offered his hand.

Raddan accepted, his grip firm.

Zaide glanced to one of the broken-born officers overhead and the man nodded in response.

They approved of the invitation, accepted the first of his freed allies.

The first sign any of this would work as he intended.

Behind him, the door opened and a pair of goborrins stepped through.

"Clean him up," Zaide instructed in Torec. He still struggled to smooth out the words, but he'd taken to practicing a few short sentences he thought would help him free however many of Sendassian's men had survived. "Take him to Whok."

"Whok?" someone asked beside the door. Not a goborrin, but one of the broken-born officers who had come to either escort Zaide from the arena or take over the situation. Perhaps both.

"The goborrin medic," Zaide explained. He didn't know how many addressed the old goborrin by name, but he guessed it was not many. "Raddan is a medic. He will be... useful."

The officer raised a brow.

The pause hadn't been intentional, more of a chance to recall the right word, but apparently the drama it added had been valuable. Zaide would have to remember that. Fewer words. Carefully chosen words. Not only were they easier to manage as he changed between languages, but he took the notion the officer was either impressed or intrigued by the lack of explanation.

The goborrins flanked Raddan and steered him toward the door—and toward a real chance at freedom.

"Welcome to the family," Zaide said as the man strode by.

Raddan met his eyes for one long second, then continued on. He didn't need words. The statement was clear enough.

I hope you know what you're doing.

Zaide hoped so, too. He worked to keep his demeanor cold and unaffected as he addressed the officer beside the door. "Call for me when the next one is ready."

"Think you can convince them all, do you?" The broken-born almost sneered.

"Not all of them will learn their place so easily, but they'll join us or die," Zaide replied.

The officer said nothing, so he excused himself before the exchange grew awkward. He stepped through the door and almost walked straight into Gadranus.

The dark-haired man glided back a step, positioning himself to the side of the main walkway. "A good display. I'm afraid I did not catch all of it, but I am pleased with the progress you're making."

Zaide would have preferred to go lift rocks, but he stepped

aside to speak instead. "He's a good swordsman. You'll be pleased with his performance, too."

"Familiar with him, are you?"

"We traveled together. Briefly. I don't know him well, but I know a good fighter when I see one." Keeping things terse was difficult. Every time they crossed paths, Zaide cursed how easy it was to talk to that man. He carried such an odd sense of openness about him, an accepting warmth that made it comfortable sharing things one often kept quiet. A shame that Gadranus seized power through violence. He would have made an impressive councilor or advisor.

"As do I." Gadranus tilted his head, indication for the two of them to walk. He set a casual pace with his hands clasped behind his back, his shoulders relaxed and his head high. Were it not for the magic that brimmed in him, Zaide might have thought him off his guard.

They walked in silence for a time, Gadranus calm and Zaide tense, his hand itching for the hilt of his sword. There was nothing he wanted more than to draw the blade and strike, but he forced himself to breathe. If he was fortunate, maybe the man would simply think him high-strung after combat.

The frustration stirred the sliver of magic that tainted him. It coiled and flexed, making the hair on his arms and the back of his neck stand on end. Trying to touch it would do nothing, even if he'd known how. For all that the power raged in him like a storm, it was but a fraction of what Gadranus had at his mercy. A blade was the only way that man would meet his end.

And the magic is for that blade, Zaide reminded himself. He prayed it would be enough.

Gadranus spoke when they reached the stairs. "There is a small matter I felt we should discuss, if you have a moment to spare."

"You're the one setting my schedule."

"Am I?" Gadranus feigned surprise. "Hmm, perhaps I shall

carve out more time for the two of us to train together, then. Tell me, Zaide. Have you noticed the hierarchy in my armies?"

"You at the top, goborrins at the bottom?" It was hard to restrain his sarcasm.

"I was more interested in your observations regarding the middle portion. Everyone knows the goborrins act as foot soldiers, but surely you have seen who is in charge of them?"

The officers weren't anything unusual. Every military had them. "I have."

"There are no Torec men in my army who do not hold some sort of rank to establish their authority over my goborrins. None except you, that is. I should like to rectify that. I have more than just skill with a sword that must be passed on, and painfully little time in which to do it." A softly pensive expression took Gadranus's face. "I do intend for this to be the last time I walk this world, and I should hate for all my experience to go to waste."

"And?" Zaide asked, though he already knew where the conversation was going.

"I will be assigning you a proper rank within my army, but I wish for you to take lessons with me regarding leadership tactics and the management of militias."

Zaide had no words for the utter lack of surprise. "All right." No matter how Gadranus phrased it, he knew it was not as simple as a wish or request. It was an order, and there was nothing to do but obey, lest he find himself stripped of the power he'd sought.

"That you will be taking my place is reasonably common knowledge, but I believe it will be easier for you to earn the favor of others if you begin near the bottom. I mean for you to begin with the rank of captain, as that will put you above most of my officers in Amrochan. Most of my men with a higher rank are on the field, working to reclaim Tinith and seize Yithel." Gadranus paused a beat. "Which brings me to the next subject."

There was always something else. Zaide waited for him to go

on and remained silent as they rounded a corner into the palace's halls. He did not need to confirm he was listening. The man always seemed ready to speak. Perhaps he enjoyed the sound of his own voice—or perhaps he'd been without a listening ear for so long that the words would not stop flowing.

They did not slow now.

"My forces in Yithel have spotted a boat bearing a number of Amrochan soldiers. They are sailing south, meaning they intend to reach us here. They will most likely attempt to enter the city through the docks, which have largely remained unused since I claimed the city. You already know the lack of fondness goborrins have for water." Gadranus glanced at him from the corner of his eye.

"Yes," Zaide said. He didn't know where they were going, but he wasn't certain he cared. Either he'd be given a new assignment to keep him busy for the rest of the day, or they'd spill out in some familiar place where he already knew what was expected of him.

"From what we have gathered, the docks are the only part of the city where defenses are questionable. It would seem Sendassian relied on the aversion my armies had to sailing as a major part of his defense. A lack of naval force meant I could never pry Lake Sian from his hands, but admittedly, I never tried." The wry smile Gadranus gave was almost enough to earn sympathy. No matter what anyone thought of the man, he had not risen to power by being a lackluster leader. To have such a hole in his military force must have been some source of embarrassment.

It wasn't enough to convince Zaide to pity him. "Defending the city against one ship should be easy with the numbers you have."

"It is also possible they are not here to fight," Gadranus said. "You did relay my original offer to Sendassian's heir?"

A strange way to refer to Lark, but it was not incorrect. "Yes."

Gadranus appeared pleased. "Then it is always possible she

has reconsidered. There is still a chance for peace, and while I will not be denied what I desire, I have no interest in unnecessary bloodshed. I have seen enough, and I am not as thirsty for vengeance as younger versions of myself were."

"Vengeance against who?" It was hard to think he could bear a grudge against anyone; from all Zaide had ever heard or read, it was Gadranus who was always the aggressor.

They turned into a familiar hall and it made their destination obvious. They were headed for the war room, with the table covered in maps. There would be no time wasted in his training.

Gadranus considered his answer for a time before he gave it. "The Maker, I suppose."

Zaide's brow twitched, but he caught it before he showed more than an inkling of curiosity.

Again, it took no prompting for the man to go on. "Or perhaps the people favored enough that they were given power to stand in my way. For a long time, I did not understand why I was made to suffer so long for my mistake, especially when the outcome was misery for everyone else, as well. But when one prays for patience, they are made to earn it through the hardest means necessary, and when one prays for peace, what follows is often the most turbulent."

Zaide had never asked for either, but he'd received turbulence anyway. He considered saying as much, then decided to keep his mouth shut. The less he shared, the better. He would not risk being known too well.

They reached the doorway to the war room and the moment Gadranus opened the door, he returned to the subject of their impending guests. "I want you to be there when the ship arrives," he said as Zaide followed him inside. He sealed them in the room without summoning anyone else. "Beside me, to greet its passengers when they seek me. I believe your presence will make Dasienna feel more welcome, especially when she sees I have done you no harm. I will accept the surrender of her crown gladly, and our war will be over. This can still end peacefully for everyone, and it is my sincere hope that it does."

That Lark would surrender to anyone was a bold assumption, but Zaide kept that to himself and made for the table and its large map, instead. "When will it arrive?"

"Soon. Within a few days. Until then, you will be allowed to train as usual. I expect you to obey your instructors, regardless of how they rank. They are here to help. And you will begin training with me. Still with the blade, first and foremost, but also in strategy, and when things with the young queen are resolved, we shall begin your training with magic."

The very suggestion made the power stir. Zaide's breath caught, and he struggled to clear his mind and let the magic sink back into obscurity before he spoke again. "And if things with Dasienna aren't resolved?"

"They will be," Gadranus said as he took a small figure of a ship and placed it on the river just north of the city. "One way or another."

All around the mark that represented Amrochan, tiny markers representing goborrins swarmed. They stretched from Yithel to Tinith and the mountains in the west. They curved around the northern edge of the continent and hung beside Ganede. They ringed the lake and flooded the now-refined marks that represented Toren and the rest of the Shattered Lands.

As Zaide studied the map, Gadranus took another pig-shaped trinket and planted it on the river in Yithel, symbolizing an impending blockade on the river.

No matter who was on that ship, they were about to be trapped.

Against all reason, Zaide silently prayed Lark was coming to surrender.

CHAPTER TWENTY-SEVEN

THE LAST TIME Lark had laid eyes on Amrochan, it had been her birthday. Smoke had cloaked the skies then, but the weather had been temperate. Now the skies were a clear, bold blue, but a bite chilled the winds and promised something worse to come.

As if anything could be worse than her. A child born on the autumn solstice was an ill omen; a life begun at the cusp of death, a harbinger of all that would be lost. No one had ever dared say it in front of her, but she knew what the people thought. The whispered speculation among palace staff was never as guarded as they believed. Even her father had dreaded her and fought to keep her out of the way.

He had not been wrong to do so.

She leaned against the railing on the narrow ship's deck and watched the city grow closer. There had been no scouts spotted along the riverbank since they'd passed through Yithel. They had taken precautions as they passed by the city, but Lark was not convinced they had not been seen and identified. There were few other vessels on the water, and none headed toward the lake. In the past day, since reaching Lake Sian, they had encountered no other ships at all.

Amrochan's walls loomed ahead. The city had always struck

her as a beautiful fortification, something strong and stern, yet sheltering and protective at the same time. Now all she saw was austere walls. The peninsula had changed little, but instead of filling her with the warmth home should have brought, she was left empty.

Just like her father's throne.

He had been right to dread her presence.

No matter how many times Lark swallowed, she could not rid herself of the tightness in her throat. After all the weeks that had passed since they fled from Amrochan, she still had not taken the time to grieve. Part of her wondered if her father deserved it, and the rest of her was ashamed for wondering.

There had been times he was loving. Moments where he brought her flowers from the garden, or sat and laughed over old stories, or offered approval of her crafts. He had often liked her embroidery, and on one occasion, presenting him with a piece she had designed herself had earned her a tender hug.

But those memories were few and scattered between the versions of him that were harsh. Bitter recollections of criticism or scorn cluttered her head, all but smothering the parts of him she'd liked.

Worst of all was that she could not blame him for being that way. Lark's grandfather had been given the gift of ruling during a time of peace; Sendassian had inherited a Rise. He'd known from the moment the crown settled on his head that he would be locked in a ceaseless fight, the last bastion of resistance that kept Gadranus's empire from claiming the world and plunging it into darkness. He'd had to be hard, merciless, and cold. There was no way a king with a tender heart could survive all they had been through.

Yet now he was gone, and all the world had left was Lark.

Something brushed against her leg and she reached to scratch Daisy's ears without thought. If the dog was close, that meant Tula was, too, and Lark did not think she could bear to look at her friend. Instead, she swallowed again and tried to find her voice. The version she found was thin and weak. "I don't want to cry again, but I sit here looking at the palace's peaks and wonder if they even buried him."

"Zaide?" Tula asked, confused and concerned.

"My father." Although Lark doubted Zaide would be treated with any more honor. She dared not think he had perished. Her heart was broken enough, and if even one more thing tore at her, she feared she would not survive.

The Magister crept forward to lean against the rail beside her. Before long, the admiral would chase them both back into the hold, but at least they had a moment. Tula said nothing, listening to the wind and the choppy water. Listening for whatever Lark had to say.

"He wanted to be buried next to my mother, someday. She was buried in the palace gardens. Not the one my father let me visit, but the larger one, adjacent to the palace walls. He took me there sometimes, but did not want me to go alone. He said it was too dangerous. Sometimes I think it's a wonder he let me outside at all." Lark did not know why she shared that, but it had been the first thing that came to mind.

Tula propped her elbows on the rail and leaned forward to cradle her chin in her hands. "Did he try to keep you locked up? Hidden up in a tower where the boys couldn't see how pretty you are?"

Lark snorted. "There was never any danger of that."

"Which part? The boys, or the tower?"

"Either one. Do you remember when we went to speak with my father? How he reacted to Zaide?" Lark had tried to forget, but the image of her father's hand wrapped around Zaide's throat was impossible to shake.

Evidently, Tula did remember, though whatever version she had in mind, it was not the same as what Lark recalled. Instead of being horrified, she grinned. "Oh, yeah. He was real mad there was a boy talking to you."

"I don't believe that was his concern." But Lark could not

deny the possibility it was, either. She would never know, and perhaps that was the worst of it. Knowing nothing of his thoughts or intentions—or even what he truly thought of her—and never being able to ask.

Daisy nudged her hand and she resumed her petting.

The clack of booted footsteps that came with someone's approach made Lark bristle. She already knew who it was; even his stride irritated her.

"Forgive me for interrupting your sight-seeing," Warinal said as he stopped behind them, "but the two of you need to remove yourselves from the decks. My men have spotted approaching scout ships. They have not yet come close enough to see you, and you will want to keep it that way."

Just the two of them? Lark bit back a snide comment about how Daisy staying on deck was fine. "And you suppose a ship full of soldiers in recognizable uniforms and armor will be better for keeping secrets?"

"They expect to see us on the water. They have not yet expanded to claim the lake itself. Now, if you please, Majesty." He gestured with an open palm, as if it was an invitation. She supposed he had to do it that way. He could not be seen trying to give orders to the queen.

Lark raised her chin. "I would prefer to stay here. If they mean to attack us, they will do so regardless of who is on board. I will not be safer for going down below." If anything, she preferred to have them know she was coming. She would not be cowed, nor would she run from them any longer. Her fingers slid along the Spectrum Blade's cross guard.

Now that they approached the city, none of it felt real. The battlefields, the artifacts, the losses and deaths—it all struck her as a dream, coated in haze and turned intangible, as if it had happened to someone else and not to her.

But it was real. The sword's presence at her side helped ground her in the moment, as painful as it was. It was all real, from the blur of the battlefields to the tragedies she would carry forever in her heart. Her grasp tightened on the Spectrum Blade until it made her knuckles ache.

The dog whined and licked the fingers on her other hand.

Lark twitched and looked down. Tula leaned closer beside her and she realized the Magister had said something. Asked something. What had it been? She worked to focus, to make herself process the question, then forced herself to smile. The expression was as thin as her optimism. Tula was checking on her. Nothing more. "I'm fine. I just wish we didn't have to be here, that's all."

"Are you sure?" Tula squinted at her, as if that might reveal something better left hidden.

The real answer was no. Lark was not fine. She would not be for ages to come. "Of course."

In the midst of her pensive gazing, she had not noticed the admiral leave. She glanced about and found him heading back to the helm.

"He seemed real cranky," Tula whispered conspiratorially. "I mean, even worse than usual."

"I cannot say I blame him. We may be sailing to our demise." In all her glancing about, Lark spotted the approaching scout ships, too. She watched them in silence.

They drifted closer, their path meandering, as if it were coincidence that brought them together. Lark expected goborrins on board, despite what she knew of their aversion to water. The broken-born man she identified on the deck of the first ship that drew near came as no surprise, but her sensibilities had not prepared her for the sight of ordinary sailors from Amrochan managing the rigging.

"Admiral," she called. "Am I seeing correctly what is on those ships?"

Tula held onto the rail and leaned back, craning her neck strangely to look across their boat. "What do you—oh, there's regular people!"

Lark's brow twitched and the Magister flushed.

"I mean—instead of goborrins, that is. Not that goborrins are people. Are they people? I guess they aren't, they're just animals, right? But maybe some animals are people, because Vorkaris—"

A blue hand clapped over Tula's mouth from behind. "I will gently suggest you should stop talking, because you are now making it worse."

Tula gave an apologetic sort of hum and Andriun let her go.

"Thank you." Lark nodded toward one of the scout ships. Now that it had come close enough to get a good look at them, it had begun to pull away. "Can you tell how many ships like that are on the water?"

Andriun squinted against the sunlight, then shook his head. "There are many ships on the water, all different shapes and sizes. I cannot tell much about them, aside from that the highest concentration is near the docks."

"Left behind when people fled, perhaps." Or when incoming cargo had arrived, leaving innocent sailors at the mercy of Gadranus. Those who had been out sailing would not have heard of the city's fall. Lark nibbled her lower lip and turned back to the harsh outline of the city's stone walls against the clear sky. A hint of movement caught her attention and she froze.

Tula grew still, too. "What is it?"

"The flag," Lark murmured. "My father's banner still flies over the city."

The three of them watched as the flag snapped and danced in the wind, and Daisy nosed Lark's hand again.

Eventually, Andriun spoke. "I came to suggest we should gather our things and determine a plan of how we are to do this, now that we know we will be able to dock. We have discussed many ideas, but beyond manipulating water to ensure we reach the city, I do not know what is expected of me."

"Nothing." Lark drew back from the railing with a measure of reluctance. She wanted to keep watching Amrochan as they approached, but she knew it was pointless. It looked the same from the outside and that had brought comfort, yet there was no denying that both she and the city would never be the same. "You won't like this, but I'll be honest. I intended to go alone."

Andriun's delayed reaction gave away his thoughts before he found his words. "You cannot go alone," he protested. "You are the queen."

Lark headed for the hatch that led below deck and Daisy trotted along beside her. They had taken little with them and consolidated their belongings to as few bags as possible once they had abandoned the goborrin warship in Chithal and commandeered their smaller vessel, yet even what little they'd taken had been enough to make the boat seem cramped. She was sorely tempted to acquire one of the larger vessels in Amrochan's harbor for their escape. "That's precisely why I think I should. I'm the one who grew up in the palace. I know more ways in and out of it than anyone."

"You didn't know the secret exit at the city gate," Tula said as she followed.

"That's because I didn't use the gates to get out of Amrochan." There was no easy way to get the dog up and down the ladder, so Lark put out a hand to signal for Daisy to wait. The white dog sat on her haunches, her tail swishing along the deck's sea-worn boards.

Tula crouched beside the hatch as Lark descended. "How'd you leave, then?"

"The docks. Trust me, I know what I'm doing." This time, at least. Lark bit that back, lest she sound uncertain. She had failed at so much, but she would not let herself foul up this rescue.

The space immediately below the hatch was something of a common space. The galley was right beside it, and a number of soldiers sat there with bowls of whatever sludge they were trying to pass off as food today. Resia's capability with cooking had improved things, but in the future, they would have to remember to bring a cook.

When Lark's boots hit the floor, the Kolmari girl glanced up from peeling vegetables. "Is it time?"

"We're approaching the city. I want you, Tula, and Andriun to help hold the docks while I get into the palace and look for Zaide." Lark was certain that was where he would be, though she did not know whether he'd be held in the prison or put somewhere else. Ideally, she'd run across someone who might have seen him, but she did not know how many soldiers might still be in the city—or how many might still be alive.

Andriun followed her down the ladder. "This does not seem like a plan. This seems like the seed of a plan, before it has time to sprout."

She cast him a dirty look. "What else do you think we're supposed to do? You may be Paragons, but we're still not strong enough to stand up to Gadranus directly, and we can't put together a plan to assassinate him until we know what to expect from the state of things here."

"I just do not think it is wise for you to go alone." He turned to Resia as if seeking her support.

The Kolmari girl nodded, the gesture as gentle as the rest of her demeanor. "I want Zaide back just as badly as everyone else, but if something were to happen to you..." She worried her hands, twisting her fingers over and over.

The worst of it all was Lark did not know how that sentence was supposed to finish. If something happened to her, a new Paragon would be chosen. One with more skill, one who could replenish the blade and accomplish what she could not.

Yet if something happened to her, it would mean all was over. She was the last in the line of succession, and no one had stepped up to claim a right to the Allied Kingdoms should she fall. No one else was willing to face Gadranus, to keep him from seizing power over Amroch. The war would be over, and he would have won.

Perhaps the reason the Oracle had not seen another Rise was because it was not necessary. The thought put an uneasy fear in the pit of her stomach and she rested her hands against it, as if the touch might quell the turning.

Lark forced herself to speak. "I don't think we have a choice. I stand the best chance of finding my way in undetected. And if I fail, then..." Her throat tightened and she struggled to keep going. "Then I'll leave the Spectrum Blade with the rest of you. It's not as if I could kill Gadranus with it, even if I saw him. If something happens to me, you have to promise to keep fighting without me. Find someone to restore the blade, and end all of this."

"This is a bad idea," Tula called, still crouched at the top of the ladder. She and the dog both peered down with disapproval.

That the *dog* dared to scorn her idea was enough to make Lark indignant. And more determined to see things through, though she was less likely to admit that. She stared up at them without blinking as she removed the Spectrum Blade and held out its sheath for Andriun to take.

He raised his hands as if to ward it off. "Me?"

"If the chosen Bladebearer becomes incapable of wielding it, the sword will choose another. I suspect it's most likely to choose you." Lark did not know if Andriun had any experience with swords. Of the other Paragons, Tula appeared to be the most competent with blades, but the Spectrum Blade struck Lark as serious and discerning. The Magister did not feel like a good fit for those qualities, though Lark would never say it to her face.

"It did not wish for me to touch it when we fled Amrochan before," Andriun protested.

"It didn't wish for me to touch it when I tried to pull it from the old Gadranus's skull, either, but here we are." She pressed the scabbard into the outward-turned palms of his hands until his fingers reluctantly closed around it. "Besides, I just need you to keep it safe for a while. If this goes well, we'll have our regular Bladebearer back in no time."

The tightening of his mouth conveyed what they'd be up against if it did not go well, but he surrendered.

"Hey," Tula called. "The admiral says we're around the corner and moving in to dock now. Are we all ready?"

Lark left the Shaman with the blade and returned to the ladder. "Yes. Tell Admiral Warinal to take the ship to the far eastern edge of the docks and tie up there, with the ship's nose against the dock, if possible. It should make it harder for anyone to make it on board, and I can have Andriun use the water to lift me to shore."

"To the docks?" Andriun asked. He still held the Spectrum Blade sideways in front of himself, as if he didn't know what to do with it now that it was in his hands.

"I suppose that's a better description, isn't it?" She scaled the ladder and paused at its top. "I'm leaving the artifacts here. You may need them."

The Shaman muttered something in his mother tongue, and it was not hard to identify it as a complaint.

Tula's hand disappeared into her red and gold coat, then emerged with a Jadoran knife. "You never did get yours back, so you should take this if you don't have the sword."

Lark took it, though not without a frown. "What about you?"

"I'll be fine. I've got these, remember?" Tula's fingers flicked outward from her palms and fireballs sparked in her hands. Just beneath the edges of her sleeves, the golden dragon marks Vorkaris had given her to represent their bond glowed. They were covered so often, Lark had almost forgotten they were there.

"I suppose that's more useful than a knife." Lark fastened its sheath at her belt where the Spectrum Blade had been, then stood. "Andriun, come lift me to the docks. The admiral doesn't need me to be here to bring in the ship."

Andriun's hands tightened on the Spectrum Blade, then he thrust the scabbard into Resia's hands and made for the ladder. The Kolmari girl stayed behind, blinking.

He gave Daisy's head a pat as he reached the top, then joined Lark beside the rail. "I wish for it to be recorded in Tula's contribution to the Great Library's history books that I said this was a bad idea."

"I'll write it down," Tula said with a grin. "You get her over there. And good luck, Your Majesty."

Lark's nose wrinkled. "I swear, if you start speaking to me with formality, I'll abdicate the throne just so I can have friends again."

"Perhaps save abdication for after this war is over." Andriun stepped back as a tendril of water draped itself over the railing and wrapped around Lark's middle like a snake. He did not give her a chance to reply before he moved it—and her—out over the remaining gap between them and the empty docks.

Lark fought back a gasp and squeezed her eyes shut until her feet hit the wooden planks. He hadn't lifted her far, but it brought back unpleasant memories of her being pulled down from the top of the goborrin warship, an experience she was not eager to relive.

The water drew itself out of her clothes when it retreated, leaving her dry. She waved to the ship and turned, bracing herself for everything to come. Small offices lined the docks, and she knew one of them connected to a merchant's house that opened into the rest of the city. Whether or not it was supposed to was something she would have to consider when Amrochan was hers again, but for now, she was grateful for the indiscretion. She sprinted for the doorway to the merchant's office and had almost reached it when the great wooden gates in the city's wall groaned.

Lark skidded to a halt and her heart leaped into her throat.

That wasn't supposed to happen. They weren't supposed to use the docks. They had no reason. Panic swelled in her and she turned back to call for retreat, but the Paragons were already preparing to leap over the ship's rail.

The parting gates revealed a party of goborrin soldiers led by a broken-born man in gleaming armor with his hands clasped behind his back.

He smiled, and her heart sank. "Well met, Your Majesty. We've been waiting for you."

CHAPTER TWENTY-EIGHT

TULA AND ANDRIUN landed on the docks almost in unison, leaving the ship behind them to fend for itself. The admiral shouted orders and men shouted back as they ran across the deck. In the midst of the noise, Daisy howled in distress at being left behind.

Lark saw it all and found herself grateful for the speed at which they responded, yet she could not make herself move.

Maybe she should have run, or retreated to join the Paragons at her back. Instead, all she did was stare down the white-haired man at the front of the unpleasant welcome party.

The goborrins stayed in formation as the gates creaked to a halt. Once they stood wide open, the streets of Amrochan were easily visible. The city was empty, but clean and whole. The tiniest brush of relief tickled against Lark's heart, though she chased it away. It was only a relief because of the lack of destruction. The absence of people was something else entirely.

Only the human officer at the front strode forward, his gait casual as he spread his hands in greeting. He held no weapon, but there was a blade at his hip.

Lark drew her borrowed knife and pointed it at his chest. "Stay where you are."

He halted and raised his hands to show they were empty, putting more distance between them and his weapon. "I mean you no harm. His Imperial Majesty has been eagerly awaiting an opportunity to speak with you. I have been sent to ensure your safe passage through the city. Your escort is more than welcome to accompany us."

Tula posted herself at Lark's side and snorted. "As if you could stop us."

Andriun took up her other flank. Both Paragons were empty-handed, but the air sizzled with the magic they both held ready.

"Forgive me." The man kept his hands up, his demeanor as serene and smooth as his accent. "I did not intend to imply anything of the nature. You are all welcome here as esteemed guests. His Imperial Majesty has been impressed by your determination and it would be my great honor to take you to meet with him. You and any escort you deem necessary." His gaze flicked to the ship as the soldiers onboard worked to bring it into the harbor.

"I'm not here to see Gadranus." Lark kept her blade steady, though everything inside her seemed to shake. "Tell me where my Bladebearer is."

The broken-born officer's cheerful expression faltered, tinged with uncertainty. "Bladebearer?"

"Zaide," Tula added. "Where is he?"

"Oh." The man gestured for them to settle and gave a relieved smile. "Forgive me, I was not here when the Emperor took the city, but I know that name. He is a formidable swordsman, is he not? Your friend is in the palace. I am certain His Imperial Majesty would be glad to let the two of you speak."

Lark did not believe for a moment that he told the truth. "Bring him to me first, and then I'll consider speaking with Gadranus."

He considered her demand for a moment, then inclined his head. "I do not have the authority to fulfill your request, but I will carry it to His Imperial Majesty. Please, wait here." He turned his head and offered quiet instructions to the goborrins behind him. They split out of formation and positioned themselves around the gate, leaving it open, but guarding the way as their leader's brisk strides carried him up the street. His wine red cape fluttered at his back.

The three of them stood in silence as he receded into the distance and then turned the corner.

"I do not like this," Andriun murmured when the man disappeared.

Tula nodded in agreement. "He was too nice."

Lark counted the goborrins. "Fourteen." All of them watching without a sound as they guarded the gate.

The Magister hummed thoughtfully to herself. "If we're welcome, how come they have the gate blocked off?"

"It is not much of a blockade. We could defeat them easily." Andriun studied the path ahead, as if rehearsing which way they would go.

"And do what, fight our way all the way to the palace?" Lark did not scoff, though she felt she might. "And here you said my plan seemed poorly conceived."

Tula lowered her hands. "Well, your plan already failed, so either we think of a new one really fast, or we go with the one where we burn this bacon and head for the castle."

"I do not believe that is where bacon comes from," Andriun said.

"Hush," Lark interjected, silencing them both. From where they were, she could see no sign of goborrins in the city. They had to be there, and in numbers she could not imagine, but the roads were empty enough that it felt like an oversight. The most obvious answer was that they'd set up a trap and were just waiting for her to fall into it, yet what other way was there to get through the city now that they'd already been seen? She crossed her arms and tried to soothe her frustration. "If we wait, the admiral will push us to retreat and give up, but I'm not leaving without Zaide."

"So we go in?" Tula asked.

It was unwise, but when had they done anything wise? Lark kept her voice low when she spoke again. "All right. Here is the new plan. Andriun, you can move between here and the ship more easily, so you'll have to deliver instructions and then rejoin us here. Have the admiral keep soldiers here to hold the docks. Resia stays on the ship. She's more useful there, since her magic is oriented toward healing and defense."

"And we go in?" Tula asked again, more excitedly.

"We go in," Lark agreed.

Andriun backed up a step. "This is not a good idea. I want it to be recorded that I said that as well." He turned to go, but not before Lark could frown at him.

"Didn't you just suggest we could defeat them and gain access to the city?"

"A suggestion is not the same as a plan. It was me thinking out loud. In the future, I will not share my intrusive thoughts." But he grinned as a coil of water rose over the harbor and swept him back toward the ship.

Zaide had rubbed off on all of them, and she was eager to have her party whole again.

Lark sighed and watched as Andriun crossed the water and stumbled onto the deck of the ship they'd only just left. "Wait for him to return, then we'll start."

No response came, and she turned back around. "Tula?"

The Magister remained fixed in place, staring at the goborrins guarding the gate. "Do you think they know we're talking about them?" she asked softly, as if concerned they might hear.

"They're goborrins," Lark murmured back. "I don't think they're that intelligent. I'm not sure they're intelligent at all." They were certainly primitive, though she admitted she knew little about them. They had only discovered the monsters could speak in human tongues once they'd made it to Toren, and even then, she did not know if that was a skill all of them possessed.

Loud protests rose on the ship behind them and this time,

they both turned. It was still too far off for the words to be clear, but Andriun cringed as he climbed and stepped off the railing and drew the water up to meet him. It rushed back to the docks and deposited him mid-stride, as if he'd walked straight from their vessel to the harbor. "Admiral Warinal agrees with me," he announced. "He thinks this is a terrible idea, although he used more words to say it. I do not believe I will repeat some of them."

"All right. Let's go." Lark strode toward the goborrins, all of which peered at her as if unsure why she was moving. She held her knife ready, but that she meant to use it took them far too long to realize.

Tula pitched a fireball at a goborrin in the center and the beast went down squalling.

The rest of the monsters burst into a frenzy and charged, but Andriun snared water in the harbor and sent it surging forward as jagged spears of ice. They whipped past Lark as she met the first of the goborrins with her knife and carved the life from its flesh.

The Paragons to either side of her drove the monsters back, buying space, giving her room to fight. She spun from one goborrin to the next, fueled by frustration and everything she'd lost.

One after another, the monsters fell to flame and ice and the bite of steel, until none were left and she stood panting for breath.

Once, it had seemed impossible to fell so many of the beasts with so few people—never mind so swiftly. How much things had changed since that first expedition to the sleepy temple in Kolmar's forest. They could tear through entire armies now, carve a path through the battlefield and make themselves known.

When the Spectrum Blade was restored, she would make them tremble.

She worked to catch her breath as Andriun snared the dead

goborrins with his magic and let the water pull the bodies into the lake.

"Well." Tula planted her fists against her hips. "That was easier than I expected."

"Don't get too excited. We still have to get to the castle." Lark pointed with her knife. "We can try to take the route I intended, but I fear the two of you are..." She trailed off and gestured at the Magister from head to foot, unsure how to say what she meant without causing offense.

Tula blinked. "Attractive?"

"What? No," Lark protested. That was not what she meant at all.

"I am attractive," Andriun replied cheerfully. "Tula has already said so. It cannot be taken back now."

The Magister's cheeks puffed. "I told you we should have dropped him."

Slapping her forehead would have been unbecoming of a queen, or Lark might have done it. "Just go, and try to stay out of sight. The two of you draw too much attention." There; that was what she'd been trying to say.

Andriun dusted his hands together after he dropped the last goborrin into the water. "In the future, you may wish to consider your traveling companions more carefully if you wish to go unnoticed. I believe Resia is the only one of us who could be considered ordinary."

"Yes, I've noticed." Lark gestured with the knife, then started up the road herself. "There's no easy way past the palace walls, but there is a place where we should be able to climb into the garden where my mother is buried. The mortar between the stones has not been pointed properly in some time."

"I'm surprised you'd climb anything, since you're so scared of heights." Tula trotted along behind her, though she cast one longing look back toward the ship. "Do you think we should have brought Daisy?"

There were few things Lark thought would be less useful

than the dog, but she considered it anyway. It was only fair; one of the less useful things was herself, yet she had deemed herself valuable enough to make the trip, if only because she could lead the way. "No. She should stay with Resia, where it's safe." That was a good enough excuse.

It wasn't as if the dog was trained for tracking, anyway. It was a wonder she was trained at all, given how far into the wilderness they'd been when they found her. It was obvious the dog had wandered far from home and would likely do so again. Keeping her on the ship was the best way to ensure she was still there when Zaide got back.

When Zaide got back. Her heart yearned. They were so close to realizing it, to winning his freedom and restoring their party. She fixed that aching hope in her chest and clung to it as she led the way through the gates and into the city that had been her prison as much as it had been her home.

Tula and Andriun fell in step alongside her, both clinging to magic, ready to fight, but the streets of Amrochan were empty. Occasional parties of goborrins filtered past the end of a street or rounded a corner, but none noticed their presence, and their progress was unimpeded. Lark chose the fastest path she knew. They could skirt the palace once they got close, find their way to the wall and get in that way—as long as the palace was not under heavy guard.

She tried to tell herself it wouldn't be. What need was there for guards when the whole city's population was now nothing but goborrins? She rounded a corner and stumbled to a halt when they came face to face with the broken-born officer who had met them at the docks.

The man blinked at them in surprise. "Oh, you've already... that's... oh, where are your guards?" He leaned to the side to look down the street, as if he expected to see the goborrins there.

"They let us pass," Tula said.

Lark bit her tongue.

"We decided to accept the offer to meet with Gadranus," Andriun added.

She bit harder.

"Oh, well, I am glad to hear that. I was just coming to tell you that you would have to come to the palace to see your friend, but this will make everything easier. Come. I'll take you to see him right away." The man smiled, a warm and genuine expression that almost made Lark feel bad, then turned to beckon them up the road to the main gate.

Lark allowed him a healthy lead before she followed. "You're going to get us killed," she whispered.

Andriun flattened a palm against his chest. "And as it shall be recorded, I said this was a bad idea."

She exhaled hard, not quite a sigh, and tried to sort out what they were supposed to do next.

"Do not sigh at me," Andriun murmured. "We must speak with Gadranus no matter what. We may as well do it now."

"I was thinking more sneaking up on him and getting him to confess wrongdoings at knifepoint," Tula added.

"We don't need him to confess anything," Lark said, irritated. "We already know what he's done." Or at least a fraction of it. She did not think they could fathom all the terrible things he had done in his many lives.

They followed at a sedate pace through front gates that were left open and unguarded. All the while, Lark's heart hammered and she worked to keep her breath even and her demeanor calm. She would not let them see her fear, no matter how certain she was they were now walking straight into a trap.

"Here," their escort announced as he opened the palace doors and motioned for them to enter. The hall beyond was empty.

Lark turned her head to speak, but Tula nodded before she could. Already, the Magister flexed her hands and the dragon marks shimmered on her skin, just visible below the hem of her sleeves. Power brimmed in her, ready to spring forth. Andriun did the same, though his gift left no visible sign he held it, nor did the way he moved betray his preparation.

By now, Warinal would have abandoned the ship and have hundreds of soldiers flowing through the city behind him as he marched to try and save Lark from her folly. Some tiny part of her—the part where fear churned like tumultuous seas—wished she had listened. Yet they were there, standing outside the door to the throne room that should have been hers, all for the rescue of her dearest friend, who she'd grown to fear lost forever.

"Be ready," she told her companions as the broken-born officer opened the door.

The man stepped aside and gestured with an open hand. "His Imperial Majesty awaits."

Lark brushed past them with her borrowed knife still gripped tight.

The once-grand throne room was now all but bare, nothing to see but her father's throne.

There, the dark-haired man she'd come to loathe reclined, and to his right stood Zaide.

CHAPTER TWENTY-NINE

FROM THE FIRST moment everything had gone sideways, Zaide had feared he would never see his friends again. He had operated on that assumption, believing he'd made the right choice by offering himself as a sacrifice for their safety; that whatever happened to him beneath Gadranus's rule, at least he'd made a difference.

Now they stood before him, bold and hale and foolish enough to repeat the same mistakes. Now, of all times. Now that he was so close to what he needed to help bring things to an end.

Now that he was at his worst.

He did not let his fingers tighten on the hilt of the Viper's Tongue, though panic surged in him like a storm. It didn't bring the same comfort the Spectrum Blade always had. Instead, he stared back at the three of them and kept his face a cool mask while he worked to still the dismay and dread their untimely arrival brought. The emotions stirred his borrowed magic, and he did not know how to make it rest.

Emptying his stomach on his boots was the last thing he needed right now.

"Welcome, Dasienna," Gadranus said, his voice booming in

the emptiness of what had once been a grand and beautifully decorated hall. "Queen of what remains of Amroch."

Sweat broke across Zaide's temples and the back of his neck as he tried to ignore the itching cold heat of the power that surged in his limbs. He fixed his eyes on Lark's face, willing her presence—her safety—to fill his mind with peace.

Instead, he saw her shifting confusion, and it only made things worse. Her attention drifted from his wine-colored cape to the armor it covered, to the sword at his side and the emblem on his chest and the insignia of his new rank pinned at his throat. Disappointment, fear, and denial crossed her features in rapid succession.

He was going to be unwell.

Somehow, she tore her gaze away from him to address the man he stood beside. "Gadranus the usurper. I've come for my Bladebearer."

A low sound of amusement rose in Gadranus's throat. "Your Bladebearer? Tell me, girl. Whose blade does he bear?"

Lark hesitated, though she looked again.

The urge to move now, to take advantage of the moment of distraction and strike Gadranus dead surged straight to Zaide's fingertips. He forced himself to remain perfectly still, his hand relaxed against the snake-headed hilt of the sword he now carried.

More than anything, he wanted the man dead. But if Lark stood before them now, they were closer to victory than he'd ever realized. She wanted him defeated, locked away by the power they hadn't yet recovered. Right now, he held the key, yet using it still hovered just beyond his reach.

Why now? The question rose in his thoughts again, stirring his dismay anew. Why when he was so close? When everything she'd ever asked of him hovered just outside his reach? The magic in him lurched like poison and he closed his eyes for half a beat, begging his stomach to settle even as the toxic power bubbled.

When Lark did not reply, Gadranus chuckled. "I had hoped your presence meant you reconsidered my offer. I hold Amrochan, but the Allied Kingdoms elude me. Such an arrogant name your family has given the place. Amroch. As if this seat of power is all that matters here."

She did not rise to the goading. "I did not come for such idle chatter. Release my Bladebearer."

"A bold demand for a girl who has brought nothing with which she may barter."

A faint pink colored Lark's cheeks. "Release him," she repeated. "Then we will discuss your offer."

Gadranus shook his head. "I fear you misunderstand, my dear. Zaide is no prisoner."

A hint of confusion returned in the subtle crease of her brow and her gaze traveled back to him. Searching for an answer, he thought. Some confirmation that the man was a liar, that he was trapped by something other than his own ill-timed and ill-conceived plan to do what he believed he must. "Zaide?" she asked, her voice steady, though the certainty in her eyes was not.

"What do you say?" Gadranus asked. "Do you wish to leave now and rejoin them?"

More than anything. More than words could express. The magic Zaide tried so hard to ignore twisted again and he worked to keep from flinching. As he wrestled with removing the power from his thoughts, he caught the subtle shift in the way the Paragons stood. Did they sense it, the way he now sensed them? Did they feel what he had done? If so, they did nothing to let him know. He tried to put that thought aside as he turned the question Gadranus posed over in his head.

Leave *now*. That word hung over him, a tantalizing escape, and he could not help but wonder if Gadranus had phrased it that way on purpose. There was no way to answer without incriminating himself. If he did not admit to wishing he could escape *now*, the assumption would be that escape would come later. His answer could not be an answer.

Zaide was tired of the games. "I have not completed my training."

A cold smile cracked across the dark-haired man's face. "Then I suppose he stays with me."

There was no way for Zaide to describe the disgust and disappointment that surfaced in his friends, but its arrival made him wish he could sink into the stone beneath his feet and disappear.

Trust me, he begged them silently, knowing they would not hear, not daring to let his wordless plea be seen in any part of him, lest Gadranus see it too.

Beside him, the man slouched in the throne with a dark laugh. His posture was a taunt of its own. "Your demand holds no weight, girl. Now let's discuss mine."

Lark stiffened where she stood. "How dare you sit on that throne and think you can make demands of me?"

"What power do you have to stop me?" The sly smirk Gadranus gave turned Zaide's stomach to ice.

He knew.

He knew who Lark was. What she lacked.

Her eyes widened.

"None," Gadranus added when she offered no reply. "No matter how you try. You can't stand against me, girl. You don't even know how."

She leaned forward as if she meant to take a step, but Tula and Andriun seized her arms and held her in place.

Listen to them, Zaide willed. *Let them keep you safe.*

Slowly, Gadranus drew himself upright. He did look imperious as he sat there, though he wore no crown. His bearing was regal enough on its own. "I believe I had told you my previous offer was the last, but you will find time has gentled me and I am far more forgiving than I once was. So I shall say it once again. Surrender your crown to me now, give me control of the Allied Kingdoms, and we will stop all this petty fighting. Let us end this war as friends. Your people will be safe. All of them." He extended one hand, a gentle invitation.

Not this. Not now. Not when the Spectrum Blade was nowhere to be seen. Zaide gave his head an almost imperceptible shake before he caught himself.

Tula's attention snapped onto him, her stare intense.

"I would sooner die," Lark snapped.

The Paragons who flanked her both winced.

"That can be arranged." Gadranus pushed himself to his feet and flexed his hand, and dark magic surged in Zaide's awareness.

He flinched as his own sliver of power roused in response.

Magic flowed down Gadranus's arm like smoke, wrapping itself around his hand and swarming between his fingers. He curled them into his palm and his sword solidified, as cruel as the man had tried to sound kind.

The Paragons shoved Lark backwards and both of them reached out with magic sparking in their hands.

Zaide bit back an oath.

Tula struck first. Her fireball tore through the smoke-like shadow where Gadranus had just been and she gasped when the shape of him disappeared.

Andriun spun with water coiled around his wrist like a whip. It snapped past the Magister's shoulder as the first hint of darkness shuddered in the air beside her. The shadows peeled back as the water struck and Gadranus spat a curse.

A surge of ugly jealousy heated beneath Zaide's breastbone.

All the weeks of training, struggling, and suffering, and the Paragon of Water was the one to finally land a blow.

"Go!" Tula cried as she urged Lark toward the door. The two of them bolted while Andriun twirled the whip into a rope and struggled to hold their enemy fast.

An anger that was not Zaide's swelled inside him, cold and dark instead of the hot fury he was used to. He leaped from the dais and sprinted after the girls as they ran.

"Seize her!" Gadranus snarled as he flew past the lashing threads of water.

Lark looked back, and the fear gleaming in her eyes stoked the fire of anger to rage.

After everything he'd done, all he had sacrificed for her—his home, his family, his *life*—she dared to look at him with fear? She didn't stop to ask why, didn't give him a chance to explain. Just ran, as if he was her enemy. As if he'd become the monsters he would have to lead.

They stumbled out the throne room's doors at the same time goborrins burst into the hall where Zaide had once waited for an audience with the king. Tula hurled flames at them, then spun to fling some at him, too, but his reflexes had grown faster and he dove beneath their arc.

Fine. Let them be scared. His plan worked better if they stayed away. He seized the Viper's Tongue with his left hand and it sang free of its sheath.

The fear on Lark's face morphed to something new, and the sudden hate that filled her stare raked its claws across his heart.

She went after the goborrins first, diving in with a flash of her blade. The Jadoran knife tore through one of the beasts as Tula struck another, but then the Magister turned and her attention was all on him.

"Don't do this, Zaide," she pleaded. Flame still wreathed her hands, but she held them with her palms out, begging him to stop.

He advanced without a word.

"You can't do this. You're our friend, remember? You're supposed to be our friend!"

Yet they abandoned you so easily, the anger whispered in his thoughts. *Left you here to suffer all you've endured. They're here now because they need you. They can't fix the sword without you.*

His eye twitched and he gave his head a shake. Wasn't that why he'd stayed here in the first place? Why he'd accepted the sword and the training, why he'd asked for the creeping magic that woke inside him now?

More goborrins flowed in through the door. Tula spun to drive them back with more of her flames. She looked back twice, but not at him. Her attention was on the throne room behind him, searching for Andriun when he failed to reappear. Worry and determination mingled at her brow as she hammered the goborrins with fire and Lark whirled in to stab and cut at those who made it through the flames.

Zaide closed the distance between them and caught her arm mid-twirl. She gasped as he wrenched her knife hand behind her back and reeled her in close.

"Lark!" Tula cried, but it was too late to free her. Goborrins swarmed on the Magister and cut her out of view as Zaide pulled the queen out of the fray.

A curve in his sinuous blade fit perfectly against her throat. "Walk."

"Traitor," Lark spat.

"Walk," he ordered again, his voice rough in his throat. The deception pained him just as much as it hurt her, but it was better that way. If she did not know, she would not interrupt him again.

If nobody knew, there would be no one to warn Gadranus the blade was coming.

Lark pressed her shoulders back against him to gain space between her skin and the edge of his blade. Her hand twisted in his grasp and he dug his fingers into her wrist to force her to drop her knife. He couldn't afford to let her take it with her other hand. She'd always been more dexterous than he, nimble with both her fine daggers at the same time.

Even unarmed, she didn't give up fighting. "It's no wonder the blade rejected you," she snapped as he herded her toward a side passage. "It saw through you, didn't you? I can't believe it ever—"

"Shut up," he hissed against her ear.

She swung her head back, aiming for his face with the back of her skull. There was nowhere for him to go, but he turned just enough that she struck the side of his cheekbone instead of his nose. Pain blossomed up the side of his head and radiated down his neck, but it was bearable, and he twirled her away from him before she could land a second blow. The pain stirred the magic and his stomach grew uneasy as the power rippled unbidden along his skin.

"I hate you," she spat as he turned her to face him.

He still used his sword against her throat to steer her backwards, guiding her step by step into one of the empty halls. "You won't."

Just as she drew breath to berate him, the man he'd prayed he might see in that passage arrived at the top of the stairs with a box of empty bottles in his arms.

"Maker's mercy!" Raddan dropped his cargo and the glass rang like warning bells as it shattered on the floor.

Zaide shoved Lark backwards into the medic, his sword still hovering a hair's breadth from her skin. "Go."

"Captain—" Raddan started, but Zaide pushed harder, forcing Lark close against his chest.

"Go," Zaide barked as a wave of nausea swept over him, threatening to bring him to his knees. Something cold licked along the back of his hand and he raised his sword just in time to see the mist-like tendril of magic slide over his skin.

The medic wrapped a hand around Lark's arm and dragged her along with him as he ran.

Shadows stole in around the edges of Zaide's vision and he staggered back against the wall to grip his head. The now-familiar cold sweat traced a path down his spine and he slid to the floor as the power swelled, sickening and exhilarating at the same time.

Faintly, as if the sound were far away, he heard the clatter of his sword as it hit the floor. He reached after it, but his hand closed on darkness instead. Everywhere around him, the shadows loomed—vicious, living things that hissed and tore at the edges of his soul.

Familiar voices brushed against him as if whispers of air on his skin. Something gray stopped before him, crackling with magic, rippling as if his eyes couldn't focus. He raised his head to look at it, but the shadows held him down, turning the words to noise and then venom.

"Lark," he answered, though he didn't know why, and the taste of her name let a sensation like drowning rush into his lungs. He inhaled and found no air and the shadows grew darker still.

Then a hand closed on his shoulder like a vise and the magic retreated like a rush of black butterfly wings, leaving him gasping for breath.

"Zaide," Gadranus prompted as he shook him, his voice thick with concern.

A handful of broken-born officers stood nearby, murmuring between themselves as they pointed or shook their heads. They hadn't been there a moment ago. How long had it been?

The hand on Zaide's shoulder squeezed again, grounding him in the moment as his heartbeat settled and the weight of invisible water left his lungs.

"I couldn't—" he found himself saying as sweat dripped from his scarred eyebrow and stung his eye. "The magic—"

"I know," Gadranus said before he could finish, soft and understanding. "It's taken to you better than I expected. It seems we've overlooked those lessons for too long."

Zaide's throat was so dry he could scarcely swallow. "Lark?"

"Gone." A grim set took the emperor's mouth. "But don't worry. You'll have another chance."

Relief let Zaide's shoulders sag and he was grateful it looked like defeat.

They hadn't found her, then.

He did not know what had become of Tula or Andriun, but if nothing else, Lark got out.

CHAPTER THIRTY

LARK DID NOT KNOW whether to follow or fight the man who dragged her through the hallways, though from how hard he gripped her arm, she doubted she stood much of a chance. She should have tried to get her knife from the floor before she was forced to stumble along behind him.

He pulled her down a narrow hall she knew led to the kitchens and for the first time, she realized he meant for them to escape.

"Who are you?" She thought she recognized him, but she'd met and dealt with so many soldiers since her expedition in the spring that their faces had begun to blur together in her mind. That he wore one of the dark uniforms all the human members of Gadranus's military sported only muddied things worse.

"Lieutenant-Medic Raddan, Majesty. We met once before. This way." He pulled her past a dozen startled members of the palace staff, all of them both human and familiar. They gaped as he hurried her through the kitchen and straight out the back door.

Lark remembered now. He'd been in the party that escorted Resia back to Kolmar after Zaide made his first trip to

Amrochan. The thought of *him* filled her with a tangle of confusion and anger.

He'd betrayed them all. Joined Gadranus and held a blade to her throat. And then he'd shoved her into the arms of one of her father's officers, a man who had aided her cause before. She looked back, half expecting Zaide to be right on her heels, but there was no one there. Not even a goborrin.

"This way," Raddan said again. He guided her through the vegetable patch and around the corner into a maze of flowers.

Lark knew the way from there, and the fact the lieutenant knew it too left her unsettled. "Over the wall?"

"It's the fastest way out. It's the way most of us have gone."

"Most of you?"

"The soldiers he's got imprisoned." Raddan didn't need to specify who *he* was; the belief that speaking the enemy's name would draw his attention was an old one, and one Lark regretted they had abandoned. "We can't go all at once, or they'll find out."

She darted around a corner and under a branch. The roses had not been tended for weeks and the tallest of them had outgrown its place. "How are you getting out?" He didn't exactly look like he belonged in that uniform, so it wasn't as if he was trying to sneak his way around the palace.

He started to speak, then shook his head and motioned for her to keep going. Elsewhere in the garden, hurried footsteps clattered against the stone walkway.

Silence was probably wiser. There was no way of knowing who could have been listening.

Lark shut her mouth tight and ran for the wall. Scaling it would leave them exposed, but what choice was there? It was better than trying to run out the front gate. It hadn't been guarded, but the goborrins were fast to appear the moment there was trouble.

At the foot of the wall, Raddan laced his fingers together and propped them against his knee as a foothold. "Up you go."

She planted her boot in his grasp and as he hoisted her as high as he could reach, she found herself grateful she'd been afforded the chance to find pants again. Her fingers dug into the shallow gaps between the stones and she worked her way up. The path between the prison and the kitchen was relatively unimpeded, one of the reasons she'd intended to enter that way. What she would have done when she'd gotten there and found Zaide wasn't in the prison, she didn't know.

The sound of footsteps behind them came faster.

Raddan almost cursed and only bit back the word at the last second. He turned with his hand on his sword, but the figure that emerged from the rose maze was not an enemy.

"Tula!" Lark gasped.

"Go, go!" The Magister waved for her to move. Her arms were bare to the shoulder, the shimmering lines of the dragon's gift glowing hot under her skin. "Climb faster, they're coming!"

Lark hurried to the top of the wall and looked out across the garden. Half a dozen goborrins crashed through the bushes instead of rounding the curves and corners of the maze, ignoring the way the thorns tore at their flesh. She leaned down to offer a hand. Raddan gave Tula a boost, too, and the height was just enough for her to reach.

The moment Tula's fingers wrapped around her wrist, Lark gripped her, heaved back with all her might, and pulled her friend to the wide top of the wall.

"Down the other side, quickly!" The lieutenant had already started his climb.

The two of them crawled to the other edge and Lark swung a leg down first. "Where is your coat?"

"Keep going." Tula waved her hands as if that might rush her to the bottom.

"Where is Andriun?" Lark asked a moment later. Between him and the Magister's coat, he was probably more important.

"I don't know. Keep going!" Tula almost planted a boot in her face in her rush to descend, and Lark chose to focus on her climb.

Raddan followed a moment later. "We have to get out of here."

"To the docks," Lark said. "If we can make it there, the ship —" She cut off with a shriek as something seized her leg and pulled her off the wall. A moment later, she landed in blue arms.

"Sorry," Andriun said as he turned her upright. Coils of water plucked the Magister and the lieutenant off the wall next, depositing them more gracefully on the ground.

"How come I don't get dropped into your arms like some kind of romantic rescue?" Tula whined.

"Oh, excuse me. I did not think you would want to smell like fish." He motioned for the three of them to follow. "Hurry. They will be coming."

Lark resisted the urge to call out the understatement. The city echoed with alerts and warning calls as they sprinted down an alley and wove their way back toward the city. "How did you get out?" And ahead of them, no less.

Andriun hesitated. "Are you going to accuse me of being cowardly if I say I ran for my life as soon as Gadranus was distracted?"

The last she had seen, they'd just started the sort of combat that could easily result in death. "What distracted him?"

Again, he hesitated. But this time his lips pressed tight and he said nothing.

The tiniest tendril of fear coiled itself around her heart, but it withered a moment later when the reality of his words sank in. "You ran away without helping the rest of us?"

"Of course not. I am just better at jumping than her and made it over the wall faster." He made a soft, floating motion with his hands and a strand of water drew itself together beneath his hands, then fell to the pavement with a rough spatter.

Raddan motioned for them to halt. Everyone stopped and the lieutenant slipped around the corner without a word to scout ahead. The streets were wider here, with fewer places to hide. At least his uniform let him blend in.

Once he indicated the way was clear, Tula spoke. "How did he get away?" She nodded after the lieutenant, then shot Lark a suspicious look. "How did *you* get away? By the time I caught up with you, Zaide was on the floor looking like you kicked him in the bits."

Lark blinked. "What?"

"You know, when you..." The Magister swung a boot up high enough to illustrate her meaning.

"She knows what it means," Andriun interrupted crossly.

"He told us to get out," Raddan said, troubled. He'd stayed so quiet through their banter that both Paragons looked at him in surprise. "He's been getting all of us out, one at a time."

"Oh." Tula grimaced, exposing gritted teeth. "Wasn't very nice of you to kick him, then."

"Nobody kicked him." But Lark had called him a traitor. She measured that against what he'd done to aid Raddan and the other soldiers—to aid *her*—and struggled beneath the weight of guilt.

Tula pursed her lips. "I may have kicked him on my way out. A little."

"Tula!" Lark cried, scandalized.

"What? He was kidnapping you, like some kind of..." The Magister trailed off, as if the words she'd chosen didn't seem right now that they tried to leave her tongue. "Some kind of villain."

The assessment wasn't wrong, though Lark did not appreciate the observation at all. "And you just kicked him? And left him there?"

"What else was I supposed to do?" Tula protested. "I was being chased by a bunch of goborrins."

Lark turned to Andriun next. "You left him there?"

He grew solemn. "I can explain my decision, though I suspect it will—"

A goborrin's bellow cut him short. The monster's spear drove straight for his head as the rest of the brutes poured out from the side street.

Andriun ducked sideways and summoned a jagged pole of ice into his hand. It shattered when he drove its sharp end into the goborrin's chest and he slid back to create another.

Tula leaped past him to assault another monster with a gout of flames.

"Hey!" he protested when the heat turned the ice in his hands slick.

Raddan, too, sprang in to greet the beasts in combat. His sword swept upward to defend against an overhead strike and behind the clash of steel and the whirling magic, Lark shrank back.

The band was small, maybe half a dozen, but the number changed nothing. Without her knife, she could do nothing to help.

She should have brought the sword.

Tula pushed forward and threw flames straight into a goborrin's face, and Raddan struck it down while it cried. Between them, Andriun honed another spear of ice.

Lark winced and looked away as he plunged it at the last monster's throat. The longer they fought, the less palatable she found the war.

Andriun panted and swept a loose strand of hair back from his face. "I wish I had seen my trident when we were in the palace. It is difficult to fight with magic alone."

Somehow, Lark had failed to realize he no longer carried it. Shame at her lack of attentiveness heated her cheeks. Shame at their failure to retrieve another thing from the palace made her wish she could disappear.

He did not seem to notice her discomfort. "This is a poor place to discuss what has happened in the palace, but yes. I left him behind. Let us get to the ship and I will explain there. Believe me when I say it was a choice not lightly made."

Nor did Lark believe it was, but they were near enough to the harbor that she could bear to wait for the story.

Raddan marched them onward at a steady pace and soon, the harbor gates came into view. Just beyond, dozens of Amrochan soldiers lined the docks.

"Back on the boat," Lark shouted as she trotted ahead. The gangplank was down and more soldiers had been on their way across it to assemble, but now they stopped and appeared unsure what they were supposed to do.

Tula gave her arms a broad wave and let fire lash upward from her fingertips, demanding their attention. "Board and sail!" she bellowed. "We're getting out of here!"

The mess of soldiers parted to let Lark and the Paragons through. Raddan walked at their heels, and a handful of men greeted him with wonder and surprise.

Warinal met them the moment they set foot on the deck. "I told you this was foolish," he groused as he directed men back onto the ship with a few gestures Lark didn't understand. He surveyed their party, then looked back at the harbor, his face grim. "Where is the boy?"

A question she desperately wished not to answer. "Set sail the moment everyone is on board."

The admiral pinned her with a hard look. "Where?"

She stared back, hoping her eyes were as cold as she felt. "He won't be joining us."

For a long moment, he said nothing. Then his attention slid to Raddan. "Who is this?"

The lieutenant snapped to attention. "Lieutenant-Medic Raddan, Admiral, at your service."

"My service?" Warinal scoffed. "Not in that uniform." His lip curled with disgust as he inspected it again.

Lark bristled at his tone. "Lieutenant Raddan has been assisting imprisoned soldiers in escaping from Amrochan. As he assisted us in escaping."

"You're out of regulation, Lieutenant," Warinal said, as if she hadn't spoken at all. "Go change."

Raddan responded with a stiff salute and hurried off to find the way to the hold down below.

If Lark had been a cat, her irritation would have stood every inch of her fur on end. "I assumed from the way I just told you he aided me that you would welcome him with a little more gratitude."

The admiral scoffed again. "Should I be expressing gratitude for the enemy army in the harbor as well? For the ships coming in from three different directions? Forgive me if I'm short on gratitude after the trouble you've gotten us into."

Tula stepped forward, her green eyes flashing with her inner fire. If they weren't mindful, she'd have a handful of outer fire to go with it soon. "How dare you speak to your queen that way?"

"I'll speak to her how she deserves after pulling me and my men into this mess," Warinal snapped back.

The dragon marks on the Magister's arms shimmered a little brighter, but before she could summon flames or let her temper loose, a soldier with a spyglass stepped between the two of them.

"Admiral," the soldier said as he gave a quick salute with his free hand, "the ships that noticed us have all passed the harbor. There's a blockade forming at the mouth of the northern river. We won't be able to depart in that direction."

Warinal turned a cold and vindicated smile Lark's way. "Imagine that. Now, if you'll excuse me, Your Majesty, I have to figure out how to undo this disaster without getting everyone killed."

"We'll go east," Lark said calmly. "To the channel that leads through the Shattered Lands."

"That's not your call to make."

Annoyance flared behind her temples. "I am your queen."

"And I am the one who knows how to sail," the admiral replied flatly. "Now get out of my way."

Even Andriun leaned closer, unable to contain his irritation.

Lark put out an arm to block him. "Don't let him distract you from what we've started. We need to tell Resia what happened."

A task none of them wanted, judging by the way Andriun's head bowed and Tula's shining marks of power flickered out. Lark had no desire to carry the news, either, but it could not be avoided. She herded the Paragons toward the hatch that led into the hold, though she paused by Warinal's side to give him a frosty sidewise glance. "I will speak with you later. For now, we sail east."

The admiral pretended to ignore her, but she caught the subtle flex of a muscle in his cheek.

Resia met them at the bottom of the ladder. She watched as they descended one by one, and when no one followed Andriun, her hands drifted together in front of her ribs. Her thumb rubbed over the knuckles of her other hand. "Where's Zaide?"

"He..." Lark didn't know what to say. "He stayed behind."

The worry in Resia's eyes grew deeper, her shoulders tense with the question she didn't want to ask.

Lark could think of no way to answer.

Hurried footsteps thudded on the deck above as the soldiers rushed to board the ship and prepare to set sail. There would be more goborrins after them soon, and if the ship was still sitting in the harbor, their aversion to water would be no help. Raddan had vanished—to change into proper Amrochan armor as directed, she was sure—but there was nowhere for the rest of them to go to avoid all that had gone wrong.

Finally, Andriun released a long sigh. "I know what you have said, that he has aided the soldiers imprisoned there, and I believe it." He caught and held Lark's gaze, his dark eyes earnest but his expression guarded. "But you asked what distracted Gadranus, and he is the answer. It was Zaide, and I know Tula must have felt it, too."

"Felt what?" Tula asked slowly, though Lark suspected she

already knew. She was never so trepidatious regarding the unknown.

Beside her, Resia worried her hands some more.

Andriun bowed his head. "I promised I would tell you why I did not aid him, but it is not easy to say. I do not know what he has done, nor will I pretend to understand why. But what I felt in him is something I have felt before, and hoped I would never encounter again."

"What?" Lark struggled to hold in her desperation. Between the power wielded by the Paragons and the immense force their enemy held, she had struggled to detect anything at all. "Felt where?"

"The corruption of Gadranus." The Shaman squeezed his eyes shut as if to seal in the pain. "The same shadow that took my father."

CHAPTER THIRTY-ONE

"THEY WILL GO EAST." Gadranus circled the table, studying the map as he took each slow, sideways step. "There are no other options. There are no small settlements between cities here, as there are in the Conquered Lands, so there will be nowhere else for them to make landfall."

Zaide listened, but only halfway. His hazy thoughts hung on the name of what should have been his homeland, so different in tone and meaning and yet all the same in the end. Shattered. Conquered. What would his home be when the war ended?

Gadranus grew still. "Do you disagree?"

For an instant, Zaide thought he was asking about his thoughts. Then the absurdity of that caught up with him and he shook his head. "No, sir."

The man's shrewd gaze landed on him and sat there like a weight. "You are unwell again."

Again was an odd way to put it. Zaide had been unwell through every miserable hour since Lark's escape. Every moment had become a war with the blackened magic he'd asked for, robbing him of rest and nourishment and clear-headed thought. He swallowed against bile in his throat a thousand times over and wondered just as often whether he'd been given power or poison.

"I'm fine." A bead of sweat traced a line down his temple as he voiced the lie.

Undeceived, Gadranus frowned. "I had hoped you would recover swiftly, so that we could begin our work while you were at full strength. I see we shall not be afforded that luxury."

Zaide tried to ignore the commentary. He leaned against the map table for support and pointed out the tiny pewter ship on the center of Lake Sian. "It won't take them long to reach the eastern tail."

"You are likely right. I have forgotten to account for the tools they carry." Gadranus planted a finger against the map, right behind the little marker. It slid smoothly toward the end of the lake when he pushed.

Whether the tools he meant were the artifacts or people, Zaide didn't know. He tried to search the map for some clue as to where they find refuge, but his eyes would not focus.

Nor would the borrowed magic settle. It ripped at him as if it were alive, and for an instant, he wondered if the beast it was might swallow him whole.

"Zaide."

He lifted his head, but his eyes would not focus on Gadranus, either. Spots of shadow swam in his vision and crackled like magic.

No; it wasn't like magic, it *was* magic, crawling across his skin like insects. He tried to swipe it away and it tingled against his hands the way the Spectrum Blade always had.

The next thing he knew, there were hands on his shoulders, guiding him to the comfortable sitting area they'd come to use for so many lessons on tactics and history. Gadranus helped him settle, then pressed a cup into his hands. It was warm, soothing, and Zaide's fingers closed on it out of reflex. Had he seen the man brew it? He could no longer recall, nor could he remember how long it had been since the illness came upon him. Had it been hours since Lark escaped? Days? Had he slept or eaten? His hands shook and he squinted at the warm brown liquid in his cup.

"Spiced tea. It will help." Gadranus sat across from him, but he took no tea of his own. "Drink. Then we will begin."

Zaide had no desire to drink. He didn't trust it, nor did he believe he could keep it down. Yet the next moment, he found himself with the teacup against his lips and the liquid flowing down his throat. His stomach did not protest. Neither did the magic. When the last drop was gone, he didn't know what to do with the cup, but Gadranus did not try to fill it again.

Instead, the man leaned forward to rest his elbows on his knees. "I am not fond of repeating myself, so listen well."

Had he felt any better, Zaide might have been excited. This was everything he'd hoped for—the last piece of what they were missing to do what their predecessors had failed to achieve.

"The first lesson is simple," Gadranus said. "You cannot grasp it. You cannot hold it. This magic will not answer to you."

"It answers to you." Zaide's voice came out rough, for all that he'd just downed a whole cup of tea in a few swallows.

"It does not. It answers to no one. But in its permanence, we can touch it, and we can channel it. This is how it differs from other magic." A grim smile tugged at the corners of the emperor's mouth. "This darkness has existed far longer than our world, and it will outlast us all. It is, it has been, and it will be. Such is the simple state of things. For what was there before all time began with the advent of light and darkness? Nothing. There was nothing, and it is beyond what you or I or any mortal man can fathom. This power, this balance between the dark and the light, is all we can hope to understand."

"And channel." Zaide was not sure he would have understood on the best of days, yet he was at his worst. "That— directing it—that's what keeps it from tearing you apart?"

Gadranus shrugged. "Perhaps. Or perhaps I am so intimately

connected to the darkness now that I cannot fathom existing without it."

"Darkness," Zaide repeated. The word stirred something at the edge of memory, but he could not recall who had said it, or if it had been said to him or someone else. He strained to pull the thought into focus, but the magic wouldn't allow it. Someone, some time, had said there was no need for a Paragon of Darkness, for it was something that had always been. Had that been the Oracle? Andriun? He could not say. "What about shadow? It's not the same."

"It is not," Gadranus agreed. "It is a third thing. The simplest concept, yet the hardest to understand. There is light, and there is dark, but shadow is the harmony between the two. It is more akin to the elements, yet nothing like them at all. The light fractures into all these other harmonies, and each aligns itself somewhere between us, but none so perfectly as shadow. For while it is of darkness, it is not simply darkness. An absence of light in varying degrees. A counterbalance to remind the light to know its place."

"And in an absence of light, this is all that's left?" Zaide grimaced as his stomach heaved. Perhaps the tea had not quelled it after all. He fought to keep his voice steady. "A shadow so deep, it consumes everything?" Was that where they had gone wrong? Why Gadranus had grown so powerful? In the absence of Lark's power, the shadow's depths had grown beyond imagination.

Gadranus leaned forward to refill the teacup. Somehow, it had moved from Zaide's hands to the low table that sat between the two of them. "No."

"Then what is it?" Zaide's hands shook when he took the cup again. This time, he could not force himself to raise it to his mouth, but the heat in the porcelain was grounding.

A chuckle welled in Gadranus's throat. "Here we have the truth of the matter, don't we? This, what we now share, is older. Ancient. Far beyond the gifts I was given, which were only the gateway to the unfathomable power of everything that lay beyond."

The formal, poetic way the man spoke was enough to make Zaide's head ache. "I don't understand."

"The power to break a world or to shape it in your hand. To move unfettered by what others see as real. Haven't you wondered why it makes you ill? Why your dreams feel as if you're being pulled apart?"

No matter how Zaide had tried, he'd never come up with a more accurate description. It was always shadows crawling, seeping through him, digging into his skin and tearing at his sense of self. A cold darkness that threatened to devour him, no matter how he struggled against it in his waking hours. "How do you stand it?" he whispered hoarsely.

"Because I am of it, now. That is what I touched unbidden. What condemned me. It is where I exist when my spirit is sealed. Where I come from, when it is time for the Rise. Where the all-consuming dark reigned before the light broke it into shadows. Where I walk, and where you, too, will learn to tread."

If he could. Right now, Zaide did not think he could do so much as stand. "That's what you hold? An unbroken darkness?"

"Don't you see, boy? What we hold is more than mere darkness." Gadranus leaned forward and curled his hand into a fist. "It is the *void*."

CHAPTER THIRTY-TWO

EVERYONE WATCHED in silence as Andriun pushed the narrow ship back into the lake. Its sails hung limp until the water turned beneath it and the boat rotated. Then the wind caught and the empty vessel glided off on its own.

For a long time, the soldiers stood and watched it skim across the waves. Lark watched, too, silent and defeated. Letting the ship drift was like letting go of her last tether to hope, and all that remained of what she'd set out to do was a broken party and a powerless sword.

Daisy nudged her hand and she pulled it away. She didn't want the dog's comfort. She didn't even want to look at the animal. When she didn't react or offer attention, the dog nosed at Tula instead.

Admiral Warinal gazed across the water until the ship was all but gone. "That's the third time I've lost a good ship to your folly. You'd best pray that it's the last."

Lark did not have the energy to rebuke him. She adjusted the bag slung over her shoulder and turned toward the muddy forest.

The leaves were gone, the trees barren, and their branches clawed the sky like hands that begged for mercy. Lark's shoulders hunched and she stared at her boots as wet leaves and clumps of mud collected at her toes. She was tired of pleading. Every cry for help had gone unanswered and she did not know how much farther she could sink.

One by one, the soldiers turned to file after her. Tula and Andriun hung close and the admiral was somewhere farther behind, but Resia took up the back of the party and shifted the plants and the earth itself to help hide signs of their passage.

Lark looked back now and then, puzzled over what the Kolmari girl was doing, and decided that although she had spent much of her life dedicated to studying, she still understood little of how magic worked.

"How does she do that?" she asked, though she wasn't sure which of the two Paragons beside her might answer.

They both looked, but Tula replied first. "Do what?"

"Manipulate the forest." Lark watched as trees shifted, closing the trail behind them until no one would ever know a small army had passed. "I know she is the Kolmari Elder, but I don't understand what Resia is Paragon of. She seems to have gifts with the trees and plants and even the earth, but the Hymnflute is tied to wind, and she has a gift with healing, too. I have thought of her as the Paragon of Forest, because I don't know what else to call it, but if she is the Paragon of Wind, how can she do such things?"

"The spectrum of magic," Andriun said simply.

More frustrating concepts Lark did not understand. On paper, in the books stacked in the palace library, it had seemed simple: magic divided itself into elements. Yet she was meant to be Paragon of Light, and light was not one of them. Nor was shadow. Both were far less tangible than what the others could do, yet what they did was beyond what her studies explained. How was she to understand her own gifts if she could not understand theirs? "Where is she on this spectrum, then?"

"Right in the middle." Tula made a chopping motion. "I'm

closer to you. Andriun is closer to... uh, the side far away from you. And Resia is in the middle."

"And that's what? Wind? Plants?" Lark waved a hand at the forest.

"That may be an oversimplification," Andriun said. "Do not think of it as simply wind. It is the breath of life. The point where all else converges into the perfect balance that is needed for life to be. That is why living things answer to her."

That, she understood. Lark considered it for a time, then sighed. "You're a good teacher, Andriun. You should be involved with Jadora's educational system."

"Andriun can't be a teacher," Tula declared as firmly as if her opinion was all that counted. Maybe it was. As Magister, she would eventually be in charge of all aspects of the desert city.

He did not appear offended, just confused. "Why not?"

"You don't even wear spectacles." Tula's fingers bent to rings and she held them up to her eyes. "You can't be a teacher until you're old."

Andriun shrugged. "I am older than you."

"How do you know?"

"That is a secret."

Lark found herself longing for times they had all been together and in better spirits. Their playful bickering had been comical then. Now, it grated on her nerves. She kept the rest of her thoughts to herself and marched onward. The dog trotted ahead.

It was not the first time Lark had crossed through this portion of the forest, yet she was relieved when the mossy roof of the forest's temple came into view at dusk. Her fingertips brushed the Spectrum Blade, back at her side where it belonged, but it did not answer. A response was too much to ask.

The temple had changed since their last visit. The space around it was cleaner, all traces of the goborrin encampment gone. Lamps burned in many of the windows and a new stone path had been laid by the front doors, which stood open to welcome the chilly night air.

It did not take long for people to notice them walking along the ridge above the temple. People pointed and shouted, none of the voices afraid; Andriun and Tula were far too recognizable to be seen as trouble here. Most of the Kolmari had spied the Paragons at least once before and they ran to welcome them now. When Resia made her appearance on the ridge, as bedraggled and worn as she was, their excitement only grew.

"At least something has gone right," Resia murmured as she brushed past the others and trudged her way down the slope.

A group of Kolmari greeted them at the bottom. Lark did not catch what was said, but it tempered the excitement on many faces and half the welcome party turned to walk with Resia along the winding path back to Kolmar.

It had been the Elder's suggestion to take refuge in Kolmar and they had approached the forest by ship the same as they had done before, when the group was just Lark and Zaide and Resia, accompanied by a handful of soldiers on a quest to reclaim the temple and the blade.

A trek west from the forest to Tinith had seemed the most obvious solution, and with luck, Gadranus would not devise where they had gone before they had a chance to gain a solid head start. Whether the protective shield anchored in the temple was strong enough to keep whole armies at bay, Lark wasn't sure, but she wasn't willing to test. The Kolmari had been through enough and she would not jeopardize them again. A brief rest in the forest was all she would allow. Then she and the Paragons would venture west with whatever soldiers still wished to follow.

They reached the village well past nightfall. The amount of work that had gone into rebuilding homes was impressive, yet seeing the progress they'd made stirred an ache in Lark's heart, too. Would any of the ills that had befallen the forest have happened if not for her? There was no avoiding the first siege, the one that happened the day of the eclipse, but everything else had been in response to her pursuit of the blade.

People appeared in doorways as they approached, figures silhouetted against the bright lights of their homes. The more people saw them, the more excited voices rose into the night and drew more people to look.

"Resia!" a familiar voice shouted.

Lark had almost placed it when a young man bolted across the grass.

"Aren!" Resia almost shrieked. She threw herself against him in a hug, and they stumbled until they almost fell. The Kolmari Elder lifted her feet as if she planned to go down, but Aren set his feet wide and held her hanging. Daisy bounded forward, barking and leaping around them as if to make herself part of the scene.

"That's Resia's sweetheart," Tula whispered to Andriun indiscreetly, one hand fanned beside her mouth.

"I would have assumed as much, thank you." The Shaman smiled, polite but unimpressed.

A jealous longing and bitter sadness rose beneath Lark's breastbone and she made herself look away. She had observed the closeness between the two during their previous expedition and was not surprised, but the show of affection hurt in ways she hadn't expected.

Aren heaved Resia up until she could plant her feet on the ground again, then he turned to the rest of them. "And—Your Majesty, I never thought I'd see you in Kolmar again. What's happened? Is everything all right?"

So Resia's letter had reached the forest safely. Had it not, none of them would have known Lark now bore the crown.

"I'm afraid not," Lark said. "But I am surprised to see you outside the city. Weren't you with my father's soldiers during the razing of Amrochan?"

Aren let the Elder go and adopted a posture more befitting a trained soldier. "I was. I tried to help hold the palace, but my commanding officer told me to make for the harbor as soon as things turned sour. I told him I would stay, but he said no soldiers had gone with the Kolmari and they would need defense, too."

"Then you have my thanks for defending them so well. It seems the forest is thriving. Perhaps the only part of Amroch that still is." Lark wished she had better news to share, but none of it was good. Armies everywhere, the Allied Kingdoms falling apart, and her without the power to save it.

"Thank you, Your Majesty." He looked at the Spectrum Blade twice, but said nothing of it. Resia must have shared a great deal in her letter.

Lark was exhausted, but she dared not sigh. Instead she tried to look regal and wished she'd had the foresight to pin her crown into her hair instead of leaving it wrapped safely in her bag with the useless artifacts she'd worked so hard to collect. "Is Verlin still Kolmar's acting Elder? I must request hospitality for myself and my men. Just for one night, then we will depart for Tinith, assuming the woods to the west of here are not infested."

"Not with anything but spiders," Aren said. "And yes, Verlin's in charge. Should I fetch him, or...?"

"No need, I'm here," Verlin called as he emerged from a house nearby. He hurried to join them, though he was unable to walk fast. If he'd had a limp before, Lark had never noticed it.

She turned to greet him, though she couldn't make herself smile. "I apologize for our sudden appearance, but there was nowhere else for us to land that might let us slip our enemy's notice."

"You are always welcome here, Your Majesty." He bowed, though stiffly, leaving her to assume their trip back to Kolmar's forest had not been smooth.

Zaide's foster mother appeared in the doorway, too, watching all of them with a hand to her chest. Her head swiveled back and forth, counting those present and then counting again.

Lark knew what she was looking for. She wished to see it,

too, but they had returned with a family member missing. Resia greeted her parents alone, exchanging hugs and murmured words of affection that left Lark hurting in a new way.

She worked to be strong. "I will reward your village for your hospitality as soon as I am able. We will rest here tonight and depart in the morning. I fear we cannot spare more time for a visit."

Verlin waved his hands, dismissing any need for repayment or apology. "Having you here is an honor. We have little in the way of accommodations befitting a queen, but—"

"I have visited Kolmar before and found it perfectly comfortable. I have no complaints against my previous lodgings." Lark had not thought they might be open, but Resia's family had all made an appearance and several of them looked that way. In the midst of all the brightly lit homes, the most familiar cottage sat dark.

"Thank you, Your Majesty. You do us honor with your visit and your kindness." Verlin gave a gentle bow with one hand flat against his chest. "Do you have any specific requests we might fulfill?"

"Settle the soldiers wherever you can and see that everyone is fed." She paused, then turned to address Andriun and Tula, who had positioned themselves close by but remained silent while she spoke to Kolmar's leader. "Help them wherever you can. We'll make for Tinith at dawn, so rest well."

"Of course, Your Majesty." Tula spread her arms wide and would have bowed until her hanging ponytail touched the earth if Andriun hadn't caught the back of her shirt to keep her from going too far.

"Let me see to our Elder and we'll be right on it," Verlin said. "And let me know if there's anything else I can do." He bowed— far more reasonably than Tula—before he headed back to his house, a new sense of duty in his step.

Daisy circled Lark's feet, but she waved her away. The dog answered with a flat whine and trotted after Verlin instead.

Zaide's foster family huddled together at their door with the dog in their midst, cozy and yet incomplete, and both Verlin and Sarma leaned close as their daughter shared the news that was not Lark's to tell.

Lark wasn't close enough to hear the words Resia shared, but she knew what they were from the answering cry of grief. She put her head down and trudged across the village alone, seeking the one space she knew that was both familiar and private. She lifted the door on its crooked hinges to draw it open and then shut herself inside Zaide's empty cottage without so much as a candle to light the dark.

Everything they did went in circles. An endless cycle of trying and failing without ever getting closer, yet each time they went around, something else was lost.

The blade's power. The Captured Spring. Her father's life. Zaide. She sat in the center of the floor, planted the Spectrum Blade's sheath against the uneven stones, and rested her brow against the hilt.

The floor was clean, the hearth was cold, and the sound of Sarma's sobs still reached Lark's ears.

CHAPTER THIRTY-THREE

For days, Zaide did nothing but train with Gadranus. From sunrise until long after sunset, they practiced swordplay and studied maps, discussed tactics and strategies used in countless battles, and worked to calm the seething shadow that thrummed within his blood.

It could not be seized or controlled, but it could be touched and directed with subtle suggestion. More importantly, it could be cooperated with, and Zaide found that when he simply did as the void asked him to do, it was more likely to respond in kind.

When it clawed at his mind, he let it in, allowed it to swallow his thoughts until he operated on instinct. When it surged along his arms and down his fingertips, he let it flow until waves of its frigid power drifted down his sword in the same smoke-black tendrils Gadranus wielded.

The closer to its edge he came, the harder the magic pulled, yet the man he'd sworn he would kill was always there to pull him back and keep him from losing himself.

Their sword fights grew faster with the magic involved. It snared them both as they fought and drew them together like magnets. It fueled Zaide's strength, fed him power and endurance like nothing he'd ever known, whispered promises of violence and death that even his darkest dreams did not hold.

And then his blade made contact.

Gadranus sucked in a breath and stepped back, shaking his hand. Crimson droplets spattered the dry earth and for a moment, he looked at his fingers in disbelief. "You've cut me."

Zaide drew back and fell into the now-comfortable stance he'd created for himself, halfway between the indifferent way Gadranus approached battle and the way he had, when their training first began. His posture was cautious, but more importantly, it was patient.

For all that he longed to do worse than shave skin off the man's knuckles, he was no longer in a hurry.

He would kill Gadranus. That fate was as inevitable as his own death.

The man regarded him with a placid, thoughtful stare, then inclined his head and released his shadowy blade to the void from where he'd drawn it. "I believe you are ready for the next step."

Zaide hungered for it. The magic hungered, too; it bubbled and swelled at the notion of drawing Gadranus into its embrace. Zaide let it carry him like a current in the sea, his head just above water. It no longer tried to drag him under. Instead, it tried to lure him in, whispering promises of peace—if only he did what he must and then surrendered.

He could not succumb now.

"What's next?" He was mindful not to let emotion show. The calmer he kept, the calmer the black tide inside him remained.

A cold grin wreathed itself on Gadranus's face. "Follow me. If you can." He stepped backwards and smoky plumes of shadow-filled power wrapped around him. His body melted to mist and he was gone.

Zaide had once wondered how the specter they fought beneath Kolmar's temple had been able to do such a thing. Now, knowing the nature of the magic Gadranus had touched, it was easy to understand. More than shadow. More than darkness. He let his eyes drift closed and whispered his request before he let go.

He plunged backwards into the frigid void, the crushing weight of nothing that had existed before time. It squeezed the air from his lungs and stripped the warmth from his skin, yet it flooded his senses in the most tantalizing way.

Stay, it begged, a whisper in his thoughts that was almost a voice—his own voice, the way it sounded in his head.

Not yet, he whispered back.

He stepped forward and the shadow peeled back, letting the heat of being strike him like the flames of a blacksmith's furnace. A shudder coursed down his spine as he emerged in the war room beside the map table.

The laugh Gadranus gave was dark, bitter, yet satisfied in ways Zaide could not describe.

"Magnificent," the man almost purred. "Truly. You are ready."

The cold faded from Zaide in a way that made him wonder that melting ice did not drip from his fingertips. "To take your place?"

"To claim your own." Gadranus slid a hand across the map and left a sword-shaped token on the desert beside Jadora. "Your queen is on her way back to her makeshift kingdom. My armies are on their way to meet her. You will join them. You will lead them."

Zaide stared as he surrounded the sword—the token of *him*—with the ugly pigs that represented goborrins. "You mean to make me a general?"

"What you are becoming has no title, but when I am gone, you may call yourself Gadranus if you wish."

The very idea made Zaide's skin crawl. "What do you expect me to do?"

"Chase Dasienna from her hiding place, like a mouse chased from its hole. Capture her, or kill her. The end is all the same."

Last of all, Gadranus placed a tiny figurine atop Jadora, right where the Magister's palace would be.

A bird.

Zaide's eyes darted to Gadranus's face.

The man stared back. "Will that be a problem?"

This was beyond anything Zaide could have hoped for. Magic to restore the Spectrum Blade. Unfathomable power at his fingertips. The ability to walk among enemy soldiers unfettered. And now Gadranus sent him straight to Lark, where the last piece needed for his demise lay waiting. He looked at that tiny pewter bird again, so like the wooden carving he'd tried to make that now lay abandoned in his room. "No."

"Good." Gadranus crossed to the sitting area and claimed the most comfortable seat, then leaned forward to pour himself a cup of tea from the ever-present serving tray. "Now go."

Zaide said nothing. He did not bow. All he did was step backwards into the void again, and the magic rejoiced with wicked glee.

The return to Jadora should have been triumphant. Lark had envisioned it as a great homecoming, as an event worth fanfare and celebration. She'd pictured herself in her coronation gown again, bestowing honor upon her chosen Bladebearer in a ceremony to honor all he had done for Amroch. He would have worn blue to match, and everyone would have rejoiced to see the Spectrum Blade in his hand again.

Instead, they stole through the gates just before dawn and slinked through the city like dogs with their tails between their legs. All but Daisy; the actual dog trotted along with her curved tail swishing and her tongue lolling from her mouth.

A small retinue of guardswomen escorted them, though the city was quiet and there was little need for protection. The soldiers who had not yet given up walked in two columns behind them, and though they had chosen to continue their service instead of staying behind in Tinith or Addare this time, not one bore any enthusiasm.

Lark could not blame any of them. All things considered, the rescue attempt had gone well; few men had been injured and fewer lost. Admiral Warinal still mourned the loss of the boat he'd acquired for their use, but Lark was the queen; any vessel in Amroch was at her disposal. There would be other boats.

Elsanna greeted them at the doors of the Magister's palace, her hair a mess and her silk dressing gown rumpled. One look at their faces revealed everything she needed to know, for she did not even ask, merely called for the palace staff to prepare their rooms and see that they were fed. There was food in Lark's room by the time she reached it, but she bore no appetite. Instead, she ordered the curtains drawn and clambered into bed with her boots still on, not caring what time it was. She drew the blankets to her chin, curled in on herself, and slept.

She had slept a full day before someone sent Tula to check on her. The Magister peeked into Lark's bedroom with some trepidation, though her own worry must have outweighed her concern about interrupting something. "Lark?" she called softly from the doorway that stood between the queen's parlor and her private bedchamber. "Are you sick? I can call for Resia."

Lark did not want to see either one of them, but of the two, she thought Tula's was the more comfortable presence. She had not been able to bear looking at the Kolmari Elder after the way things had gone wrong.

Zaide was Resia's brother.

It was her fault he'd been lost.

"I'm not sick." Lark pushed herself upright, though she did not want to. It was far preferable to stay in bed and wallow in her failures. "I just don't want to be queen anymore. That's all."

"Oh." Tula's fingertips drummed against the door frame. "Well, I don't really want to be Magister of Jadora, so I guess I understand."

Lark didn't have the energy to snort. All of them bore unfair fates. She fiddled with the edge of her blanket and stared at her fingernails.

When she did not reply, Tula stepped inside. "I think you'd feel better if you had a bath. Can I help you wash your hair?"

"I was under the impression you disliked water," Lark said.

"Hot water is different. It's halfway between my magic and Andriun's, and everyone likes a good cup of tea. Not that you'd be a cup of tea. That is, I'm sure someone would think you're as good as tea, but—"

"All right," Lark interrupted before that subject got any more out of hand. "Draw a bath. I would appreciate the help with my hair."

The faintest smile flickered on Tula's face. Then she hurried into the private bath connected to the bedchamber. There was a large bronze tub there that was always filled with water, but most of the time, it was cool. With the desert's heat, that had been preferable.

Lark dragged herself from the bed and shuffled in to find Tula gripping the edges of the tub and steam already rising from the water.

"Not too hot." Tula dipped a finger into the tub as if to prove it. "No Dasienna tea for breakfast."

"I don't know," Lark mused as she pulled her hair down from its ponytail and shed her boots and clothes. "It might be better if you just go ahead and boil me alive. Maybe the next Paragon of Light will know how to fix things."

"Or maybe you know, and you just haven't figured it out yet." The Magister plucked a half-dozen bottles of who-knew-what out of a basket on the floor.

"That makes absolutely no sense." A single touch of Lark's big toe proved the water was a perfect temperature. She climbed in and slid down until her chin touched the water and her golden hair floated on the surface.

There was a pitcher on the washstand Lark had used every

day leading up to her coronation. Tula retrieved it and scooped water from the surface. "I think you know what I'm trying to say. You're just pretending you don't."

Lark held her breath when her friend doused her, then leaned back so her hair could be tended. Clouds of dust and dirt already swirled in the water, obscuring her skin. She could not debate that, so she didn't try.

"And I think you know what you need to do, too," Tula added, softer.

A moment later, suds rolled down the side of Lark's head as the Magister worked her hair into a lather. She watched them float across the water's surface and imagined they were clouds, that she looked down on the world and all its problems with some great perspective.

It told her nothing.

When she didn't speak, Tula went on. "You've always been good at figuring things out. Even when everything is stacked up against you. You never give up."

"I want to," Lark whispered. "I don't think I can win this."

"Of course you can. You're already winning, aren't you?"

Nothing could be farther from the truth. "I've lost everything that matters to me. He'll never stop hunting me." In what world was that winning? Certainly not Lark's.

"But he can't chase you forever. Eventually, he'll get old and wrinkly and he'll be hobbling around on a cane and there's no way he'll be able to beat us then." Tula sounded so sure. So confident.

Lark's shoulders curled forward and she hunched until her mouth was just beneath the water's surface. She blew bubbles and scowled as they pinged against her nose.

"All right, so maybe that's not the best idea I ever had. I guess we'd all be tired if we had to keep running for our lives and commanding wars for 50 more years before we can see him tip over and die like a regular old person." Tula kept scrubbing. The number of suds grew.

The piles of foam drifted toward Lark's knees and clustered where they protruded from the water, the bubbles like white surf against island shores. Lark stared at them for a long time before she lifted her chin from the water. "I need to leave."

Tula's hands grew still. "What?"

"You said I know what I need to do. I need to leave." Lark brushed the foam away from her kneecaps and let her legs dip beneath the water. "As long as I'm in Jadora, I'm a danger to the city. He's going to keep hunting me for as long as he draws breath. So if I'm going to keep my people safe, I need to go somewhere else."

The Magister rinsed her hands, then scooped up another pitcher full of water to dump over Lark's head. She upended it so fast, it splashed everywhere. "All right, so where are we going?"

Lark wiped her face hard to remove water and opened her mouth to speak. A second pitcher full of water poured over the top of her head, leaving her sputtering. She wiped her mouth with the back of one wet hand and found it only marginally better. "*We* aren't going anywhere. Jadora needs you here to protect it. I'm going to Sast."

"By yourself?" Tula crouched beside the tub and crossed her arms on its rim.

"I don't think I'll be found easily there. I'll have Andriun help me across the water, and then..." Lark did not know what came after that. It was more running. More hiding. But if it kept Gadranus hunting instead of drawing all his attention down on her people, it would be worth it. She'd have to figure out how to orchestrate military movements and coordinate with the Paragons, but it would keep them safe. There was little else she could do.

Tula's eyes softened with sympathy. "There's nobody in Sast but the monks who protect the walls. Don't you think you'd be lonely? You should have someone with you."

"I'll take Daisy," Lark said, though the idea of having the dog as her only company was the most miserable punishment she could imagine.

"Or maybe you should stay here. Jadora is a strong city. We can hold off goborrins for a long time, now that all the holes are plugged. We have a dragon here and everything. Sast doesn't have any dragons, and they don't have an underground supply river full of good-looking fish people, either. They get their supplies from Estkel, across the bridge. And it's a really long bridge." Tula walked her fingers along the edge of the tub.

"And I'm just one person. I don't need a whole army's worth of supplies there with me. Or any Paragons. The lot of you are more useful if you stay here and protect this city until they figure out I'm not here." The idea of leaving made Lark's throat tighten, but she did not know what else to do.

Tula shook her head. "I don't think this is your best idea. This isn't like a bad Zaide plan, it's just a regular bad plan. What difference is it going to make if you're here or somewhere else? He's going to attack every city. You know that."

Yet if Lark stayed in the heart of the war, she could not fulfill her role. She needed more time, and where else could she find it? The month they'd spent in Nimultis had not been enough to uncover her power, but if she found somewhere to hide and focus on her magic instead of the war, perhaps things would be different. "But it will distract him for a while. You won't have his full attention. And while he's looking for me, I can try to fix the blade. You, Resia, and Andriun have already done your parts. My part is all that's left, and I can do that alone." If she could figure out how. The unlikeliness of that tore at her, but she tried to ignore it and convince herself this was the best strategy. "The rest of you can manage armies without me. You'll have Elsanna and General Jobe to help."

"And Admiral Warinal?" The scrunch of Tula's nose emphasized her displeasure.

Lark sighed and slumped in the bath. "I'd prefer not to take him with me."

Tula heaved a sigh and seemed about to lodge a complaint, but someone pounding on the door to Lark's quarters forestalled it. She held up a finger, asking to pause the conversation, and hurried out of the bath chamber to see who was there.

In the silence that followed, the fizz of the soap bubbles popping seemed loud. Lark slouched in the tub until the water reached her nose and let her eyes slide shut. The water was warm, comforting, and as the tension seeped out of her body, everything else drew into focus.

Leaving was the right choice. It had to be. She'd go somewhere she had no ties, somewhere her enemy wouldn't suspect, work until she discovered what she was doing wrong, and return triumphant with the Spectrum Blade glowing in her hand.

She raised her arm and curled her fingers as if to hold the blade overhead and had just begun to regain an ounce of confidence when Tula returned. Lark pushed her toes against the end of the tub to thrust herself upright and turned to speak.

The grim look on Tula's face forestalled any conversation.

The Magister shut the door and leaned back against it. "We have a problem."

CHAPTER THIRTY-FOUR

Lark ran. Her tangled hair dripped around her shoulders and down her back, making the fabric of her shirt cling to her skin in the most uncomfortable way. She shrugged and rolled her shoulders, but in the end, she was forced to ignore it.

"Show me," she called as they reached the wall. Already, hundreds of soldiers clustered around the gate, a mix of her army and Elsanna's. The guardswomen, mage-guards and Amrochan soldiers stood straighter as she passed, leaving one of the higher-ranking guardswomen to respond.

"This way, Your Majesty." The woman offered a stiff bow, then led the way into the wide walls of the city.

Lark had been in the questioning rooms before, but the woman led her past them now. Tula trotted along at her heels without a word. They passed the long row of rooms and scaled a staircase hidden behind them. The moment they emerged onto the top of the wall, she shaded her eyes.

The approach of evening had brought cooler winds, but the air was still blistering and the sinking sun burned a hot red in the western sky, directly behind the vast army now marching across the sands.

They covered the desert like a dark blanket and she

despaired at the number. "I don't understand. Where did they come from?"

"We don't know, Your Majesty," the guardswoman said. "They just arrived. There was nothing, and when the guard changed and the new watch looked out to sea, they were coming across the horizon."

There was nothing due west but the ocean. Steep cliffs meant it should have been impossible for the goborrins to scale the western rim of the continent. The other options were slim and few. "Any sign of ships?"

"Nothing, Majesty. It's been days since any vessels tried to enter between the peninsulas."

Which meant they had to have crossed the desert. Lark swiped wet hair away from her face when it stuck to her cheeks and stared down at the ranks of figures below.

The guardswoman watched her face. "What are your orders, Majesty?"

Lark did not know. Jadora's terrain gave them advantages; the narrow road up the plateau made the city's entryway easy to defend, and the enemy's inability to climb or swim meant the only way in or out was through the gates. The tunnels beneath the city led only to water now, and Andriun had already gone to ensure they were empty. If the Paragon of Water could not flush out those tunnels, no one could.

But the same things that made Jadora defensible made it hard to move soldiers outside the city, and she had no wish to send people to be slaughtered.

And it would be a slaughter. She searched the horizon with one hand shading her eyes, yet there was no end to the marching army that worked its way across the sand. It stretched as far as she could see, cresting dunes and creeping forward without cease. The sheer number of goborrins made her quail.

"They'll surround the city," Tula said, breaking the long silence that hung around them. "But as long as the gates hold, they're unlikely to breach it. The walls go right up to the edges of the plateau's cliffs, so it's not like they can chisel through anywhere else. Their focus will be the gates. They may think they can starve us out."

"Assuming they don't know we're using the underground river." Lark wished someone would carry them word from Andriun, but it was too early to hope for that. "Or perhaps they do know, and the station at the end of the river will be under attack as well."

Tula nodded. "We can ask the Desheni for help defending the river entry. The tribes that live out in the ocean have a lot of water mages. Between them and Andriun, our supply line should be safe. Are they called tribes? Have I asked him that?"

Lark almost scoffed. "You're the one writing the book on Desheni history and customs, not me."

"Well, my notes are all back in my room." The Magister pouted, but only for a moment. "I'd say our defenses need to just focus here, but we'll increase patrols along the top of the walls to ensure they don't come at us with any sneaky surprises. They won't be able to climb the cliffs, but they had those bombs before, and if they figure out how to get one to the walls, it could blow another point of entry."

"Having Vorkaris will help with defense, I'm sure." Lark tried to untangle a strand of hair with her fingers, but it was drying fast in the desert's heat and she worried it would mat before she had a chance to brush it.

"He can hold the gates on his own if he has to, but we should see if he has any ideas for how to handle all of that." Tula pointed and swept her finger at the horizon.

Goborrins still emerged from the distance. Lark watched them and tried not to feel helpless. How was she supposed to flee to Sast with so many eyes on her? She glanced back at the city, toward the plaza where the supply well waited. Perhaps she could flee by water. Then again, perhaps they'd be waiting at the mouth of the river. Frustration welled in her until she thought she might cry. "The battle hasn't even begun, and we're already at a stalemate."

Tula stared at the approaching army, a thoughtful frown drawing her brows together. "Maybe that's the point."

"What?"

"Maybe he's not trying to actually take the city or starve us out. Maybe he's trying to trap us here until we lose hope." The Magister patted the pockets of her loose-fitting robe, looking for the notebook she didn't have. She sighed when she found nothing and planted her fists against her hips instead.

Lark studied the monsters below as she puzzled over the suggestion. "I don't see how planning an offense against our morale is supposed to work."

"Because people give up when they're hopeless. He wants you to surrender."

A stubborn anger flared in Lark's chest. She'd had the chance to surrender in the throne room. She had refused it then and she refused it now. Her people needed support, not a leader who gave up the moment she was challenged. "He'll never live to see that happen."

Tula opened her mouth to say something, then seemed to think better of it and shut it again.

In the silence that followed, the guardswoman who had taken them to the top of the wall cleared her throat. "What are our orders, then?"

Lark's cheeks warmed. She had almost forgotten the woman was still standing there, waiting for direction. "Continue defense of the gates. Increase the number of guards patrolling the wall to ensure no goborrins approach from elsewhere. Should any parties be spotted somewhere other than here, notify me, Tula, or Elsanna at once."

"Tula, Your Majesty?" The guardswoman's eyes cut toward the red-haired former librarian with a hint of confusion.

A crinkle pinched one side of Lark's nose. "Of course. She is your—"

The stricken look on Tula's face cut her short.

"—Official Jadoran Ambassador to the Crown of Amroch," Lark finished smoothly. "If I am unavailable for any reason, consider her the next best thing to my own ears."

"Of course, Your Majesty." The guardswoman bowed, accepting Tula's new title without any hint of surprise. Given how much time the two of them spent together, perhaps there was no room for surprise, but the arrangement of treating Elsanna as Magister had grown cumbersome now that they were all in the desert. They would have to address that, but Lark did not know when. She had brought enough trouble to the city already.

"Let me know when they make it up the road." There was little else Lark could do.

Another bow from the guardswoman. "Yes, Majesty."

Lark nodded back, then excused herself to trudge back down the stairs with Tula at her side.

Unwilling as she was to give up, in truth, she held little hope. Jadora was a well-stocked and easily defensible city, and with the help of the Desheni, their supplies would not run dry any time soon. But the army at their doorstep had to be at least fifty thousand strong, and she had come to know the ways of war.

No matter how strong their defenses were, they were only human, and eventually, they would run out of bodies to fuel the fire.

The cadence of the marching was a strange balm to Zaide's aching spirit. It was steady progress, tangible movement, and the one thing he'd always wanted. He'd always envisioned himself as part of an army.

The only difference was he'd always thought he'd be on the other side.

Heavy drumbeats set the pace, the vibrations both energizing and grounding. A gentle coastal wind pulled at his cape and for a moment, he shut his eyes. Swirls of something darker than shadow crept around the insides of his eyelids, begging him to fall into them again, but he ignored them and focused on the sound of the drums and the marching goborrins. The harsh clack of their feet along the rocky coast was different from the sound boots would make, keeping his daydreams from drifting too far from reality.

He couldn't believe he was doing this.

Leading an army.

Leading it against his friends.

He'd spent so many foolish years wishing for an opportunity to march and now that he had it, it was the farthest thing from what he'd wanted.

At least, on the surface, he reminded himself.

No one knew his goal, and as he moved with the goborrins from the coast to the rising dunes, he held it fast and close to his heart. A small confidence that he'd done what he had to. That he'd found his way to fix things. Now all that remained was convincing everyone in the city of Jadora that he led an army of fifty-two thousand goborrins to their doorstep to *help*.

The absurdity struck him hardest of all, and he was the one doing it.

But he held what he needed. Magic and shadows brimmed within him, begging to be released, and Gadranus had set up everything perfectly for him to try this sort of madness.

Gadranus had made the offer more times than what was reasonable. If Lark surrendered, the war would be over without an ounce more violence. He would be crowned emperor of everything, would submit to the endless death he craved, and Zaide would be left to lead the goborrins in his stead. The latter part had never been part of his intentions, but he recognized the need. Without someone on Amroch's side to lead them, the monsters would overrun everything in no time. There would be no end to the violence when

Gadranus died—if anything, the lack of clear direction would make it worse.

Zaide had no desire to rule the beasts, yet if someone had to make that sacrifice, it might as well be him. He'd be accepted more readily through the Shattered Lands due to his Torec heritage. He'd grown competent with the language through his months of imprisonment. It was the one way he could serve indefinitely, and he would embrace it if it meant sparing Lark.

But there was no sparing her feelings.

He did not know how to request an audience without raising suspicion, save to present the opportunity to surrender one last time. His heart begged her to trust him, but all he saw in his mind's eye was the hateful way she'd looked at him as he'd worked to get her out of the palace.

That ill-timed attempt at a rescue left him frustrated beyond measure. If only she'd been a little slower. If only she'd arrived after he'd learned to channel the magic he'd stolen. They could have worked out the plan then; to surrender to Gadranus—or at least pretend to—and replenish the Spectrum Blade to strike him down once he thought he held the world in his hand.

But she'd come early, and without the blade. Zaide despised the situation, but the frustration of a plan gone awry bothered him less than it once had. He had more patience now, a more level head and the strategic skill needed to look ahead to alternatives. Loath as he was to admit it, his time with Gadranus had shaped him for the better.

Now if only Lark would see it that way.

Zaide shut his eyes and tried to focus on the march.

He had positioned himself near the back of the army, either a plan or some delusion of grandeur planting the thought in his head that he would draw more commanding attention that way. They would reach the desert city, the goborrins would arrange themselves in ranks, and then the columns would part to let him proceed alone. He would stride past his army—the army that would soon be his in truth, he reminded himself with uneasy resignation—and make it clear what sort of authority he now held. He would request an audience with Lark once he reached the gates, and then… well, he still didn't know how exactly he was supposed to restore the power in the Spectrum Blade, but that was what the magic was for. It was older, wiser than he, and it did not answer to him.

If he asked it for guidance, the power would grant it.

He only hoped he would be given a chance to speak.

The desert heat bore down on them as they marched and he found himself frustrated with how the goborrins faltered and stumbled in the sand. Their narrow feet were ill-suited to keeping them steady on such unpleasant terrain, slowing their progress to a crawl. But they did make progress. Zaide willed himself not to feel the merciless power of the sun or the sweltering temperature that made his skin slick with sweat beneath his dark armor.

The shadows in his head whispered promises of comfort. Trusting them would have been foolish, but if light was heat, perhaps shadow was the answer. He asked for shade, a silent request to the strange entity that was the magic he held. It considered. Then something collected around him, defying the light and bringing sweet respite. The shadow hung around him in ways that did not make sense, cool and mist-like, though it crackled with power that stung his senses and filled him with the most gratifying sensation at the same time.

Zaide never knew if he was supposed to thank the power. He considered it, but the notion made him uncomfortable, so he did not. If it was offended, it told him nothing.

The fact that it told him anything should have been disturbing.

Hour by hour, the march went on, and he played through the plan in his head again, a dozen times over. There were other broken-born officers with the army, but for this expedition, they answered to him. He would request an audience, ask to speak with

Lark in private. There, he would offer an explanation and propose his plan of using borrowed magic to replenish what the blade had lost. With any sort of fortune at all, Lark would have made progress with her own power. If she was ready, the task should be simple.

The heady magic within him danced at the notion of touching the Spectrum Blade and he tried to take it as a reassurance he was on the right path. He let it flow as it pleased, swirling in the shadows that cloaked him.

And then, at last, the city of Jadora came into view.

Zaide had already given orders to be passed to the goborrins; they knew what to do and the moment he stopped walking, they did it.

The long columns swayed and separated, and the entire vast army parted to create a wide avenue between their ranks. When enough of them had stepped aside, he started forward through the gap.

The setting sun blazed at his back as he walked. Plumes of darkness poured from his body like smoke and cascaded across the sand.

As he moved, the city's lights came to life, illuminating the plateau against the darkening sky.

They would see him coming. It would likely fill them with dread, but the intimidation was important; they had to believe he was there on behalf of Gadranus, the same as what the goborrins believed.

Their drums still throbbed, and now each goborrin matched the sound with the steady stomping of a foot. It sounded as if the whole army still marched along with him, and he wondered at the show.

Was this what the rest of his life would be like? Followed and revered by thousands of those ugly brutes? Zaide almost dared regret he'd left his quiet home in the forest at all.

When he reached the front of the army, a small procession broke away to accompany him and they climbed the long, zigzagging trail to the city's gates with a pair of broken-born and a handful of goborrins at his back.

The number of guards on the walls increased as he approached. More lanterns sparked to life along the fortifications. Zaide willed himself to breathe.

This was his chance, he reminded himself.

One more chance to set things right, carved out of an endless cascade of problems through sheer determination and more sacrifice than he thought he could bear.

There were no guards outside the gates when they arrived, but no fewer than a hundred peered down at them from above.

"State your business," one of the guards called, a man who looked nervous enough that it was a wonder his armor did not rattle.

Zaide lifted his head to search their faces, hoping beyond reason that he might see someone familiar. "I've come to speak with Queen Dasienna." He kept his voice firm and more confident than he felt.

It was not enough to impress.

"Who are you?" a guardswoman demanded.

"Tell her..." Zaide trailed off. What did he call himself? *Bladebearer* had been the first thing to come to mind, but the Spectrum Blade was in her hand, and he dared not say anything that might make his escort question him. When he met with Lark in private, all could be explained, but for now, he still had a part to play. He surveyed the broken-born men to either side, then raised his head to meet the guardswoman's stare.

"Tell her the Hand of Gadranus has arrived."

CHAPTER THIRTY-FIVE

Lark had just finished combing the snarls out of her hair when the messenger arrived. She'd leaped from her chair and almost left, but a nagging uneasiness pulled at the edges of her thoughts until she turned back to retrieve the Spectrum Blade and belt it at her side. Her stomach turned somersaults as she hurried through the palace, but she worked to project an outward sense of calm.

If Gadranus wanted to play at diplomacy, so be it. She would not cooperate with his demands, lest her people suffer for it, but she would not snub an emissary and be seen as petty, either. The thought of how history would remember her had begun to weigh heavily on her mind and as she walked, she worked to shape the image she wanted to offer in her head.

There was no way to know if she would be recalled as the last queen to stand against Gadranus before his armies consumed everything, or if she would be honored as the one who finally ended the Rise. Either one could come to pass, and while she prayed it would not be the former, she would not deny the likelihood of that outcome.

But she could be remembered with honor, even if she lost.

She could be seen as strong and dignified, protective of her people and determined to keep them safe. Perhaps she would be remembered as kind but firm, determined and unrelenting. She'd given up on ever being seen as a hero, but noble was a quality she could still aspire to.

The Paragons waited by the palace doors. They turned to greet her in silence, all of their faces as troubled as she felt. None of the three said a word, but the unspoken question of what they were getting into hung thick on the air, magnified by the way they all noted the blade at her hip.

Lark offered a nod of acknowledgment and nothing else. She continued through the palace doors and into the courtyard where dozens of soldiers waited to provide an escort. For one fleeting moment, she recalled the way the courtyard had looked after the dragon's awakening. Every hint of char had been removed from the palace, and even the fire-blackened stones had been scrubbed clean. It was as if the battle had never happened.

If only all of them were so easy to forget.

"We'll meet them at the wall and see what they have to say." Lark glanced behind her to ensure all three of the Paragons had heard. Andriun and Tula nodded in response, but Resia just twisted a curl of her hair and looked troubled. There was no blaming her for that. Lark was troubled too, but what other options did she have?

She did not expect anything ground-shattering from whatever the broken-born men at the city gate had to say, but she would hear them out, all the same. They would demand she surrender, claim she had the opportunity to spare her people and end the war.

Nonsense, all of it. Kings had surrendered in the past. All of them were dead, their lands as broken and empty as the rest of the world.

It took the entire walk to the gates for her to think of responses she could offer that would befit a noble queen, rather than the scathing commentary she wished to give.

Surrender would do nothing but see her dead.

Guards swarmed around the gates. Dozens of worried faces turned her way, but she ignored them and continued to the doorway she'd passed through with Tula before, the one that led to the stairs.

"Is it wise to appear where you can be seen?" a guardswoman asked softly as they walked. "They may have arrows."

"Don't worry. I'm already good at torching them out of the sky." Tula raised her hands and curled them to fists. Lark half expected them to erupt with flames, but nothing sprang forth. The Magister was being cautious today, it seemed.

"I trust the Paragons to keep me safe. Andriun's ice makes an effective defense, I have the blade, and should the situation grow dire, Resia is a gifted healer. We will be fine. Ensure the gates are reinforced, though. Have all guards ready for defensive measures all the way around the city's walls." Lark did not think there was any risk to the rest of the city's perimeter, but she wasn't willing to take chances. "Where is Magister Vorkaris?"

"Scouting," Tula said, earning herself a few curious looks. She answered them by sticking out her tongue. "Before he left the palace, he said he was going to fly over the desert and get a full count of the enemy army."

"Good. We'll need a proper tally so we can plan accordingly." Lark needed a tally of her own army, for that matter. She knew they had lost a number of soldiers by allowing them to remain with family in Tinith and Addare, but she had not asked General Jobe for the actual figures. Foolish of her, in retrospect; she'd simply wished she could ignore the problem and pretend it wasn't real, but that had never been an option. Letting anyone leave the army had been foolish, too, no matter what Admiral Warinal had advised. Her tender heart had gotten the better of her, but she would not make that mistake again. Once this was over, she would call for a full draft. They would need every ounce of help they could get.

She stopped at the bottom of the stairs to brace herself and gather courage, then continued.

The last sliver of the sun set the sky ablaze far to the west, beyond where the goborrin army sprawled across the desert. Lark strode to the edge of the towering wall and when she looked down to meet her enemy, every ounce of composure slipped her grasp.

"Zaide," she breathed.

He stood with broken-born men at his flanks, his eyes colder than they'd ever been. "Queen Dasienna," he offered in greeting, his tone so neutral and placid that it almost sounded like scorn.

The Hand of Gadranus, her messenger had said. She took in his stance, the armor he wore, the emblem that marked his chest and the shadows that fell from the folds of his cape. The sensation of magic teased her senses and stirred her stomach into violent churning.

"What have you done?" she whispered. Her eyes stung and her heart twisted, but he gave no answer. How could he? He hadn't heard.

"I come bearing an offer," Zaide called. He never so much as blinked. "Allow me through the gates, and we will speak."

Allowing him in was foolish, considering the size of the army that marched at his back. She raised her chin and stared down her nose. "State your offer now. There is nothing you must say that cannot be said before all of Jadora."

Neither his posture nor his expression changed, but she took the sense her response displeased him.

"You knock him down," Tula murmured to Andriun, none too discreetly. "I'll kick him again."

Lark was tempted to help.

Unaware of their exchange, Zaide spoke again in the same calm, measured tone. "I suggest we speak privately. I carry an offer with the power to end this war. Forever."

"Carry it to your grave," Lark snapped back.

A rush of wing beats drew Zaide's attention skyward and he turned to watch as Vorkaris banked overhead. The dragon did not land, but circled twice before he swept out across the desert, far above what ordinary arrows could reach. Zaide did not return to their conversation right away; instead, his head turned as he tracked the dragon's movement.

"He counts the monsters in your army. The flames come next," Lark said, hoping to goad him into some sort of reaction. That still, level way he spoke was not the Zaide she knew. The thought he could have changed so greatly in such little time made her ill.

Zaide did not react.

Let him in, Vorkaris rumbled into her thoughts, his voice louder and more forceful than anything she'd heard from him before.

Lark stumbled over her own disbelief before she managed to respond. *What?*

I have spoken to him. I know why he is here. Let him in, but be cautious. A heavy shadow lies on his soul.

Her belly tied itself into knots. She had not wanted to acknowledge Andriun's claim that he felt corruption. She hadn't felt anything at all. Now, as she stared down at the stern figure that had been her closest friend, she wondered if she had not felt it because she had not allowed herself to. It was easier if she didn't, if she denied any chance that what her own eyes told her was true. It couldn't be. She couldn't bear it. Yet there he was, slowly turning to face her again, his eyes as cold and his face as impassive as if he were carved of ice.

I can't open the gates to him, Lark thought back at the dragon, unable to restrain her desperation. *The people of Jadora will think I'm willing to negotiate with a man who wants them all dead.*

A noise like rushing wind echoed in her head. A sigh, she realized, just before the dragon growled, *Must I do everything myself?*

The dragon wheeled in midair and dove toward the gates. The goborrins and broken-born cried out and ducked, leaving Zaide alone to stand tall. Vorkaris snared him in his claws and gave his wings such a powerful stroke, smoke and ashes clouded the air and left everyone coughing. He shot upward and spiraled into the sky, leaving Zaide atop the wall's battlements.

Zaide threw his arms wide to catch his balance as a wave of shouts went up from the soldiers that lined the wall. Most of them gripped their weapons and shifted uneasily, unsure what to do. Any other time, they might have pushed him off the stone and let him fall to his death. But the draconic Magister had put him there. Did that make him an enemy, or a guest? Lark did not know, herself.

He slid off the stone and landed on the wall's walkway with a soft thud. More than a dozen spears and swords pointed his way, but he raised his gloved hands with his palms out and his fingers spread, presenting himself as no threat.

"Do we kick him now?" Tula asked.

His gaze turned to her, but her suggestion drew no reaction at all.

Lark suppressed a shudder.

"Vorkaris feels you should listen to what I have to say." Zaide did not move again, just stood still as stone and let his eyes travel between them. None of the three Paragons were happy, but Lark had never seen such a range of expressions. Tula looked angry. Andriun wore suspicion like a mask, and Resia looked as if she was about to cry. Zaide studied each of them in turn before he returned his attention to Lark. "I will gladly speak in front of the Paragons, but what I have to say is for the four of you alone. Dismiss your guards and I will share my offer."

"Not likely," Tula said.

Lark motioned for her to be quiet. "Remove your sword and lay it on the wall behind you."

Andriun made a sharp sound of disagreement, but Zaide complied. Ever so slowly, he lowered his hands to his belt, unfastened the buckle, and slid the leather free of his waist without ever touching the strange, golden-hued sword he carried. He sat it atop the tall stone at his back and spread his empty hands again.

"Step away from it." Lark pointed to the other side of the wall.

He obeyed, his steps slow and cautious. He positioned himself precisely where she'd pointed, then looked to her for directions again.

She searched his eyes, but found nothing. No hint of spirit or humor. None of the tender connection she thought they'd had when they last had a chance to speak in earnest, standing together on the balcony. It was as if he was hollow, and she feared that might be the truth.

Lark swallowed hard. "What did you tell me on my birthday?" They had been the only ones present; there was no way anyone else could know the answer. If this was some sort of trickery, his answer would make it clear.

For the briefest of moments, the ice thawed, and she caught a hint of emotion in the way his breath quickened and his shoulders tensed. Then, just as swiftly, it disappeared and that shield was back up. He swallowed, too, and she doubted it was from nerves.

"For as long as you need," he said. "No matter what."

There were a dozen things he could have chosen. Hearing his promise again threatened to shatter what little of her heart remained unbroken.

He was supposed to be helping.

He was supposed to be *hers*.

"I know what it looks like," Zaide added when she did not respond. "I know what you think. But I need you to trust me. Send your guards away so we can speak."

She didn't want to. She wanted to have him seized, carted off to the dungeon and punished for everything he'd done.

Trust him, he said.

How was she supposed to trust him when he'd led fifty thousand goborrins to her door?

"Leave us," Lark called over her shoulder.

Andriun gave a long hiss, but the guards shuffled to obey, retreating to either side. They did not disappear completely, but moved back until they were no longer within earshot. As long as they kept their voices low, nothing would be overheard.

Resia started to step forward, then seemed to think better of it and sank back into her place, her eyes lowered. Tula rested a hand on her shoulder, a silent offer of reassurance.

That left Lark to address things, and it took everything in her power to pry her attention from the tusked ram's skull emblazoned on Zaide's chest.

"There. The guards aren't listening." She took a slow step forward, as if to challenge him. Would he try to strike her? Draw a hidden weapon? She had no doubt there were a few tucked about his person. "Tell me what offer you brought, O Hand of Gadranus." The title made her lip curl. She did not try to hide it.

Zaide met her stare, still and calm. "To strike him down, you need the blade at full strength. To restore it, you needed the Paragon of Shadow."

As if she didn't already know that. She lifted her chin.

He lowered his, and his eyes darkened. "Give me the sword, Lark. Together, we can fix this, and then you can end everything."

"Or you can seize the blade and run back to your new master." She gripped the sword's hilt tight in her hand and angled her body away from him as if to protect it.

A hint of annoyance crossed his face and was swiftly quashed. "I asked you to trust me."

"Then give me proof that I should."

Zaide stared at the Spectrum Blade at her side and his fingers twitched as if he longed to touch it. Maybe he did. She did not know what sort of bond he'd formed with the blade; perhaps losing it had been a greater blow than she imagined. "The fact

I'm here should be enough. You needed magic. You needed shadow. So I've brought what you were missing."

"Which means what?" she asked, then sorely wished she hadn't, for she already knew the answer.

His eyes hardened until they shone like a storm in a looking glass. "I've taken his magic."

CHAPTER THIRTY-SIX

"You are a madman," Andriun spat.

Any other time in his life, Zaide might have thought that a compliment.

"That's impossible," Tula said a moment later.

Zaide shrugged and peeled off one glove, then offered his hand. There were other ways to show the power he'd brought, and he wasn't sure he understood the doubt, given what they'd already seen. There was no mistaking the way the dark mists rippled and fell from his body, but they did not do it now. Explaining how he had no control over it and his intention to ask the magic to help with the sword would be interesting.

Tula glowered at his hand and did not move. Resia was the one to creep forward. She reached for him, her fingers trembling. They slid against his palm before her wrist turned and she laced her fingers with his.

Show her, he suggested to the creeping magic that already simmered just beneath his skin. It responded as if delighted. A cold tingle crept down the back of his arm, a thread of power that twined itself around their hands and forced a shudder down her spine.

He expected surprise, maybe relief at seeing what he'd brought to aid them.

Instead, she lifted her dark eyes to his, tears brimming against her eyelashes. "How could you do this?" she whispered. Her hand still shook, but she did not let go.

"There's a lot to that story and I don't think I'll like telling it. But it's there. You feel it." He squeezed her hand, hoping it would reassure her and still her trembling. "I don't know how much time we have, but we can restore the blade with it if we're fast. If you're ready." The latter part was more for Lark than Resia, but Lark shook her head.

His heart sank.

All this time, he'd hoped she'd be able to unravel whatever blocked her magic and be ready for him when he arrived with the other half of the power. He'd never accounted for what might happen if she failed.

The disappointment almost broke through to his face. He caught it at the last second, tamped it down with the rest of his smothered emotions and hid it away for later, where the magic couldn't see it, react, and make him ill. Either the feelings would fade after being ignored, or there would be time to deal with them after he spent whatever little power he'd been given. He wasn't foolish enough to believe it was his to keep; not while Gadranus still lived.

"We can still try," Zaide said. "This magic is... it's like the sword. It knows things. Maybe it will know how to release your power, too."

As if to confirm, the sliver of magic pulsed within him, eager to be used.

Lark hesitated, watching as Resia released his hand and shuffled backwards, more troubled than ever before.

He hadn't convinced them.

They didn't trust him.

Anger swelled within him and the magic reacted, feeding off

it and wrenching his insides with the sort of sickness that had become all too familiar.

After everything he'd suffered while seeking this moment, after all he'd risked in seizing the other half of the power they needed so he could bring it to their door, they still thought him a traitor.

He struggled to twist his hurt and frustration back under control and held out his bare hand toward Lark. "Just try."

She eyed his hand with uncertainty.

"Don't do it." Tula shifted close to Lark and gripped her arm as if to keep her from drawing the Spectrum Blade. "I have a bad feeling about this."

Zaide dropped his hand and scowled. "Why are you afraid? This is everything we wanted. If we do this, we can take the fight right back to Amrochan."

"And pass through all these monsters?" Lark waved a hand at the desert beyond the wall. "Just leave them here at our doorway, without paying any price?"

"They answer to me," Zaide said. "If I order them to stand down, they will."

Andriun scoffed. "You are an idiot and a fool. I have always known you were reckless, but I did not realize you were stupid, too."

The anger was fast to return. Zaide couldn't contain it and the magic roiled until his stomach lurched and sweat that did not belong to the desert's heat flecked his temples. "What else was I supposed to do?" He wanted to snarl it, but it came out frosty, strangled by the sickness that tried to take him.

"Not join the villain, to start with!" Tula planted her fists on her hips and gave him such a pouty stare that he wished he could clean it off her face.

"You have no idea what I've done." He took a step forward and all of them moved back.

Hurt and fury warred within him. The magic burned so intensely that his skin rose in gooseflesh.

He took another step. "Everything I've done has been for you. Every choice I made, every sacrifice and scar was for you."

"Stop it, Zaide." Lark stood her ground. "You're not yourself."

He almost laughed at how right she was. No; he didn't think he'd ever be himself again, not after the way the toxic magic boiled through his veins. "You have no idea," he whispered, his voice gone hoarse.

And neither do you. The words crawled along the inside of his skull like a centipede, rumbling with amusement.

That wasn't the magic. Or was it? Zaide froze in place and felt his brow furrow, though the crinkling of his skin was somehow strange and distant, as if it belonged to someone else. His breath quickened and sweat rolled down the sides of his face as a crackling gray crept in around the edges of his vision.

Not this. Not again.

He tried to force it back with willpower, struggled to make his eyes focus on Lark's face.

Her mouth moved, his name on her lips, but it came as broken and garbled as if they were underwater.

The world tilted beneath his feet.

Thank you for making this easier for me, the same voice whispered.

Lark leaped forward, but the gray swallowed her too as Zaide fell backwards into his borrowed magic's embrace.

Lark's hand closed on empty air where Zaide had been. Frigid shadows kissed her skin and then exploded a short distance away to reveal him again, right beside the battlement where the dragon had left him before. His hand closed around the hilt of his abandoned sword and a roar of protest rose from the watching guards. They rushed to meet him, but he disappeared the moment one got close, only to emerge behind the man and strike him dead.

Resia screamed.

"That's not Zaide!" Tula cried as he turned to face them again.

He chuckled as he pulled his sinuous blade free. "Are you certain?" It was his voice, but the savage way he smiled at them held nothing of the forest boy Lark had come to know.

Her hand went to the Spectrum Blade. "Release him!"

"After all the time spent on his training?" He whirled to deflect a guardswoman's curved blade and teach her the shortcomings of their traditional armor.

More guards flowed in to seize him, but the dark magic swallowed his form before they arrived.

Fireballs struck the stone wall where he'd been. Tula stomped a foot in frustration. "Where did he go?"

Rather than answering, Andriun leaped off the wall.

Resia shrieked at the display, but he eased his fall with a coil of water and landed in a crouch on the pavement below.

Lark climbed onto the battlements to follow. "Catch me!"

The Paragon of Water seized her with his magic before her feet even left the stone, sweeping her to the ground with deft speed. She didn't have a chance to register her fear before she spun to face the gates.

Zaide flashed her the same vicious grin as he freed his blade from another guard and black tendrils of power lashed out to tear the gates open wide.

Soldiers and guardswomen swarmed around him, but the strike of magic kept them at bay and let goborrins pour in. The monsters stormed through the dark mists unimpeded, and the cacophony of hooves warned them of more storming the trail.

Guards from atop the wall rushed down the stairs to challenge him. Over all the noise, Lark barely caught Andriun's grunt of effort as he rolled a tendril of water into an ice spear and hurled it past the writhing coils of magic.

Its jagged tip raked across Zaide's cheek and he turned toward the Shaman as a single bead of crimson pooled in the cut and slid down his face.

Lark gripped the Spectrum Blade, only to peel her fingers off its hilt a moment later and turn to run.

"Where are you going?" Andriun cried.

She could not spare the time or breath to explain. Her feet carried her up the street, her boots drumming against the stone so fast, their rhythm almost matched the hammering of her heart.

With the blade still depleted, there was only one thing she could do—only one power that could chase away the shadows that had stolen her friend.

Snakelike tendrils of darkness raced alongside her feet, swiping at her ankles and only missing because fire scoured them away.

Tula's legs were longer and she caught up with Lark within a few strides. "I don't know why we're running, but I'll help you do it."

Lark nodded back.

All across the city, warnings sounded and people shouted a call to arms. Soldiers from every faction in the city poured into the streets as battle erupted behind her, but she dared not look back. There had not been so many goborrins outside the gates that they could not close them again, but the army would be swift to spring on the opportunity to strike.

More footsteps joined hers and she prayed they were friendly.

"I take the running to mean that you have a plan?"

Relief swept over her at the sound of Andriun's voice. "Yes," she replied, though she was not sure of her idea's strength. It would only work if Zaide followed her. So far, she had only seen tentacles of dark magic darting up the road.

Then, abruptly, the air before her burst and he sprang out of a dark swirl, his sword flashing for her throat.

Lark squealed and dropped to her knees, letting the slash pass harmlessly overhead. She should have collided with Zaide, but all she encountered was that strange cloud of bitter cold.

"You can run all you want, Dasienna," Zaide snarled, his voice coming from everywhere and nowhere, "but you can't escape your fate."

"Neither can you." She stumbled the first step, but Resia caught her arm and helped her find her stride again. Lark shot her a thankful look and kept running.

Once Gadranus eliminated her, he could afford to wait for the Spectrum Blade to be restored. He'd pursue her anywhere now, determined to strike her down and bring things to an end.

Again, Zaide erupted from nowhere and tried to strike, but the Paragons were ready. Andriun snared him with a coil of water and flung him back, clearing the way for them to run.

"This had better be a really good idea," Tula said.

Lark hoped it was.

Somewhere overhead, the dragon's furious roar split the night.

"That takes care of the gates," Resia panted between breaths.

The palace loomed just ahead, its gates open wide to let countless guardswomen and soldiers pour into the city. More than one looked her way as she bolted past, but none of them stopped to help her. She didn't know whether to laugh or be angry, but she didn't have time for either, for Zaide appeared before the palace's doors and blocked the way. He shifted his stance, one shoulder drawn back, his posture deceptively calm.

If she had not known before, she would have been certain now. She would not pretend to understand how such magic worked, but now, they'd seen it twice; once as the apparition of Gadranus they fought beneath the forest's temple, and now in the power that had overshadowed her friend.

She drew her blade. "Stand down."

"It's delightful that you think you can best me." He took a slow step forward, the movement as smooth as flowing water, yet there was no mistaking the way every muscle in his body coiled tight.

Lark had no doubt she couldn't. All she needed was an opening to get past him.

It arrived a moment later, when a woman with twin blades leaped through the doorway and chased him back into the mist.

"What in the sun's blazes?" Elsanna spat the moment he disappeared.

The shadows collected closer to Lark, but a shrill note whipped them away and the Hymnflute's wind exposed Zaide's hiding place before he was ready. Then the barrier wrapped around them as Resia began its song.

Lark released a trembling breath as he drove the tip of his sword against the barrier and found it blocked.

Her relief was short-lived, for magic crawled down his arm like lightning and streaked across his blade. The barrier shattered like glass and the shrieking winds threatened to knock all of them to the ground.

Only Zaide remained steady on his feet—if Lark could think of him as Zaide at all.

Lark's hands trembled and the Spectrum Blade quivered, but she dragged herself upright and pointed its end at his chest.

"We both know you wouldn't," he almost purred. "You care too much about those who surround you."

Fire streaked past Lark's head and shot straight for his face, only to glance off his sword.

"My quarrel is not with you Paragons," he said as he strode forward. "Nor with the figurehead you've placed in charge of your city. Give me Dasienna, and all can be resolved right here. Not another drop of blood shed."

"None but mine?" Lark spat back.

"Some sacrifices are necessary for peace. You've had more than your fair share of chances to resolve this. I have been patient. Generous. Every time, you have snubbed my kindness."

He stalked toward her until Tula and Andriun stepped between them. His eyes narrowed.

A spear of ice drew itself together in Andriun's hand and Tula angled herself away from him, sheltering his ice from the fire she summoned.

Resia grabbed Lark's elbow and pulled her toward the doorway. Elsanna darted in behind them to defend their backs and together, they ran.

"What's your idea?" Resia struggled to keep up and her breath came hard, yet her equanimity never faltered.

Lark wished she could be half as composed. Fear shoved her heart into her throat and threatened to choke her. "The Sunshard," was all she got out.

It was enough. The Kolmari girl darted around the corner and strained to move ahead, waving for palace guards and serving staff to get out of the way.

A faint prickle coursed up Lark's arm, startling her so badly she almost dropped the Spectrum Blade. Did it agree with her? Or was it trying to share some kind of warning?

I won't hurt him, she promised silently, hoping it would be enough to placate whatever awareness the blade possessed.

The sensation faded and Lark's heart ached.

What she wouldn't have done to have the sword be in his hand. Maybe then, none of this would have come to pass.

The cold brushed her face before the magic did and Lark shoved Resia to the other side of the hall before Zaide's sword carved the air between them. Elsanna rushed forward to intercept and deflect the strike, aiming to throw him off balance. He slid to the side instead and spun to bring his sword up in a vertical slash. Their blades rang, yielding a curse from the former guardswoman.

The other Paragons closed in from behind, both nimble in the narrow hall. Andriun ducked a sword and sprinted to catch up, his arms spread as if to herd Lark and Resia in a new direction.

Behind them, ice sealed the passageway, blocking Zaide, Tula, and Elsanna out of sight.

"I don't think that's going to hold him," Lark said without slowing.

Andriun's mouth took a grim set. "I fear you are right. Maker's mercy, but I wish I knew how he moved like that."

"I don't think it's him." Resia's whole body betrayed her anxiety, but she kept moving. It was all they could do. Just keep moving.

The ice shattered behind them and Andriun stifled a hiss.

"Just run," Lark ordered. They weren't far from the dragon's rooms now.

Shadows sprang from the wall ahead and she brought the Spectrum Blade up just in time to shave sparks from the edge of Zaide's sword, but the force of the blow made her stagger. He was far stronger than she remembered and she didn't know how much was magic and how much was his own might. He drew back a step and then swung again, the one-handed strike hard enough to knock her backwards.

Before she hit the floor, Elsanna surged into the gap and rained blows against his blade with both of hers, driving him back against the wall. "Get her up!"

Andriun and Resia seized Lark's arms and dragged her back to her feet. The Spectrum Blade dangled in her grasp, her fingers all but numb after the force with which he'd hit.

A low growl of annoyance escaped Zaide's throat. He faded into the wall and reemerged at Elsanna's back as a thrust of his sword tore through her ornate robes and cut into her side.

"No!" Lark spun back, but Tula bounded forward to shove her farther up the hall.

"Keep moving!" the Magister shouted.

Lark stumbled and started, and Resia spun back to go to the guardswoman's aid.

The next strike came as if from thin air. Andriun's spear of ice intercepted it and shattered, yet the Shaman spun the fragments into a whip of water that snared Zaide by the waist and slammed him backwards into the wall. Lark glanced back only once, then bolted ahead.

The grand doors to the rooms Vorkaris kept for himself lay just ahead. She summoned every scrap of strength she could find and raced for them, but Tula beat her there and flung the doors wide.

Daisy sprang from the gap and both girls shrieked. The dog landed just behind them, her teeth bared and her hackles raised.

Another crash signaled how well the fight was going and Lark hurried into the dragon's quarters. She almost shut the door, then realized there was no point. She'd seen Gadranus wield that same strange power before, phasing in and out of reality as he swirled across the water to challenge each of them beneath the temple, and then again in Amrochan's throne room. He would be there in an instant, whether the door was shut or not.

"We need the Sunshard," she said as she ran for the table where they'd held their meetings. The last she knew, Vorkaris had taken them to examine. They had to be in his room.

"Sunshard. Got it." Tula veered toward the pile of pillows that constituted the dragon's bed. She all but dove in, tossing cushions to the left and right.

Daisy hovered in the doorway, barking and growling until something startled her and she skittered back a few steps. Andriun crashed into the room, flung by a coil of dark magic, but he tucked into a roll and came up on his feet. Water spiraled around him and struck toward the hallway.

Lark did not look to see if the lash made contact. The bag she'd kept the artifacts in wasn't near the table. Nor was it on any of the shelves scattered about the vast room. She hissed through her teeth. "Tula!"

"I got it!" the Magister shouted back. She sprang up from the cushions with the Sunshard gleaming in her hand.

The same tendril of magic that had thrown Andriun raced

toward her and she stabbed at it with the crystal. It recoiled and Lark's heart leaped.

It worked. The light repelled it.

She ran toward the pile of pillows and hacked at the threads of blackness that tried to snare her ankles with the Spectrum Blade. They retreated from it, too. Daisy snapped at the receding shadows and posted herself at Lark's side, growling all the while.

Gold flashed in the doorway and ice shattered. Shards chimed against the stone floor as it fell and Zaide crossed the threshold, his step slow and dangerous.

Lark braced herself to face him, the Spectrum Blade in one hand and the Sunshard in the other. She extended the latter and pointed it as his chest. "Release him."

A low chuckle welled in his throat. "Foolish girl. You don't even know how to use that." His sword flicked up to deflect a fireball, his eyes never leaving her face. Flames leaped up in front of him, drawing a circle on the floor. His amusement faded.

Andriun's water whipped for his head and snapped through nothing.

Tula scuffed a boot against the floor in frustration. "How do we pin him down?"

At Lark's feet, Daisy turned to bark.

There. Lark spun with the Spectrum Blade ready and intercepted a stab as Zaide reappeared. The faintest flicker of surprise lit his eyes, but he adapted quickly, sliding right and then bringing his sword back in a hard horizontal swipe.

Lark ducked and Daisy launched herself at his arm. Her teeth snagged against the etched shapes in his armor and he shook his arm hard to dislodge her.

Flames burst around Tula's hands and laced their way down a Jadoran blade. Lark glanced at it, startled, then let her eyes sweep the dragon's quarters. Dozens of fine weapons decorated the walls. A handful lay on the floor where Tula had knocked them down.

"Andriun!" Lark had no hands free to point, but she looked that way and hoped it was enough. Two more blocked strikes jolted up her arms and made her shoulders ache. There were no openings in his form, no gaps into which she could try and return blows.

A second later, a spear skimmed just below Zaide's chin and clattered against the far wall. He jerked back in surprise and water coiled around his neck to drag him backwards.

He stumbled a few steps and cut at the water with his blade, but it remained, unhindered. His upper lip curled back and he faded out of existence.

"Make him stop that!" Tula cried.

Lark didn't know how, but Daisy spun to look in a new direction. Despite the early warning her bark gave, Tula was not ready, and Zaide came at her from the side. His sword tore through the fabric of her silk coat and left it hanging, though the tip just missed flesh. Tula whipped her Jadoran blade up in response and a shower of embers sprayed across his armor and burned holes in his cape.

The Magister slammed a foot against the ground, summoning flames beneath him, but he didn't stay in one place long enough to be burned. His serpentine sword swept down against hers, hammering with blow after blow until she stumbled over one of the displaced pillows and fell. Lark did not see where the stab landed, for a wave of water surged between them, yet she knew the blade made contact by the way Tula screamed.

The water crashed against Zaide's back, wrapped around him like a cloak and hardened into ice. Andriun lunged in with a spear, its needle point cracking through the ice and striking nothing at all.

Lark gripped the Sunshard until her fingers hurt. *Do something!* she begged. She tried to seize the power within the stone or shake it free.

Zaide burst from shadow behind Andriun and drove a boot

into his back to send him sprawling on the floor. Beside him, Tula twisted on the pillows and tried to rise. Black coils snared them both and held them fast.

Andriun gritted his teeth and spread a hand as if to reach for his magic, but whatever power held him held the water at bay. Zaide's boot landed on his wrist and ground downward, yielding a cry of pain.

Do something, anything! Lark pleaded again. No magic answered her. The Spectrum Blade in her hand remained silent.

"I have run out of patience," Zaide's voice hissed as he dropped the tip of his sword on Andriun's hand. The Shaman's gasp of pain grew into something more as the razor edge of the strange weapon carved a line down the sides of his fingers, shaving the webbing from each digit.

Daisy lunged forward and her teeth snapped shut on Zaide's sword hand and drew an angry cry. He flung her back and snared her with magic to pin her down, too. Blood stained her teeth and the hair around her mouth. She never stopped snarling.

Hot tears traced darkened paths down Lark's cheeks, fear and fury and desperation all woven inside her until she could not contain it anymore. She leaped toward him with her teeth bared and swung with all her might. The Spectrum Blade slammed against his sword with such force, it almost tore free of her grasp.

Shadows surged around her and she swung the Sunshard, driving them back as she stabbed with the powerless blade again, cursing the lightless colors on the steel.

He met and deflected her blows twice more before she brought the sword down hard overhead and he knocked the blade aside and rammed his shoulder into her chest. Lark toppled backwards with a cry and when he leaned forward above her, she swiped at him one last time.

Instead of blocking with his blade, he snared it in his gloved hand. The Spectrum Blade's edge cut through the leather and the scent of blood hit the air, but his grip was iron and his blue eyes were just as hard.

Slowly, he twisted, wrenching the blade out of her grasp. She gasped as he cast it aside.

"I gave you every chance to end this," he said softly as he lunged down to seize her throat in his bare hand. His sword clattered to the stone. "Take the knowledge that I could have let you live, and hold it close when you see me on the other side."

His other hand wrapped around her neck.

Lark shut her eyes and held her breath as his fingers pressed into her skin, unwilling to let the bitter grin that contorted his face be the last thing she saw.

Heat tingled in her fingertips and she cracked open one eye.

The Sunshard flashed and glowed in her grasp.

His grasp faltered. Instead of that icy grin of victory, his face twisted into something else, flickering between effort and surprise. His fingers stayed locked tight around her neck, neither loosening nor tightening, and her eyes widened.

The magic's hold on him weakened. For an instant, she saw something else in his eyes.

Fear.

"Zaide," Lark gasped. "Fight him! Push him back!"

The hatred that was Gadranus burned back through. "I will not lose," he snarled through gritted teeth, and his hands tightened on her throat again, squeezing out the last of her breath.

Spots swam in her vision and a darkness that was not his magic stole in around the edges of the world. Heat magnified in her hand and the Sunshard grew brighter, telling her what to do.

Lark gritted her teeth and slammed the sharp end of the Sunshard into his chest.

Power flared and a blinding light seared her vision as the stone sank through his armor and dug into flesh.

A scream unlike any other tore from his throat, anger and agony twisted into one long, painful note. Magic lanced up her arm—not from the stone, but from *her*, driving into the wound and scorching every last shred of shadow out of existence.

Zaide collapsed sideways and rolled over. His heels skidded against the stone and his back arched as he clawed at the base of the Sunshard in vain.

Lark scrambled to seize the Spectrum Blade and gripped it tight in both hands as the light swelled, enveloping everything, blotting him out of sight.

Glass shattered and a roar split the air. Tula's voice cried something over the sound of Zaide's screams, the words lost but their hope clear, and massive claws emerged from the light to wrap around Lark's waist.

"Wait!" she cried, leaning over the dragon's paw and stretching one hand after Zaide, but Vorkaris spun and launched himself from the floor without a word.

Great wings spread and carried them out of the fractured windows of the Magister's quarters as the light burned brighter and brighter, until the whole palace glowed like a beacon in the night.

Lark choked on her breath and slumped in the dragon's grasp as the pure white light mingled with the rich orange of fire, then blurred behind the tears in her eyes.

Once again, Jadora burned.

CHAPTER THIRTY-SEVEN

Theʏ ꜱᴘɪʀᴀʟᴇᴅ down to the desert north of the city, where there were no goborrins to be seen. Vorkaris released Lark while he was still a few feet up. She hit the ground hard and fell backwards, kicking up sand. A protest sprang to her lips, but she saw why he'd dropped her before it left them. He needed both forepaws to handle the Paragons.

He lowered Andriun with a bit more caution, then sank to the ground with Tula, using an abundance of care. The Magister's face contorted, but she sucked in a deep breath through her mouth and worked hard to remain composed. Tears tracked down her face as freely as blood ran down her arms, and the first look at her injury was enough to make Lark sick.

The Spectrum Blade dropped tip-first into the sand and drove deep enough to stand upright on its own. "We need a healer." Lark hurried forward, though she didn't know what to do. "Resia is—Maker's mercy, what about Elsanna?"

She is all right, Vorkaris said with a low rumble, though he sounded resigned. *The Kolmari Elder has ensured she will survive, though she will not wield a blade again soon.*

Tula's shoulders twitched as if she wanted to let them slump, but she could not relax. Her breath shuddered and she fought to keep it coming and going at a steady rate. "Jadora will n-need her. I can... I can..." The word *wait* hung obviously on the air, but it didn't seem true. Ugly cuts marred the insides of both her upper arms.

Lark shook her head, then turned to Andriun. "What's he done to you?"

The Shaman's face was grim and a little gray, but he held his composure far better than Tula as he crouched beside her to inspect her injuries. "He sought to remove us from battle without causing lasting harm. I am right-handed, so he has injured my hand. Tula uses both of hers, so he has injured her arms. A wound in such a sensitive place prevents her from moving them easily." He gave a long, slow exhale. "The cuts are so precise. Just deep enough to disable her arms, yet not deep enough to cut through the artery. Had it been any deeper..." He did not need to finish.

He had not done anything to draw attention to his own injuries, though Lark looked at them now. The blood on his hand was darker than normal, an ugly contrast to the rich tones of his skin. The gaps between his fingers wrenched her heart and she looked away.

Behind them, Jadora still glowed, though it was only the soft, warm hue of firelight that remained.

"The fires?" Lark asked fearfully.

A low, muddled grumbling sounded in her head and she glanced up at the dragon, confused.

"He did it," Tula said, her voice high and strained. "Killing goborrins. Dragon fire isn't very controlled."

The city is secure, Vorkaris added, uncharacteristically defensive. *The gates are closed and the army beyond the wall has been dealt a blow. The fires will be extinguished shortly.*

"And Zaide?" This time, Lark's voice quavered.

The dragon said nothing.

She did not think her heart could have dropped any farther.

A long moment passed before Vorkaris turned away. *I will*

retrieve the Elder. The three of you are to stay here. I will not move my Magister again with those injuries. I will trust you to defend her.

Lark squeezed her eyes shut. She was the worst choice he could possibly make for that. She hadn't been able to protect anyone.

You protected yourself, the dragon replied, an unwelcome reminder that he could see into her thoughts. *Congratulations on the awakening of your powers.*

Then he backed away and launched himself into the sky.

Lark snorted softly and tucked in her chin. A long, weighty silence passed before she opened her eyes again and found her companions staring at her.

"The light was not what I expected," Andriun said when she met his gaze. "But I am glad you found it."

"It doesn't do us any good," Lark muttered. "I don't know what I did. I don't know *how* I touched it. And even if I did, we don't have..." She couldn't make herself finish.

All three of them sat in morose silence.

In the still, Lark felt her hopelessness bubble back to the surface and she could not hold it at bay. Her vision blurred, tears obscuring the city in the distance.

For the briefest instant, she had allowed herself to believe that maybe it was true—that Zaide had found a way to fix the bind they'd gotten into. Everything had gone wrong so fast, she could hardly grasp it.

Had it been foolish to hope? To think there was a chance the struggle might have ended? She watched the city as if it might give her some sign to serve as an answer. It didn't.

Eventually, a glowing spot rose into the sky over the city. It wasn't hard to identify it as Vorkaris, nor was it long before he came close enough to pick out his smoldering wings. He spiraled down and let Resia off his back a short distance away. The Kolmari Elder picked up her skirt and ran across the sands, stumbling more than once.

"Let me see," she called as she approached. Her face was

already pinched with exhaustion, but she went straight for Tula anyway.

The Magister stayed where she was and did not so much as move. Pale salt tracks marked where tears had run down her face, but most of them had dried.

Lark stood back and watched helplessly as Resia poured water from a skin over the wounds in Tula's arms, then touched the flesh beside the injuries to work her healing.

I have spoken with the chief officers of your military, Vorkaris said, interrupting her dismal thoughts. *They have suggested it may be wise for you to move your base of operations elsewhere. As long as you remain in Jadora, your army must split its focus between defending you and defending your people.*

"I've already thought of that." It had been no more than a handful of hours since she had discussed that very thing with Tula. "I will go north and seek refuge in Sast. The monastery fortress can be evacuated. If I am the only one there, no one else will be at risk."

Very well, the dragon replied.

Lark gazed up at him, hoping for more information or updates on everything else she wanted to know. He did not notice, his attention solely on his human companion.

"Magister Vorkaris?" She felt bad to interrupt, but her heart still ached with all she knew and all she didn't.

One large reptilian eye tilted her way.

Her throat tightened even before she asked. "What about Zaide?"

He stared for a long time, then returned his focus to Tula and the Elder who worked to heal her. *Your officers elected to arrest him.*

A flutter in her chest made her heartbeat soar. "Is he all right?"

They approached my quarters to take him in chains, but there was... no need. The dragon held his head high, his gaze distant.

She stared, waiting for him to continue. Her chest constricted with fear when he did not. "Is he—did I free him?"

In a manner of speaking.

Lark's heart plummeted and she sank to sit in the sand.

I am sorry, Vorkaris added softly, the closest to a whisper he'd ever come. *The soldiers reached him too late.*

Everything inside her wound so tight, she thought it would splinter and fall apart.

She had failed. Again. Even after tapping into her magic in her moment of dire need, she was simply not enough. And now...

Her breath caught and seized and when at last she made a sound, what escaped was no more than a hiccuping sob.

Every step of the way, Zaide had been the one to support her. To stand by her side and offer belief in her and her cause. To chip away at the thick walls she'd erected around her heart until he carved a place for himself and become a part of her world she couldn't live without.

Tears came hot and fast, blurring everything around her as every last shred of hope within her crumbled to dust and pain unlike anything she'd ever known swelled in the hollow it left behind.

Someone touched her. She didn't see who, nor did it matter.

Her power was supposed to save them. Instead, it stripped her of the one thing that had come to matter most of all. The hand on her shoulder tightened, yet it offered no comfort. The hurt still grew until it tumbled out in broken words.

"I didn't tell him," she gasped between sobs. "I never told him. He didn't know."

And now he never would.

She curled in on herself and cried until she was too empty to breathe, and even the dragon bowed his head.

For a long time, she sat with her forehead against her knees and her arms wrapped around herself, yet they could not sit in silence beneath the glow of the burning city forever. The firelight faded, and eventually, Vorkaris spoke again.

The devastation is immense, he said slowly. *Whatever your power has done, it has settled enough that your officers and the palace guard have begun clearing what remains of my quarters. I will not pretend to understand the nature of whatever power he claimed in his efforts to aid you, but a dark power lingers, and whatever was left has been taken. I am sorry.*

Lark could not make herself open her eyes. Her mourning would be like what she offered for her father, then; not so much as a grave left behind where she could cry. Her eyes stung, too dry for more tears.

"Hey," Tula interjected, her voice shaky.

Vorkaris turned his head as Lark struggled to lift hers.

The Magister looked no better, still tear-streaked and bloodstained, but she pushed herself to her feet and the partially-mended gashes in her arms appeared to pain her less. "Where's Daisy? Did you see her? Did she get out?"

I will look, the dragon replied, *but I will not try to carry a dog in flight. If she remains in the palace, she will be cared for. For now, we must determine what shall be done next.*

As if Lark could simply move on. Her world was collapsing, yet the rest carried on without her, turning with the wheels of war. She drew a shuddering breath and forced herself to nod and think of all that remained undone. "Did you see the Sunshard? Was it left behind?"

No.

"Is the Shadowsliver still there?"

It should be. The dragon tilted his nose toward the city as if thinking. *I will look for it while I wait for provisions to be brought for your journey. I shall carry you to Sast myself. The Paragons should go with you and serve as your guardians. Do you desire your military officers to be there, as well?*

Lark could think of little she wanted less, but she tried to be reasonable. It was a stretch; rather than feeling responsible, all she felt was hollow. "Someone should stay here and help manage the defense of Jadora. Order Admiral Warinal to stay here, as his naval expertise will be relevant to the defense of the underground river. We cannot afford to have Jadora cut off from supplies."

And the other? Vorkaris asked.

"General Jobe should gather whatever number of soldiers he thinks will be necessary to defend Sast and meet us there. I trust he will be capable of moving without drawing suspicion." Truthfully, she didn't trust that at all, nor did she know how such a thing could be done. It was hard to disguise an army.

The dragon must have noted and shared the thought, for he rumbled. *I shall suggest they travel with empty wagons. It will not slow their progress much, but it will give the illusion they travel to seek supplies for Jadora's people.*

"Which should help hide what the Desheni are doing to aid us," Lark concluded. "All right. That's a reasonable plan."

Then I shall return to the city to gather what you need. He spread his wings.

"Thank you," Lark added, the words all but lost beneath the roaring whoosh of him taking flight. She watched him work his way higher into the sky, then turned to face the others.

All of them stared at her, yet the moment she looked their way, they dropped back to what they were doing and pretended they'd never stopped. Tula and Resia both hovered over Andriun, examining his hand and the damage done. He stood still, his fingers spread and his hand steady, but the soft way he stared at it hurt.

"Are you all right?" Lark knew before she asked that he wasn't—she was not, either—but she didn't know what else to say to invite him to share words. They had to keep going, regardless of how they felt.

One by one, his fingers curled into his palm. He held them there for a long time before he relaxed them. "I would be less ashamed if he had cut my hair. At least hair will grow back."

Lark didn't know what else to say.

"Are you in need of healing, too, Your Majesty?" Resia's voice was small and worn and tears stained her face, but she still presented herself to offer what she could.

Seeing what injuries the others had sustained, it struck Lark as unfair. She alone had escaped without injury—at least physical ones. She and Resia both were stricken by the internal hurt that would take an eternity to mend, but Lark knew that was not what the Kolmari girl meant. The tenderness of the skin at her throat made her suspect there would be bruises left behind, but what were bruises compared to the cruelty of what the Shaman and Magister had suffered? Her hand went to her throat, but she shook her head. "No. I'm all right." It was only her heart that had broken, and no amount of healing could aid that.

"Thank goodness," Tula sighed. "When I saw him grab you like that, I thought... I thought..." Her green eyes turned glassy and she did not finish. She didn't have to. They'd probably all thought it, that their resistance had reached the end of the line and all was lost.

Had it not been for the single moment where the Sunshard's power had driven back Gadranus's influence and allowed Zaide's resistance to shine through, it might have been.

The glassiness shifted to something else, distant and unfocused, and Tula bit her lower lip.

Lark had seen that expression enough times to know it meant Vorkaris spoke. Whatever bond he held with Tula, it let them speak over greater distances than what he could manage with ordinary people like her. "What's he saying?"

"He has the Shadowsliver." Tula squinted as if it might let her hear better, though the voice was only in her head. "He still doesn't see any sign of the Sunshard, though, and he says he doesn't see Daisy. She's probably hiding after the fight. He says he'll have the palace staff look for her and make sure she's treated well when they find her."

Something positive, something negative, and something that had no answers yet. The same as it had been in every other matter. "Tell him I said thank you."

"He also says the general and the admiral are real unhappy."

No surprise there, either. The predictability of it all made Lark sigh.

"Must be nice to be a dragon. He can just talk orders into people's heads any time they're in the city, so he gets things done fast." Tula's gaze refocused and she lifted a hand to explore the edges of the cut on the inside of her arm. No matter Resia's skill, there was only so much a tired healer could do. The scabbing was ugly, but it was better than bleeding wounds. She frowned. "He cut right through the dragon marks. I hope that's not symbolizing something."

"If anything, let it symbolize your determination. It will heal." And probably scar, though Lark didn't say that. "The edges look clean and fit close, so it will hardly leave a gap once it's better."

"An advantage you are lucky to have," Andriun added. He had lowered his hand to his side, but there was no hiding the slump of defeat in his shoulders.

There was no way to comfort him and Lark saw no use in platitudes, so she simply moved on. "We need all the advantages we can get. If I can figure out what I did back there, that would be a good one to gain." A rising flood of guilt rose within her and she struggled to drain the mire of self-pity before it got too deep. She would not feel bad for focusing on herself. Not now, not when she was so close to achieving what she'd been born to do. "When I used the Sunshard, did you feel anything? Any of you?"

"Yes," Resia said, earning herself a measure of surprise from the others. She hadn't even been present, still elsewhere in the palace tending Elsanna.

"Something was there," Andriun agreed with more hesitance.

Tula nodded. "I felt a lot. Maybe we can use that to help you figure it out."

Lark prayed that was so. She glanced back to the Spectrum Blade, still standing upright in the sand. "Good. We've suffered a setback, but we're not done yet."

It was far more positive than she felt, though as she wrapped her hand around the sword's hilt and returned it to its scabbard at her side, she found the conclusion brought a subtle sense of resignation. There was no undoing mistakes or bringing back what was lost. All they could do was move forward, the same way they always had.

She did not know where Gadranus was, but the first clue to unlocking everything she was missing had been found, and that meant the blade's restoration was nigh.

CHAPTER THIRTY-EIGHT

Raindrops hissed and steamed as they landed across the dragon's wings. Lark made herself focus on those droplets instead of their descent, though the flight had been smooth.

It had also been silent, a drastic change from the rides they'd taken before. The mood was heavy, but it provided ample time for Lark to puzzle over what she might have to do to summon the light within her again—and to let silent tears track down her face while no one could see. She tried to stay focused, reminding herself how little time she had to spare for the feelings that would both overwhelm and cripple her. Her magic had to be the highest priority, no matter how she grieved.

The power had carried an unmistakable sensation, but try as she might, she could not tap into it on a whim. Eventually, she concluded she was too distracted by flight and her heartache to give it the attention it deserved, and she put the thoughts aside for later.

When they landed, it was in the main courtyard of Sast's monastery, a structure so fortified she couldn't help but wonder why it had only ever been home to monks. The monastery sprawled across the entirety of the island, a space ringed by walls so high, they shut out the sun through all but midday. Cool shadows fell across her now, making the rain feel colder, and she braced herself for the gloom.

Tula made a sound of disgust at the wet and ducked under one of the dragon's wings the moment she slid from his back. Resia joined her, leaving Andriun alone to be unbothered.

At least, Lark assumed he was unbothered. He had been so withdrawn following the incident, she could no longer read him at all.

Monks in drab, undyed linen appeared in doorways to watch. They were neither surprised nor alarmed by the dragon's sudden arrival, though curiosity painted a number of faces.

Lark's familiarity with the monastery was limited, but she supposed everyone's was. It was isolated, after all, and few were allowed to set foot on the island. With that in mind, perhaps her surprise at discovering the robed figures were both male and female was uncalled for. She gazed back at them for a long moment before Vorkaris gave his wings a shimmy, encouraging her to get off.

An older man with tired eyes, a shiny, hairless head, and an unshaven chin was the first to greet them. He scuffled across the stones with his head bowed against the rain, and rather than greeting Lark or any of the Paragons, he stopped before the dragon.

"Greetings, noble Magister." He bowed just enough to be meek without appearing to grovel. "We are honored to receive you. You have not graced our island with your presence in such a long time, but you will find we are ready."

Vorkaris gave a gentle puff and steam, rather than smoke, rose from his nostrils. The damp made the air cool, though it was so humid it felt rather like sitting in cold soup. *Greetings, Grandmaster Hyar. Your correspondence since my awakening has been welcome.*

Lark did not frown, though her puzzlement likely showed anyway. *You know him?*

I know everyone worth knowing, Vorkaris replied dryly, his mental voice scarcely a whisper. He flicked his wings and folded one. The other remained half-spread, allowing Tula and Resia their makeshift shelter. *Has Grandmaster Sidoya recovered from her illness?* It was strange to think of him as having volume, but his voice carried a certain presence when he spoke to more than one person.

"I am afraid not, noble Magister." Hyar bowed again.

Perhaps it is fortune that brings us here, then. I am accompanied by the Paragon of Wind, a skilled healer. The dragon's wing bobbed, funneling attention toward the two beneath it. *I am sure she will be happy to see if Sidoya's condition may be improved through less traditional means.*

Wind, then. Lark tucked Resia's proper title away in the back of her mind.

"All of us would be grateful if the Paragon can spare such effort on our behalf." The monk smiled and took in the rest of their group, too. "I see you are also accompanied by the Paragon of Fire, and the Paragon of Water."

And the Paragon of Light, Vorkaris added, dipping his muzzle toward Lark.

The dragon's appearance had not deserved attention from those nearby, but that drew a series of surprised murmurs.

Lark bowed her head and tried to ignore the heat in her cheeks.

Hyar regarded her thoughtfully. "We have heard of the armies that march for Jadora. News reached us as swiftly as they reached your gates. For the Paragons to stand before me means the time has come, then?"

So it would seem, the dragon agreed.

What does he mean? Lark thought at him, wishing she'd chosen to take shelter under his wings, too. She would have been more comfortable huddled with her companions, rather than standing in the rain, but she did not want to seem rude by retreating now.

Vorkaris gave his tail a swish. *Did you think you were the only people to receive messages from the Oracle?*

Her brows twitched, but she kept them from rising and managed to look composed when Hyar's attention turned her way.

"My queen," the Grandmaster said with a gentle bow much like what he'd offered the dragon. "Word of your father's passing has spread across Amroch and has brought much grief. We are deeply sorry for your loss. I know there is little that can be said to ease your pain, but know that we, too, have mourned."

"Thank you." Lark couldn't make herself smile. Had she mourned? Her father's death had brought emotions, certainly, but somehow the spells of sadness she had experienced since his demise did not strike her as mourning—especially compared to the pain that followed losing Zaide. Perhaps grief for her father was a part that came later, after she'd had time to sort out the unhappy realities his death had exposed.

Hyar went on, unaware of the tangle of thoughts that rolled over in her head. "In spite of all you have suffered, Your Majesty, we are grateful to have you here, for it will allow us to fulfill our vows at last. Please, come inside."

At the invitation, Vorkaris folded his one outstretched wing and stepped back. *I will take my leave now, as there are no accommodations here that are suitable for my kind, and I find the weather unpalatable. Be at ease, Majesty, and be prepared for your army's arrival.*

Lark turned in place to watch him spread his wings and prepare for flight. "Thank you, Vorkaris. It seems I am eternally in your debt."

Don't worry, little queen. I shall find some way for you to repay my favors. With an expression she could only describe as a draconic smirk, he launched himself into the air.

Lark waited for the Paragons to gather around her, then progressed into the ornate stone archway where Hyar indicated they should go. "You've expected the dragon's visit for some time now, haven't you?" She posed the question casually, as if there could be no other explanation for the calm way the monastery's people had greeted them.

"Oh, yes," Hyar said with a smile that only made his eyes more weary. "We have been prepared for his visit since word first came from Jadora that he had awakened. The Oracle promised he would arrive after that, accompanied by all five Paragons."

"All five?" Tula looked at each member of their party as if she thought she might have miscounted.

"Our records indicate there have always been variances within her visions. If all is not exactly as she foretold, we can only assume the Maker has chosen it is better this way. Come. I will take you to where your work must begin." The monk smiled again and Lark found herself trying to count the creases at the corners of his eyes.

They had gone a short way down a long hall when Resia cleared her throat. "I don't mean to pry, but Vorkaris mentioned a Grandmaster Sidoya and that she was ill?"

"Oh, of course. Yes. Rest assured, her illness is the slow sort and she will not suffer for seeing your group settled before you visit. Here, this is where you may begin your efforts." Hyar stopped at a pair of simple wooden doors and pushed them wide.

Tula's gasp came accompanied by a murmured oath from Andriun and Lark stood in the doorway, too astounded to make any noise at all, for the rows of bookshelves rivaled the Great Library of Jadora.

Resia alone retained her wits and strode in a few paces, tilting her head back as her gaze traveled up the towering stacks. "What is this place?"

"A collection of things we hope will be useful to you." The monk's chest puffed. "Since the moment the Oracle first foretold your coming, we have worked to preserve every piece of knowledge related to the Rise, including documenting every Rise that has happened since."

Lark looked up, too, but the height made her dizzy. "And... how many Rises has that been?"

"All of them," Hyar said. "Since the Oracle gained her gift."

Knowledge lost through countless ages. Knowledge Lark had always assumed lost, at least, due to how little remained in the palace library or in Jadora. "But why? What am I supposed to learn from all this?" Given how much of it there was, she didn't know if she would learn anything from it at all. One could spend their entire life in that sort of repository and never touch every volume, never mind read them.

"Has she not told you?" The Grandmaster looked between them.

One by one, Lark and all three Paragons shook their heads.

His face softened, and the smile he offered then was the most genuine by far. "Then allow me, my friends. Our order exists to preserve this knowledge so that you might someday use it. Here is where the end of everything begins. And yes," he said with a glance toward the Spectrum Blade, "where you regain all that has been lost."

Sast had been an arbitrary decision.

That bothered Lark more than anything; that she had chosen the island solely because of its fortifications and the reclusive ways of its inhabitants, only to arrive and find they'd been expecting her all along.

Had Vorkaris known? He hadn't given any indication he might, but he hadn't been surprised, either. The possibility he had withheld information that could have spared them all left her ill, yet she was no longer surprised. Everywhere she went, people knew more about her fate than she did. She had grown tired of it, and resentment swelled in her chest.

The days in the archives were long and dry, in more ways than one. The weather outside the monastery remained dreary and wet, while the air inside was dusty and dry enough that it made Lark's nostrils sore. The books and scrolls and tablets and other sorts of knowledge were so numerous and plentiful that none of them knew where to start, but by the end of each day, the piles of texts on the study tables had grown higher and Lark felt more lost than before.

The nights were no better. Each moment she was alone brought back her tears, but at least she was not alone in spirit or grief. More than once, she'd caught Resia with tear-stained cheeks, though the Kolmari girl remained diplomatic and smiling any time the others were around. The two of them were alike in that regard, Lark decided; both dedicated to their cause, perhaps to the detriment of themselves. But the name of their hurt never left anyone's lips, and each day, they all reported back to the strange library to resume the search.

The monks who came and went and helped direct Lark to subjects for study were kind, but they offered little in the way of real help. Their job had been documenting and preserving information, not learning it, and while they could direct her to each Age and era of information, they did not know which volumes held what.

Tula grumbled as she opened yet another book and rubbed the bottom of her nose to stave off a sneeze. "This one's not even written in a language I can understand."

"Then I suppose you've gone too far." Lark had encountered a few of those, herself, but she had no time to wonder what they might say. "Just keep looking. Anything with a title that jumps out at you might be useful." There had to be something about how the Paragon of Light was meant to access power; she could not fathom she was the only one who had lacked a teacher. Thus far, the only noteworthy thread she'd found was the occasional mention of vessels for power, which she had taken to mean the artifacts—and the Sunshard and Shadowsliver, most specifically, with the vessel for shadow repeatedly named. How they were meant to be used, though, it did not say.

Resia sighed, leaned against the table, and propped her chin in her hands. "I don't mean to be rude, but is there a reason no one asked the Oracle about these sorts of challenges?"

"She is the one who can see the future, not us." Andriun turned a page, though he looked as if he would have preferred to put his head down and take a nap. "We did not know what to ask when we were there."

"It's also not as if she was forthcoming with information." Lark knew that best of all; surely Oroduna had seen what was necessary to unlock her power, yet the Oracle had given her no hints beyond showing her how to focus and breathe. If there was more to it than that—which Lark had concluded there must be—then that knowledge had not been shared.

"At least, not with us. Maybe we didn't ask the right questions." Tula clapped her book shut and put it on a stack to be returned to their shelves. "But we're probably not the only ones. I'm not sure these people understood their assignment, either."

Lark had chosen not to discuss the monastery's inhabitants or their practices out of politeness, but she was less surprised by the mess of information than the Magister. The Oracle had given their founder a specific piece of knowledge; someday, Lark and the other Paragons would bring the Spectrum Blade to the island, and she would need some secret from a Rise in the past to unlock its true potential.

What that secret would be had never been disclosed, and so their order had recorded every Rise since that prophecy had been given to them. Thousands of years of information, gathered in spite of war and conflict, conquering kings and wicked ones, all with Gadranus and his armies slowly seizing pieces of the world.

That dedication was the reason the monks were all still there. Lark had suggested both gently and firmly that they should depart while it was safe to do so. None of them had complied and the Grandmasters, Hyar and Sidoya, had been just as firm in their declaration to stay and preserve this Rise the same way their order had for generations.

Given the mess that had made of their archive, Lark wondered how it was supposed to help at all. She rubbed her temples and sighed.

"It seems Your Majesty may be ready for a break?" That gentle voice belonged to Sidoya, and the woman's face practically dissolved into wrinkles when she smiled.

Resia shoved herself up from the table. "Oh, Grandmaster! Are you sure you should be up?"

"Oh, don't fret over me, dear. Thanks to your help, I feel more sprightly than I have in years." A hint of a wheeze still hung in the woman's laugh, but there was no denying she'd improved from the shriveled and weakened state she'd been in when they'd arrived the week before. Her eyes reemerged first, creating dark pools in her weathered face. "I would apologize for the interruption, but it sounds as if I have come at a convenient time. Your soldiers have been spotted on the bridge, Your Majesty. They will arrive at the monastery's gates soon."

Lark had expected it would take longer to move men across the desert and then the marshes along the coast, but she did not know the terrain. "How many are there? Will you be able to accommodate all of them?"

"We did not count, but we would be happy to help you do so once they arrive, if your general does not know the number." Sidoya remained so serious, it took a moment to realize she was joking.

Tula snickered first.

"I suspect Jobe will have figures for us. Thank you, Grandmaster. I will go meet him on the bridge." Lark pushed her book aside and stood with a wince. Her back creaked like that of a woman twice her age and she made herself stretch before she made for the door.

"I will go with you." Andriun stood, leaving his text wide open.

"And I will stay right here, where I don't have to get rained on or have the humidity turn my hair into a million corkscrews." Tula patted the top of her head to smooth any stray curls, then pulled another book from her stack.

Lark had little patience left for the Magister's fussing. She rolled her eyes and continued outside.

They had done little to explore the monastery, which was truly more like a city. The towering walls sheltered it from the outside, but buildings had grown up against the walls and crept almost as close to the sky. The structures were a maze of doors and stairways and bridges that often made no sense or led to nowhere, artifacts of an earlier era left behind when the monastery changed or grew. Even now, monks in their drab linen carried stones and buckets of mortar through the courtyard where Vorkaris had landed to let them off. Lark had come to understand that open space was the largest, and the closest thing to a city square or plaza Sast had, although there were parks and gardens scattered throughout the place.

The courtyard was not adjacent to the monastery's gates, though, and Lark only hoped she was going the right direction. They had received a tour the day they arrived, but the path they used each day since was simple and triangular. There was a series of rooms for the monastery's long-anticipated guests, the five spaces beautifully furnished and a stark contrast to the austerity of the rest of the island. One sat empty, of course; Lark had not dared to peek inside, but the others had all been pleased with the state of their rooms.

There was the massive library that archived the Rise, where she had spent most of her waking hours, be they day or night.

Then there was the communal dining hall, where all the monastery's inhabitants were expected to take all their meals, including the two Grandmasters who seemed to be in charge of the entire island. Lark had spoken to them little but found them pleasant enough. When things calmed—if they ever did—she would have to get to know them better, if only so she could thank them properly for their aid. As it was, she knew nothing about their order. She did not even know if all the people in the dull linen robes were monks, or if the men were monks and the women nuns, or if some were neither and were simply occupants of the city who had taken no vows. It was easy to blame their insular nature for that, yet she found she could blame them for nothing.

She did not know what might call a person to forsake a life outside Sast's walls and become a hermit who documented history, but there were far more of them than she ever expected. In this part of the world, it couldn't have been that unusual.

The part where they never had to deal with anything outside could have been a boon, though. Were she not already queen, Lark might have been bold enough to ask to join them and hide for the rest of her life.

"Your mood is as good as the weather," Andriun remarked as they walked. He trailed a step behind, never at her side. Lark figured he meant it as some gesture of respect, but she would have preferred a closer companion. She should have asked Resia to come along.

"It's hard to be chipper, knowing what I'm walking into." As much as she liked General Jobe as a person, he would be full of strong opinions after the events in Jadora. None of them would be fun to deal with.

Her sense of direction had not failed her, and they reached the island's gates without trouble. The first time she'd seen them, she'd been taken aback by the simplicity, but as the surprise settled, she concluded it was a good way to defend the records they kept. It never would have functioned for a city that needed to welcome commerce or travelers, but for the scant handful of people who came and went from Sast, it was good.

The old man who sat beside the gate got up from his stool as they approached. Had his back not been so stiff, he would have bowed; all he offered now was a polite dip of his head. Everyone on the island already knew who she was, and she could not decide if that was convenient or uncomfortable.

"Good afternoon," Lark began, though the rain meant she did not know if it was afternoon or if it was still morning. It was too bright to be evening, so she made peace with her choice. "Grandmaster Sidoya has informed me of my general's arrival. Open the gates to the bridge so I may welcome him."

The gate guard said nothing, but he bowed his head again and reached for the heavy ring of keys at his belt. His hand trembled as he sorted through them to find the one needed to open the plain wooden gates beside him. They were more like doors, Lark thought, ordinary and person-sized and set into the monastery's massive wall. The moment the monk had the gates unlocked, they swung open to reveal another set. The ingenuity of such defense came in how many pairs of gates there were. Lark had seen seven before she'd declared she needed to see no more, but there were seven sets of seven, with the final, larger fiftieth gate waiting where the monastery's wall met the bridge.

One by one, each pair opened until they were through the first set of gates. Each bore fortifications and the time it took to unbar each gate meant progress was sluggish. The gap between the seventh gate and the first in the next set was larger, and another man in monk's robes sat in the space. He stood when they arrived.

"All the way out," the first man told him before he closed the last of his set of gates at Lark and Andriun's heels.

The first gate of the second set was steel, rather than simple wood, and she examined it with interest. The monk noticed as he prepared his keys. He offered a small smile. "There are seven gates of steel. One at the beginning, and one at the end of each set."

"The doors on the monastery side are wooden," Andriun said. "Why?"

The man shrugged. "Steel reflected the midday sun. It was painful to view."

The explanation was so ordinary that Lark put her face in her hand. Then the steel gates groaned on their hinges and she shuffled forward for the next pair to be unlocked.

There was no further conversation as they crawled along beneath the wall, leaving her to marvel at the distance they traveled. The speed with which they moved meant there was plenty of time to do it.

For the gates to be built into the wall, it meant the wall itself had to be sixty yards across. The size left Lark stunned. Were they solid stone? Were there rooms built within them? She doubted the monks would tell her, but she vowed to ask the Grandmasters anyway, if only to sate her curiosity.

Eventually, the last gate in the seventh set swung open and they stepped into a larger room filled with crates, barrels, and sacks. Steel gates large enough to allow a wagon through waited on the other side. To Lark's surprise, Grandmaster Hyar was the one sitting beside them. He stood to greet them, looking less haggard but no better rested. "Welcome, Majesty. Paragon."

"It's good to see you, Grandmaster, though I didn't expect to find you out here." Lark did not wish to be too casual; she still did not know what they thought of her. She was less formidable than her father, but she still hoped to make a good impression.

"I chose to relieve the gate guard when we saw your army approaching. I thought it would be most proper for Sidoya or myself to greet the general. I had not realized you meant to join us." His thick eyebrows—the only hair left on his head—traveled upward as he spoke.

"Just as it is good for the body to rest after a long day's work, it is good for the mind to rest after many challenges have been thought through." Andriun spread his hands with his shrug, though Lark noticed he kept the fingers of his right hand curled as if to hide what was missing.

"Oh, yes. The labor of the mind is often overlooked, but you are right. The wisdom of the Desheni has always been spoken of with great respect. I am not surprised to hear such conclusions from the Paragon of Water." Hyar smiled again, then drew the ring with its single large key from his belt. "Shall we greet the general?"

Lark nodded.

The Grandmaster pushed the pulleys to open the gate bars and fitted the key to the lock. The large doors swung open and on the other side, a handful of soldiers shuffled back in surprise.

In the lead was Jobe.

"Good afternoon, General," Lark said.

He took in the three of them on the other side of the gates as he settled back into his usual calm demeanor, then cleared his throat. "Your Majesty," he began, stiff and formal but offering the proper respect. "I bring news."

"Yes." Lark had to steel herself to keep from sighing. "I thought you might."

CHAPTER THIRTY-NINE

Lark stepped back as Jobe signaled for the soldiers he led to move, but Hyar stepped into the center of the open gateway and cleared his throat. "Twelve men may pass the first set of gates before the next dozen is permitted to enter."

Jobe's eyes went from the monk to the first pair of wooden gates and back, then swept over the army behind him. "You can't be serious."

"These are our rules," the Grandmaster said in the same stern but placid way.

The general looked to Lark as if he expected her to order the monk to stand down.

All she did was smile.

Jobe relented, though the corners of his mouth settled into the faintest show of displeasure. "Eleven will accompany me. The rest will wait here until I have spoken with the queen in private. We will choose what to do about the others after she has heard all the news I carry."

So he did not anticipate they would be there long. Lark bit the inside of her cheek to keep her face still and let her gaze wander across the bridge and the water beyond it. It would have been a beautiful place to stand and gaze out to sea, where the wind and roaring waves could drown out the noise of her thoughts. "Very well. Come inside and we will speak."

Jobe selected the men for his party from those at his back, and they progressed to join Lark, Andriun, and Hyar in the supply room just inside the gates.

The Grandmaster drew the steel gates shut and made everyone wait while he barred them. Then he strode to the wooden set that led back into the monastery. It was only then that Lark realized she did not know how one was supposed to signal for anyone to open the door. The other monks were behind a barrier of seven gates; there was no way for any of them to hear someone knock.

Her momentary puzzlement was relieved a moment later when Hyar pressed a stone beside the gates and it slid sideways beneath his palm, revealing a series of cords. He pulled them in what appeared a random order, but Lark took it to be a code.

"Bells?" Andriun guessed.

"Yes. Brother Basfoth will have the gates open in a moment. For now, we wait."

All of them stayed in one place, shifting uncomfortably.

Eventually, the gates rasped and the monk Lark and Andriun had only just passed opened the way. Progress was faster going back. With the gates just opened by the monk, they could pass all seven at once. He closed each gate behind them and rang the next bell.

It had not been bad when it was just Andriun beside her, but with the Paragon of Water and another dozen men packed into the tiny holding chamber between the end of one set and the beginning of the next, Lark began to feel claustrophobic.

They remained silent until the last set of gates opened and they filed into the narrow lane on the other side. The courtyard was not visible from the monastery's entry, and Lark suspected it had been built that way on purpose as another defensive measure.

"We can speak privately in the archives." She turned to the bridge-shaded path that led toward more familiar territory.

"They will not be allowed into the archives," the old monk beside the gate said before she took more than a step.

Lark turned back on her heel. "What? Why not?"

"No outsiders are allowed. It is part of our code." He gave the general and his men a skeptical once-over before he turned back to Lark. "You are allowed into the archives because you are Paragons and they were built for you."

She fought back a sigh. "To my quarters, then. Andriun, will you accompany us?"

The Shaman gave a single nod.

"Very well. This way." She started off in the same direction as before, and this time, no one stopped her.

The soldiers marched along in single file behind them, earning more than a few curious glances from the men and women who called the monastery home.

Lark led them through hallways and around corners, under the bridges that connected the strange, blocky buildings and up flights of stairs bearing steps of all different heights. Eventually, they reached the corridor where the Paragons' private quarters waited. "Your men may wait in the hallway," she said as she opened her door.

Jobe signaled them with his hand and they arranged themselves along the far wall as he followed Lark and Andriun inside.

"Shall I call for the others to join us?" Andriun asked.

Lark shook her head and closed the door. "If there is any need to discuss matters with them, we will reconvene as a group. I would prefer to know everything now."

The general did not delay. "Word arrived in Jadora just after our departure. Magister Elsanna sent a bird to find us."

Lark wondered what sort of bird could find a traveling army, but it was a question for later. "And?"

"A handful of soldiers were able to infiltrate Amrochan.

Gadranus is missing. His officers hold the city, but they don't appear to know where he is."

"Gone back to Toren, most likely," Lark murmured. It would be easy for him now, with Lake Sian under his control. The river connected to the easternmost tail of the lake would carry him almost all the way back to the capital of the Shattered Lands.

"That is what we believe, as well. There has also been no sign of..." He trailed off.

"Zaide?" Lark guessed, though his name put a lump in her throat.

Andriun's eyes hardened.

"We don't know what we're fighting," the general admitted. "I know what I saw and what Magister Vorkaris reported to you, but we cannot risk making assumptions until we have his body in our possession. Until an enemy is buried, we must treat him as if he is alive."

Lark didn't know which part of his cold statement made her flinch harder, but the latter tore a hole in her heart.

Jobe clasped his hands behind his back and continued his report. "At this point, we recommend sending scouts to Toren. If we have an opportunity to strike Gadranus by surprise, we should take it. And if we have made any errors in judgment and his officer lives, we should kill either one while we have an advantage."

"*Either one*?" She shook her head. "I'm sorry, did I hear that correctly?"

His stern expression never faltered. "If he was taken back to Toren, whether dead or alive, he is our enemy."

"You can say his name," Lark said crossly. "It's not a curse."

"It might be," Andriun muttered.

She shot him a glare and he turned away, his head down.

"Either way," Jobe put in, steering the subject back the way he wanted, "we believe sending a small force to Toren is the best course of action. Scouts and a handful of assassins. Your father had intended to send assassins for just such an attempt after you brought back information about the enemy's territory."

Lark folded her arms over her chest. "And assassinating him just puts us right back at the beginning. Without the Spectrum Blade being fully restored, he'll be reborn immediately, and we're back in this exact position in another twenty years when the Rise starts over."

"Twenty years is a lot of time for us to regain ground," the general argued.

"It is also a lot of time to lose it. There are still goborrins in Amrochan, outside of Jadora and north of Ganede, and they will be eager to reclaim Tinith, too." Andriun exhaled so hard that the normally flat gills on his neck flared. "How are we to drive back so many? His forces are greater now than they have ever been."

"And we are at a disadvantage," Lark added. "My armies are scattered. By splitting what I hold, he has weakened my grasp on Amroch and I no longer believe twenty years is enough to replenish my armies after the blow we've been dealt. If we can wait until the blade is restored, we'll have a hundred years to—"

"We don't have time to wait for things that aren't a guarantee, Majesty." The general shook his head as he cut her short.

She drew herself up and curled her hands to fists. "We have time to wait for whatever I order, General." She emphasized his title with a quirk of her brow, reminding him where he stood on the ladder of authority.

Jobe grew quiet.

"There have been changes. You saw what happened in Jadora. You know what that means." At least, Lark hoped he did. She hadn't seen anything, herself, and she did not know if the aftermath of the power that had so briefly awakened in her was devastation or a disappointment.

He considered her face for a long while before he spoke again. "Then you have made progress?"

Her stomach rolled over at the question. "Yes," she lied.

Andriun's head turned, ever so slightly, but enough to let her know she'd have questions to answer later.

"But like with all things, it will take time," Lark added.

"A luxury we don't have." Jobe's voice grew heavy, thick with insistence. "I've brought men to protect Sast, but even this fortress cannot be defended against what we face forever. We need to strike, Your Majesty, and every moment we delay puts us at risk of losing the opportunity."

She stared at him—at the way he subtly avoided meeting her eye—and understanding hit her so hard that she almost shrank. "You mean to do it anyway. Regardless of my commands."

The general hesitated for too long.

Stinging betrayal twisted up inside her and left her cold. "You've already sent them, haven't you?"

"A meeting of council was drawn in Jadora," he replied slowly, testing each word and measuring her response. "As leaders of Amroch's military force, we are allowed to make some decisions regarding tactics without a ruler's immediate approval. Against an established enemy, the dispatch of specialized attacks falls within what is permitted."

"And if I forbid it? What then? Were you counting on coming here and having me immediately approve to absolve you of your clear overstep?" Her voice rose until Andriun put a hand on her shoulder—the one with fresh scars where the webbing should have been. The touch calmed like a lid dropped over the flames of her outrage.

When she grew quiet, Andriun spoke. "How were these soldiers deployed? From where, and how many?"

Jobe remained still and calm as he answered. "The orders were sent to those stationed in Tinith. A number of our best soldiers remained behind to help aid refugees fleeing Amrochan. By now, they will have traveled through the southeastern forest and be well into their trek toward the north."

"And what were the orders?" the Shaman pressed. "The exact orders relayed to your men?"

Again, the general hesitated, then locked eyes with Lark. "To deploy five of our best scouts and three assassins to Toren, to strike down Gadranus and any of his commanding officers. And to spread the word among our remaining forces that any broken-born not drafted into our military should be treated as a threat and eliminated at once."

"You can't do that! It's an egregious overstep, there are innocent refugees from the Shattered Lands scattered all throughout my kingdom." Her hands shook and she wished she could clench them tighter.

"Then they can serve your kingdom, the same as anyone else," Jobe said.

"And Zaide?" He'd served her better than anyone, yet he had never been part of Amroch's military. "He did more to help soldiers escape Amrochan than anyone else, and he was never drafted. Is his example not enough to prove your orders are too broad?"

The general's expression grew cool. "As I said, *any* broken-born."

The chill that dominated Lark's insides turned to ice.

CHAPTER FORTY

Cold water lapped against Zaide's face. It drew his skin into gooseflesh, and the tightening sensation made him too aware of the wet cloth that clung to his body. His ears were underwater, its movement simultaneously a soft whoosh and a roar that blotted out all other sounds.

Something cold pressed against his nose, followed by warm and wet. He flinched and turned away from it, his neck stiff. It followed until he drew a hand from the water and pushed it away. Wiry fur greeted his fingertips and he forced his eyes open.

An ice blue gaze so much like his own greeted him, although set in a white face with a dark nose that hovered just above his.

Daisy's pink tongue swiped up the underside of his nose and Zaide snorted as he twisted away in disgust.

Pale sand and scattered pebbles shifted beneath him as he moved. The white dog licked his face as he sat upright and then she frisked along the water's edge, though she paused after a few steps and stood alert, staring across the pool.

They were not alone.

At the far side of the circular room, Gadranus sat atop a

stone. He held his sword by the pommel, using two fingers to rotate its tip against the ground. He watched it, bored, yet Zaide took the sense the man saw every move he made.

In response, Zaide grew still.

"I never thought I would come here again," Gadranus said without looking up. "One hundred years spent in this place was more than long enough."

Every muscle in Zaide's body ached, drawn tight by the cold water in which he sat. He rubbed the back of his neck, but his hand was so cold it brought no comfort. "I thought you said you spend the time between Rises in the void."

"I do. But a part of me was here. I doubt you have forgotten." A hint of a smile curved the dark-haired man's mouth, though it lacked the sincerity it had once held and it came off as more of a sneer.

Zaide had not forgotten, but he, too, had assumed he would never see this pool again. Water still poured from the font at one end. The ripples it cast flowed between the two of them like some great divide, currents pushing in two different directions. He brushed his fingers along the pool's edge. "How did I get here?" And of all the places to be, why Kolmar's temple?

"How do you suppose?" Gadranus shrugged. "It was the last thing you did, when you consumed the last scrap of what magic I'd given you. Perhaps you thought you'd be safe from me here."

"Is anyone ever safe from you?"

Gadranus gave a harsh but amused laugh.

Daisy's fur bristled and the dog growled. Zaide put out a hand to soothe her. His wet fingers picked up every loose hair in her thick coat.

"In spite of all the training I've given you, it seems some of that wild impulse still remains untamed. But no, Zaide. You are not safe. Not here, not anywhere. Not when we were in Amrochan and not in Toren, either." The black sword in Gadranus's hand melted into shadows and disappeared. "I had hoped to guide you until the end, but it seems someone else has your fetters now."

Zaide's brow furrowed and he was not sure what that was supposed to mean until Gadranus lowered his gaze. Zaide touched his chest. His fingers sank into a gap in his armor and he looked down, surprised. Where one of the eye sockets on the ram's skull emblem had been, there was now a scorched hole. Pale skin showed through and he brushed it with wonder.

He'd been aware—painfully so—through much of what happened in Jadora. Nothing could compare to the agony of the Sunshard striking his chest, yet there was not so much as a wound to mark it had been there. Aside from the ache brought about by floating in a pool of cold water for who knew how long, he was well. Whole. There should have been pain. There should have been the perpetual queasiness in the pit of his stomach, too, but it was also gone.

His heart skipped a beat and he tried to find the power that had all but consumed him.

Nothing answered.

"It is gone," Gadranus said, as if he knew what Zaide looked for. "You are again as you were. An empty vessel. Nothing more."

Gone.

A profound sense of emptiness and longing stirred within him and warred with elation, which surged and then sank into disappointment.

He had tried so hard to give Lark the power she needed to restore the blade.

He had failed.

"If that is what you believe," Gadranus murmured.

Zaide's head snapped up. "Get out of my head."

"I can do many things, but I cannot read minds. If you don't wish for me to know your thoughts, then don't think them with your face, and I will not." A dry smile graced Gadranus's features. He rose from the stone where he perched, then sobered. "Our time together has reached an end, but I wish for you to know that I enjoyed it. Truly. You are a young man of remarkable skill and your father would be proud to see all that you can do, and all the determination you do it with. When we meet again, I pray that we can do it as friends."

"I was never your friend," Zaide fired back. "I never will be."

"Then that is my loss, and I hope you will believe my grief is real." Shadows swelled behind Gadranus and he stepped backwards into their embrace, leaving mist to fade into the empty air where he had been.

Zaide stared at the space until he was positive there were no tricks at play. Then, against his better judgment, he focused his attention inward and searched for the magic that had almost destroyed him before.

Nothing.

He was weaker. Empty. Devoid of the incredible power he'd tasted and learned to crave. He was nothing but himself, the same as he'd always been, and the shadows of magic that had haunted his mind and itched against his bones had disappeared.

Even the spring he sat in, something he knew was magic, was nothing more than cold water on his skin.

The silence in his spirit was so great, he did not know if he should rejoice or weep.

He did neither.

Instead, Zaide pushed himself up with a grimace. Water poured from his clothing and armor and he regarded them both, trying to decide how to proceed.

He had nothing else. He was in Kolmar, but his old home was empty—he'd packed all his clothing when he'd made that first expedition to Amrochan. Hanging what he wore beneath his armor so it could dry was an option, but there was nowhere to put it down here. If he hung it anywhere, it would have to be in his cottage, where he could sit in private until it was dry enough to wear.

But he couldn't very well walk through Kolmar as he was. He was ashamed enough after all that had happened; the last thing he needed was to explain to the few remaining people who might love him why he wore the enemy's crest. He dug his fingers against the buckles of the cuirass, but they were numb from the chill of the water and he could not unfasten anything. He gritted his teeth in frustration and reached for his sword. The moment his hand closed around its hilt, he paused.

He didn't remember sheathing the Viper's Tongue at his side. All he remembered was light and pain before darkness swallowed him. If he still had the sword, it meant someone had picked it up and returned it to its sheath.

The idea Gadranus had saved him nagged at the corners of Zaide's mind and he refused to give it notice.

Gadranus was his enemy.

Zaide owed him nothing.

He drew the blade and tried to hook it under one of the straps at his side, but the angle was wrong and he didn't have enough space and in the end, he let his hand drop with the sword still in his grasp.

Beside him, Daisy huffed at his apparent defeat.

"I tried, all right? If I had a regular knife, I could do it." He shoved the blade back into its sheath and waded out of the water. "But I guess it's better to keep it on, just in case we run into goborrins. We'd better get to the surface."

The dog's tail swished and she all but pranced toward the exit. Zaide didn't know what lay beyond the temple anymore, but he prayed it would not be trouble.

He remembered the stairs. They were easier to traverse than the slope he'd taken to the space beneath the temple the first time, but that had been a different room, not the pool where they'd slain a specter and found the Shadowsliver.

That strange purple prism was their only hope now. Zaide struggled not to feel defeated. Through all the time they'd carried it, they'd never figured out how to work it or what it was meant to do. But there was one difference, he reminded himself; now, he had experience working with the brand of magic Gadranus held. If anyone could determine how to redirect its magic into the Spectrum Blade, it would be him.

"Looks like we'll be headed back to Jadora," he told Daisy as they walked.

She looked up at him with her tongue lolling past her white teeth and he questioned her presence for the first time.

"How did you get here, anyway?" He reached to scratch the top of her head. From the way she leaned into his touch, he guessed she enjoyed it. Odd, considering the last he remembered of her was her fangs in his hand. He tilted it and found the bite marks were still there. A hint of disappointment tugged at his heart. "I guess I can't be mad at you for that. You were a good girl, keeping Lark safe." Something he hadn't been able to do.

Daisy looked up at him again, but her mouth was closed and he could have sworn her eyebrows had drawn close. Did dogs have eyebrows? He wasn't certain of their anatomy, but she looked worried.

He scratched her again. "I'm all right." Or he would be, once they made it to Jadora. How he was going to achieve that sort of a trek, he didn't know.

They emerged into the wide, empty room where he'd first seen the mark of Gadranus. Its peeling paint still marked the floor and he studied it for a long time, though it was dark outside and only a faint light filtered in from elsewhere in the temple. It had not yet been a year since the first time he'd set foot there, yet experience set it so far behind him that it felt like a memory long lost. He'd never imagined then that the man would someday be his mentor. Maker's mercy, the version of him that first entered that room hadn't imagined the man could really *exist*.

Yet here Zaide was now, clothed in Gadranus's colors and bearing a sword that had belonged to him. He shook his head in mild disbelief and made for the stairway he knew led to the second floor. The room with the emblem was empty, but the lights in the doorways at the far end of it still burned and soft voices reached his ears.

He would not distress the Kolmari with his appearance tonight.

Daisy trotted along at his side as he walked the hallways and tried to recall the various paths he'd taken through the temple before. Eventually, his memory served him well and he found the wooden doorway that he and Lark had first entered through, back in the spring. That doorway had been rocked over the last time he'd been there, but much of what the goborrins had damaged was now repaired. The temple looked better than it ever had, to his knowledge.

"And there are no spiders," he muttered to himself as he led Daisy to the balcony and shut the door behind him.

There were lights outside the temple, too. Armored guards stood at each corner and he reconsidered his plan of escape. Kolmar had never been home to guards, but he should have expected that, too, would change. Now it was one of few places in the world that was safe from goborrins, the forest's protective barrier anchored to the spring whose water still dripped from his clothes.

Yet perhaps the barrier protected less than he'd assumed. Gadranus had pierced it easily, sat right beside its anchoring power and appeared unconcerned.

If that wasn't a sign of what sort of devastating power they were up against, Zaide didn't know what was.

He glanced in both directions before he considered the cliff straight ahead. The light was dimmer there, but he did not think he was equipped to make that climb. Nor did he think trying to make for his home in Kolmar was wise anymore, either. He rubbed his forehead and tried to come up with some alternative that didn't involve presenting himself to the guards and wallowing in guilt as he tried to explain himself. He had little left; shredding the last scraps of his ego was not high on the list of things he was eager to do.

Beside him, Daisy gave a soft whine and nosed his thigh.

"You're right," he sighed. "I need to just..." What? Admit the idiotic plan that had almost gotten their queen killed? Tell his family about all the things he'd learned in service to the man who meant to conquer the world? Zaide fought back a groan.

There was no way for any of this to end well.

"We'll go around the back," he told himself as much as he told the dog, as if he could reassure himself the idea would work. "We'll hope for a guard that recognizes me and see if he'll let me past."

Idiocy, the more reasonable part of him whispered as the words left his mouth. But it was the only choice he had left that he thought might spare him a scrap of grief.

He climbed down the back side of the balcony and opened his arms to invite Daisy down. She pawed the edge of the stone for a moment before she jumped and landed on the earth beside him with a whump. Zaide winced, but she scrambled back to her feet and ran straight for the guard at the back corner of the temple.

The man shouted in surprise as the dog ran a circle around his legs and streaked off into the night, her white coat aglow in the moonlight. Calls of alarm rose from the other guards and armor rattled as they ran to help.

Zaide cringed and shrank back into the corner where the balcony's support wall met the temple.

That was not part of the plan, yet the guard from the front of the temple ran past without noticing him there. The man disappeared around the corner, and so did the light of the lantern he carried.

A moment passed without any more disturbances. Zaide pushed himself off the stone wall and peered around the corner.

The front of the temple was dark now, the lights concentrated at the back.

He considered for only a moment before he sprinted into the dark and prayed there would be no one on the path.

That side of the forest was more familiar. Two guards stood beside the temple's front entrance, but neither looked up as Zaide cut his way up the steep, angled hill that rose beside the path to Kolmar. He wove between the trees and his sodden cape snagged more than once, but it was heavy enough that shaking it snapped branches and let him loose.

Please think the noise is just a deer. He certainly wouldn't have if he were one of the guards, but who knew how safe they thought they were? They didn't know what he did, that the man who meant to destroy them all had been beneath the temple not even an hour past.

Eventually he found a game trail and the path grew easier. He ran for as long as he could, but the weight of his wet clothing and armor combined unpleasantly with the exhaustion that came from everything else he'd been through, and he had not yet gone a mile before he was out of breath.

White darted between the trees ahead.

Daisy.

Zaide dared not call her, but seeing her free in the woods without anyone pursuing her was enough. She'd find her way back to him, the way she'd found him in the first place.

He walked for as long as he could, but the adrenaline from the brief escape was gone and his limbs ached with fatigue and cold. It was winter now, after all, and for the first time, he noticed that his breath misted on the air.

Should have gone back to Kolmar, he grumbled silently to himself. It certainly would have been wiser, not that he was known for wisdom. With that in mind, he unfastened his cape and twisted it between his hands to wring out the excess water. It was wet but still useful, and if he fashioned it into some sort of cover suspended above him, he could use it and dry leaves for insulation to stay warm until his energy returned.

He'd just chosen a bush he thought would suffice as a hiding place when a bark from Daisy split the night and his whole body turned in the direction it had come.

A blade pricked the corner of Zaide's jaw and he froze.

CHAPTER FORTY-ONE

"Turn around." The order was low, rasping and dangerous.

Zaide let his cape fall and spread his hands wide as he raised them, showing he held no weapons. His heart threatened to choke him, but he cooperated, turning as the blade rotated and slid to a tender hollow just beneath his chin. Their eyes met and the fact recognition brought no relief threatened to make Zaide sick.

He spread his hands a little wider and lifted his head a shade more, as if that might spare him the prick of Aren's blade. "I can explain."

The moonlight through the bare trees made it easy to see Aren's face as he took everything in. He examined the fresh scars on Zaide's face, the blue earrings he wore, the sword at his right side and the fine armor, sullied by both the emblem it bore and the scorched hole made by the Sunshard. None of it brought any change to the expression Aren wore. "Start with why you're wet."

"I was in the pool under the temple."

Aren's blade remained still. "Why?"

"I—" Zaide's breath caught. Maybe he couldn't explain. "I woke up there. I don't know."

The quality of that response made itself evident in the way Aren's mouth pressed thin.

"I can explain," Zaide repeated, though he was no longer sure. "I just need time. Put down the sword and I'll tell you everything that happened."

Aren gave him another quick inspection. "I think I can guess."

"I promise you can't." Zaide would have laughed if not for the danger he was in. The absurdity of the situation made his head reel.

Faint creases formed between Aren's brows as he considered his next step. His eyes flicked to the sword at Zaide's side several times over.

"I can lay it down if that'll make you feel better." Zaide did not want to be parted from his only defense, but he did not want his oldest friend to believe he might wield it against him, either.

Aren snorted. "I don't think there's anything you can do to make me feel better right now."

"I could leave," Zaide suggested.

"That's going to happen whether you do it by foot or by funeral."

Zaide didn't think he was supposed to laugh at that. He swallowed. "All right. Quick version, then. I was captured when Amrochan fell but convinced Gadranus I would join him, so they let me out. I helped a bunch of imprisoned soldiers escape, then I helped Lark escape when she came back, too. I sparred against Gadranus so I could try to kill him, but I wasn't good enough with a sword because he's had thousands of years of practice and I've had about ten."

Aren stared at him, his expression unchanging, but he did nothing to interrupt the story so Zaide went on.

"I convinced him to give me a piece of his magic and I tried to take it to Lark so she could use it to restore the Spectrum Blade's power and we could go kill Gadranus together, but he used that magic against me and I woke up here underneath the temple and now I have to figure out how to get back to Lark to help with Jadora because the city is in danger." He paused to wet his lips in the heavy silence that followed. "Any questions?"

"Yeah," Aren said. "You think I'm stupid?"

Zaide offered a slight shrug. "I think you're my friend. That's probably the same thing."

"You're probably right." Aren shifted back and lowered his sword. "The officers who got here after Amrochan was evacuated ordered us to kill any enemy broken-born who try to cross through the forest."

"Good thing I'm not your enemy," Zaide said. He dared not show his relief, his heart still drumming in his chest.

"Lucky you ran into me, or you wouldn't have a chance to try and convince anyone. Resia's barrier keeps goborrins out, but it doesn't always work on people."

Which might explain why Gadranus was able to move so freely within the temple. Zaide didn't know if he should mention that or not. He had no desire to rob Kolmar of what little sense of safety they had.

Aren drew back another step, then pointed west. "Go."

Zaide hesitated.

"I don't believe half of what you said. But some of these guards from Amrochan won't believe any of it, and I can't protect you if anyone else sees you like this. So get out. Before they do." Aren held his finger steady, but he turned his face away.

The doubt stung in ways Zaide hadn't expected. "I'm not lying, Aren. Not about any of it."

"Prove it, then."

Zaide didn't know how. "I can't."

"Then I don't have to believe you. Now go, before I change my mind." Aren did not look at him again.

It was not the exit Zaide wanted to make, but it was the only one he was going to get.

He scooped his cape from the ground and headed west.

The forest hadn't changed. The same trails Zaide knew led him to the river that had once been the boundary dividing his life from the rest of the world. The living bridge of woven trees still stood, and the road beyond it was still held by Lark's forces.

Daisy trotted alongside him the whole way. More than once, she brought him some squirrel or rabbit she'd managed to catch, but he had nothing with which to make a fire. His only provisions were the things he could forage; nuts and seeds and occasional handfuls of peppery watercress leaves whenever he found fresh water. By the time he'd made it to the edge of the forest, he'd lost enough strength that he spent more time hunting for food than traveling, and the raw meat Daisy offered had begun to look more appealing.

Then the scent of something cooking struck his nose.

He'd passed through this part of the world before and knew there were no permanent installations nearby. That meant a camp, but whether it would be friendly or full of enemies, he did not know, and that he wasn't sure which side of that distinction humans or goborrins fell on was both strange and darkly amusing.

The dog smelled it, too. Her nose tilted to the wind and she looked back, questioning.

Zaide weighed his options. The best chance he had to reach Jadora was to make for Tinith and find a ship, but he had no money with which to hire one and doubted he could make it that far without questioning, anyway. A stop at a camp—if it was a human camp, anyway—might let him evaluate his chances in a way safer than strolling into a city that was likely still under siege. The last he'd known, Tinith was still holding out against advancing goborrins, but that had been before he'd joined the army destined for Jadora. He prayed the city still held.

"Guess we can see if they have some food for us." Zaide removed his cape and unbuckled his cuirass, the only things he suspected were necessary to hide. He'd have them handy if it proved to be a goborrin camp, but the food smelled far too palatable for that to be likely. As far as he knew, goborrins didn't use spices.

He rolled the discarded armor in his cape and slung it over his shoulder like a travel bag, then beckoned for Daisy to walk with him. The dark gambeson underneath gave nothing away on its own, save that he'd been through some sort of skirmish. There was no hiding the burnt hole in the chest, or the pale circle of flesh it left exposed. Perhaps he could convince someone he'd found it that way.

Zaide crested the hill beside the camp and went down on one knee to evaluate what waited ahead.

Daisy hung close beside him, her nose continually twitching.

"I know," he murmured. "Me, too." He tried to ignore his stomach's grumbling, though it grew hard. He couldn't afford to make stupid mistakes because of hunger, though, and the long training sessions with Gadranus had curbed his impulsive impatience.

Every sentry stationed around the camp was armed with a bow and Zaide doubted they would hesitate to shoot if he tried to approach. All he needed was a chance to speak with someone, explain who he was and why he was there, but there was no easy way to get it. Even without the ram's skull on his chest, he'd look like an enemy, and he could not fault any of the soldiers for being on edge after Amrochan's fall. But he could not put his life on the line for a full belly, either.

Zaide shook his head and inched backwards. There were too many archers. He couldn't justify the risk. "Into the woods, girl. We'll find you a rabbit or something."

Daisy whined and he held up a finger to silence it. Her pale blue eyes grew round and mournful, but she quieted.

A meal would have been nice, but Zaide was happy with the information he'd gained, too. For a camp to be settled here, right at the edge of where Kolmar's forests ended and the hills northeast of Tinith began, it meant Tinith had to be safe. How he was supposed to make it onto a boat was still a problem to work out, but it meant there would be a boat, and that was a good start.

He slid between the trees with a plan to disappear and made it a handful of steps before an axe sailed past his head to slam into a tree.

Zaide stifled a shout and leaped back with his hand on the hilt of his sword, but a hand snagged him by the collar and thrust him back against the tree, just below the axe's blade. It knocked the air from his lungs and he wheezed as he reclaimed enough to speak. "Portran!"

The blacksmith froze with his other hand curled to a fist, surprise and recognition lighting his eyes.

Daisy leaped around their feet, barking, and Zaide motioned with a flattened palm to silence her.

"Maker's mercy, boy!" Portran loosened his grasp, but didn't let go. His empty hand went for the handle of his axe.

Zaide twitched as it came free and damaged bark crumbled into his hair. "What are you—"

"Shh." The blacksmith examined him for all of two seconds before he unfastened his coat, peeled it off, and flung it over Zaide's shoulders.

Another question leaped to the tip of Zaide's tongue, but he managed to swallow it as Portran jerked the hood over his head. Then the man seized the dark red bundle of the cape and cuirass from the ground.

"Walk with me," the blacksmith ordered, his voice low. "Walk fast." He added a few chunks of cut wood to his arms and stuffed some into Zaide's arms, too, then led the way out of the woods.

They crossed the field in a hurry. More than one of the sentries looked at them twice, though they appeared more interested in Daisy than the two of them.

"Don't look at them," Portran ordered in a murmur.

Zaide did as he was told, his attention fixed on the wood he carried as they hustled through the camp.

"Found yourself a friend?" someone called.

The accusation made Zaide's pulse leap before he realized the man meant Daisy.

"Dog's a better friend than any of you here, and I only just met it," the blacksmith shouted back, earning a hearty laugh.

They passed between the rows of tents until they reached one larger than the others. A workbench outside marked it as a makeshift forge, or at least some sort of repair station. Portran opened the tent's flap and motioned Zaide inside. He ducked in, still clinging to the wood he'd been given, and the smith followed close at his heels. Daisy squeezed in before the flap swung closed.

A woman in the corner rose from a cushioned barrel. "Maker's mercy! I thought we talked about bringing animals—"

"In a moment, love," the smith interrupted mildly. He dropped his wood by the door and plucked the rest of the logs from Zaide's grasp, then seized him by the arm and steered him toward the back of the tent. Another flap opened into a smaller space where tidy pallets on the floor offered an explanation of its use.

Before Zaide could ask what they were doing, Portran took hold of the shoulders of his coat. Zaide shimmied out of it with ease, in spite of his armor; the blacksmith was a much larger man than he.

"Don't you 'in a moment' me again, or I'll—" The flap snapped open and Portran's wife froze with the thick canvas still in her hand. She stared and Zaide stared back. He'd expected a negative reaction, yet the uncertainty and fear with which she regarded him was different from the animosity he'd braced for.

She slid inside and let the tent's makeshift door close behind her. "Is he...?"

"Aye," Portran said.

The simple exchange reminded Zaide of so many looks and

questions he'd received that it rubbed his hackles the wrong way. "I'm Kolmari," he said, a shade defensively. "I just came from there. I'm on your side."

With timing that could not have been worse, Portran unwrapped the cuirass he'd hidden in his cape, and the man's wife inched closer to see it, too. Her hand drifted to her chest.

Zaide regretted approaching the camp at all. "Portran—"

"Calm down, lad. Keep your voice down. Fetch him a bowl, Etta, and one for his pup. They're fit to be starving if they've come from Kolmar with only leather to eat." The blacksmith raised a brow.

His wife was unimpressed. "It's hardly been a day. If anyone finds him here—"

"Then they won't," Portran said. "And if they do, they'll go through me to get 'im. I know his father. I worked with him in the forge. He's a good lad, Etta. No matter what they say."

Wariness stirred in Zaide's veins. "What who says?"

Etta cast him a worried frown, then ducked out of the small sleeping room. That left Portran, and the blacksmith did not look happy. He folded the deep red cape back over the discarded armor. "How long since you left Kolmar?"

Zaide tried to recall. He hadn't counted, nor could he, looking back. He'd slept so poorly that the days blurred together in his head. "I don't know. A week?"

Portran blew out a sigh. "Maker's had mercy on you after all, if that's the case. You missed them by a day and must have passed them in the woods without either of you noticing."

"Who?"

"Men from Jadora, carrying the queen's orders. Every soldier in the country's been ordered to watch for broken-born, and especially for you." The blacksmith tucked his chin and looked Zaide in the eye.

Zaide stared back for a long time, unable to find words. His hand drifted to his throat, and Portran gave a single nod.

That told him everything he needed to know. Had he been a

day earlier, or too late in leaving Kolmar, he would have run afoul of the party looking for him. Now it was worse; now the entire camp was looking for him, and soon Kolmar would be, too.

He had no words for the way everything left inside him began to crumble.

"A lot has happened since Amrochan," the blacksmith said with a note of apology. "Nowhere's safe. Not for us, not for you. Goborrins camp outside Jadora and the queen's men march for Estkel. Tinith is ours, but the messengers have already been there and gone. They'll be waiting for you there. I don't know where you're going, lad, but I'll do what I can to get you back on the road."

"Lark," Zaide said, though his voice cracked. "I have to get to her."

Portran's brow furrowed. "She means to have you killed, boy."

Something inside him had already died at the thought. Zaide struggled to contain it, keep it from falling apart, but it was as if it fell to dust and slipped through his fingers. His breath quickened and he fought to keep it steady, but it was a fight he couldn't win. He sank to the floor and stared at the blacksmith's boots without seeing. Daisy whined and nudged his shoulder.

A long silence hung between them before Portran spoke again. "Word from Jadora is you tried to kill her."

Zaide's head whipped up. "I would never," he spat as fury sent heat up his neck and to the tips of his ears. "Gadranus tried to kill her. He'll do anything to kill her. I did everything I could to keep her safe."

"Easy, lad." The smith patted the air with one hand, telling him to settle. "I never said I believed it, I'm just telling you what you'll be up against. Rumor has it she's calling for a draft. There'll be a lot of people looking for you. A lot of ways to die."

"I don't care." Zaide almost startled himself with the strength with which he said it, but the moment it left his lips, he knew it was true. "I still have to find her. I have to—I have to fix this."

"And if fixing it costs your head?"

Was there any other way? Zaide dropped his head into his hands, but it did nothing to soothe the growing ache that swelled in his chest. If that was what Lark wanted, she could have it. He wouldn't run away. He'd claim the title of idiot and accept what a fool he'd been, but he wasn't a coward.

A rustle in the front of the tent announced Etta's return before she shrugged her way under the flap to the back room. "Supper time," she announced, presenting a bowl in either hand.

Daisy leaned forward, her nose twitching, and when the woman knelt to leave a bowl in front of her, the dog's tail swished, but she stayed still and waited for permission.

The second bowl, Etta pushed into Zaide's hands. "Eat while it's warm. It looks like it'll do you some good."

"Thank you," Zaide said. The warmth of the wooden bowl was a comfort he'd sorely missed and he cradled it close as he tapped Daisy's bowl with a foot. "Eat."

The dog tore into her meal.

Portran cleared his throat above the noise. "I can't promise you'll get anywhere alive, but I'll do what I can to help. Provisions for the trip, and..." He cast the wrapped armor a disdainful look. "Something more tasteful to wear, perhaps. We'll get you out of here tomorrow."

"Thank you," Zaide repeated. He didn't know what else to say.

The blacksmith nodded and took his wife by the arm to steer her out of the room. "You stay here and rest for now, and eat up. Stay out of sight, but let Etta know if you need anything. I'll be back tonight." The two of them slipped out, and in their absence, the darker back room of the tent felt colder.

Zaide looked at the bowl in his hands.

For all that he was starving, he found he had no appetite.

CHAPTER FORTY-TWO

THE BLACKSMITH and his wife dragged their bedding to the front portion of their divided tent to sleep, leaving the back portion to Zaide and the dog. It was his first chance since leaving Kolmar to sleep without his armor on, and the comfort meant exhaustion was quick to claim him.

At some point in the night, Zaide jerked awake with a gasp and found Portran kneeling beside him with a hand on his shoulder.

"Best find something sweeter to think about," the man whispered. "Whatever's in those dreams right now will have half the camp knowing you're here."

A flush of embarrassment warmed Zaide's face. He didn't want to speak of the things that haunted him, the ugly amalgamations of every waking nightmare he'd faced since leaving home. He scrubbed his eyes with the side of his hand and rasped an apology.

The blacksmith patted his shoulder and slid to the front room of the tent. Daisy slipped in beside his legs.

"And where were you?" Zaide asked. He couldn't make himself lay down again, not yet; not while it still felt like shadows and spiders and the bitter cold of nothing crawled across his skin.

The dog sprawled out beside him, her back pressed close to his thigh, and her yawn exposed all her teeth. He hadn't expected she'd give an answer, but her profound lack of guilt worried him more than if she'd put her head down or avoided his eye. If she was off gallivanting around the camp all hours of the night and getting in the way, it wouldn't be long before someone came to discuss it with Portran, and Zaide did not know how long he could hide.

He sat until his eyes felt heavy again, then settled down with an arm draped over the dog. She nestled close, the warmth of her fur welcome in the chilly night air, and eventually, sleep took him again.

When he woke the next morning, she was still there, curled close beside him, and Zaide found he could not muster the will to rise.

He had to get up. He had to leave. To remove himself from the camp, to figure out how to cross the country without encountering any of Lark's soldiers, to find her and finally offer an apology for everything he'd gotten wrong.

Yet turning himself in meant death. Even as hopeless as he was, he wasn't eager to march to his end, and the longer he thought about it, the less strength he found in his limbs.

Eventually, a stirring in the front room caught his ear and Etta slipped in with a bowl in each hand.

"Good morning," she whispered, an unpleasant reminder of the need for secrecy. A number of shadows had passed over the canvas as men strode by, but it was easy for Zaide to ignore them when all he did was lay there and wallow under the weight of despair. With another person there and the possibility of conversation in front of him, he could not afford to ignore anything, lest he make a mistake and meet his end before he so much as had a chance to clear the air.

Zaide pushed himself upright as Daisy turned to try to stick her nose straight in his bowl.

"Ah-ah," Etta scolded as she lifted it beyond what the dog could reach. "Yours is here." She lowered the other bowl and tilted it to display the meat scraps inside. Daisy had her muzzle in it before the bowl touched the ground.

"Thank you," Zaide murmured as he accepted his own breakfast. He'd had no desire to get up and pursue it, but now that it was in his hands, he couldn't ignore his appetite.

Etta shrugged and folded her skirt under her knees as she settled on the ground beside him. "Thank my husband, whenever he makes it in here. He's putting a lot at risk for you."

"I'm sorry. If I'd seen him before he saw me, I would have spoken to him in the woods instead of coming here." He kept his voice low, but they both fell silent as booted footsteps passed the tent.

Once they faded, Etta replied. "He's fixing up a piece for your armor now, and I've packed up some food. The skies look like snow, so it'll be easier for you to sneak off during the day, before it falls."

Zaide fought his disappointment and focused on his food. It wasn't that he wanted to stay; his presence was a risk for them. But he didn't want to leave, either. The camp was quiet and offered a strange illusion of safety. Anyone else in the camp might try and kill him, and while Zaide was confident he'd grown enough as a swordsman to stave off a handful of attackers at once, there was no hope for any one man to defend against an entire camp.

Etta watched him eat for a time, then raised a finger. "One moment." She ducked out and he finished his meal before she returned with something in her hands.

A white muzzle dipped into Zaide's bowl from the side, searching for remnants of stew with a wide pink tongue. He wrestled Daisy back with an elbow and stacked their bowls to return them.

Whatever it was Etta held, she offered it with one hand as she accepted the bowls with the other. "I made this for you, this morning."

Zaide took it, puzzled, and turned it over twice before he got it right side up. He couldn't tell what color it was, but it was a hat knitted of soft, dark wool. It snagged against his rough skin as he rubbed it between his fingers. "You made this for me?"

"Just said I did," she muttered, then went quiet as a shadow passed the tent. "Thought it might help with... well, at a glance... you know."

His hair would probably doom him faster than his armor. Without the cuirass, there was only the color of the cape to mark him as a part of Gadranus's army. He ran his thumbs over the tidy knit stitches again. It wouldn't be as helpful once he reached Jadora, but for as long as he was in the parts of Amroch that saw winter, it would be invaluable. "Thank you."

"Thank Portran." She shrugged and departed without another word, but the brusque way she spoke couldn't hide the sincerity and thoughtfulness of the gift.

Zaide smoothed back his white hair and pulled the hat onto his head.

He considered laying down again, but feared he wouldn't find the strength to rise if he did. Instead, he stayed sitting upright and inspected his injuries. Part of him reasoned it was pointless to monitor them when certain death waited on the other end of Amroch, but there was the small matter of getting there. For a single, fleeting instant he considered whether there was anywhere else he could go, but the thought went nowhere. There was nowhere else. If it wasn't Lark hunting him, it would be Gadranus, and whatever fate the latter had in store for him would only ensure the former never stopped.

"It really was all for nothing, wasn't it?" He scratched between Daisy's ears, then went still. There was no power for the Spectrum Blade, no leader to save anyone from the goborrins, no helper on the inside to let men trapped in Amrochan escape.

Everything he'd planned and all he'd struggled for had only made things worse in the end.

Daisy shoved her head up into his hand with a soft whine.

He resumed scratching. "I ruined everything."

"That might be taking a bit more credit than you deserve."

Zaide jumped at the voice, but it was only the blacksmith. He ducked in with the leather cuirass in his hands and tilted it to display the repair.

Only it wasn't just a repair. The hole where the Sunshard had burned through the armor had been patched with an attractively shaped piece that spanned the breast and was riveted in place, but what drew Zaide's eye was the fresh tooling across and beneath it—a white wolf surrounded by dark stain, all but obscuring what remained of the ram's skull.

Portran cleared his throat. "Well, what do you think? Might have taken a few liberties. She's not all that frightful in real life."

"You never do anything halfway, do you?" Zaide accepted the armor and traced the edges of the new design with a fingertip.

The compliment bounced off the man as if he had an iron hide. All Portran did was shrug. "If a man's going to make something, it ought to be something worth looking at. That should last you a long time, though. Well past Estkel, maybe to the end of all things."

"Estkel?" Zaide lifted his head.

"The scouts who passed through let a few things slip. Easy to do, when you're hungry and sharing a meal and a good drink with a few old friends." The blacksmith offered a grim smile. "The decision to deploy their band was made by the officers left in charge of Jadora, not the queen. What does that sound like to you?"

"Like..." An odd sinking in Zaide's chest made him glad he'd chosen to stay sitting. "Like she's not there." And the last thing he recalled clearly before the moment the Sunshard pierced his skin was her face, cutting through the shroud of gray so he could see his hands around her neck.

What had happened after the crystal drove the shadows back? Had it been too late? He shut his eyes and a wave of nausea like the void's taint swept over him. If he'd hurt her...

He swallowed hard. Maybe marching west to die was the best thing he could do with himself. He already knew he couldn't live with himself if that moment had brought Lark's death.

"That was what I gathered, too. I hope they're more mindful of their tongues moving forward, because that could be dangerous for wherever Her Majesty has gotten to. My guess is Estkel, though." Portran nodded, as if that made his conclusion firmer.

"Why there, though?" Zaide tried to picture the city's location in his head. It was in marshland similar to what was found outside Amrochan, and it sat on the coast of the Ellean Sea, but that was all he recalled.

"The scouts who came through mentioned a draft, and that a small army was traveling there from Jadora," Portran said. "But Ganede would be a closer place to start and would bolster Jadora's defenses sooner. Addare has solid connections with Jadora for trade, so they'd be happy to send troops to the desert. So why head for Estkel first?"

Zaide nodded slowly. "Estkel is waterfront, and the road between there and Tinith is bound to be easier than the one that crosses the desert."

"Easier to move troops once they're gathered," the blacksmith agreed. "Now you're thinking. Get your armor on, lad. You've got a long way to go."

~

The storm's first snowflakes had begun to fall when Zaide determined he was ready. He ran his hand over the white wolf on his chest before he donned his gloves—a new pair Etta had provided, since he'd only had one and the fingers on it were cut through and stained with blood. She'd brought him a fresh linen tunic to put on beneath his gambeson, too, leading him to believe she cared far more than she let on. Though the hat had been proof enough of that. He'd taken it off when he'd changed. He picked it up now and rubbed it between his fingers. Its softness was lost with his gloves on, but it didn't reduce the value at all.

Last of all, he slung the pack of provisions the blacksmith had procured over his shoulder. "My armor will stand out," he remarked to Portran as he ducked out of the small room at the back of the tent that had been his for the night. "I don't think—" He stopped short as the door opposite his flipped open.

The soldier in the entryway froze and his eyes locked with Zaide's. Then he cursed and turned to run.

Portran spat an oath and leaped for him, but it was too late and he caught nothing.

Daisy bolted after the man, barking. Zaide bounded forward as if to go after her, but the blacksmith snagged him by the cape and hauled back so hard, he choked. He stumbled twice before he found his footing again and shot Portran a glare. "I have to—"

"You have to get out of here, is what you have to do," the blacksmith said. "Cut a way out the back, I'll go out front and—"

"No. I won't have you punished for me being here. Not after everything you've done." Zaide jerked himself free of the larger man's grasp.

Portran tried to seize him again, but Zaide snatched the Viper's Tongue from its sheath and leveled it with the blacksmith's throat. The man's eyes widened, but there was no fear in them. He took in the sword with wonder. Slowly, he raised a hand to touch its asymmetrical blade. "Where did you get this, lad?"

Zaide gave the weapon a flick, neatly escaping Portran's

touch while maintaining the threat. "Stop being a blacksmith and be afraid. If they think I forced you to help, you won't be punished."

Undeterred, Portran reached for it again. This time, he snagged the tip of the blade between his forefinger and thumb. "Dragon-forged. I'm sure of it, but I've never seen anything like this."

Shouts and warning bells rose across the camp and a moment later, Zaide jerked the sword from the man's grasp and ducked out the door just in time to meet a soldier head-on. The clear note of their blades striking almost drowned out the shriek of a woman nearby, a harsh reminder that it was not a military camp.

Another man lunged at Zaide from the side and he sorely wished he could call for the void to swallow him now, carry him far away and leave these people in peace. But he had no magic anymore. He couldn't so much as sense it, and the only gift he had to protect him now was the expertise Gadranus had drilled into him with a blade.

He ducked and deflected, struck and parried, never letting them get close, yet he could only hold out for so long. Already, more men were coming, ranging from fully armored to barely dressed, and Zaide regretted that he hadn't run when Portran suggested it. He feinted to give himself space and saw the flash of fear in a soldier's eyes when not a single stab landed.

They were not ready for an opponent of his caliber, yet they knew how to fight him.

Surround and overwhelm.

Six enemies.

Eight.

Without warning, a soldier leaped in beside him. Zaide's heart skipped a beat and he twisted in anticipation of a blow, but none came—instead, the armored man surged forward to drive back the attackers.

Another slid in at his other side as more opponents came.

Bewildered, Zaide could do nothing but continue the fight and his desperate attempts to hold death at bay.

More soldiers. More men. Half a dozen more fell in beside him, but three times that many joined the fight against him, and Zaide was running out of breath fast.

He blocked a stab and his strength faltered.

"Enough!" Portran roared.

A few more weapons clattered before the men grew still.

Zaide fell to one knee, gasping for breath.

Somehow, fighting was harder when the goal was to defend without wounding anyone.

A soldier stepped closer to Zaide, hefting his sword in a manner that made it clear any further attacks would be intercepted by him.

Portran stepped in front of Zaide, too, and the handful of men who had come to his aid shuffled to form a barrier around him.

Moments too late to do anything of value, an Amrochan officer stormed toward them. "What is the meaning of this?"

"You can kill as many broken-born as you want," Portran said, "but this lad's not one of them."

The officer's lip curled and he reached for his sword. "Stand aside."

"No, sir," the soldier by Zaide's elbow said, his voice both gruff and familiar. "The boy's Kolmari."

"He's a war hero," someone else added.

"He rescued dozens of men in Amrochan," said another.

Daisy contributed a long, keening *roo*.

Zaide managed to lift his head as the officer shoved Portran out of the way. The soldier to his left stepped forward, blade ready, but the officer motioned for him to settle.

Rather than striking or giving orders, the officer squatted to put himself on Zaide's eye level. His sword remained in his hand, but its tip dug into the earth to offer support. "Lot of battle scars for a Kolmari boy."

"They're fresh," Zaide replied dryly.

The man gave a thoughtful nod. "Who are you? You've got a lot of my men on your side, considering you're a stranger."

Zaide's hand tightened on the hilt of the Viper's Tongue, but he dared not move the blade, lest the man take it as a threat. "Dasienna's Bladebearer."

"Rumor has it the Bladebearer turned on us."

Before Zaide could offer any sort of retort, a handful of the men who had come to his defense shifted as if they meant to challenge their officer.

He raised a hand to stop them. "He can speak for himself. I already know where you came from."

For the first time, Zaide paused to inspect those who had aided him. Several were faces he recalled from the arena where he'd persuaded Raddan and a number of others to change sides for a chance to escape. Others were more familiar still—he scarcely masked his surprise when he recognized Murk to his left.

"Well?" the officer prompted.

Zaide worked on breathing deeper instead of faster and it brought back stability to his voice. "I faced Gadranus and drew blood twice. The next time I see him, he's going to die."

The man shook his head, yet he never broke eye contact. "It's easy to pledge a fight against a lord who's not looking over your shoulder. I'm going to need more proof than that."

What better proof was there? Zaide almost scoffed. "For Dasienna's eighteenth birthday, I carved a wooden fork for her hair."

The officer stayed silent and searched his eyes for a long time.

Zaide stared back without blinking.

Whatever it was the man was searching for, he found it, for he extended a hand. "Sergeant Karj. Queen Dasienna left me in charge of getting refugees from Amrochan to Tinith."

"Zaide. Looks like you've done a good job." He clasped the

sergeant's hand, though only briefly. Daisy squeezed in between the two of them, looking for attention, and he motioned for the dog to sit at his side when he rose.

"You were mentioned by name as a person to kill on sight." Karj stood, too. "Is there a reason for that?"

"There is." Zaide saw no need to elaborate. "But I made a promise, and I mean to keep it. I'll serve the queen for as long as she wants it. If she wants me dead, I'll accept that, too, but only by her hand."

"I believe it," the sergeant said. "I've seen men who could hold off multiple opponents before, but not like that. No one touched you."

"And I didn't touch them," Zaide replied. "I'll keep it that way, if you let me go."

Karj gave a low chuckle. "Doesn't sound like I have a choice."

"Don't think you do," Murk put in. "I've traveled with the boy. More stubborn than a dead donkey."

Somehow, it was not the strangest compliment Zaide thought he had been given. But it was also a subtle cue for him to do something less stubborn, in hopes it might sway the sergeant to his side.

He sheathed his blade.

One by one, the men around him did, too.

"If I may, Sergeant," Portran said slowly, "I think the lad has given your men the slip."

"I think you're right." Karj was the last to put away his sword. "Hard to track a broken-born in the snow. Got away from us in the woods."

"That could be your head, Sergeant," Zaide said.

"Then the queen's free to take it, same as she'll take yours." Karj motioned for his men to disband and a number of them fell back or shuffled away. The sergeant moved back, too, though he studied Zaide for a long time before he simply turned to leave.

Portran let out a long whoosh of a sigh.

Had Zaide any less self-control, he might have done the same. Instead, he turned to scan the ground. At some point, he had lost hold of his hat. He looked until he located it, but another familiar soldier was the one to pick it up. The unremarkable-looking man nicknamed Plain handed it back to him with a wry smile. "Best cover your head. You've got a long walk."

Zaide tugged the cozy knit cap on over his white hair. "Seems I do."

A long walk on a long road, and he doubted this brush with Dasienna's soldiers would be his last.

CHAPTER FORTY-THREE

THE ROAD ZAIDE took let him avoid Tinith, but not people. Not long after the expedition began, he dipped off the main road. Scattered camps of soldiers, refugees, and the goborrins they ran from lined the way along the path into the mountains, and Zaide would not risk being seen again.

Snow fell in thick curtains, obscuring the terrain, and progress slowed. Daisy proved an effective scout—the first truly useful thing she had done, Zaide admitted—and he followed the path she cut through the growing snow drifts in the woods. Bare branches rattled above him, the noise reminding him of chattering teeth and clattering hooves, and he found himself wishing for a horse.

The provisions Etta had packed for him were enough to last for several days, and he worked to stretch it farther. The hardtack was easier to eat with melted snow to soften it, and the dried meats and fruits were best saved for emergencies. Daisy hunted for the two of them, and since Portran had been thoughtful enough to pack flint and steel, he built a fire to cook with each night.

In the absence of a tent or any bedding, that fire became his dearest friend. He curled close to it to sleep and Daisy curled up on top of him, and the firelight and warm fur helped hold the nightmares at bay.

Foraging was better in the mountains. Brown-striped turkey tail mushrooms made a good broth for his hardtack and bold red wintergreen berries stood out against the snow, making them easy to find. Zaide twisted dead grasses into a coil as he walked and made himself a basket for his spoils. Most of the sweet, waxy berries ended up in his mouth, but before he reached the top of the mountain range, he carried a respectable number of nuts, berries, mushrooms, and seeds in his basket of supplies.

He could not see Estkel's marshes from the mountains, but the thick haze of humidity on the horizon offered clues for where he would find it, and it did not take long for the warm western winds to chase away the winter chill. He put away his hat and gloves—though not without trepidation, knowing how many watched for him.

He still did not know whether goborrins would be a threat. Gadranus had done nothing to indicate they would harm him, but with the white wolf on his armor instead of the crest the monsters knew, Zaide could not be sure they would recognize him as a friend.

If he was a friend. That question hung heavy in his thoughts as he traveled each day.

Gadranus had never been more than a tentative ally, and now that bond was severed.

Lark and the others had been... far more than that, yet his foolish overconfidence had torn that away, too, and he had no choice but to believe that Portran and the others had been sincere when they said the queen had called for his death.

Now he marched toward it of his own accord, but there was no other way forward.

The Spectrum Blade's power still had to be replenished, and Zaide recalled the Sunshard still in his chest when he'd fallen into the void. Without it, he did not know if Lark could restore the blade at all, but at least he could take her some scrap of knowledge for how the shadow in the prism they'd found so long ago might be handled. If he shared that and nothing else before his death, at least his soul might rest knowing he'd done what he could to save his home.

Days of travel carried him down the mountain slope and into a dreary fog that hung thickest along the rivers. Once Zaide found the water, it was easier to follow; all the waterways that fed the marshes had to reach the sea eventually, and Estkel would be right on the coast.

The number of farms that hung along the marshes came as a surprise, and Zaide worked harder to distance himself from them, lest he be seen. Fish were as plentiful as the water, so the dog did not go hungry, but nowhere was dry enough for a fire. It was likely better that way. Even in the heavy fog that hung in the unpleasantly sticky air, a fire would have drawn attention. Zaide took comfort in knowing they were close when his foraged supplies ran dry.

Daisy whined often about the soggy ground and muddy puddles they crossed, and both their legs were stained dark with mud.

"We're getting close," Zaide reassured her, though he was only certain of it once they reached a wide body of water covered in swampy greens. Wide, flat-bottomed boats drifted sleepily in the misty rain and he took care to stay out of sight while he located the main road. He had no intention of approaching Estkel that way, but roads provided information. As long as he'd avoided camps and stayed in the wilderness, he'd seen no clues that he was headed the right way, and he needed them now.

The road was not hard to find. Nowhere offered a comfortable place to camp, so he stayed awake and watched from the shelter of an old tree with moss-covered branches.

People moved along the road all night, undeterred by the rain. They came wearing all manners of clothing in styles Zaide knew and some he didn't recognize. All of them were men, and many carried weapons. Portran had mentioned a draft, and it seemed he was right. If everyone reporting headed for Estkel, a city known for nothing in particular, the chances Lark was there seemed good. And if not Lark, then someone close to her. One of the Paragons, maybe. He could work with that.

"Next we just have to find where they're going," Zaide murmured as he absently scratched the base of Daisy's ear.

The dog gave him a mournful look, but her opinion didn't matter, and he tried not to acknowledge it. Would she interfere when he surrendered? Try to protect him? He hoped not, but he found he scratched a little harder, yielding a soft whine. Daisy shifted closer and swiped his cheek with her tongue. She'd taken to doing that a lot when his thoughts grew heavy, leaning into him or nosing at his hands or face. Sometimes he appreciated the distraction. Right now, a distraction was all it was, and he gently steered her away.

"We'll follow the road," he remarked, though he wasn't sure if he was explaining the plan to the dog or himself. "Skirt the edge of the city and see if we can figure out where people are flowing. There has to be some sort of staging point where they're supposed to meet." Knowing his luck, it would be some sort of fortress and he'd be bristled with arrows by the time he made it close.

"Maybe I'll send you first," he muttered.

The dog cocked her head.

"Not to get shot at," Zaide added hastily. "To carry a message or something. Are you clever enough for that?"

The idle swish of her tail wasn't reassuring.

"Yeah," he sighed. "I didn't think so." He slid from his hiding place and motioned for the dog to follow. Together, they trailed after a pair of men in clothing that indicated they'd come from Beshnai.

Zaide followed until midmorning, when they reached the edge of the city, then found somewhere to put himself out of sight and kept an eye on them for as long as he could. Rather than turning in any direction, Zaide swore they continued straight through the city.

"Headed for the harbor?" he asked, as if Daisy might have the answer.

She huffed obligingly in response.

"We can try going down to the waterfront." If nothing else, it would give him a clear idea of how large the city was and how many soldiers were in it. He made up his mind, gave a slight nod, and delved back into the swampy forest to find his way around the city.

Only once, when the sucking mud was halfway to his knees, did he stop to consider that there could have been an easier way to handle the whole situation. Had he sent Daisy with a message earlier, he could have spared himself trouble.

Had he sent a letter from Karj's camp of refugees, rather than bringing himself on this suicide mission, he could have spared his life.

After all the patience and strategy Gadranus had drilled into him, he'd still managed to act without thinking things through.

And so what? He turned the thought over in his head until it tumbled like a worry stone in an anxious hand. He'd done the first thing that came to mind, the first thing that felt right, and it was the first time he'd felt like himself in... he didn't know how long. A reckless choice based on instinct instead of reason, and he'd made it this far.

He'd defied the master who tried to train him, and the vindication swelled in his chest with a white-hot anger.

So what? It didn't matter. He could walk to the gate and confess his wrongs, or he could cower and hide until someone hunted him down. The ending was the same—he was going to die either way.

Zaide found solid ground some ways west of the city with its tall wood and plaster houses. He emptied the water from his boots and squeezed it out of his socks, ignoring the numbness of his toes. Good earth let him move faster and a few hours later, he reached the sandy shore of the Ellean Sea, where the swamp waters turned brackish and dark.

There was a harbor, though it was smaller than he expected. What he had not expected was what appeared to be a bridge just beyond the docks, a bright stone structure that stretched into the sea farther than the eye could follow.

The harbor did not seem to be where the would-be soldiers had gone, but he found his attention drawn to that bridge a dozen times over as he tried to determine his next action.

"We'll rest here," Zaide told the dog. Or maybe he told himself, as if to justify the choice. The winter days were short and night would be along in a scant few hours. They would get through the harbor easily when business concluded for the night, and then he could investigate that bridge.

Daisy flopped down on a sandy ledge and gave a long, slow sigh while Zaide pulled the last of the provisions from his bag. Strange, he thought, that it had been just enough to be his last meal.

He did not sleep, though he rested until long after sunset, watching the placid water and the way the soft rain disappeared into its waves. It was calming, though it put no such peace in him. Everything in him was a storm, raging winds and torrents of hate and frustration that churned like a white-capped sea. Above it all, a deep regret and a strange new sense of self-loathing floated on the tumult like a slick of blackened oil. Zaide shut his eyes and tried to picture something more peaceful inside, something like the easy waves that rolled and sighed before him, but the dark grew deeper and the water grew harder to see, until at last its expanse was as black as his thoughts.

Gently, he nudged Daisy's leg with his boot. "Come on, girl. We have to go."

The dog groaned and stretched, none too eager to move, but she plodded along when Zaide chose a path along the shore. They had to wade only twice.

A chilly breeze swept in from the sea and Zaide retrieved his dark woolen hat from his bag, grateful for how it would help him hide. There was no moonlight, and his armor was dark. Even his cape blended into the night.

He ghosted along the harbor, staying on the shoreline when he could and avoiding porters and sailors the rest of the time, and eventually he reached the footings of the bridge.

Rather than being part of the harbor, the bridge connected to a road that ran straight from the heart of Estkel. He found himself beneath it with no easy way up. For a moment, he considered discarding the bridge as a distraction. He paced past the stone piers before he started up the shore toward the city's edge, only to stop when he saw the guards at the bridge's mouth.

Men in the plain steel armor of Amrochan's guard blocked the way from the city, giving directions to those reporting for the draft. None of the reporting men were allowed through, and so the bridge's span stayed empty, shrinking off into the distance without a soul to be seen.

There was only one reason to guard the path and keep the bridge clear, and there was only one way up.

Zaide stared up the side of the bridge, examining each arch and the walls on both sides. The west side, from which he'd approached, bore heavier shadow. He waded into the shallows and called Daisy over with a quiet click of his tongue.

The dog abandoned her inspection of the foundation beneath the piers and trotted to the water's edge.

"Come," he whispered.

Daisy stepped forward, then eased back and moaned, unwilling to get her feet wet again.

Zaide almost scolded her, then thought better of it. What was he doing? A dog couldn't climb. He unfastened his cape and trudged over to meet her. "Be quiet," he ordered, though he had no faith she would obey.

She pranced about on the sand when he tried to loop the fabric under her, but he caught her in both arms and held her until she stayed still. He scooped her into the cloth and knotted it into a sling around his chest, then grunted as he stood. The dog was heavy. The climb would be hard.

He made it all of three feet up the wall before her yowling protests came, and he winced with bemusement at how little she sounded like a dog. Long, sorrowful notes whined out her nose and strangely round keens bubbled from her mouth.

More than a few spooked sailors shouted oaths from the harbor nearby, but no one appeared brave enough to investigate. Zaide gritted his teeth and focused on climbing. This close to the city, the bridge's roadway was no more than fifteen feet up. With the wiggling and whimpering animal on his back, it felt more like fifty.

Deep gaps between the weathered stones provided ample handholds and places to tuck his toes, but sweat coursed down his back and plastered his hair to his face by the time he swung a leg over the wall and dropped to sit close beside it. It was dark out at sea, but a shadow standing on the bridge would still stand out.

Blessedly, the wind had warped the dog's howls and the soldiers at the bridge's mouth some distance away did not seem to know which way they had come from, for they pivoted back and forth in search of the noise.

"You're going to be the death of us," Zaide muttered as he leaned back and slid the makeshift sling off overhead. The moment Daisy sprang free, she bolted down the long and empty avenue that reached toward the heart of the Ellean Sea, and he watched after her with forlorn resignation. That statement wasn't true and he knew it. Between the two of them, Daisy would be the one to survive.

With the soldiers at his back still puzzling over the strange rise and fall of the ghastly sounds that carried on the bitter winds, Zaide pushed himself to his feet and followed after the dog, careful to crouch low in the shadow of the wall where he wouldn't be seen. Those shadows had come to feel welcoming, and he hated it with everything in him.

The moment he passed beyond sight, he made a point of thrusting himself away from the wall, though the shadows of night only deepened as he moved farther from shore.

Against all that he desired, Zaide fought his rising pulse with all the serenity his worst enemy had taught him. The farther he went, the more it reminded him of falling into the void, and nausea knotted his stomach—not from fear of the dark, but of what waited for him in it, when the light of life was driven out of him at his final destination.

He walked until dawn, and as the sun spilled over the far eastern horizon, a fortress rose from the sea.

CHAPTER FORTY-FOUR

IT HAD NOT TAKEN LONG for the archive to become Lark's sanctuary, rather than just a place to study. As soon as Jobe arrived with soldiers in tow, it felt as if her plan of becoming unnoticeable had been torn to pieces.

She had called for a draft, but men came to Estkel instead of heading for Tinith or Jadora, because that was from where Jobe had issued the call and instructions had gotten tangled along the way. She could not fault the people reporting for duty; for some, reaching Estkel was far easier than the other options.

Jobe's soldiers had taken over a portion of the city and worked to settle and train the new recruits, but a large number of soldiers remained in the monastery with the general, who insisted she needed defense.

She wouldn't have needed it so desperately if he hadn't made himself so visible. If she'd known her location would become common knowledge within so few weeks, she would have stayed in Jadora.

Yet then she wouldn't have had the chance to look over the records in Sast's archive.

Progress had been slow, but it was progress, and the pile of notes that at least came close to being useful had grown. But so had the pile of paperwork that was Lark's responsibility as queen. She carried most of it to the archive, where she could study it in peace, but every minute spent going over supply counts and battles and the number of lives that had been lost was another minute she was left with no power at her fingertips and a slumbering blade at her side.

With how many reports were carried to her each day, it was little surprise when someone knocked at the door. Lark had hardly been awake and already, they needed her.

Grandmaster Hyar had ordered a rotating shift of door watchers to ensure the soldiers never went where they were not allowed. The woman on the current shift rose to answer, but Lark had already pushed herself up from her seat, knowing she would be needed for yet another consultation or question or handful of written reports.

The soldier on the other side of the door removed his helmet as he nodded in greeting to the monk, then bowed to Lark. "Your Majesty, there's a problem."

There were a lot of them. She tried to stay patient. "Yes?"

The man rubbed a nervous finger along the helmet's edge. "An enemy soldier has been spotted on the bridge and approaches the monastery. He is alone. We believe he is a messenger from Gadranus."

"What?" Lark jerked the door open wider. Chairs skidded against the stone floor behind her, betraying all three of the Paragons for listening in, but she was out the door and into the hall before any of them found their feet.

The soldier jogged a few steps to catch up with her. "General Jobe is in the courtyard, giving orders. He thought that you—"

"I should have been informed before any orders were given," Lark snapped before she caught herself. It wasn't the messenger's fault.

"Of course, Your Majesty," the soldier said, all the same.

She bit her tongue to keep from unleashing it on anyone else who didn't deserve it and hurried toward the courtyard.

Outside, two dozen of the fifty soldiers Jobe had kept in the monastery stood in formation before him. Or, rather, they broke out of formation and jogged toward their assigned stations.

Lark reached Jobe a moment later. He had the nerve to look surprised, though he recovered with a gentle bow.

"The situation is under control, Your Majesty." He worked to sound placating. "There are archers on the wall already and I'm sending more up. I'll be taking a handful of men through the gates myself to confront the messenger, but I fully expect he'll be full of feathers by the time we're through."

"How dare you?" Her lip curled back in a snarl. "Giving orders regarding a direct messenger without my consent?"

"Your Majesty, we act out of an interest for your protection. You cannot forget what happened the last time." The general's eyes darkened.

Lark scoffed and spun on her heel.

Jobe hadn't expected her to take off in the middle of the conversation, and he sputtered as he chased after her. "Your Majesty, please. Everything is well in hand."

"It will be in my hand, as it should be." She stormed through the narrow corridors and under the arching bridges of the maze-like monastery until she reached the one and only entryway.

The monk with the first ring of keys stood so fast, he almost knocked over his stool.

"Open the gates," Lark ordered as she drew the Spectrum Blade.

The man gaped, then fumbled with the keys.

Someone drew close behind her, but the musty smell of the archive still clung to the clothes of the Paragons and she knew who was there without turning.

Jobe strode after her as the squad he'd called for began to assemble at his heels. "Don't be ridiculous, Majesty. You're doing exactly what he hoped you would."

"No," she fired back as anger heated in her breast. "I'm sending a message right back." She had come to expect nothing but audacity from Gadranus, yet this was a new low. A taunting repeat of what he'd done in Jadora, knowing how it must have pained her. Every inch of her stung with the salt it rubbed into the wound of loss, still raw with the hole in her heart and the tears she cried whenever she was alone. The mourning left her empty, and the emptiness made her a vessel for rage.

The general stormed after her through the gates. "This is foolishness. You exposing yourself now is exactly what he's after. This kind of reckless nonsense is going to get you killed, and then where will Amroch be?"

"In the hands of you and Warinal, which I'm sure you'd both be more than happy with. What's wrong, General? Don't you believe your soldiers can protect me?" Lark flicked her head so her ponytail snapped behind her.

That shut him up, but she caught his low hiss of frustration and a cold and short-lived sense of satisfaction rolled through her.

One by one, the gates opened, and her heart beat faster every time one shut behind her.

She would not be trifled with anymore. She would not be baited or mocked. Her hand tightened on the Spectrum Blade until her fingers hurt and her pulse throbbed in her ears, and silence ruled all else.

Footsteps ticked against the stone in a steady cadence as they marched to the very last set of gates. The poor monk beside it looked at them, flustered, surprised, and confused all at once.

"Open the gate," Lark ordered as the one behind her slammed shut. The three Paragons fanned out at her heels and Jobe's men spread behind them. Her hand trembled so the Spectrum Blade quivered in her grasp, but she could not make her monstrous pain be still.

The lock clanked and the gates groaned open. The golden light of sunrise poured in through the gap and seared the sight from her eyes, but she stepped forward anyway, her pointed ears flush with the heat of her temper.

Then her vision resolved and frigid shock coursed through her from head to toe.

Of all the wicked tricks, she had never expected this.

Zaide.

She tried to find some of the angry words she'd prepared on her way through the gates, but her mind and mouth were empty and all she could do was stare. They locked eyes and he was just as shocked as she.

He stood with his arms wide and his hands raised level with his shoulders, his gloved fingers spread to show he held nothing, but he wore the same armor—though with a different marking on the chest.

By his side, Daisy keened a greeting, her curved tail wagging hard.

Lark took a slow step forward, shaking her head in disbelief.

He recalled himself then, for he reached for his sword.

Dozens of arrows clacked against bows on the wall overhead.

"Hold!" Jobe shouted when Lark did not stop. She moved forward as if drawn, inching toward him with slow steps.

She had driven the Sunshard into his chest.

She had poured every shred of power she'd never realized she had into destroying whatever darkness he'd become.

She had watched him fall and die, yet there he was before her, somehow whole.

Zaide dropped to one knee and held up his strange sword, flat on the palms of his hands.

Lark stopped before him.

"Your Majesty," he began, his voice hoarse and unsteady. "I failed."

A chill unlike any other crawled over her skin, but he went on.

"I—I tried to kill him. I failed. I cut his face. I cut his ear, but I failed. I tried to bring you the magic you needed so you could do what I could not. I failed. I tried to take power over enemy armies so I could protect your people by commanding them to do no harm, but I failed." His voice cracked and for the first time since Lark had known him, she heard tears. He kept his head down, as if he might keep her from seeing—or as if he feared what he might see if he looked at her—but the sudden dark spots that marred the stone beneath him betrayed the rising emotion.

"I failed as your Bladebearer. I failed as a friend and as the Elder's apprentice and at everything else I've ever done, but I won't fail to take responsibility for my mistakes." He raised the sword a little higher. An offering. A surrender. "I'm sorry. For every mistake I made. For the foolishness and pride that led me to them, and for my failure to serve you the way you deserve. I am here to accept my punishment."

Lark's throat tightened until she struggled to find her voice. "Zaide."

He remained still, his sword still raised, though his breath came hard and fast.

"Zaide—" she choked.

His head lifted and his eyes—his bold, beautiful, summer-sky eyes—held worry for her instead of fear.

She'd never seen who he was reflected so clearly.

A reckless idiot. A fool who would walk the world to seek his own death. And a brave but gentle heart who always put the well-being of others first—even now.

She hated him. And she loved him more dearly than her polished words could ever say.

The Spectrum Blade fell from her hand as she fell forward and flung her arms around his shoulders, and it clattered at her feet as she squeezed him hard and let herself cry sweet tears of relief.

He dropped his sword, too, and buried his face in the crook of her neck.

"I thought I lost you," she whispered beside his ear—the whole one, to be sure he caught every fragile word.

His arms slid up around her ribs and he held her close. "I thought I lost me, too."

Daisy bounded around the two of them, barking with delight.

Lark savored the warmth of him and the strength of his arms around her middle and wished that she could linger, but their embrace was cut short the moment a hand grasped the back of her shirt and dragged her backwards out of Zaide's arms.

"Hey," Tula protested, but the general was undeterred.

Jobe forced Lark back several steps and then posted himself in front of her, his sword drawn and pointed at Zaide. "Only a fool would fall for the same trap twice."

"I beg your pardon?" Lark bristled at the accusation.

"What proof is there he's not using your affection as a weapon against you? First Jadora, now Estkel? How many fortresses will he raze before you guard your known weaknesses?" The general held his sword level with Zaide's throat.

"I'm here for myself," Zaide said as he unfurled himself from the ground. He stood tall—almost as tall as Jobe—and held himself with a bearing Lark hadn't seen before. There was a wary tension in his shoulders, a coiled strength and new confidence.

Jobe's upper lip twitched with distaste. "And how are we to know you're yourself? What evidence do we have?"

"Stand down, Jobe," Lark said.

The general did not move. "Letting him through these gates would be a mistake you might not live to regret. Think, Your Majesty. Use your head and not your tender heart."

"Test him," Resia called.

Jobe remained still, but Lark and Zaide both looked to the Kolmari Elder in surprise.

The dark-haired girl shrank as if startled they'd paid attention. "Make... make him do something only the real Zaide could."

Lark had done exactly that in Jadora, asking something only Zaide would have known. He had answered. It had been him. But it had been Gadranus, too.

"Make him take the sword," Andriun said. The Shaman lowered his chin and his expression grew dark. "If he is corrupted, then he will not be able to touch it."

"Andriun," Tula almost scolded.

Lark shook her head, but Jobe glanced to the blade at Zaide's feet, where it lay crossed with the sinuous bronze sword.

"A suitable test. How about it, Bladebearer?" Jobe laced the title with contempt.

Zaide's jaw tightened, but his eyes flicked down.

"Don't," Lark protested. "You don't have to prove anything to him."

He stared for a long time, weighing his options. Then, slowly, he crouched beside the two swords.

Irritation raced up the back of Lark's neck. At the same time, warm fondness swelled in her heart. He'd changed, yet some parts remained infuriatingly the same. The stubborn streak, the reckless behavior, the determination she had so often envied.

Yet there was something else when he lowered his hand and let it hover above the hilt of the iridescent sword.

Hesitance. Uncertainty. A deep-seated doubt that made his fingertips flex and his frame grow still, though none of it changed the hardened resoluteness in his stare.

A muscle in Zaide's cheek twitched as his jaw clenched tighter and he curled his hand around the Spectrum Blade.

Lark's breath caught and she pressed a hand to her heart as if to keep it from leaping free.

He slid the blade out from under the other sword, stood, and turned its tip toward the sky. Relief washed over his face as its colors shifted in the early sunlight, promising it knew who held it, and Zaide's eyes slid shut before more tears could get free.

Resia clasped her hands before her mouth and looked as if she might cry, too. Tula leaped and whooped, and Daisy woofed and danced with her, though the dog had no way to know why they celebrated.

Lark made herself smile, but a lump formed in her throat as she watched the sword gleam.

Once again, she was left without a purpose.

Beside them, Andriun's shoulders sagged with disappointment and he turned back to the gate with a shake of his head.

"Now, General," Lark said as she stepped forward, "let my Bladebearer pass."

Reluctantly, Jobe lowered his sword and then returned it to its sheath. He didn't like the outcome, but he'd been the one to select it as the test. He retreated and motioned for his guards to pass back through the first gate.

Zaide let his hand sink, then rotated the Spectrum Blade to present its hilt to Lark. She eyed it, unsure why he offered.

"It was always meant to be yours," he said.

She shook her head. "It chose you."

"When it thought that was best. I don't know why it did. But it should have been yours, and you're the queen now. It belongs in your hand." He looked as if he wished to smile but couldn't summon the strength, so he bowed his head and nudged the blade still on the ground with the toe of his boot. "I've got my own. Dragon-forged, I'm told. Whatever that means."

"I'm sure Tula will know." Lark didn't want to take the blade from his hand, but when she tried to push it back, he only pressed it more insistently toward her. Reluctantly, she let him place it in her palm and curl her fingers around it.

Then he bent to reclaim his own and return it to its sheath.

"Are we all going back in, then?" the monk by the gates asked.

"Back to work," Tula said, though she pumped a fist in the air as if to declare victory. "The team's all back together!"

Daisy ran loops around their legs before she bounded

through the gate alongside the Magister. Resia followed them, giggling.

Zaide motioned for Lark to go first, but she posted herself at his side instead. "Walk with me?" she suggested.

"Of course."

She took the first step and he moved easily alongside her, as if it was where he belonged. It was, she decided, and she glanced at his hand as they walked.

She wanted to touch him, to reassure herself he was a flesh-and-blood companion and not some ghost or dream. There was nothing in the way, their swords on opposing hips, and her fingers twitched at the idea of twining with his.

But then she found herself looking at him from the corner of her eye and noticed how his gait had changed, and a slender thread of worry wormed its way through the delicate hope she'd almost reclaimed.

It should have been like old times. It should have offered relief and joy to know her friend was back, when just the night before she had wept for his death. Yet as they walked and the dangerous tension in him remained wound tight, a small sense of fear tugged at the heart that had been soaring in her chest only a moment before.

Zaide was there, but some gentle part of him was lost, and she did not know if she would get it back.

CHAPTER FORTY-FIVE

HE'D TOUCHED IT.

He'd wrapped his fingers around its hilt. Lifted it and felt the soft tingle of awareness that showed it knew him.

Zaide had not dared believe he would ever see the Spectrum Blade again, never mind hold it.

Yet it had accepted him. Welcomed him, even, after everything he'd done.

He curled his hands to fists at his sides, but he couldn't stop them from shaking.

They should have killed him. Should have peppered him with arrows and thrown him to the sea, or left his body for the goborrins, or any number of other horrific yet well-deserved things that were too much for him to think of right now.

All he could think of was the soft prickle of power that had been in his hand... and the sweet fragrance of Lark's hair.

Zaide glanced at her beside him, then let his gaze slide to the Spectrum Blade at her side. She walked with it on the other side, away from him. He didn't think it was deliberate, but at the same time, the distance left him unsure.

She scarcely looked at him as they walked, her face back to the stern and regal facade he'd grown used to. The familiarity should have made it comfortable. In the wake of their brief but tearful reunion, it left him unsatisfied.

Had it been too much to ask that they might have a moment to savor? That he might find a single scrap of peace in the security of her presence and the forgiving warmth of her embrace? Annoyance at how swiftly that had been taken from him made his shoulders itch, but he remained still. His eyes settled on the back of the general—a man he'd heard about, but had never spoken to before Amrochan's fall. The men he'd encountered in the capital's dungeon and in Karj's camp had spoken well of him. After their introduction, Zaide had a hard time feeling any sort of warmth for the man, though he begrudgingly admitted respect.

It had been wise to demand proof of good intentions.

It simply hadn't been *kind*.

"So," Lark began, a soft note of hesitance in the single word. "The Paragons and I have been combing the archive here in search of clues."

Zaide turned his head enough to look at her, while still keeping the soldier ahead of them within his peripheral vision. The presence of the Paragons between them was a small comfort, but he didn't trust Jobe an inch.

"About the magic, I mean," Lark added. It wasn't like her to be flustered, but he remained calm and quiet, hoping it might encourage her to go on. A nervous sort of smile played at her lips, but she never looked at him, even when they paused in the odd chambers between sets of gates. She worried her hands, too, rubbing her fingernails. Was she concerned? Afraid? He'd have to be mindful of what he did and how. The last thing he wanted to do was scare her.

"For you? Or the sword?" he asked.

"Both. We've made a little progress, but only a little. The residents of the monastery here have dedicated themselves to documentation of the Rise. There is more information about it here than anywhere else in the world, even the library in Jadora." Lark rubbed her thumbnail longer than the rest.

Zaide considered offering a hand, then discarded the idea as swiftly as it had come. She had never been eager to seek physical comfort or reassurance, and the few times it had happened, he suspected it was because she simply had nothing else to cling to. Instead, he nodded and listened. Nothing else.

"We thought they might have recorded something about management of the blade's power, or maybe how my magic is supposed to work. I tried so many things when we were in Nimultis, but nothing ever stirred it. It wasn't until I—" She stopped abruptly and her mouth worked a moment before color rose in her cheeks and she turned her face away.

Did she think he'd be angry? Offended? Neither were reasonable responses. She had only done what he'd forced her to do. The choice might not have been his, but Zaide would not deny that it had been his fingers bruising her throat. Had her magic not restored some scrap of his humanity for long enough that he could resist, well... he had chosen not to think of how else things might have ended.

"One of us had to die," was all he said.

Her brows drew together and he regretted the words immediately.

He'd misunderstood. *She* was hurt. He did not blame her for the choice she had made and he never would, but she blamed herself, and he had failed to see that pain. He inwardly scrambled for something he could say to soften his mistake and came up short.

Lark shook her head. "I don't understand." A tiny quaver shook the statement and again, he felt the impulse to reach for her and offer comfort. Then again, maybe the comfort was for him. Something to ease his guilt for putting her in that situation in the first place.

She went on before he decided how to react.

"I don't know how you're here. I don't know how you

survived. The soldiers saw you. They said—Vorkaris said—he told me—" Her voice cracked and her breath hitched. The tears that glittered in her eyes remained unshed, but they twisted like a knife in his heart, all the same.

He'd done that.

He'd failed to protect her in every conceivable way.

Zaide bowed his head and swallowed. "I woke in the spring beneath Kolmar's temple. That's all I know." He dared not mention Gadranus or how the man must have dragged him there—not simply for her comfort, but for his own. He could not so much as think of the man without the heat of anger rising within him, and though none of the void lingered within him to respond, he still worked to dull the rising hate.

Just ahead of them, Resia stopped and turned. "The spring?" She clasped her hands in front of her chest, as sweet and endearing a gesture from her as he'd ever expected. It softened the edges of the harsh feelings Zaide's thoughts had stirred within him, as soothing as all the healing she'd ever offered.

"Where you found your magic," he added, though it struck him as a pointless addition. Simple confirmation, maybe. Even so, it caused Andriun to pause and look back, a shadow of suspicion in his dark eyes.

Resia smiled and her whole demeanor brightened. "Yes, exactly! It's the anchor point for my magic, so some of the same power is there. The soldiers had to be wrong. The waters there are strong enough to bring you back from the brink of death."

"Just like the Birthplace of Water and the Captured Spring," Lark mused, earning herself a glare over Andriun's shoulder. She didn't notice, but Zaide did, and he cast a dark look back.

"I don't understand, though," Resia said as the last set of gates opened and they were left squinting in the morning light. "How in the world did you get there?"

Zaide didn't want to answer. He paced out into the monastery instead and allowed himself a moment to look up at the strange, maze-like construction of awkwardly angled buildings. The shadows cast by the towering walls covered everything and left him chilled. The soldiers dispersed, though when he turned to look at the wall behind him, there was no missing the dozen or so men who stood atop it with their bows still ready. He stared up at them for a long time.

When he finally lowered his gaze, Tula stood directly in front of him, her hands on her hips.

He did not so much as flinch.

"How *did* you get there?" She leaned closer as she asked.

Foolish to think he'd be able to avoid the question. He answered slowly. "I learned things, while I held magic."

"Yeah? Like what?" The Magister squinted at him in suspicion.

"How he moves so fast. From Toren to Amrochan and back. Across the battlefield. Around the throne room." The same nausea Zaide always felt when directing the magic himself clawed at his belly and he willed it to settle. Associations were powerful things, but he needed to break that. As long as the mere thought of power made him sick, it was a weakness. "Whatever happened in Jadora, afterward, I did the same thing. Went through the void."

"Through what?" Resia asked.

Lark, too, looked at him with puzzlement.

Andriun was gone, and so was the dog.

Fickle, Zaide thought, though he kept that to himself. He'd been asked a question. All he had to do was answer. "I don't know how to explain it. It's just... dark. Empty. But he can move through it, and for a while, so could I." It was how he'd joined the army that landed outside Addare and marched north to Jadora. If there was a limitation to how far void walking could take someone, he did not know.

Deep worry creased the space between Lark's eyebrows. "How are we supposed to fight someone who can do that?"

"Easy," Zaide said. "If we manage this right, then when the time comes, he won't fight us."

"Didn't he try to strangle Lark?" Tula asked.

He shifted away from them before he caught himself.

Lark shook her head. "Never mind that. We need to take this one step at a time, and the Spectrum Blade still needs our attention. If Zaide had a chance to see how Gadranus wields magic and..." She faltered, but tucked in her chin and made herself go on. "And used some of it himself... then maybe he can help us see what we're missing."

It was what he'd tried to do in the first place, yet now, the suggestion left him tired. He had not slept in more than a day, and all that had transpired since his arrival had sapped every bit of strength he'd had left. "Maybe," he agreed, "but right now I just want to sleep."

"Of course." Lark gave a flustered smile and pointed toward a narrow side passage that did not strike him as a pathway to anything. "This way. I'll show you to the rooms. Or, that is, a room. You can stay in mine for now. There's an empty one near the rest of us, but we'll need to make sure it's all right for you to use it. The monks are particular about who they allow into which parts of the monastery."

"We'll find something. I'm sure there are a lot of extra rooms in a place like this." He studied the height of the buildings and the surrounding walls as they meandered through the monastery. The place was like a city in its own right, or like a strange combination of a city and a palace. "Strange that no one ever really talks about it."

"Well, when the monks never leave the island, I suppose there's not a lot to be said about what they've built here. We've always known the people of Sast were secretive. Now that I've seen the archive, I understand why." Lark fidgeted with her hands while they walked. "I hope they're willing to let you in. I haven't asked."

"I can find one of the Grandmasters and explain the situation," Resia offered.

Lark exhaled in relief. "Oh, would you?"

The Elder nodded. "You go rest, Zaide. We'll have someone bring you to the archive when you wake up, assuming the Grandmasters say it's all right. None of the soldiers have been allowed inside, so we have to be sure it's all right for you."

"I don't have to go in. If they say no, I'll wait outside and you can just ask me what you need." Between the soldiers and the Paragons, he figured himself far more likely to be included with the former than the latter.

"We'll see." Resia smiled at him, a warm and welcoming expression that almost made him feel as if he belonged. He would have to make time to sit with her after he rested, to go over everything that had happened and update her on the state of everything in Kolmar.

For now, he just followed Lark as she led him into a building and through a meandering series of halls.

"I don't think they have many guest rooms," Lark said when they reached their destination. "I don't think they have many guests. I'll speak with the Grandmasters about accommodations for you, but for now..." She shouldered open a door and motioned for him to pass through.

Desite the cold austerity of the outside of the buildings, the interior of Lark's room was lavishly decorated in shades of yellow, white, and gold. Zaide examined the regal gilded furniture, the plush rugs underfoot, the sweeping curtains and fabric streamers that draped the walls.

"It's a lot, I know." Lark ducked her head. If he didn't know any better, he might have called it sheepish.

"No, it suits you. It just makes me feel like I don't belong." Maybe he never would. He'd grown up in the forest, after all. Not a palace.

"Then maybe you should take off that armor," Lark said.

Zaide turned to look at her and her face turned so red, he thought she might burst.

Her mouth worked a moment before a few broken words escaped. "That is—I didn't mean—"

"No, you're right," he reassured her. Portran might have changed the emblem on the chest, but it was still the armor Gadranus had given him. Still a shadow of everything that had gone wrong. "I'll sleep better without it."

Lark still blushed, but she responded with a vigorous nod. "I'll leave you to it. When you wake, just ask any of the monks to be taken to the archive doors and I'll speak with you there."

"Of course." He didn't have much else to add.

She lingered by the door for a long time, as if she had something else to say, but in the end she just nodded again. "Rest well." She spun on her heel and darted into the hall, shutting the door behind her and leaving him alone.

Zaide stared after her for a while, then released a long sigh.

Removing his armor would have been wise, but he was so wearied that all he did was unbelt the Viper's Tongue from his side and let it fall to the floor before he dropped face-first into the luxurious cushion of Lark's bed.

CHAPTER FORTY-SIX

SLEEP CAME LONG, deep, and dreamless—all luxuries Zaide had given up on experiencing again. Had it not been for a vigorous knock at the door to rouse him, he thought he might have slept through to the next morning. Then again, Lark would have had to sleep eventually, and that meant someone arriving to oust him from bed no matter what.

He answered the door, still rubbing his groggy eyes, and found a small-statured elderly woman smiling up at him.

"Good evening." It was such a mild greeting that he wondered how she managed to knock loud enough to wake him.

"Evening," Zaide repeated, unsure if it was good or not. He was still alive; that was either good or terrible. In rubbing his eyes he found ridges from the folds of blankets pressed into his face, and that, too, could have had multiple meanings. Either he'd slept wonderfully, or he was so exhausted that he was not even aware of discomfort.

"I am sorry to interrupt your rest, but quality rest also demands food, and there is a freshly cooked meal in the dinner hall. I suspected you might appreciate having something to eat." She smiled until her eyes disappeared in the crinkles and crags of her aged face.

"Oh. Sure." He blinked a few times to clear his vision, then glanced down at himself. Armor didn't wrinkle, so he was presentable enough, but he thought of Lark's suggestion that he remove it. "I'll just..."

"I'll wait here a moment while you refresh yourself," the old woman said before he explained himself. She leaned forward to point through the doorway. "There should be a washbasin with anything you need in the corner there." Then she pulled the door shut, giving him no say in the matter.

Zaide started with his armor. Piece by piece, he piled it on the floor at the foot of Lark's bed. He'd figure out what to do with it later; it needed to be cleaned and conditioned, but so did the rest of him. He spent more time at the washbasin than anything else, scrubbing as much of himself as he could with what little water the basin's pitcher offered, starting at the top and working his way down so his hair had time to dry. The soap beside the basin was sweetly floral, an excellent choice for Lark but one that made him feel silly.

Not, however, silly enough to forgo a proper cleaning. There was a straight-edged razor tucked in with the combs, too, and while his beard had rudely not yet acknowledged that his birthday and proper coming of age had passed, there were enough quarter-inch white hairs along his jaw after a few weeks of travel that he had come to look unkempt. It was not until he had the blade against his skin that he stopped to wonder what Lark was supposed to do with a tool like that. He'd heard of ancient customs where women were expected to do absurd things like shave off their eyebrows to look more mysterious, but surely Sast's monastery had not been cut off from the rest of the world for so long that they still believed such things were done. In the end, he decided all the rooms had to be stocked the same way, and he was glad to look a little more like himself when he was done.

"Sorry," he said when he opened the door again and found the old woman still waiting. "I didn't mean to take so long."

She waved a hand as if it didn't matter. "Such is the way of the world. Nothing happens when we believe it must. Come, Bladebearer. I am Grandmaster Sidoya, chief nun of Sast and supervisor of all the monastery's women. I'll see that you're fed, and then I shall take you to your friends."

Bladebearer. There had been a time he'd been proud of that title, but none of that feeling remained. Nor did he feel he deserved to be called by such a title, not when he'd been so fast to give the blade back to Lark. He bore no guilt or envy over it; part of him had longed for the sword, but he saw it better now for what the concern truly was.

Without the Spectrum Blade in his hand, he had nothing to offer.

"Are they in the archive?" he asked as they walked.

"Yes. It is where they spend most days."

"I thought soldiers weren't allowed inside."

Sidoya cast a patient smile over her shoulder. "While that is normally true, I have discussed the matter with Grandmaster Hyar and we agree that if your party's purpose is restoration of the Spectrum Blade, the hand chosen to wield it deserves access to the archive."

Zaide was not reassured. "But Lark is the Bladebearer now. She carries the sword with her. You know that, you have to have seen it."

She shrugged. "All the other Paragons confirmed that they saw you take the blade on the bridge outside our gates."

Why the blade had allowed it, he did not know. It couldn't be that he was chosen again, or it would have refused when he had passed it back to Lark. Even in its weakened state, it had remained opinionated, and the magic it held was quick to snap at anyone else who dared try to touch it.

Which meant it had to have chosen him. At least in that moment, when General Jobe posed his little test.

Zaide could not understand why. After everything he had done, everything he had ruined, no one could deserve it less.

He said nothing else when Sidoya ushered him into the dining hall. Dozens of people in the same bland, gray linen robes lined the tables, eating and conversing in companionable comfort. The food was kept near the kitchen and part of him was disappointed to see no meat, but he conceded there was likely no easy way to obtain it on an island where there was no space for animals to be kept. The walls barricaded them from the sea, too, promising no fish. But the dense bread and roasted vegetables they provided were good, and he admitted he felt somewhat rejuvenated by the time he finished and the Grandmaster led him to the archive doors.

She smiled at him and waved him through.

The Paragons sat at a long table not far from the doorway. Lark rose when she saw him, while Tula and Resia greeted him with smiles. Andriun glanced up once, then resumed his studies. He gripped a pen tight in his hand and scrawled hasty notes across an already-cluttered page.

"You look better," Lark said as she approached.

"Less tired." That was Zaide's assumption, anyway. "Less... travel."

The corners of her mouth drew up, but it wasn't a smile. Not a real one. "Have you eaten?"

He nodded.

"Good. Come look at this. Maybe some of the knowledge you've picked up will help us decipher something." She beckoned him to the table, though he did not sit down when she did. There were only four chairs.

While she paged through her notes, he scanned the space they were in. The library in Jadora had been impressive enough. The archive left him without words. One thing was missing, though, and he looked around and behind him before he glanced at the others. "Where's Daisy?"

"In my room," Tula said with a sigh. "The monks said dogs don't belong in archives full of fragile and precious ancient history. For some reason."

"Do you disagree?" Resia asked, amused.

"Well, no," Tula conceded. "I don't think she knows how to read."

Andriun snorted.

"Sometimes the texts in here make me wonder if I can read." Lark shuffled her notes into order. "Right now I can hardly decipher my own handwriting, and I've been the one writing out the plan."

"And what is the plan?" Zaide tried not to sound too eager, but the flat way the words came out instead made him sound skeptical.

Lark hesitated. "From what I've heard, it sounds as if Gadranus has gone back to Toren. That might give us time before he resumes his push against Tinith, Ganede, and Jadora. The other cities don't seem to be a concern, but to be fair, these are where my forces are most concentrated."

"And Beshnai," Zaide said. "A lot of people from Yithel and Chithal went that way. They'll be a considerable force, but we don't know if they mean to stay in Beshnai or push west toward Ganede."

"We?" Andriun asked without lifting his head.

Zaide grew still. That had come out wrong, but also without a thought. He would have to watch his words more carefully.

Lark ignored it and added a line to her notes. "That's valuable. What else do you know about our troop movements?"

"A lot more Amrochan refugees are headed toward Tinith." That, at least, he could explain; Murk had shared a few choice pieces of information in hopes Zaide would be able to carry them all the way to the queen's ears. "There are a few camps collecting stragglers still, but there doesn't seem to be any push against Tinith at this time. Gadranus is holding back his forces."

Tula leaned against the table and tapped the end of her pen against her cheek. "Why would he do that? Tinith is the closest to his seat in Amrochan. It would be the easiest to take."

"He's more interested in Jadora right now." Zaide caught and held Lark's gaze. "More interested in you."

She accepted it without trepidation. "Does he know I am here?"

"Not that I know of. I only knew because some of your soldiers figured it out when those scouts carrying draft orders came through." More than one questioning expression turned his way, so he added, "I ran into some friends at one of the camps. Soldiers I helped escape from Amrochan after they were imprisoned."

Resia hummed thoughtfully to herself, coiling and uncoiling a curl of her brown hair around a finger. "He'll probably figure it out soon, considering the directions people are going to report for the draft. There are only so many cities left outside his control, so the number of places we could be isn't very impressive."

"Which is why we need to restore the blade as soon as possible," Lark concluded. The look she gave him was so hopeful, it made Zaide wish he could shrink out of sight.

To his disappointment, he stayed exactly where he was, the size he was, and Lark, Tula, and Resia all stared at him with hope in their eyes. The look he got from Andriun was cooler. Skeptical.

Zaide was skeptical, too. His hand drifted to his chest, to the mark the Sunshard had left behind and Kolmar's spring had healed. Without that shard, there was only one option left. "Your magic?"

"I touched it once, but I..." Lark trailed off and her eyes slid to his hand. Her shoulders grew tense and for a fleeting moment, he saw past all the shields she kept around her heart and recognized the pain.

And why shouldn't it hurt? It was easier for him; he'd never thought himself dead, though he knew he had to have been close. Yet the lack of pain on his end meant he did not know what to say to soften things. He almost touched her shoulder, then thought better of it and dropped his hand.

They were talking about the war right now. Talking about the blade. A time for them to clear the air and find comfort would have to come later.

Lark drew herself up straight in her chair and sucked in a shaky breath. Steeling herself, as always. Ignoring her own needs and trying to push on. They were alike in that respect, Zaide mused.

"My magic is only half the problem," she said as she reached for something underneath the table. "Everything we've found in the archive talks about the Paragons of Light and Shadow working in tandem, which is something we already knew, but it reinforces what we lack. I can't figure out what I did that might have been different. Maybe it was the Sunshard drawing it out of me. But I'm still here, so there's still hope for my magic. The real question is, after everything you've seen and everything you've learned... can you tell us anything about this?"

She drew the Shadowsliver from her travel-worn satchel and held it out before him.

Zaide stiffened in place.

The others remained silent, tense, as he stared.

Inside the prism atop her fingers, magic flickered and rolled like smoke above an extinguished candle. It stung in his senses—something it shouldn't have done—and the discomfort made his stomach twist.

"The texts mention a vessel for shadow, over and over again," Lark said slowly. "But it implies that my power should manifest when the vessel is there to seize shadow. This is the only thing we think it could mean, but no matter what I've tried, I can't seem to make it work."

Zaide reached for the purple stone and she let him take it. The facets were cool against his fingers, but the sting did not recede, and when he wrapped his hand around it, magic crackled across his skin. Cold. Hungry. Anger sparked within him as the familiar power called to him from where it was trapped.

He spun and flung the Shadowsliver at the floor.

Resia shrieked and Andriun snarled something profane, and both were too late.

The prism exploded and the smoky mists of the void screeched inside Zaide's head as they spilled across the floor. Crystal shards bounced across the stone, cackling as they went.

"Zaide!" Lark cried.

He slammed the heel of his boot atop the last remnants of Gadranus's magic and ground it into nothing.

She scrambled out of her chair, but there was nothing she could do. The color faded from the thousand shards scattered across the archive floor, leaving them plain and powerless. "What have you done?"

"He lied to us," he snapped. "That is not the shadow."

"It was all we had!" Tula exclaimed. "It was the only tie to his magic there was. Without that vessel, what are we supposed to do?"

Zaide shook his head, hate and fury burning so hot within him that it chased away the last chill of the dark magic he'd dispelled. "It's void, darkness, it's corruption and filth and it—"

He stopped short and his breath caught.

A vessel.

"It's me," he breathed.

Lark stared at him in devastation and disbelief.

His hands drifted to his head.

You are again as you were.

An empty vessel.

Nothing more.

He squeezed his eyes shut and exhaled hard, drawing his hands down over his face, confusion and rage and understanding and despair all spiraling together until everything made sense.

"Zaide," Lark started cautiously. The other Paragons rose, and more than one looked ready to fight.

He didn't know whether to laugh or cry. "It's me," he repeated. "He knew the whole time. He told me we had everything we needed. That I was the closest thing to his power, that his power was more than shadow. Because it's not shadow. It was right there the whole time, why the sword picked me when I was nobody, why the Elder kept me in the forest—"

Lark shook her head. "Zaide, what are you talking about?" She put out a hand as if to stop him, but he backed away before she could.

"Lark's power awakened when she was pouring it into me." He touched his chest where she had stabbed him, when her magic had been set free. "The—the empty vessel, like Gadranus said. The counterbalance she was missing. Don't you see? It's me." His fingers dug against his skin. "I'm the other Paragon!"

And a fool for never figuring it out sooner. Looking back, every subtle sign was so painfully obvious that it threatened to drive him mad.

"Zaide, that doesn't make sense." Resia put all her practiced diplomacy into the gentle words. "You don't have any magic."

"That's the point," he said. "I'm empty. A vessel. Something to catch whatever shadow is cast by Lark's power, not hold my own."

Andriun scoffed. "You are an idiot."

"I know." Zaide had just thought as much, himself.

Tula clapped her hands to her pockets and then felt all over her coat, searching for some of the notes she always had on her person. "Hang on a minute. Did anything ever say the vessel we were looking for was a thing and not a person?"

Resia and Lark exchanged glances. Andriun shook his head, though whether the Shaman was replying or just voicing more disapproval, it was hard to say.

Zaide would address that later, too. For now, he held out his hand. "Just try it, Lark. Please."

She looked at it with a sliver of fear and he knew what she thought. He'd done that before, had reached out to her right before he'd lost himself to the magic he'd so arrogantly thought he could contain.

But this is different, he promised himself. *This is Lark's magic. This is light.*

She held his gaze until all her fear and worry had run its course and all that remained was doubt, but still she did not move.

"I suppose we have nothing to lose," Resia sighed.

"Yeah, because he already broke it." Tula waved her pen at the shards of the Shadowsliver still scattered across the floor.

"Please," Zaide repeated, softer.

Instead of taking his hand, Lark reached for the Spectrum Blade. His stomach flopped and he almost took a step back, but instead of brandishing it, she turned its hilt up and held it between them.

"We'll do it this way. There's no sense in wasting any more time. If you're right, then…"

"Then we restore the blade," Zaide said.

"And if he's wrong?" Resia tugged anxiously at the hair beside her ears.

Andriun muttered a curse, and the Magister dutifully wrote it down.

Zaide curled his hand around Lark's and squeezed her fingers tight to the hilt, then slid his grasp up so that he was touching the blade directly, too. It tingled slightly against his skin. Hopeful. Eager.

He swallowed hard. "Ready?"

"No," Lark whispered.

"Me, either." But the blade's reaction gave him confidence, so he squeezed her hand again.

"I don't know how to do this," she protested.

Zaide reached for her other hand and drew it to his chest, pressing her palm flat above the strange scar the Sunshard left behind, holding it there when she trembled. "Put it there. Like you're pouring it into me. Just like you did before."

She stared at him for a long time, studying his face. Searching his eyes. Waiting for something to happen.

"You can do this," he whispered. "I believe in you."

Lark shifted her focus to her hand resting above his heart.

Then she closed her eyes.

Two breaths.

Three.

A slow, drowsy warmth spread beneath her hand and seeped into his chest. His muscle twitched at the strangeness of it, but he stood still.

Then it began to flow. A trickle at first, strange and tingling and warm, like fresh teardrops seeping through his skin, but growing into a flood that threatened to knock him from his feet.

It was nothing like the darkness Gadranus had poured into him before. It was sunlight on his skin and the heat in his veins, a pure, vibrant sensation of *life*. He squeezed both her hands tighter and gasped as the magic surged, spreading everywhere, filling every last corner of his body and mind and swelling until he was sure it would tear him apart. Somewhere, vaguely, Zaide thought he heard an exclamation, but the voices were so dim beneath the roar of magic that he did not understand any words.

Then a wave of cold swept over him, faster and harder than either power he'd experienced, and it was Lark's turn to gasp. It pushed back against her light, small but growing, driving the power she'd summoned out of his body and back into hers.

Her hands shook and he held her firm, and between their fingers, the Spectrum Blade began to hum.

Magic sizzled where they touched the sword, crawling first up Zaide's arm and then coiling around Lark's, and the hum grew until the blade vibrated in their grasp. Light and shadows coursed down the blade, stirring the colors that once whirled across its surface, sinking in and racing around the edges until the steel began to glow.

Heat bloomed under their joined grasp and Lark gave a soft whimper, but she did not let go.

All at once, the magic stabilized between them and stilled on the blade.

One side light. One side dark. Marbled colors glowing across them both.

Power flickered across the sword's surface like lightning, then faded as magic drained from them both.

"Did—did we—" Lark started, though she could not make herself finish.

The comforting heat and soothing chill of magic left Zaide as the pins-and-needles sensation he had so long associated with the blade's awareness surged in his hand, triumphant and stronger than ever before, and for the first time, something almost like a voice brushed his mind in a long, satisfied sigh.

Finally.

The Spectrum Blade lived.

GLOSSARY

Addare – (uh-dare) – An oasis city on the western coast of Amroch.

Amroch – (AM-roke) – The Allied Kingdoms ruled by King Sendassian. Originally a number of smaller kingdoms, unified as an empire for defense purposes.

Amrochan – (am-ROW-kan) – The capital city of Amroch.

Andriun – (AN-dree-un) – The Desheni Shaman's son.

Aren – A soldier stationed at the garrison outside Kolmar. Friend of Zaide and Resia.

Arkosh – A well-respected Master Librarian and one of Tula's mentors.

Athradan – The Desheni Shaman and the Paragon of Water. Leader of the Desheni people.

GLOSSARY

Beshnai – (besh-NIGH) – An isolated city on the northern coast of Amroch.

Broken-born – People born in the western kingdoms destroyed by Gadranus. Many seek refuge in Amroch, but face difficulty integrating due to their history in the war.

Bugrak – (BUG-rack) – Small, flat-faced and ugly gray creatures. Hunt in packs and use primitive weapons.

Captured Spring – One of the three artifacts. A vial that contains a self-replenishing healing tonic.

Chithal – (chee-thal) – A large port city and trade hub

Daisy – Zaide's dog.

Dasienna – (das-EE-en-uh) – The princess. King Sendassian's daughter.

Desheni – (duh-SHEN-nee) – A settlement named after the race of aquatic people who live there. The Desheni people bear blue-tinged skin, fin-like ears, webbed fingers, and gills on their necks.

Elder – Kolmar's chief overseer and most skilled mage. Zaide and Resia's mentor. Also known as the Paragon of Forest.

Elsanna – (el-san-nuh) – Chief of the Magister's guardswomen.

Estkel – (est-KELL) – A marshy city at the edge of the Ellean Sea.

Gadranus – (guh-DRA-nuss) – Breaker of the Shattered Lands, leader of the army that threatens to destroy Amroch. According to legend, he has been cursed to be reborn a thousand times as a punishment for his misdeeds.

Ganede – (gan-NEED) – Jadora's sister city. A port of trade on one of the peninsulas that frame the Ellean Sea.

Goborrin – (guh-BOR-rin) – Bipedal man-like monsters with pig-like faces and tusks. The smallest of the goborrins are the size of an adult man.

Ikan – A high-ranking Desheni hunter and a relative of Andriun.

Jadora – (jah-DOR-ah) – Ganede's sister city. Referred to as The Watcher. A fortress atop a desert plateau.

Jobe – General of Amroch's land-based armies. Stern, but regarded as level-headed and reasonable.

Kolmar – (coal-mar) – A small forest village in the southwestern region of Amroch.

Lark – The name Dasienna uses while traveling to protect her identity.

Magister – The leader of the fortress city of Jadora. Also known as the Paragon of Fire.

Molten Dagger – One of the three artifacts. An obsidian dagger that appears to have veins of magma trapped within it. Contains fire magic.

Moros – The warden of Jadora's prison and Elsanna's sweetheart.

Murk – A soldier from the garrison outside Kolmar.

GLOSSARY

Oroduna – The Oracle of Nimultis, blessed with visions of the future.

Paragons – Leaders entrusted with the protection of the three magic artifacts. Considered to be perfect representations of their type of magic.

Parral – (puh-rawl) – A port city at the southernmost tip of Amroch.

Plain – A soldier from the garrison outside Kolmar.

Portran – A blacksmith and former jewelrysmith.

Raddan – A lieutenant and medic in Amroch's army. Stationed at the garrison outside Kolmar.

Resia – (ree-see-uh) – Zaide's foster sister and the new Elder. Bears a strong magical bond with the forest and wields earth magic.

Salamander – Bipedal lizard-like creatures found in Jadora's caverns. They attack anyone they deem an intruder.

Sarma – Resia's mother and Zaide's foster mother.

Sast – A fortress outpost on an island in the Ellean sea. Home to a monastery that is closed off to visitors, in order to protect knowledge documenting every Rise.

Sendassian – (sin-das-see-an) – King of Amroch.

Shadowsliver – A prism in which a piece of Gadranus's magic is trapped. Found under Kolmar's temple after a specter of Gadranus was slain. Believed to be the sixth artifact.

GLOSSARY

Shaman – The leader of the Desheni. Entrusted with the protection of the Captured Spring.

Shattered Lands – The western kingdoms destroyed by Gadranus.

Spectrum Blade – The fourth artifact. A legendary weapon said to be the only thing that can strike down the cursed knight Gadranus.

Sunshard – A crystal containing light magic, left by the previous Paragon of Light. Believed to be the fifth artifact.

Tinith – (ten-nith) – A marketplace large enough to be its own city.

Toren – The current capital of the Shattered Lands.

Tula – (too-lah) – An apprentice librarian at the Great Library in Jadora. Fancies herself an archaeologist and adventurer.

Vale Hymnflute – One of the three artifacts. A set of wooden pan pipes that serves as anchor for Kolmar's Vale magic. It bears power over earth and wind.

Vale magic – A spiritual shield that lays over Kolmar's valley and protects the forest from evil.

Valla – (vah-lah) – A high-ranking Jadoran guardswoman. One of Elsanna's most trusted soldiers.

Verlin – Resia's father and Zaide's foster father.

Viper's Tongue – A bronze blade forged by dragon fire.

GLOSSARY

Vorkaris – The Magister who sealed away the Molten Dagger. Also known as the Dragonster, according to Zaide.

Yithel – (yee-THEL) – A trade city along the river north of Amrochan.

Warinal – Admiral of Amroch's navy. A stern man of bad temper.

Whok – A goborrin who oversees medical care of those imprisoned by Gadranus.

Zaide – (zayd) – A broken-born refugee fostered in Kolmar after his mother's death. Accidentally involved in helping the princess recover the artifacts and saving Amroch.

ABOUT THE AUTHOR

Beth Alvarez has enjoyed writing since childhood and is a ravenous reader.

A visual arts major, Alvarez has worked as a freelance web designer, graphic designer, illustrator, and video game programmer. When not writing, she enjoys drawing, playing video games, driving, and sewing for her unusual collection of Asian ball-jointed dolls. Her collection can be seen on her YouTube channel, Lomi's Playground.

Raised in southern Illinois, she now resides in the suburbs of Memphis, Tennessee with her husband and daughter, their Siberian husky, and a very mean cat.

If you enjoyed this story, consider signing up for Beth's author newsletter so you'll never miss a future release: http://www.ithilear.com/newsletter

OTHER BOOKS BY BETH ALVAREZ

The Assassin's Bride

The Spymaster's Prize

The Artificer's Wife

Gale's Gift

Of Blood and Rain

To Steal the World

To Steal the Crown

To Steal the Queen

Serpent's Mark

Serpent's Tears

Serpent's Bane

Serpent's Wake

Serpent's Crown

Serpent's Blood

Spectrum Blade

Paragon of Fire

Paragon of Water

Paragon of Light

Paragon of Shadow (Thanks for reading!)

Spectrum Legacy (Coming soon)

9 781952 145346